PENGUIN (🐧) C

TYPHOON AND OTHER STORIES

JOSEPH CONRAD (Józef Teodor Konrad Korzeniowski) was born in December 1857 in Berdichev (now in the Ukraine) of Polish parents. His father, a poet and translator, and his mother were exiled for nationalist activities and died when he was a child. H: ɡ ɛw up and was educated informally in Lemberg (now L'viv) and Cra ow, which he left for Marseilles and a career at sea in 187 ɤ. A   voyages to the French Antilles, he joined the Bɪ   Mɛ ɪ t Service in 1878, sailing first in British coastal waᴛɛ s an tɪ   to the Far East and Australia. In 1886, he became a Britisɪ ɛct and received his captaincy certificate. In 1890, he w ɛˀly in the Congo with a Belgian company. After his career aɪ a ended in 1894, he lived mainly in Kent. He married in 18 ɴd had two sons.

Conrad began writing, in his third language, in 1886. His tɪɪ ʼɴovels, *Almayer's Folly* (1895) and *An Outcast of the Islaɴ* 1896), were immediately hailed as the work of a significant n alent. He produced his major fiction from about 1897 to 19ɪ ɪ period that saw the publication of *The Nigger of the 'Narcis: ɛ* 1897), *Heart of Darkness* (1899), *Lord Jim* (1900) and ʼolitical novels *Nostromo* (1904), *The Secret Agent* (1907) ɪ ɪ: ʼnder Western Eyes* (1911). Considered 'difficult', his wriɪ :eceived considerable critical acclaim, but not until 1914 afteɪ appearance of *Chance* did it win a wide public. The dazɛ narrative experiments and thematic complexities of Conɪ ɪ earlier fiction are largely absent from his later writings, pitched ɔ ɪ more popular audience.

Fame saw the offer of honorary degrees and a knighthood (both ʼleclined) capped by a triumphal publicity tour in America ɪn 1923. In addition to novels, Conrad produced short stories, ʃ ɪ s, several essays and two autobiographical volumes, *The Mirɪ of the Sea* (1906) and *A Personal Record* (1908–9). He diɪ ɪn August 1924 at the age of sixty-six.

J. H. STAPE has taught in universities in Canada, France and the Far East. Author of *The Several Lives of Joseph Conrad* (2007), he has edited *The Cambridge Companion to Joseph Conrad*

(1996) and Conrad's *Notes on Life and Letters* (2004) and co-edited *A Personal Record* (2007) and Volumes VII and IX of *The Collected Letters of Joseph Conrad* (2005 and forthcoming) for Cambridge University Press. He has also co-edited Conrad's *An Outcast of the Islands* and *The Rover* for Oxford World's Classics, and has written on Thomas Hardy, Virginia Woolf, William Golding and Angus Wilson. He is Contributing Editor of *The Conradian: The Journal of the Joseph Conrad Society (UK)*.

JOSEPH CONRAD

Typhoon and Other Stories

Edited with an Introduction, Notes and Glossaries by
J. H. STAPE

6 464 235 000.

General Editor
J. H. STAPE
PENGUIN BOOKS

PENGUIN CLASSICS

Published by the Penguin Group
Penguin Books Ltd, 80 Strand, London WC2R ORL, England
Penguin Group (USA) Inc., 375 Hudson Street, New York, New York 10014, USA
Penguin Group (Canada), 90 Eglinton Avenue East, Suite 700, Toronto, Ontario, Canada M4P 2Y3
(a division of Pearson Penguin Canada Inc.)
Penguin Ireland, 25 St Stephen's Green, Dublin 2, Ireland
(a division of Penguin Books Ltd)
Penguin Group (Australia), 250 Camberwell Road, Camberwell, Victoria 3124, Australia
(a division of Pearson Australia Group Pty Ltd)
Penguin Books India Pvt Ltd, 11 Community Centre, Panchsheel Park, New Delhi – 110 017, India
Penguin Group (NZ), 67 Apollo Drive, Rosedale, North Shore 0632, New Zealand
(a division of Pearson New Zealand Ltd)
Penguin Books (South Africa) (Pty) Ltd, 24 Sturdee Avenue, Rosebank, Johannesburg 2196, South Africa

Penguin Books Ltd, Registered Offices: 80 Strand, London WC2R ORL, England

www.penguin.com

First published in 1901, 1902, 1903
Published in Penguin Classics 2007
1

Editorial matter copyright © J. H. Stape, 2007
All rights reserved

The moral right of the editor has been asserted

Set in 10.25/12.25 pt PostScript Adobe Sabon
Typeset by Rowland Phototypesetting Ltd, Bury St Edmunds, Suffolk
Printed in England by Clays Ltd, St Ives plc

ISBN: 978-0-141-44195-5

Contents

Acknowledgements

I should like to thank my editors at Penguin, Laura Barber and Marcella Edwards, for their assistance and encouragement. As ever, I am grateful to Owen Knowles and Allan H. Simmons for sharing insights and for sage advice and to The Joseph Conrad Society (UK) for support.

I am also indebted to the Humanities Research Center at the University of Texas at Austin for an Andrew W. Mellon Fellowship in 2006, which allowed me to undertake some of the textual work related to this volume, and to The Institute for Bibliography and Editing, Kent State University, for providing me with a photocopy of the typescript of 'Typhoon'.

Thanks are due to David Watson and Janet Tyrrell for their help in preparing the manuscript.

Chronology

1857 Józef Teodor Konrad Korzeniowski, coat-of-arms Nałęcz, is born on 3 December in Berdichev (Ukraine), the only child of the Polish poet and translator Apollo Korzeniowski and Ewelina (or Ewa), née Bobrowska.

1862 Apollo Korzeniowski, his wife and son are exiled from Warsaw to Vologda, northern Russia.

1865 Ewa Korzeniowska dies of consumption.

1868–9 Permitted to leave Russia, Apollo Korzeniowski relocates to Austro-Hungarian territory with his son, first in Lemberg (now L'viv, Ukraine) and vicinity and then in Cracow, where he dies (May).

1870 Becomes the ward of his maternal grandmother and maternal uncle, Tadeusz Bobrowski, and begins private studies with Adam Pulman, a medical student at Cracow's Jagiellonian University.

1873 Tours Vienna, Swiss Alps and northern Italy with Pulman. Private studies in Lemberg.

1874–7 Arrives in Marseilles to work for the shippers Delestang et Fils, sailing to the French Antilles in the *Mont-Blanc* and *Saint-Antoine*. A period of biographical mystery ensues, involving a possible brief side voyage to Venezuela, gun-running in the Basque country for the doomed cause of the pretender to the Spanish throne and smuggling near Marseilles.

1878 After amassing debts and gambling losses, attempts suicide (February or March). Leaves Marseilles in the British steamer *Mavis* for Mediterranean waters (Malta and Constantinople) and then lands at Lowestoft, Suffolk. Employed as ordinary seaman in the *Skimmer of the Sea* (Lowestoft to Newcastle).

1878–80 In the *Duke of Sutherland* (to Australia) and then the *Europa* (to Genoa, Sicily and Greece). Passes the British Merchant Service second mate's examination.

1880–85 Third mate in the *Loch Etive* (to Australia); second mate in the ill-fated *Palestine* (bound for Bangkok, but sinks in the Straits of Malacca), ships out of Singapore in the *Riversdale* (to Madras) and after crossing India by rail joins the *Narcissus* in Bombay (to Dunkirk). Passes the examination for first mate (1884).

1886 Second mate in the *Tilkhurst* (Hull to Wales, Singapore, Calcutta, Dundee). Submits first story, 'The Black Mate', to a competition for *Tit-Bits*. Becomes a British subject and passes the captaincy examination, receiving his 'Certificate of Competency as Master'.

1886–8 Second mate in the *Falconhurst* (London to Penarth); first mate in the *Highland Forest* (Amsterdam to Semarang) and *Vidar* (Singapore to Celebes and Borneo ports); captain of the *Otago* (to Bangkok, Australia and Mauritius).

1889 Living in Pimlico (London), begins *Almayer's Folly*. Visits Bobrowski in the Ukraine.

1890 In the Congo Free State, working for the Belgian company Société Anonyme du Haut-Congo; second-in-command, then temporarily captain, of Congo River steamer *Roi des Belges*.

1891 Recuperating from African experience in the German Hospital, London, then in Geneva for hydrotherapy. On return, works for warehouse and shippers Barr, Moering, Company.

1891–4 First mate in the passenger clipper *Torrens* (to Australia), meeting John Galsworthy (1893), later novelist and playwright awarded a Nobel Prize. Second mate in the *Adowa* (Rouen to Quebec and Montreal, but making only a return voyage from London to Rouen as the company collapses). Sea career ends.

1894 Tadeusz Bobrowski dies. Meets Edward Garnett, his literary mentor and advisor, and Jessie George, his future wife. Though still looking for a berth, turns to professional authorship in earnest.

1895 *Almayer's Folly*. In Geneva in the spring for hydrotherapy, and in Paris in August on business for Fountaine
(G. F. W.) Hope, his first English friend.

1896 *An Outcast of the Islands*. After marrying Jessie George,
honeymoons in Brittany (April–September), later settling in
Stanford-le-Hope, Essex, near Hope and family. Christmas
holidays in Cardiff.

1897 Meets Henry James. Writes 'The Return' and 'Karain: A
Memory'. Befriends American novelist Stephen Crane and
R. B. Cunninghame Graham, socialist and writer. *The Nigger
of the 'Narcissus'*.

1898 Alfred Borys Conrad born in Stanford. *Tales of Unrest*.
Becomes friendly with Ford Madox Hueffer (later Ford) and
H. G. Wells. In Glasgow, looks for a command. The Conrads
move to Pent Farm, near Hythe, Kent, sub-let from Ford.
'Youth, A Narrative' in *Blackwood's Magazine*.

1899 Works on *Lord Jim*. *Heart of Darkness* serialized in
Blackwood's Magazine. Meets Hugh Clifford, writer and
civil servant in Malaya. The Boer War begins.

1900 Becomes a client of J. B. Pinker's literary agency. Crane
dies. Working-holiday in Belgium with Ford. *Lord Jim*.

1901 Queen Victoria dies. Works on 'Amy Foster', 'Falk' and
Romance (with Ford). *The Inheritors* (with Ford).

1902 The Boer War ends. Writes 'The End of the Tether'.
Youth: A Narrative and Two Other Stories.

1903 Works on *Nostromo*. *Typhoon and Other Stories* and
Romance (with Ford) appear.

1904 Two-month sojourn in London. Engages 'typewriter'
Lilian M. Hallowes, his secretary on and off for twenty years.
Nostromo.

1905 In Capri (January–May). *One Day More* staged in
London. Writes sea papers and critical articles.

1906 In Montpellier (mid-February–mid-April). John Alex-
ander Conrad born in London. *The Mirror of the Sea*.

1907 In Montpellier (January–May). Writes 'The Duel', and
then in Geneva (May–August) *The Secret Agent*. The
Conrads move to Luton, Bedfordshire.

1908 Works on *Under Western Eyes* (then 'Razumov').

Involved with Ford's *English Review*, in which 'Some Reminiscences' appears (later *A Personal Record*).

1909 The Conrads move to Aldington, Kent. *The Nature of a Crime*, with Ford, with whom he quarrels and breaks off relationship. Writes 'The Secret Sharer' and more of *Under Western Eyes*.

1910 Suffers a mental and physical breakdown, recovery extending into the summer. The Conrads move to Capel House, Orlestone, Kent. Reviews for the *Daily Mail* (July) and writes 'A Smile of Fortune' and 'The Partner'.

1911 Writes 'Freya of the Seven Isles' and works on *Chance*. Meets novelist André Gide, who later translates 'Typhoon' and oversees Conrad's French translations. *Under Western Eyes*.

1912 *A Personal Record* in America, then as *Some Reminiscences* in England. Writes two articles on the *Titanic*. *'Twixt Land and Sea*. Writes short stories. Meets Richard Curle, journalist and short-story writer, in effect the unofficial private secretary to Conrad's later career.

1913 *Chance*. Becomes friendly with Cambridge philosopher Bertrand Russell through Lady Ottoline Morrell. Works on 'The Planter of Malata', 'Because of the Dollars' and *Victory*.

1914 Visiting Cracow in late July, the Conrads are caught by the outbreak of war. Taking refuge in Zakopane in the Tatras, return home via Vienna and Genoa (October–November).

1915 Writes 'Poland Revisited'. *Victory* and *Within the Tides* appear. Borys Conrad in basic training in the Army Service Corps, and fights in France for the next few years.

1916 Writes 'The Warrior's Soul' and 'The Tale'. For the Admiralty, visits naval bases, tours in a minesweeper, takes a flight, and sails in a Q-ship in the North Sea.

1917 Writes prefaces for new editions of *Youth*, *Lord Jim* and *Nostromo*. *The Shadow-Line* appears. Meets London-based French music critic and journalist Jean Aubry ('G. Jean-Aubry'), later his first biographer, who succeeds Gide in overseeing the French translations.

1918 Becomes friendly with novelist Hugh Walpole. Writes

articles about the Merchant Service and Polish events for the newspapers. Borys Conrad is shell-shocked and gassed. The war ends (11 November).

1919 Basil MacDonald Hastings's adaptation of *Victory* has a successful London run, including a royal performance. Moves to Spring Grove, near Wye, Kent. *The Arrow of Gold*. Moves to Oswalds, Bishopsbourne, near Canterbury.

1920 Polish relative Aniela Zagórska visits the Conrads for six months. *The Rescue*. Writes, with Pinker, *Gaspar the Strongman*, a film version of 'Gaspar Ruiz'. In December, collected editions begin publication in England by Heinemann (in the early new year in America by Doubleday, Page).

1921 Conrad and wife sojourn in Corsica (January–April), celebrating silver wedding anniversary in March. *Notes on Life and Letters* (collected essays) appears.

1922 J. B. Pinker dies in New York on a business trip, his son Eric taking over management of Conrad. Meets composer Maurice Ravel and poet Paul Valéry. Dramatic version of *The Secret Agent* flops in London (November).

1923 Triumphant publicity tour in New York, with excursions to Connecticut and Massachusetts (May–June). Briefly in Normandy to arrange for French immersion experience for son John (September). *The Rover*.

1924 Declines a knighthood. Succumbs to fatal heart attack on 3 August. After Roman Catholic rites, is buried in Canterbury Cemetery. *The Nature of a Crime* (with Ford) and *The Shorter Tales*. Ford rushes out *Joseph Conrad: A Personal Remembrance*.

1925–8 Posthumous works published: *Tales of Hearsay* and the unfinished *Suspense* (1925); *Last Essays*, edited by Richard Curle (1926); *Joseph Conrad: Life and Letters* (1927), edited by G. Jean-Aubry; the unfinished *The Sisters* (1928).

Introduction

*New readers are advised that this Introduction may
make details of the plots explicit.*

By the time *Typhoon and Other Stories* appeared in 1903,
the short story had come into its own. As literacy increased
dramatically throughout the Victorian period, popular maga-
zines burgeoned, spawning a community of journeymen-writers
ready to satisfy the public's insatiable demand for fiction. On
the other hand, more serious writers, inspired by Flaubert,
Chekhov and Maupassant, were intent on exploring short
fiction's artistic potential. James Joyce's *Dubliners* (1914), a
volume unified by setting, theme and political intention, vividly
testifies to this.

While Conrad had to write short stories to support himself
and his family, he clearly belongs to the second group of writers
– 'artists', as they would have tended to think of themselves –
whose work was directed to an audience interested in more
than simple entertainment and open to the experiment and
innovation that rapidly followed on the heels of the Victorian
age. The transition from highbrow monthly magazine to book
was, however, another matter. Collections of short fiction are
often made up of work that happens to be lying about on a
writer's desk, and, unless the writer is well known, can prove
difficult to place. Even when the writer or his agent succeeds in
finding a publisher, a collection of stories typically appears in
a smaller print-run than a novel. For the author, such collections
none the less have several advantages. They earn a second
payment for writing already done; they give work that previously appeared in periodicals or newspapers a securer and
longer life; and they have the advantage of keeping an author in
the public eye. However much they might embody a consistent

outlook, such collections more often than not have only a circumstantial or mechanical unity.

Typhoon and Other Stories stands in stark contrast to this general state of affairs. The stories included in it were written over a short period of time, and from the outset were destined for this collection. Conrad began 'Typhoon' in September 1900, and by June 1901 had completed it, as well as 'Falk' and 'Amy Foster'. After a gap of half a year, he finally rounded out the book with 'To-morrow' in January 1902. The volume enjoys a high degree of thematic and stylistic unity; its two novella-length pieces, 'Typhoon' and 'Falk', dealing with sea life, are followed by short stories set in Kent. The work, to evoke an old-fashioned term, emerges from but a single 'mood', varied but consistently recognizable.

Conrad's return to writing stories came at a significant moment in his career. Having recently completed *Lord Jim*, he was collaborating with Ford Madox Ford on *Romance*, another long project. Stories would not only provide ready cash but would represent a manageable creative commitment. *Lord Jim*, begun as a short story, had surprised Conrad by developing into a 130,000-word novel. Conrad first mentioned 'Typhoon' and 'Falk' to his literary agent on 8 October 1900, one day before *Lord Jim* appeared in book form; the first was estimated to be 12,000 words, the second a mere 5,000 (*Collected Letters*, vol. II, p. 295). Brevity, then, was a conscious aim, and although both fictions typically expanded during their writing, Conrad seems to have been more than usually sensitive to the fact that their writing was intended 'to prolong' his 'wretched existence' (*Collected Letters*, vol. II, p. 298). (The preoccupation with money in 'Typhoon' and of survival in 'Falk' can be related to Conrad's desperate concern with earning his living by his pen.)

Conrad found his mature voice in *The Nigger of the 'Narcissus'* (1897) and *Lord Jim* (1900). These stories prove him to be fully in control of his materials, confidently handling and developing ideas that reappear throughout his fiction. As much as they obviously differ in setting, the stories all share an awareness of constraint and of power, portraying individuals tightly hemmed in by circumstance and facing limited moral choices. Shipboard existence, for all its uniqueness and specificity, mimics the hierarchical organization of society generally. Moreover, it has rules, both written and unspoken, that regulate daily life and set out the status and duties of each crew member. The enclosed societies depicted in 'Amy Foster' and 'Tomorrow', with their weak links to the great world, are not so radically different from societies aboard ship. And in all four tales the protagonists confront an unexpected danger, struggling against it armed mainly with a handful of inadequate truisms.

Another strong link is Conrad's preoccupation with *Homo economicus*, with the unvarnished fact that one's daily bread must be earned by dint of diligence and compromise. He unflinchingly shows individuals – and societies – in competition with one another for their basic survival, and it is hardly surprising that love often enough turns out to be self-love, portrayed as monstrous in 'Falk' and in 'To-morrow' where tyrannical fathers rule the roost, and more subtly in 'Amy Foster' where pity, rarely a firm basis for love, mutates into disgust.

Whether such a vision of humanity is seen as 'pessimistic' or 'realistic' will depend upon one's starting-point. Conrad's contemporaries, not overly concerned that the universe presented was a dark one, praised the collection for its masterful craftsmanship and skilled delineation of character.[1] Typically divided over which story was most accomplished, critics were unanimously impressed with Conrad's achievement as a 'sea-writer'.

Typhoon

Conrad's first title for 'Typhoon', 'Equitable Division', squarely places the story's major interest on an event that occurs quite late in the final version and hints at a smaller role for the storm. His second working-title, 'A Skittish Cargo' (*Collected Letters*, vol. II, pp. 169, 237), likewise focuses on the fate of the two hundred Chinese coolies making their way back to China aboard the luckless *Nan-Shan*. The eventual title 'Typhoon' – surely more commercially viable – shifts the reader's attention to the storm itself, and to some extent even misplaces it, for much as Conrad describes the storm with vivid detail, his interest lies less in the natural event as such than in the problem it raises for the crew and how they varyingly handle it. What he claimed of *The Nigger of the 'Narcissus'* can, with slight adjustment, also be applied here:

> 'I give the psychology of a group of men and render certain aspects of nature. But the problem that faces them is not a problem of the sea, it is merely a problem that has arisen on board a ship where the conditions of complete isolation from all land entanglements make it stand out with a particular force and colouring.'[2]

Conrad's first title is subtler and more evocative than his final one, immediately focusing on an incident fraught with moral problems. How are the coolies' dispersed monies to be fairly divided? How just is the division Captain MacWhirr makes, and how is that division arrived at? Moreover, the original title seems to nod to a readerly problem. How are we to apportion *our* sympathies in this tale – to Captain MacWhirr, to Jukes, or to neither?

Judgement, fundamental in the plot, is one of the story's central themes. Conrad requires the reader to evaluate the bases of action and to judge how men deal with natural forces and social conditions. An allusion to the wisdom of Solomon – in a richly comic context of misunderstanding – underlines the theme's centrality, just as the tale's comedy itself requires a fine discrimination of stylistic ploys and rhetorical devices, actively encouraging the reader's collaboration as a necessary step towards comprehensive judgement. Thus, even if Conrad renamed his story for the sake of saleability, its main thrust altered little.

The opening scene sets up an antagonism that extends to its ending. Young Mr Jukes, competently furling his captain's umbrella, implicitly criticizes Captain MacWhirr's ability to deal with the world, while Jukes's final words are a withering judgement of the man he serves under: 'he got out of it very

well for such a stupid man' (83). And yet Jukes has revealed
himself time and again to be touchy and conceited, overly sure
of himself and – a charge he lays at his captain – of limited
imagination. His limitations are partly revealed as well by his
racism. Believing himself racially superior to the coolies, he
treats Bun Hin's representative with condescension. As he
gives him a tour of the ship, he reveals his small-mindedness in
his recourse to the racial cliché 'John' and in a pidgin English
that he mangles 'cruelly' (13). His racism is no less an issue in
the Siamese flag episode. Deriving his prestige from being a
very small cog in the British Empire, Jukes resents having to fly
under another nation's flag, seeing a dramatic and personal
affront where none is intended. By contrast, MacWhirr adopts
a staunchly pragmatic and unemotional attitude to the change
of the ship's register, understanding that the owners will benefit
from more favourable trade terms by sailing under the local
flag. The contrast is basic and one of sensibility. Wedded to
life's surfaces and 'facts', MacWhirr's taciturn approach to life
errs on the side of too great an equanimity and a failure to
probe beneath those surfaces, whereas Jukes, given to vivid
expression, writes 'out of the fulness of his heart and the liveliness of his fancy' (17). As Captain MacWhirr points out,
Jukes's use of language lacks discipline and precision; his feelings tend, similarly, to exaggeration, and he is thus the vehicle
for and butt of some of the novella's comic moments.

Rare in Conrad, for comedy suggests a natural ease with
one's audience, the jocular elements in 'Typhoon' are not incidental but functional. For humour, even of the serio-comic kind
exploited here, sets up complicity between narrator and reader,
just as it distances us from the characters and limits identifica-
tion with them. It offers a perspective on Jukes and MacWhirr,
exposes foible and alerts us to the play of temperament in the
shaping of everyday life.

Divergent in their approaches to life, MacWhirr and Jukes,
like the mismatched tall and thin man and short and stout
one of farce and low comedy, face the typhoon from nearly
opposite ends of the universe. Having set them up as foils,
Conrad proceeds to construct the storm as a test of mettle, as

an opportunity to interrogate the grounds on which they have built their lives. And yet, even in the face of death, they remain pretty much as they are, emerging from the experience somewhat like the *Nan-Shan* herself, battered and bowed but essentially the same. MacWhirr is no less stolid, Jukes no more charitable (and, as Conrad suggests in 'Amy Foster', fundamental change requires an imaginative capacity to feel empathy). The failure to learn and to feel is a sad part of the human condition. Perhaps the most darkly comic sequence in this novella, in which Conrad consciously attempted to treat the subject 'jocularly' (*Collected Letters*, vol. II, p. 304), is that of the coolies fighting tooth and nail for their dollars in the face of imminent death. The scene rings several changes. Their struggles suggest a crude, unarticulated optimism, a refusal to concede in the face of extinction. There is, concomitantly, a sheer inability to realize one's mortality, as the struggle for survival goes on mechanically, almost without reason or motive. Their below-deck position is symbolic. Like the fires that keep the steamship moving, they represent the life-force: undifferentiated, relentless in their energy, unintellectual and undaunted, they are as powerful and as terrifying as the storm.

And, as Conrad's contemporaries rightly proclaimed, what a storm it is! Conrad lapses only occasionally into the pathetic fallacy, an earlier mode of apprehending Nature as either sympathetic or hostile to human design. (The symbolic storms of Shakespeare are a classic example, with unrest in the microcosmic world of humanity reflected in the macrocosm, 'the heavens'.) The ship, metaphorically 'alive', is even human, while the storm lashes at her with malevolent intention: 'she sprang up again to her desperate plunging, as if trying to scramble out from under the ruins . . . There was hate in the way she was handled, and a ferocity in the blows that fell. She was like a living creature thrown to the rage of a mob' (40). To assign intention to Nature is to suggest that the battle has meaning, yet doubts are sown about this, partly by the use of language.

The story has a metaphoric density that verges on saturation. The repeated reliance on 'as if' and 'as though' clauses shows

Conrad himself engaged in a struggle with representation as the tale enacts its subject. The hard and precise technical vocabulary of seamanly routine by which a certain reality is mastered, clashes with a language that aspires to abstraction and abandons present-ness to recollect prior linguistic experience. Conrad's reliance on 'as if' and 'as though' is partly a verbal tic, an influence from his native Polish, but the device also suggests a characteristic means of apprehension.

The density of figurative language is perhaps most aptly symbolized by the speaking-tube that links the *Nan-Shan*'s upper and lower decks: 'He sent up his words tripping over each other, crowding the narrow tube' (59). It is 'as if' (to use Conrad's own overused stylistic device) words, too, were alive, competing with one another and striving to be heard, to be noticed and to gain significance. And here resides one of the novella's great interests – its self-conscious use of conflicting languages and its depiction of attitudes towards language. Conrad's preoccupation with this is an aspect of his literary impressionism. If in the Preface to *The Nigger of the 'Narcissus'* (1897) he famously declared his intention as 'before all to make you *see*', he emphasizes equally here the capacity of the written word, in the hands, as it were, of the artist, 'to make you hear'. Thus to the large array of literary strategies that insist on the reader's 'seeing' the storm, he adds onomatopoeia and alliteration, palpable in such sentences as 'The wind howled, hummed, whistled, with sudden booming gusts that rattled the doors and shutters in the vicious patter of sprays' (52). At times, Conrad seeks an aural effect that strains the possibilities available in print, as in the half-heard, elliptical dialogues that pepper the description of the crew's attempt to cope with the gale.

And while such attempts at communication are obviously frustrated by circumstance, more formal and controlled ones are subject to the same general law that seems to posit that communication is always partial and fated to misunderstanding. The letters Captain MacWhirr, Mr Jukes and Solomon Rout send to their various correspondents underline this theme, just as they increasingly play a role in structuring the story and

the reader's responses to it. On the one hand, they deepen a
sense of character and widen the novella's social range. The
egotistic and selfish Mrs MacWhirr, concerned less about her
husband's welfare than about her material comfort, and the
good-natured Mrs Rout serve as foils to their respective mates,
just as Mr Jukes's emotional limitations are partly suggested by
his having only one friend.

   More importantly, these letters add to the play of perspective
operating in the novella. Already singled out as loquacious
(never a positive sign in Conrad where the taciturn seaman
embodies an ideal of service), Jukes literally has the last word,
but there is a question as to how final it is. His resentment of
MacWhirr's literalness is the protest of the imaginative man,
yet Jukes's imagination stops short at fellow sympathy, and in
a work that follows quickly upon *Lord Jim* where the imagination is a double-edged sword, the reader is actively engaged in
balancing alternative visions. In 'Typhoon' superficial simplicity often collides with fathomless depth, much as MacWhirr
has overly long 'sailed over the surface of the oceans' (18)
unaware of its potential perfidy, terror and violence. Conrad,
in bringing these to the fore, tests his characters, but offers no
less a test of the reader's mettle, requiring him or her to sort
out the various simultaneously developed strands in a story
that has justly been called 'an artistic feat of the highest order'
(Kirschner, p. 13). Its interest might be suggested by the fact
that an artist of the stature of André Gide, a particular admirer
of *Lord Jim*, chose to translate the novella for the French
audience.

Amy Foster

While Conrad wrote 'Falk' directly after 'Typhoon', his ordering of the volume's stories plays up contrast, in length as well
as subject. 'Amy Foster' variously offers relief to 'Typhoon'. Its
land setting and expansion of character range allow for more
immediate social commentary, although its interests are typical
of Conrad in being mainly moral and philosophical. The alteration of the narrative method – Conrad opts for a frame-

narrator as he had in 'Youth', *Heart of Darkness* and *Lord Jim* – encourages a polyphony of ideas.

Just as the special conditions of life at sea determine 'Typhoon', so the stuffy provinciality of a coastal village in Kent is central to the tragic events depicted in 'Amy Foster'. Based partly on an anecdote Conrad had picked up from his friend and sometime collaborator Ford Madox Ford, the story painstakingly creates the claustrophobia and xenophobia of village life. Nor is it incidental to its creation that Conrad was living in Kent at Pent Farm among the two hundred souls of the village of Postling at the time he wrote it. He drew on the names of his real-life neighbours, mainly farmers and labourers, to populate his fictional Colebrook; according to his wife, he based some of Amy's placidity on the character of his own servant, Nellie; and he may have drawn on his physician John Hackney for Kennedy.[3]

The story opens with an uneasy tension between the small world within and the great world outside. Colebrook's physical setting itself suggests hostility, defensive barriers and enclosures, separation and boundaries as Conrad draws attention to the Martello towers on the shoreline, to the Coastguard, to Admiralty charts marking out 'trustworthy' anchorages (87) and to 'a wide green trough of pastures and hedges' that merge inland 'into a vista of purple tints and flowing lines closing the view' (87). In a sense, he uses two frames: the physical setting, presented in an almost painterly way at the outset, and a narrator to whom the story is told and who in turn passes it to the reader. Not specifically alluded to but forming another and larger frame for the action is the parable of the Good Samaritan. The interplay between a deeply rooted historical and social setting and wider frames of reference adds to the story's thematic depth and complexity.

Conrad's summary statement that the story's main idea was 'the essential differences of races' (*Collected Letters*, vol. II, p. 402) is an overly simplistic account of its interests. As much as his energies are directed to presenting a precise atmosphere and specific cultural context, the story develops into a wider study of the impulses, noble and ignoble, of the generality of mankind. Its continuing power as a work of fiction lies scarcely at all in its offering convincing portraits of a Kentish serving girl and a Carpathian peasant or of English and Austro-Polish sensibilities at the turn of the twentieth century. Rather, Amy Foster and Yanko Goorall, as well as the supporting characters, are recognizable human types. The extremity of Yanko's alienation is, however, specifically modern, with Conrad responding imaginatively to the large upheaval of populations during the nineteenth century's closing decades.

The story has often been seen as autobiographical, that is, reflecting upon Conrad the immigrant's own period of cultural adjustment on arriving in England in 1878, a young man not quite twenty and with a rudimentary knowledge of the language. There is, however, no evidence that the event was signally traumatic for him, and the story's autobiographical element can be, and sometimes has been, exaggerated. Indeed, the reader need know nothing of Conrad's life to appreciate the story's searing analysis of the archetypal figures of the outsider and the scapegoat. Mary Shelley's *Frankenstein* (1818) compellingly establishes that former archetype, but Conrad, if he needed models at all, had a more contemporary precedent in *The Invisible Man* (1897) by his then-friend and neighbour H. G. Wells. With its rural setting and dark subtext of prejudice and discrimination, Wells's novel also rewrites Shelley, just as Conrad, in some sense, updates and revises *Robinson Crusoe*.

Unlike those seekers for knowledge, however, Yanko Goorall is simply in quest of 'a better life'. The victim of an immigration scam, he nearly drowns in a shipwreck and is cast ashore (the story's original title was 'The Castaway') in an alien environment where his only reassurance is that he has landed in a Christian country, though, for all its churches, Colebrook's religion notably lacks the cardinal virtue of charity. So deprived in his native environment, Yanko scarcely knows that the world outside his own exists, and his psychological integration, singularly painful at the outset of his encounter with the English, is destined to be incomplete. Amy Foster's sentimental embrace of his terrible circumstances and real pain allows him a degree of assimilation into the human community, but he always stands at one remove from Colebrook, uncertain of its customs and lacking the power to break down its prejudices. Love saves him, but it also, ironically, leads to his death, for Amy's sentiments, initially kindly, are not so deep-rooted as to withstand repeated challenge and assault. The climactic moment comes when she and Yanko struggle for emotional and cultural 'ownership' of their child, with Yanko wanting 'Little John' to speak his language and adopt his religion, and Amy's maternal sentiments pulled in an opposite direction, towards integration and convention. In her way, too, Amy, as much an outsider in this parochial community as Yanko, is driven by the need to belong.

As much as Conrad distances the reader from this tragedy of misunderstanding and miscommunication by a frame, the technique of defamiliarization demands, on the contrary, an active and constant sharing of Yanko's point of view. Conrad repeatedly insists on the reader's collaboration by forcing the decoding of the familiar. References to the 'Emperor of America' and the 'American Kaiser' (96) are comic instances of this, but much of the technique emphasizes Yanko's linguistic and cultural deprivation. The following sentences demand the words 'tugboat', 'ship', 'deck' and 'masts', unavailable to Yanko's experience but shared between narrator and reader: 'the steam-machine bumped against the side of a thing like a house on the water. The walls were smooth and black, and there uprose, growing from the roof as it were, bare trees in the shape of crosses, extremely high' (95). This brilliant dramatization of perspective enacts insight. The reader's sympathy with Yanko is achieved not merely by the sympathetic recounting of his plight by Dr Kennedy (himself an outsider–insider in Colebrook) or by an instinctive alignment with the narrator's view of Colebrook's narrowness, but also by vicarious participation, however remote, in it.

Decoding, then, is one of the story's essential techniques. Just as Dr Kennedy spent his youth in the pursuit of specimens for a 'famous traveller' who makes learned contributions to science in papers on the flora and fauna of 'continents with unexplored interiors' (88) so the inhabitants of Colebrook attempt, willy-nilly, to classify the unknown Yanko. Thus, the ladies from the Rectory, who represent the woefully limited extent of Colebrook's knowledge of the wide world, attempt their book-learned smatterings of German and Italian on him in the vain hope of 'placing' him. The scene is one of grim comedy, for the 'cultured' classes fail to understand the work of Goethe and Dante in more than one way. On the other hand, there is about Yanko something doggedly resistant to the effort of 'understanding', whether of the head or the heart. Difficult as that condition may be to accept, Conrad's vision is bleaker still. He proclaims the heavens empty as his protagonist dies in a ditch. Love fails to transform, competition is the firm rule of nature and Yanko's suffering and death are meaningless. That this story first appeared in the *Illustrated London News* in three issues bridging the Christmas holidays of 1901, with illustrations of a terribly overly gentrified Amy, is one of the most mordant ironies of Conrad's publishing career.

Falk: A Reminiscence

Although likewise dealing with an outsider, 'Falk' is closer to 'Typhoon' thematically in treating of the will to live and the struggle for survival against Nature. The novella also returns to the Far Eastern setting of Conrad's earliest fiction. The story's sources, however, are diverse. The Bangkok locale draws on his own single foray into Siamese waters in 1888 (as does 'The Secret Sharer'), while the plight of Falk's ship derives from reality considerably transmuted: ' "Falk" owes its inception to a well-known at the time (1886) fact of a broken-down steamer drifting for 3 weeks in the Southern Ocean. She had plenty of provisions, and the people on board . . . suffered only from awful boredom.'[4] Conrad also draws inspiration from his childhood reading of Leopold McClintock's *Voyage of the Fox in Arctic Seas* (1859) about Sir John Franklin's ill-fated expedition of 1845–6 to the Arctic in the *Erebus* and *Terror*, which possibly involved cannibalism, and there are hints of a knowledge of the legend of the *Flying Dutchman* (whether from Wagner or other sources), and a knowledge of the Classics evidenced in allusions to Diana and centaurs.

The story's amalgam of sources may account for some of its structural awkwardness, for it effectively breaks into two stories, the more engaging and dramatic being that of the horrors aboard the *Borgmester Dahl*. The ship's derelict condition and the descent into cannibalism are vividly rendered. By contrast the 'main' story, a tale of love and desire with a happy ending, seems over-elaborated. Length apparently proved a practical problem, too, for Conrad's literary agent failed to find a serial willing to take the novella. The 'taboo' topic of cannibalism is sometimes blamed for this. Jessie Conrad claimed to have felt 'quite physically sick' when typing up the story, but only one of the book's contemporary reviewers, the influential A. T. Quiller-Couch, commented on his 'natural repugnance' to the subject.[5] (He also judged 'To-morrow' to be the collection's most accomplished story.)

Conrad seems, in fact, to have been somewhat unclear about his aims. He told his French translator that the novella's idea was the 'contrast of commonplace sentimentality with the uncorrupted point-of-view of an almost primitive man (Falk himself) who regards the preservation of life as the supreme and moral law' (*Collected Letters*, vol. II, p. 402). Yet the situation is less contrastive than a question of shades. Falk proves highly sentimental and sensitive, while Hermann and his wife, who live aboard a ship that resembles a 'cottage in the country' (123), prove mercenary and ruthlessly pragmatic. True, Falk's will to self-preservation knows no bounds, but he is placed in the most extreme circumstances, all semblances of organized society having dissolved around him. Hermann, on the other hand, seems willing, after some conventional expressions of horror and disgust, to marry off his niece to a self-confessed cannibal so that he can avoid paying her fare back to Germany. Having exploited her for her labour, she has now become a liability. There are, of course, differences in commodification: in the one case, a fellow human being is viewed as food, in the other as an economic commodity. Conrad claimed that he 'wanted to *do*' Hermann and his wife, with 'the story of Falk being more or less a foil to the main purpose' (*Collected Letters*, vol. II, p. 441), but the sensationalistic nature of Falk's story in which the disintegration of a human community and the consequent quest for survival take on an archetypal scale is such that it necessarily deflects the reader's attention. Moreover, the development of the narrator and of Schomberg, another rapacious figure, makes for over-crowding in such a short compass.

It is frequently pointed out that the love-interest, the un-named girl (she is merely 'Hermann's niece') of Falk's desiring speaks not a single word. Conrad, however, develops her by descriptions giving her mythic stature, with her tears of pity and compassion (shades of Amy Foster) speaking more elo-quently than any words she might muster. And the story – or at least the narrator – disapproves of, and is, perhaps, even hostile to displays of emotion. Recalling a rag-doll that is falling to pieces, he acidly comments, with a distinctly Conradian sideswipe at the German temperament: 'It was wonderful the way these children would work up their compassion for that bedraggled thing ... I suppose they were exercising and developing their racial sentimentalism by the means of that dummy' (131). Pity, too, can be suspect, and Falk must be pitiless in order to survive. Conventional morality and feeling, Conrad suggests, are the privileges of refined conditions. As in *Heart of Darkness*, the utterly solitary individual, lacking society's restraints, becomes either predator or prey.

The story of the narrator's being robbed, Schomberg's dys-peptic view of human life in economic terms and Falk's monop-olistic control of the ebb and flow of river trade extend this central idea. Conrad sets out to shatter the myths with which we comfort ourselves. In this light, Schomberg's boast that he has set up his table d'hôte almost as a charitable act is not only a warning about self-blindness and rampant egoism but also a comment on the nature of altruism.

As Tony Tanner has pointed out, the centrality of eating in 'Falk' (and of orality) begins at the very outset with the 'execrable' dinner that was a 'feast' only 'for the eyes' (121), much as Hermann's niece is for the narrator: 'she was built on

a magnificent scale' (126). This dehumanization is functional
in a tale where extremity rules and a sense of proportion proves
difficult to find. Falk's pained hunger and unbearable physical
sufferings are paralleled by no less pressing a psychological
need/desire for the girl: 'He was hungry for the girl, terribly
hungry, as he had been terribly hungry for food' (184). But this
other hunger, apparently fundamental and instinctive, is also
sophisticated. While Conrad is keenly alert to the needed sexual
component, Falk's deepest want is for love, a means, as the
allusion to the story of the *Flying Dutchman* makes clear, of
social reintegration for the wrongdoer and the outcast. Even
more, Falk's is an existential hunger for significance, and,
implicitly, for continuity, further attempts to stave off extinction. And, thus the extremity of his 'desire', a word of several
meanings in the novella.

To sate a need is to extinguish it, and Conrad, perhaps
nowhere more clearly in his canon than in this novella, links
Love and Death in the narrator-captain's last view of the triumphant couple who, in the fashion of generic comedy, have
overcome societal objections to their match and can finally
celebrate their union: 'They were a complete couple. In her grey
frock, palpitating with life, generous of form, olympian and
simple, she was indeed the siren to fascinate that dark navigator,
this ruthless lover of the five senses' (196). But sirens, as Conrad
well knew, do not give life but take it, dragging hapless sailors
to their doom, and when the narrator returns to Bangkok five
years later, Captain and Mrs Falk are gone, replaced by a
tale (yet another instance of oral obsession and gratification)
involving himself. This ironic substitution reveals his complicity
as more than an involved onlooker in his narrative. He is a
voyeur, part of a triangle, not fully aware of his sentiments
or the nature of his participation in the union of Falk and
Hermann's niece. The tale of 'a certain Falk ... who had won
his wife at cards from the captain of an English ship' (196) still
doing the rounds in Bangkok when he returns there has far
more psychological truth in it than he is able to acknowledge.

In this sense, he feeds off what he is witness to, not only
freely indulging the 'male gaze' but also sharing his booty in

that circulation of women that forms an important element of male heterosexual camaraderie. His attempt to pass off the whole business jocularly, a matter of chance, is typical of his willed impercipience, for he also eats at this table, devouring the girl with his eyes and, in turn, satisfied orally by talking of her. Thus, the story's opening at the river hostelry, a scene parallel to the fireside rituals of primitive man, features more than one kind of consumption. The 'execrable' dinner is followed by 'tales of experience—the tales of hunger and hunt—and of women, perhaps!' (121). As it turns out, and as the reference to Diana the huntress suggests, the tales are, if not interchangeable, variations on a theme.

It has sometimes been suggested that among the volume's structural juxtapositions is a pattern of hope and despair, but if 'Falk', by contrast with 'Amy Foster', is optimistic, it is difficult to see wherein its positive note lies. Formally a comedy, the tale none the less ends with dissolution both enacted (the disappearance of Falk and his wife from Bangkok) and unstated (the breaking-up of the dinner-party after the telling of this tale on the part of the presumably unmarried narrator). The only affirmative hint at the end is the act of sharing, both the communal meal and the narrative act, the reader also participating in the latter. Such rituals conquer the instinct for total monopoly, but, looked at dispassionately, this adds up to a singularly muted triumph for civilization.

To-morrow

The bleakness and horrors of 'Falk' are reprised under a domestic guise in 'To-morrow', a story Conrad turned into a chilling one-act melodrama, *One Day More*, in 1905. The short story title preserves the motif of stasis, for, as the adage has it, 'Tomorrow never comes', whereas the play's title, whatever its weary resignation, suggests forward movement, however halting.

The setting is the fictional Colebrook of 'Amy Foster', with Conrad again drawing on a medley of sources both autobiographical and literary. Captain Hagberd's villa draws on an unhappy experience of residing in Stanford-le-Hope, Essex, a nondescript town on the Thames estuary. The Conrads' first home there, a newly built semi-detached villa, was, in his own words, 'a damned jerry-built rabbit hutch', a 'blamed hole' lacking room enough 'to swing a cat'.[6] His status as an outsider among the petty bourgeoisie and tradespeople was obvious. Having reproved some local youths for pinching fruit from the orchard of his second, much more congenial, house, Ivy Walls Farm, Conrad in gout-sling and with untidy hair and beard became a legendary local bogeyman, his wife for some time after taunted by the query 'Hi, Mrs Conrad, how's your wild man?'[7] Conrad also imports into the story memories of his earliest days in England, with Hagberd drawn in part from the captain-owner of the *Skimmer of the Seas*, a coasting trawler (its name appears in the story) in which he served at Lowestoft in 1878. But the story's memories may go back farther still, its two domestic tyrants perhaps unconsciously drawing on Conrad's father, Apollo Korzeniowski (1820–69), who, after his wife's premature death, became morose, increasingly self-preoccupied and moody and even more engaged by the hopeless *idée fixe* of national liberation as he jealously clung to his only child.

The reader need not, of course, know anything of these sources to experience or appreciate the story's emotional intensities. The plight of Bessie Carvil is slowly developed, hinted at in the opening before being fully dramatized. Mentions of fences, walls, lines and 'stone-bordered' flower-beds emphasize a world of boundaries, with limits and no-go zones as prevalent images. The opening, then, describes less a scene of domesticity than a domestic prison where any aspiration is severely limited. Even the 'simple flowers' Bessie optimistically grows are 'somehow extravagantly overgrown, as if belonging to an exotic clime' (200), their displacement and alienation a metaphor for her predicament and barely expressed longings.

For all its obvious linkages to 'Amy Foster', the story's greater affinities are with 'Falk', for Bessie, engaged in a struggle for psychological survival, is constrained and devoured not only by her blind father and Captain Hagberd, but also by the society in which she lives. Grotesque versions of the *senex iratus* (angry old man) of Greek new comedy (the father who blocks his daughter's marriage and thus symbolically opposes the alteration of society), the father and father surrogate here are figures from nightmare, the one literally blind, the other a 'heavy figure of a man of stone' (200). Bessie's best and, for that matter, only hope of escaping them lies in marriage – ironically, in dependence on and submission to another man, and she is reduced to pleasing everyone but herself, a dry run for the self-sacrificing Winne Verloc of *The Secret Agent* (1907).

The essential drama here, like that in 'Falk', centres on predation, for Bessie, devoured by her father, is no less preyed on by Hagberd, who uses her to sustain and nourish his delusions. With every teapot secreted into his house, he puts into place another brick in his mad castle in Spain, being built with her passive complicity. The essentially predatory nature of human relationships is developed further in the drama played out with his son Harry, who having previously escaped his tyranny, comes to Colebrook only to obtain money from his father. No prodigal son happily welcomed back, Harry's own predatory nature is somewhat overdrawn. In need of money, he also takes what opportunity he can for a 'kiss'. An outsider and adventurer, he lives beyond boundaries and to the side of social norms; a restless man, he makes no commitments, indeed is incapable of them, his loyalty that of a Gambusino – 'no wife, no chick, no home, never a chum' (221). His at least seems a deliberate choice, whereas Bessie apparently has none. The song of the Gambusino is somewhat too obviously her own: 'It's all about a pretty girl that tried hard to keep hold of a Gambusino lover, so that he should bring her lots of gold. No fear! Off he went' (222).

Harry's alienation and solitude seem chosen – a Byronic pose – whereas Bessie's are enforced. His resentment of the possibility of being 'a blamed tame rabbit in a cage' (223) is paralleled by a free-and-easy sexual adventurism. For Bessie, however, the act of being kissed, a symbolic deflowering or even rape, is tantamount to annihilation and loss of identity: 'the measured blows and sighs of the rising tide accompanied the enfolding power of his arms . . . It was as if the sea, breaking down the wall protecting all the homes of the town, had sent a wave over her head' (225). Drowning in this newfound emotion, she is also ready to grasp any means to escape the death-in-life she experiences. But Harry, an illusion for his father, proves no less illusory for her as she is drawn back into reality by the antiphonal appeal of mad Captain Hagberd, now reassured that his son will return to him in but 'one day more', and of her father calling her back to his service, a monster from whose thrall no one will come to save her. That Conrad relies upon archetype at the story's end is appropriate, the allusion to Dante poignantly highlighting that Bessie is returning to a hell from which there is no escape.

As it turns out, even Harry, who roams in and out of the story, is not quite as free as he seems. For all his devil-may-care attitude, his marginal social existence does not free him from want, economic or sexual. His attachment to his chum, seemingly his only emotional tie, is a makeshift one, and his choice of a life at sea an apt correlative for his lack of rootedness and commitment. The gossipy barber, with his eight children and fixed social and economic functions, serves as a stark and unattractive contrast, his life sacrificed on the altar of domesticity. For all the sympathy Conrad creates for Bessie, or even for Hagberd trapped in his terrible delusion, no viable alternatives are presented in this bleak story.

There is still less room for sentimentality, for one of the most basic of human ties – that of child and parent – is chillingly presented as a system of emotional or financial exploitation. A twist on this theme is that Hagberd, who plays pander to his idealized son, uses the idea of Harry as a means of articulating his own sensuality. The winks he showers on Bessie are more than a simple gesture of complicity, and the story's closing irony is that, in a very real sense, Hagberd 'gets the girl'. By rejecting Harry as an impostor, he assumes even greater emotional dominance of her than in the past as, with 'terror upon her heart', she hears his crazed shouts of 'trust in an everlasting to-morrow' (226), shouts she will continue to hear.

In writing the story, Conrad revised not only his original

emphasis (its first title was 'The Son') but his initial plot in which Harry runs off with the spoons and a shipmate of Harry comes to the rescue, convincing Hagberd that Harry is his son. Harry receives the girl as his 'consolation' (*Collected Letters*, vol. II, p. 367), but precisely for what Conrad leaves tantalizingly unstated. The domestic theme is not his natural territory, but the story's evolution from its original inspiration is a happy one. As haunting as the portrait of Bessie is, however, the confines of the short story form give the exposition a forced quality – the device of the barber creaks as badly as those stagey scenes of overhearing favoured by Hardy. Mentioning that he had unwillingly cut some 2,000 words to fit the straitjacket of acceptable magazine length, Conrad lamented to his agent: 'I hate restraint in size and tone.' His revision, too, may account for what seems some abruptness in the handling, with the melodramatic aspects heightened by virtue of compression.

Typhoon and Other Stories may be dipped into, the stories read and enjoyed on their own, but reading them in the order of their appearance, that is, as Conrad himself shaped his book, proves productive critically, their contrasts heightened and the sense of continuity strengthened. No other arrangement would have quite the same effect as the one he struck upon: 'Typhoon' rather than 'Falk' must self-evidently come first, just as 'To-morrow' rather than 'Amy Foster' should close the collection. There is, if not precisely a progressive treatment of ideas, then an appropriate symmetry in the way themes repeatedly loop back and are centrifugally developed. For one, the collection circles round the imagination, the literalist Captain MacWhirr being set off not only against Mr Jukes but also against Amy Foster and the extravagantly imaginative Captain Hagberd, who places his naive faith in a tomorrow destined never to come.

Conrad's deepest engagement in this collection is with the modern sensibility. These stories handle alienation, cultural displacement, economic exploitation and the erotic (in its widest sense). They have lost little of their relevance or fascination in the century since they were first published. Resolutely of his time and place – the turn of the twentieth century – Conrad, rather like Beethoven who, when a violinist reproached him about the extreme difficulty of his work, could reply, 'It is not for you, but for a later age.' Conrad's address is, likewise, arguably more to our time than to his.

J. H. Stape

NOTES

Works cited in the text of the Introduction can be found in Further Reading.

1. For a selection of contemporary reviews, see Sherry, ed., pp. 143–58.
2. Joseph Conrad, *Joseph Conrad: Life and Letters*, ed. G. Jean-Aubry (London: Heinemann, 1927), vol. II, p. 342.
3. On the story's origins, place-names and surnames, see note 1, p. 238; note 6, p. 239; and note 14, p. 240.
4. Inscription by Conrad in a copy of *Falk, Amy Foster, To-morrow: Three Stories* (New York: McClure Phillips, 1903), cited in George T. Keating, ed., *A Conrad Memorial Library: The Collection of George T. Keating* (Garden City, NY: Doubleday, Doran, 1929), p. 115.
5. Jessie Conrad, *Joseph Conrad as I Knew Him* (London: Heinemann, 1926), p. 118; A. T. Quiller-Couch, 'Four Tales by Mr. Conrad', cited in Sherry, ed., p. 156.
6. Cited in Jessie Conrad, p. 44.
7. James Whitaker, *Joseph Conrad at Stanford-le-Hope* (Stanford-le-Hope: Bream Press, 1978), p. 13.

Further Reading

LETTERS

The Collected Letters of Joseph Conrad, ed. Frederick R. Karl and Laurence Davies, with Owen Knowles (vol. VI), J. H. Stape (vol. VII) and Gene M. Moore (vol. VIII), 8 vols. (Cambridge: Cambridge University Press, 1983–).

Conrad's Polish Background: Letters to and from Polish Friends, ed. Zdzisław Najder (London: Oxford University Press, 1964).

A Portrait in Letters: Correspondence to and about Conrad, ed. J. H. Stape and Owen Knowles (Amsterdam: Editions Rodopi, 1996).

BIOGRAPHICAL STUDIES

Batchelor, John, *The Life of Joseph Conrad: A Critical Biography* (Oxford: Blackwell, 1994).

Knowles, Owen, *A Conrad Chronology* (Basingstoke: Macmillan, 1990).

Najder, Zdzisław, *Joseph Conrad: A Life*, trans. Halina Carroll-Najder (1983; revised edn London: Boydell, 2007).

Najder, Zdzisław, ed., *Conrad under Familial Eyes*, trans. Halina Carroll-Najder (Cambridge: Cambridge University Press, 1983).

Ray, Martin, ed., *Joseph Conrad: Interviews and Recollections* (Basingstoke: Macmillan, 1990).

Stape, J. H., *The Several Lives of Joseph Conrad* (London: Heinemann, New York: Knopf, 2007).

REFERENCE

Knowles, Owen, *An Annotated Critical Bibliography of Joseph Conrad* (Hemel Hempstead: Harvester/Wheatsheaf, 1992).
Knowles, Owen, and Gene M. Moore, *The Oxford Reader's Companion to Conrad* (Oxford: Oxford University Press, 2000).
Sherry, Norman, ed., *Conrad: The Critical Heritage* (London: Routledge & Kegan Paul, 1973).

CRITICAL STUDIES

Berthoud, Jacques, *Conrad: The Major Phase* (Cambridge: Cambridge University Press, 1978).
Gordan, John D., *Joseph Conrad: The Making of a Novelist* (Cambridge, MA: Harvard University Press, 1941).
Guerard, Albert J., *Conrad the Novelist* (Cambridge, MA: Harvard University Press, 1958).
Lothe, Jakob, *Conrad's Narrative Method* (Oxford: Oxford University Press, 1989).
Moser, Thomas C., *Joseph Conrad: Achievement and Decline* (Cambridge, MA: Harvard University Press, 1957).
Najder, Zdzisław, *Conrad in Perspective: Essays on Art and Fidelity* (Cambridge: Cambridge University Press, 1997).
Simmons, Allan H., *Joseph Conrad* (London: Palgrave, 2006).
Stape, J. H., ed., *The Cambridge Companion to Joseph Conrad* (Cambridge: Cambridge University Press, 1996).
Watt, Ian, *Conrad in the Nineteenth Century* (London: Chatto & Windus, 1980).
Watts, Cedric, *Preface to Conrad* (London: Longman, 1990; 2nd edn 1993).

JOURNALS

The Conradian: The Journal of the Joseph Conrad Society (UK), published twice yearly by Rodopi of Amsterdam.
Conradiana: A Journal of Joseph Conrad Studies, published thrice yearly by Texas Tech University Press, Lubbock, Texas.
L'Époque Conradienne, published once yearly by the Société Conradienne Française at Les Presses Universitaires Limoges, Limoges, France.

ON *TYPHOON AND OTHER STORIES*

Criticism

Curreli, Mario, and Fausto Ciompi, 'A Socio-semiotic Reading of Conrad's "Falk"', *L'Époque Conradienne* 14 (1988), pp. 35–45.
Fraser, Gail, *Interweaving Patterns in the Works of Joseph Conrad* (Ann Arbor, MI: UMI Research Press, 1988).
Graver, Lawrence, *Conrad's Shorter Fiction* (Berkeley: University of California Press, 1969).
Kirschner, Paul, Introduction to Joseph Conrad, *Typhoon and Other Stories* (Harmondsworth: Penguin, 1990), pp. 3–31.
Tanner, Tony, '"Gnawed bones" and "Artless Tales": Eating and Narrative in Conrad', in Norman Sherry, ed., *Joseph Conrad: A Commemoration* (London: Macmillan, 1976), pp. 17–36.
Watt, Ian, 'Comedy and Humour in *Typhoon*', in *The Ugo Mursia Memorial Lectures: Papers from the International Conrad Conference, University of Pisa, September 7th–11th 1983*, ed. Mario Curreli (Milan: Mursia International, 1988), pp. 39–56.

Textual matters

Johnson, Bruce, 'Conrad's "Falk": Manuscript and Meaning', *Modern Language Quarterly* 26 (1965), pp. 267–84.

Fraser, Gail, 'Conrad's Revisions to "Amy Foster"', *Conradiana* 20 (1988), pp. 181–93.

Purdy, Dwight H., 'Conrad at Work: The Two Serial Texts of Typhoon', *Conradiana* 19.2 (1987), pp. 99–119.

A Note on the Texts

The copy-text for this edition is the first English edition, *Typhoon and Other Stories*, published by William Heinemann on 22 April 1903. The volume collects 'Typhoon', serialized in *Pall Mall Magazine* (January–March 1902) and in the *Critic* (February–March 1902) in the United States; 'Amy Foster', serialized in the *Illustrated London News* (December 1901); and 'To-morrow', serialized in *Pall Mall Magazine* (August 1902). 'Falk' was published for the first time in the volume. The copy-text for the 'Author's Note' is, for reasons argued below, that of its publication in Doubleday's 'Sun-Dial' edition (1921).

The manuscript and typescript of 'Typhoon' are held in a private collection. The manuscript of 'Amy Foster' and the manuscript and an incomplete typescript of 'Falk' are preserved in the Beinecke Rare Book and Manuscript Library, Yale University. Two folios (*recto*) of the 'Typhoon' manuscript have matter related to the opening of 'Falk'. The manuscript of 'To-morrow' and a typescript of the volume's 'Author's Note' are in the Berg Collection, the New York Public Library.

Although this is not a critical edition, emendations to the copy-text have been made to correct outright errors and to take into account the complex circumstances of drafting and printing and thus to supply missed-out punctuation and to rationalize minor inconsistencies. Where intrusive house-styling has been imposed on the text, such as the comma and dash in combination, it has been removed. Likewise, the opening quotation marks prefacing each paragraph of Kennedy's narratives in 'Amy Foster', another matter of house-styling, have been removed. This styling convention does not appear in 'Falk', a much longer text, and the rationalization adopted here gives a more coherent texture to the stories in the volume. The opening and closing of the first-person narrative in 'Falk' have been marked off.

A number of faintly impressed semi-colons in the 'Falk' typescript, which were mistaken as colons by compositors rapidly setting the text, have been restored. Hyphenation has been resolved on the basis of majority practice in a given text; where no clear preference exists, hyphenation is resolved by spelling of the period. Thus, for instance, where the copy-text of 'To-morrow' has 'rabbit hutch' and 'sea wall', majority practice in these texts is to hyphenate these words, and hyphens have thus been supplied. The exception here is 'wheel-house', varying in both 'Typhoon' and 'Falk' (in which 'wheelhouse' appears). It has been altered in both, where required, to 'wheel-house'. Where commas in series are a majority practice in a given text, commas have been installed to conform with this. The use of ellipses varies, in part an inheritance from the practice of the typescript. These have not been systematically altered, but in a few cases have been emended where their proximity warrants it, and not doing so would be disruptive.

Two outright errors that Conrad himself caught after the first book publication are corrected as a matter of course: (i) a letter of 17 August 1915 to Eugene F. Saxton (*Collected Letters*, vol. V, p. 499) draws attention to the fact that 'wicker-gate' should be 'wicket-gate' (115:27), and (ii) in a letter to R. B. Cunninghame Graham of 21 May 1903 (*Collected Letters*, vol. III, p. 35), Conrad concedes that 'Gambusino', not 'Gambucino', is the word's correct spelling. The latter, systematically corrected in its singular and plural forms, is emended without further notice. Also corrected is a mistake in German (150:36). Stating that Conrad later revised 'queerly' to 'quaintly' (14:33) and 'trump' to 'trombone' (130:7), Paul Kirschner, in the previous Penguin edition (1990), makes these changes but cites no evidence. Cedric Watts in the Oxford World's Classics edition (2002) makes the latter change, citing Kirschner as his authority. This edition, which follows the first English edition, retains the original readings in both cases.

Although the texts have not been systematically regularized, certain elements have been brought into conformity with the general practices in them.

It goes without saying that spellings and usage have not been modernized (thus, for example, 'battle-ship', for which authority can be found in *The Marine Engineer* of April 1884 as cited in *The Oxford English Dictionary*, and 'for ever', 'decrepid' and 'blurr' stand here). In *Typhoon*, however, 'Jukes'' has been altered to 'Jukes's', and the anomalous 'bo'ssn' and 'bo'ss'en', which have no precedent in the *OED*, have been regularized, without notice below, to the normal period use 'bo'sun'. Foreign words have been italicized. When used as terms of direct address, 'captain' and 'bo'sun' have been capitalized, and lowered, if required, otherwise. Such alterations, made silently, are not drawn attention to in the list of emendations below.

The text of the 'Author's Note' in the 'Sun-Dial' edition has been preferred over that in Heinemann's Collected Edition for several reasons: (i) the text is arguably more polished, with 'deliberately intended' (228:17) replacing 'definitely intended', 'I insist not on the events but on' replacing 'it is not the events I am insisting on but' (228:42–229:1) and 'Mr. Maurice Grieffenhagen' (229:35) replacing 'Mr. Grieffenhagen'; (ii) the Heinemann text is typically more heavily punctuated, the work of a copy-editor; and (iii) the spellings are more Conradian, Conrad more often than not using '–ize' forms than '–ise' ones.

LIST OF EMENDATIONS

The rejected reading of the copy-text appears to the right of the square bracket.

Epigraph

1.2   round] around

Typhoon

36:32   helplessness;] helplessness:
37:17   wheel-house] wheelhouse
38:9   resolution,] resolution
39:38   mouths,] mouths
40:30   tumult:] tumult.
40:35   lonely,] lonely
40:37   Never . . . Anyhow] Never — Anyhow
41:4   men. . . .] men . . .
41:14   ice; he shivered. It (TS)] ice: he shivered — it
41:36   demeanour,] demeanour
41:38   imbecility;] imbecility:
42:22   'tween-deck] 'tween deck
44:37   away. . . .] away . . .
45:11   anything] anything,
45:30   globe-lamps] globe lamps
47:20   bolt;] bolt:
47:21   as though] though
47:22   him;] him
47:34   glared;] glared
48:2   nothing;] nothing:
48:32   wheel-house] wheelhouse
50:6   energy:(TS)] energy
51:2   East End] East-end
51:28   ship;] ship:
51:32   yellow face] yellow-face
52:31   striped] stripped
53:2   sea water] sea-water
53:7   wheel-house] wheelhouse
53:12   now. Ain't (TS)] now: ain't
53:23   compass-card] compass card
53:26   wheel-house] wheelhouse
53:29   wheel-house] wheelhouse
53:30   bulkhead] bulk-head
54:2   neck —] neck, —
54:17   steering-gear] steering gear
54:22   right. . . .] right, . . .
54:23   man . . . "Hackett (TS)] man, ". . . Hackett
54:32   donkeyman] donkey-man

55:25   wheel-house] wheelhouse
56:13   exotic,] exotic
56:33   below,] below
56:35   big-jointed] big-jointed,
57:7   carpet-slippers] carpet slippers
58:7   him —] him; —
58:21   hummed;] hummed:
59:3   me — blast (TS)] me? blast
59:9   peace,] peace
59:22   talk;] talk:
60:19   you . . .] you . . . ,
61:26   Steering-gear] Steering gear
63:9   them;] them:
63:13   dust;] dust:
64:11   said] said,
67:32   smash! (TS)] smash
67:34   done . . ."] done . . . ,"
68:27   floor;] floor:
69:5   fingers,] fingers
71:14   steering-gear] steering gear
71:23   MacWhirr] MacWhirr,
72:21   Jukes?] Jukes.
73:17   plumet] plummet
74:6   VI] V
74:15   aspect;] aspect:
76:19   ". . . A] ". . . . A
76:38   soldier.] soldier,
77:7   one. . . .] one . . .
77:9   No. There (TS)] No: there
80:13   French,] French
80:14   a row (TS)] row
80:24   hot] angry hot (see p. 238, n. 53)
81:13   happened. Another (TS)] happened: another
81:31   Bun Hin's] Bun-hin's
82:2   Bun Hin's] Bun-hin's
82:3   hand,] hand
82:4   better.'] better.
82:22   month;] month:

82:29   Bun Hin's] Bun-hin's
83:5   sight;] sight:

Amy Foster

87:13   anchoring-ground] anchoring ground
87:14   Ship Inn] "Ship Inn"
87:15   nearby] near by
88:18   dog-cart] dogcart
88:26   low brick] low, black
91:34   overburdened] over-burdened
92:3   supple,] supple
92:12   startled —] startled,
93:6   all directions] all-directions
93:23   jasmine;] jasmine:
93:26   ". . . The] ". . . .The
93:31   dislike,] dislike
95:11   cart —] cart: —
95:31   straightaway] straight away
96:28   only those] those only
96:33   over-full] over full
97:6   of true] or true
97:21   sea-sick] seasick
97:27   Norton,] Norton
97:28   speak;] speak:
97:30   countryside] country side
99:4   conviction,] conviction
99:7   back door] back-door
101:6   scatheless] scathless
101:31 Ship Inn] "Ship Inn"
104:9   here?] here.
104:38 market-days] market days
106:25 Norway-pines] Norway pines
106:30 overshadowed] over-shadowed
107:12 grandchild] grand-child
107:19 horse-pond] horsepond
109:4   good-will] good will
109:13 notables,] notables

109:24   acrobat] accrobat
109:26   expostulate;] expostulate:
109:26   forcibly;] forcibly:
110:3   heart,] heart;
111:1   in all] all in
111:27   earned;] earned:
111:13   munificence;] munificence:
112:28   Coach and Horses,] 'Coach and Horses,'
113:23   doctor] Doctor
113:33   home-sickness] home sickness
113:34   half-dressed] half dressed
115:23   haunted] hunted
115:27   wicket-gate] wicker-gate

Falk: A Reminiscence

122:8   Plate] Platte
122:8   jury-rudder] jury rudder
122:9   rations,] rations
122:21   short] short,
122:36   "This] This
123:4   tug-boats] tugboats
123:6   Hermann."] Hermann.
123:12   "Not] Not
123:12   all,"] all
123:12   "No] No
123:24   adventurer,] adventurer
124:16   mutilated,] mutilated
124:20   neck-openings] neck openings
124:26   Diana—] Diana,—
124:38   well-behaved] well behaved
125:10   running-gear] running gear
125:23   twice,] twice
125:29   pleasant;] pleasant,
125:33   niece,] niece
126:6   wit,] wit
126:29   word,] word
127:2   head] head,

127:11   Earth] earth
127:18   Platt-Deutsch,] Platt-Deutsch
127:21   mankind),] mankind)
127:27   smoking-match] smoking match
127:29   shirt-sleeves] shirt sleeves
127:36   state-rooms] staterooms
127:37   cross-legs] cross legs
128:11   opened hopefully,] opened, hopefully
129:9   sickly;] sickly,
129:25   Commissioner,] Commissioner—
130:12   my] any
130:15   sea;] sea:
130:19   world-proof] world proof
130:35   *in extremis*] "in extremis"
131:10   extent;] extent,
131:22   ironwork,] ironwork
131:24   Arcadian] arcadian
132:31   heart;] heart:
133:9   mail-boat] mail boat
133:31   moonbeams] moon beams
134:25   pole-mast] pole mast
134:35   centaur;] centaur:
134:38   one especially,] one, especially
134:38   prancing,] prancing
135:8   upstream] up stream
136:3   closely;] closely,
136:15   Falk] Falk,
136:21   *gehts?",*] gehts,"
136:23   slightly;] slightly:
136:33   neither;] neither:
137:24   racket,] racket
137:25   paddle-wheels,] paddle-wheels
138:26   Falk,] Falk
138:26   us,] us
138:32   glared;] glared:
138:38   odd,] odd
139:10   this,] this
139:33   thrifty,] thrifty

139:35 sea travelling,] sea travelling
140:32 look-out] look out
142:5 stem;] stem,
142:5 howl—] howl,—
142:30 brought out] brought
142:33 sun-rays] sun rays
143:6 arose;] arose:
143:15 *table d'hôte*] *table-d'hôte*
143:19 Mistake,] Mistake
143:27 Hermann,] Hermann
143:38 can] man can
144:2 itself] itself,
144:3 has] have
144:11 *table d'hôte*] *table-d'hôte*
144:11 out,] out—
144:19 it,] it—
144:27 home,] home—
144:28 dear,] dear
144:36 presences] Presences
145:2 coolies.] coolies:
145:6 whitewash;] whitewash:
145:15 wheel-house] wheelhouse
145:32 turtle-steak] turtle steak
146:5 half-stunned] half stunned
147:10 appear] appear,
147:24 brother] brother,
147:25 water-side] water side
147:37 man,] man—
148:3 ears,] ears—
148:12 the extent] that extent
148:14 home—] home,
148:22 Well,] Well—
148:22 keyhole,] keyhole—
148:33 that,] that—
148:35 remarked that "It] remarked, "that it
149:1 half-open] half open
149:25 billiard-tables] billiard tables
149:29 side-whiskers] side whiskers

149:31   night-shirt] night shirt
149:36   tam'] tam
150:14   whip-hand] whip hand
150:15   Hermann,] Hermann
150:36   *Gottverdammt*] Gottferdamm
150:36   Schomberg,] Schomberg
151:2   me,] me
151:17   mail-boat] mail boat
152:10   *Diana!*] *Diana!*
152:17   should,] should
152:36   reiterated,] reiterated
153:15   East End] East-end
154:16   iron-grey] iron grey
154:18   a uniform] an uniform
154:21   harsh,] harsh
155:16   lived,] lived
155:31   thoroughfare,] thoroughfare
155:32   away] away, away
155:37   ankle-deep] ankle deep
156:9   river-bed] river bed
156:33   ruin,] ruin
157:15   hussars] Hussars
157:38   information;] information:
158:15   compound;] compound:
159:27   humiliation,] humiliation
160:2   tug-boat] tugboat
160:11   horribly,] horribly;
161:24   billiard-balls] billiard balls
162:7   desires,] desires
163:13   billiard-cues] billiard cues
164:21   he "didn't] "he didn't
164:23   this,] this
164:24   said,] said
164:26   who,] who—
166:16   courting] courting,
166:29   Why . . .] Why.
167:34   me;] me —
167:38   time,] time —

170:26   step-dance] step dance
171:5   red-hot] red hot
171:12   overborne,] overborne;
172:5   shore,] shore
173:31   so] So
175:4   called,] called
175:10   six foot seven] seven foot six
175:33   quarter-deck] quarter deck
176:12   knees,] knees
176:30   long-drawn] long drawn
176:31   hawse-pipe] hawse pipe
178:15   cheek,] cheek
179:1   one,] one;
179:2   maybe,] maybe;
180:12   stockinged] stocking
180:27   quarter-deck] quarter deck
180:33   silent,] silent;
182:8   streaming;] streaming,
183:6   He, for instance,] He—for instance—
183:7   if, said I,] if—said I—
183:13   story;] story—
183:27   half-hoped] half hoped
184:17   gnawing;] gnawing,
185:10   imbecile,] imbecile
185:29   Break-down] Break down
185:33   sink,] sink
185:38   of,] of
186:6   said:] said—
186:35   everyone] every one
187:21   covetousness,] covetousness
188:12   spoken to] spoken
188:18   whaler;] whaler:
188:23   apathy;] apathy:
188:29   ropes'] rope's
188:36   one;] one:
189:3   were carried] carried
189:22   Falk,] Falk—
189:28   lug,] lug

189:31   reasserted] re-asserted
190:18   suffering,] suffering
190:21   ruled,] ruled
190:38   after-deck] after deck
191:12   but,] but
191:25   fresh-water pump] fresh water-pump
192:7   brass-framed] brass framed
192:14   cunning,] cunning
192:24   second-best] second best
192:34   The fable] —the fable
192:35   wraith] wreath
193:4   after-deck] after deck
193:13   three,] three
194:6   charms,] charms
194:26   Lena,] Lena
194:28   rag-doll] rag doll
195:10   hand,] hand
195:15   Yes] "Yes
195:17   went . . .] went . . ."
196:10   drawn,] drawn
196:34   ship."] ship

To-morrow

199:23   expectation,] expectation
199:27   clothes-line] clothes line
200:28   Colebrook;] Colebrook,
201:9   describe,] describe
202:32   forgotten] forgotten,
202:33   forgotten,] forgotten
203:8   miser,] miser
203:25   face,] face
204:6   coasting-skipper] coasting skipper
204:11   animosity,] animosity—
204:31   land] land,
204:34   grass-plot] grass plot
205:18   columns;] columns,

205:21   her] her,
205:30   anywhere,] anywhere
206:6-7   cunningly. "The] cunningly: "the
206:10   sailor,] sailor
206:27   mahogany-coloured] mahogany coloured
207:15   tenant] tenant,
208:7   slow,] slow
209:7   derangement,] derangement
209:20   side-glances] side glances
210:19   sail-cloth] sail cloth
211:17   chair;] chair,
213:34   scornfully. "Just] scornfully: "just
214:24   murmured] murmured.
216:10   said. "I] said; "I
216:18   grinning] grinning,
217:8   shoulder] shoulder,
218:10   say,] say,—
218:21   arm-chair] armchair
218:22   hair,] hair —
218:33   A sailor] — a sailor
219:4   said,] said;
219:8   rabbit-hutch] rabbit hutch
219:14   sea-wall] sea wall
220:26   mountain-top] mountain top
220:33   bullocks—] bullocks,—
222:1   rest;] rest:
222:14   laugh,] laugh;
223:15   think?] think.
223:27   grinning] grinning,
224:8   excitedly. "Never] excitedly; "never
224:34   Go] go
225:38   alone] alone,
226:14   globe-lamp] globe lamp

Author's Note

227:8   *Youth*] "Youth"
227:31   required:] required;
229:19   *Tales of Unrest*] "Tales of Unrest"
229:31   "Typhoon"] The "Typhoon"
230:1   *One Day More*] "One Day More"

Far as the mariner on highest mast
Can see all round upon the calmed vast,
So wide was Neptune's hall . . .
　　　　　　　　　—KEATS

TO
R. B. CUNNINGHAME GRAHAM

Typhoon

Captain MacWhirr,[1] of the steamer *Nan-Shan*,[2] had a physiognomy that, in the order of material appearances, was the exact counterpart of his mind: it presented no marked characteristics of firmness or stupidity; it had no pronounced characteristics whatever; it was simply ordinary, irresponsive, and unruffled.

The only thing his aspect might have been said to suggest, at times, was bashfulness; because he would sit, in business offices ashore, sunburnt and smiling faintly, with downcast eyes. When he raised them, they were perceived to be direct in their glance and of blue colour. His hair was fair and extremely fine, clasping from temple to temple the bald dome of his skull in a clamp as of fluffy silk. The hair of his face, on the contrary, carroty and flaming, resembled a growth of copper wire clipped short to the line of the lip; while, no matter how close he shaved, fiery metallic gleams passed, when he moved his head, over the surface of his cheeks. He was rather below the medium height, a bit round-shouldered, and so sturdy of limb that his clothes always looked a shade too tight for his arms and legs. As if unable to grasp what is due to the difference of latitudes, he wore a brown bowler hat, a complete suit of a brownish hue, and clumsy black boots. These harbour togs gave to his thick figure an air of stiff and uncouth smartness. A thin silver watch-chain looped his waistcoat, and he never left his ship for the shore without clutching in his powerful, hairy fist an elegant umbrella of the very best quality, but generally unrolled. Young Jukes, the chief mate, attending his commander to the gangway, would sometimes venture to say, with the greatest gentle-

ness, "Allow me, sir"—and possessing himself of the umbrella
deferentially, would elevate the ferule, shake the folds, twirl a
neat furl in a jiffy, and hand it back; going through the performance with a face of such portentous gravity, that Mr. Solomon
Rout, the chief engineer, smoking his morning cigar over the
skylight, would turn away his head in order to hide a smile.
"Oh! aye! The blessed gamp[3]. . . . Thank 'ee, Jukes, thank 'ee,"
would mutter Captain MacWhirr heartily, without looking up.

Having just enough imagination to carry him through each
successive day, and no more, he was tranquilly sure of himself;
and from the very same cause he was not in the least conceited.
It is your imaginative superior who is touchy, overbearing, and
difficult to please; but every ship Captain MacWhirr commanded was the floating abode of harmony and peace. It was,
in truth, as impossible for him to take a flight of fancy as it
would be for a watchmaker to put together a chronometer with
nothing except a two-pound hammer and a whip-saw in the
way of tools. Yet the uninteresting lives of men so entirely given
to the actuality of the bare existence have their mysterious side.
It was impossible in Captain MacWhirr's case, for instance, to
understand what under heaven could have induced that perfectly satisfactory son of a petty grocer in Belfast to run away
to sea. And yet he had done that very thing at the age of fifteen.
It was enough, when you thought it over, to give you the
idea of an immense, potent, and invisible hand thrust into the
ant-heap of the earth, laying hold of shoulders, knocking heads
together, and setting the unconscious faces of the multitude
towards inconceivable goals and in undreamt-of directions.

His father never really forgave him for this undutiful stupidity. "We could have got on without him," he used to say later
on, "but there's the business. And he an only son too!" His
mother wept very much after his disappearance. As it had never
occurred to him to leave word behind, he was mourned over
for dead till, after eight months, his first letter arrived from
Talcahuano.[4] It was short, and contained the statement: "We
had very fine weather on our passage out." But evidently, in
the writer's mind, the only important intelligence was to the
effect that his captain had, on the very day of writing, entered

him regularly on the ship's articles as Ordinary Seaman. "Because I can do the work," he explained. The mother again wept copiously, while the remark, "Tom's an ass," expressed the emotions of the father. He was a corpulent man, with a gift for sly chaffing, which to the end of his life he exercised in his intercourse with his son, a little pityingly, as if upon a half-witted person.

MacWhirr's visits to his home were necessarily rare, and in the course of years he despatched other letters to his parents, informing them of his successive promotions and of his movements upon the vast earth. In these missives could be found sentences like this: "The heat here is very great." Or: "On Christmas day at 4 P.M. we fell in with some icebergs." The old people ultimately became acquainted with a good many names of ships, and with the names of the skippers who commanded them—with the names of Scots and English shipowners—with the names of seas, oceans, straits, promontories—with outlandish names of lumber-ports, of rice-ports, of cotton-ports—with the names of islands—with the name of their son's young woman. She was called Lucy. It did not suggest itself to him to mention whether he thought the name pretty. And then they died.

The great day of MacWhirr's marriage came in due course, following shortly upon the great day when he got his first command.

All these events had taken place many years before the morning when, in the chart-room of the steamer *Nan-Shan*, he stood confronted by the fall of a barometer he had no reason to distrust. The fall—taking into account the excellence of the instrument, the time of the year, and the ship's position on the terrestrial globe—was of a nature ominously prophetic; but the red face of the man betrayed no sort of inward disturbance. Omens were as nothing to him, and he was unable to discover the message of a prophecy till the fulfilment had brought it home to his very door. "That's a fall, and no mistake," he thought. "There must be some uncommonly dirty weather knocking about."

The *Nan-Shan* was on her way from the southward to the

treaty port of Fu-chau,[5] with some cargo in her lower holds, and two hundred Chinese coolies returning to their village homes in the province of Fo-kien,[6] after a few years of work in various tropical colonies.[7] The morning was fine, the oily sea heaved without a sparkle, and there was a queer white misty patch in the sky like a halo of the sun. The fore-deck, packed with Chinamen, was full of sombre clothing, yellow faces, and pigtails,[8] sprinkled over with a good many naked shoulders, for there was no wind, and the heat was close. The coolies lounged, talked, smoked, or stared over the rail; some, drawing water over the side, sluiced each other; a few slept on hatches, while several small parties of six sat on their heels surrounding iron trays with plates of rice and tiny teacups; and every single Celestial[9] of them was carrying with him all he had in the world—a wooden chest with a ringing lock and brass on the corners, containing the savings of his labours: some clothes of ceremony, sticks of incense,[10] a little opium maybe, bits of nameless rubbish of conventional value, and a small hoard of silver dollars, toiled for in coal-lighters, won in gambling-houses or in petty trading, grubbed out of earth, sweated out in mines, on railway lines, in deadly jungle, under heavy burdens —amassed patiently, guarded with care, cherished fiercely.

A cross swell had set in from the direction of Formosa Channel[11] about ten o'clock, without disturbing these passengers much, because the *Nan-Shan*, with her flat bottom, rolling-chocks on bilges, and great breadth of beam, had the reputation of an exceptionally steady ship in a sea-way. Mr. Jukes, in moments of expansion on shore, would proclaim loudly that the "old girl was as good as she was pretty." It would never have occurred to Captain MacWhirr to express his favourable opinion so loud or in terms so fanciful.

She was a good ship, undoubtedly, and not old either. She had been built in Dumbarton[12] less than three years before, to the order of a firm of merchants in Siam—Messrs. Sigg and Son.[13] When she lay afloat, finished in every detail and ready to take up the work of her life, the builders contemplated her with pride.

"Sigg has asked us for a reliable skipper to take her out,"

remarked one of the partners; and the other, after reflecting for a while, said: "I think MacWhirr is ashore just at present." "Is he? Then wire him at once. He's the very man," declared the senior, without a moment's hesitation.

Next morning MacWhirr stood before them unperturbed, having travelled from London by the midnight express after a sudden but undemonstrative parting with his wife. She was the daughter of a superior couple who had seen better days.

"We had better be going together over the ship, Captain," said the senior partner; and the three men started to view the perfections of the *Nan-Shan* from stem to stern, and from her keelson to the trucks of her two stumpy pole-masts.

Captain MacWhirr had begun by taking off his coat, which he hung on the end of a steam windlass embodying all the latest improvements.

"My uncle wrote of you favourably by yesterday's mail to our good friends—Messrs. Sigg, you know—and doubtless they'll continue you out there in command," said the junior partner. "You'll be able to boast of being in charge of the handiest boat of her size on the coast of China, Captain," he added.

"Have you? Thank 'ee," mumbled vaguely MacWhirr, to whom the view of a distant eventuality could appeal no more than the beauty of a wide landscape to a purblind tourist; and his eyes happening at the moment to be at rest upon the lock of the cabin door, he walked up to it, full of purpose, and began to rattle the handle vigorously, while he observed, in his low, earnest voice, "You can't trust the workmen nowadays. A brand-new lock, and it won't act at all. Stuck fast. See? See?"

As soon as they found themselves alone in their office across the yard: "You praised that fellow up to Sigg. What is it you see in him?" asked the nephew, with faint contempt.

"I admit he has nothing of your fancy skipper about him, if that's what you mean," said the elder man curtly. "Is the foreman of the joiners on the *Nan-Shan* outside? . . . Come in, Bates. How is it that you let Tait's people put us off with a defective lock on the cabin door? The captain could see directly

he set eye on it. Have it replaced at once. The little straws, Bates
. . . the little straws. . . ."[14]

The lock was replaced accordingly, and a few days afterwards
the *Nan-Shan* steamed out to the East, without MacWhirr
having offered any further remark as to her fittings, or having
been heard to utter a single word hinting at pride in his ship,
gratitude for his appointment, or satisfaction at his prospects.

With a temperament neither loquacious nor taciturn, he
found very little occasion to talk. There were matters of duty,
of course—directions, orders, and so on; but the past being to
his mind done with, and the future not there yet, the more
general actualities of the day required no comment—because
facts can speak for themselves with overwhelming precision.

Old Mr. Sigg liked a man of few words, and one that "you
could be sure would not try to improve upon his instructions."
MacWhirr, satisfying these requirements, was continued in
command of the *Nan-Shan*, and applied himself to the careful
navigation of his ship in the China seas. She had come out on
a British register, but after some time Messrs. Sigg judged it
expedient to transfer her to the Siamese flag.[15]

At the news of the contemplated transfer Jukes grew restless,
as if under a sense of personal affront. He went about grumbling
to himself, and uttering short scornful laughs. "Fancy having a
ridiculous Noah's Ark elephant[16] in the ensign of one's ship,"
he said once at the engine-room door. "Dash me if I can stand
it; I'll throw up the billet. Don't it make *you* sick, Mr. Rout?"
The chief engineer only cleared his throat with the air of a man
who knows the value of a good billet.

The first morning the new flag floated over the stern of the
Nan-Shan Jukes stood looking at it bitterly from the bridge. He
struggled with his feelings for a while, and then remarked,
"Queer flag for a man to sail under, sir."

"What's the matter with the flag?" inquired Captain Mac-
Whirr. "Seems all right to me." And he walked across to the
end of the bridge to have a good look.

"Well, it looks queer to me," burst out Jukes, greatly exasperated, and flung off the bridge.

Captain MacWhirr was amazed at these manners. After a

while he stepped quietly into the chart-room, and opened his International Signal Code-book[17] at the plate where the flags of all the nations are correctly figured in gaudy rows. He ran his finger over them, and when he came to Siam he contemplated with great attention the red field and the white elephant. Nothing could be more simple; but to make sure he brought the book out on the bridge for the purpose of comparing the coloured drawing with the real thing at the flagstaff astern. When next Jukes, who was carrying on the duty that day with a sort of suppressed fierceness, happened on the bridge, his commander observed:

"There's nothing amiss with that flag."

"Isn't there?" mumbled Jukes, falling on his knees before a deck-locker and jerking therefrom viciously a spare lead-line.

"No. I looked up the book. Length twice the breadth and the elephant exactly in the middle. I thought the people ashore would know how to make the local flag. Stands to reason. You were wrong, Jukes. . . ."

"Well, sir," began Jukes, getting up excitedly, "all I can say —— " He fumbled for the end of the coil of line with trembling hands.

"That's all right." Captain MacWhirr soothed him, sitting heavily on a little canvas folding-stool he greatly affected. "All you have to do is to take care they don't hoist the elephant upside-down[18] before they get quite used to it."

Jukes flung the new lead-line over on the fore-deck with a loud "Here you are, Bo'sun. Don't forget to wet it thoroughly," and turned with immense resolution towards his commander; but Captain MacWhirr spread his elbows on the bridge-rail comfortably.

"Because it would be, I suppose, understood as a signal of distress," he went on. "What do you think? That elephant there, I take it, stands for something in the nature of the Union Jack in the flag. . . ."

"Does it!" yelled Jukes, so that every head on the *Nan-Shan*'s decks looked towards the bridge. Then he sighed, and with sudden resignation: "It would certainly be a dam' distressful sight," he said meekly.

Later in the day he accosted the chief engineer with a confidential, "Here, let me tell you the old man's latest."

Mr. Solomon Rout (frequently alluded to as Long Sol, Old Sol, or Father Rout), from finding himself almost invariably the tallest man on board every ship he joined, had acquired the habit of a stooping, leisurely condescension. His hair was scant and sandy, his flat cheeks were pale, his bony wrists and long scholarly hands were pale too, as though he had lived all his life in the shade.

He smiled from on high at Jukes, and went on smoking and glancing about quietly, in the manner of a kind uncle lending an ear to the tale of an excited schoolboy. Then, greatly amused but impassive, he asked:

"And did you throw up the billet?"

"No," cried Jukes, raising a weary, discouraged voice above the harsh buzz of the *Nan-Shan*'s friction winches. All of them were hard at work, snatching slings of cargo, high up, to the end of long derricks, only, as it seemed, to let them rip down recklessly by the run. The cargo chains groaned in the gins, clinked on coamings, rattled over the side; and the whole ship quivered, with her long grey flanks smoking in wreaths of steam. "No," cried Jukes, "I didn't. What's the good? I might just as well fling my resignation at this bulkhead. I don't believe you can make a man like that understand anything. He simply knocks me over."

At that moment Captain MacWhirr, back from the shore, crossed the deck, umbrella in hand, escorted by a mournful, self-possessed Chinaman, walking behind in paper-soled silk shoes, and who also carried an umbrella.

The master of the *Nan-Shan*, speaking just audibly and gazing at his boots as his manner was, remarked that it would be necessary to call at Fu-chau this trip, and desired Mr. Rout to have steam up to-morrow afternoon at one o'clock sharp. He pushed back his hat to wipe his forehead, observing at the same time that he hated going ashore anyhow; while overtopping him Mr. Rout, without deigning a word, smoked austerely, nursing his right elbow in the palm of his left hand. Then Jukes was directed in the same subdued voice to keep the forward 'tween-deck clear of cargo. Two hundred coolies were going to be put down there. The Bun Hin[19] Company were sending that lot home. Twenty-five bags of rice would be coming off in a sampan directly, for stores. All seven-years'-men[20] they were, said Captain MacWhirr, with a camphor-wood chest to every man. The carpenter should be set to work nailing three-inch battens along the deck below, fore and aft, to keep these boxes from shifting in a sea-way. Jukes had better look to it at once. "D'ye hear, Jukes?" This Chinaman here was coming with the ship as far as Fu-chau—a sort of interpreter he would be. Bun Hin's clerk he was, and wanted to have a look at the space. Jukes had better take him forward. "D'ye hear, Jukes?"

Jukes took care to punctuate these instructions in proper places with the obligatory "Yes, sir," ejaculated without en-thusiasm. His brusque "Come along, John;[21] make look see" set the Chinaman in motion at his heels.

"Wanchee look see, all same look see can do," said Jukes, who having no talent for foreign languages mangled the very pidgin-English cruelly. He pointed at the open hatch. "Catchee number one piecie place to sleep in. Eh?"

He was gruff, as became his racial superiority, but not unfriendly. The Chinaman, gazing sad and speechless into the darkness of the hatchway, seemed to stand at the head of a yawning grave.

"No catchee rain down there—savee?" pointed out Jukes. "Suppose all'ee same fine weather, one piecie coolie-man come topside," he pursued, warming up imaginatively. "Make so—Phooooo!" He expanded his chest and blew out his cheeks. "Savee, John? Breathe—fresh air. Good. Eh? Washee him piecie pants, chow-chow topside—see, John?"

With his mouth and hands he made exuberant motions of eating rice and washing clothes; and the Chinaman, who con-cealed his distrust of this pantomime under a collected demean-our tinged by a gentle and refined melancholy, glanced out of his almond eyes from Jukes to the hatch and back again. "Velly good," he murmured, in a disconsolate undertone, and hastened smoothly along the decks, dodging obstacles in his course. He disappeared, ducking low under a sling of ten dirty gunny-bags full of some costly merchandise and exhaling a repulsive smell.

Captain MacWhirr meantime had gone on the bridge, and into the chart-room, where a letter, commenced two days before, awaited termination. These long letters began with the words "My darling wife," and the steward, between the scrubbing of the floors and the dusting of chronometer-boxes, snatched at every opportunity to read them. They interested him much more than they possibly could the woman for whose eye they were intended; and this for the reason that they related in minute detail each successive trip of the *Nan-Shan*.

Her master, faithful to facts, which alone his consciousness reflected, would set them down with painstaking care upon many pages. The house in a northern suburb to which these pages were addressed had a bit of garden before the bow-windows, a deep porch of good appearance, coloured glass with imitation lead frame in the front door. He paid five-and-forty pounds a year for it, and did not think the rent too high, because Mrs. MacWhirr (a pretentious person with a scraggy neck and a disdainful manner) was admittedly ladylike, and in the neighbourhood considered as "quite superior." The only secret of her life was her abject terror of the time when her husband would come home to stay for good. Under the same roof there dwelt also a daughter called Lydia and a son, Tom. These two were but slightly acquainted with their father. Mainly, they knew him as a rare but privileged visitor, who of an evening smoked his pipe in the dining-room and slept in the house. The lanky girl, upon the whole, was rather ashamed of him; the boy was frankly and utterly indifferent in a straightforward, delightful, unaffected way manly boys have.

And Captain MacWhirr wrote home from the coast of China twelve times every year, desiring quaintly to be "remembered to the children," and subscribing himself "your loving husband," as calmly as if the words so long used by so many men were, apart from their shape, worn-out things, and of a faded meaning.

The China seas north and south are narrow seas. They are

seas full of every-day, eloquent facts, such as islands, sand-
banks, reefs, swift and changeable currents—tangled facts
that nevertheless speak to a seaman in clear and definite language. Their speech appealed to Captain MacWhirr's sense of
realities so forcibly that he had given up his state-room below
and practically lived all his days on the bridge of his ship,
often having his meals sent up, and sleeping at night in the
chart-room. And he indited there his home letters. Each of
them, without exception, contained the phrase, "The weather
has been very fine this trip," or some other form of a statement
to that effect. And this statement, too, in its wonderful persist-
ence, was of the same perfect accuracy as all the others they
contained.

Mr. Rout likewise wrote letters; only no one on board knew
how chatty he could be pen in hand, because the chief engineer
had enough imagination to keep his desk locked. His wife
relished his style greatly. They were a childless couple, and Mrs.
Rout, a big, high-bosomed, jolly woman of forty, shared with
Mr. Rout's toothless and venerable mother a little cottage near
Teddington.[22] She would run over her correspondence, at
breakfast, with lively eyes, and scream out interesting passages
in a joyous voice at the deaf old lady, prefacing each extract by
the warning shout, "Solomon says!" She had the trick of firing
off Solomon's utterances also upon strangers, astonishing them
easily by the unfamiliar text and the unexpectedly jocular vein
of these quotations. On the day the new curate called for the
first time at the cottage, she found occasion to remark, "As
Solomon says: 'the engineers that go down to the sea in ships
behold the wonders[23] of sailor nature,'" when a change in the
visitor's countenance made her stop and stare.

"Solomon . . . Oh! . . . Mrs. Rout," stuttered the young man,
very red in the face, "I must say . . . I don't . . ."

"He's my husband," she announced in a great shout, throwing herself back in the chair. Perceiving the joke, she laughed
immoderately with a handkerchief to her eyes, while he sat
wearing a forced smile, and, from his inexperience of jolly
women, fully persuaded that she must be deplorably insane.
They were excellent friends afterwards; for, absolving her from

irreverent intention, he came to think she was a very worthy person indeed; and he learned in time to receive without flinching other scraps of Solomon's wisdom.[24]

"For my part," Solomon was reported by his wife to have said once, "give me the dullest ass for a skipper before a rogue. There is a way to take a fool; but a rogue is smart and slippery." This was an airy generalisation drawn from the particular case of Captain MacWhirr's honesty, which, in itself, had the heavy obviousness of a lump of clay. On the other hand, Mr. Jukes, unable to generalise, unmarried, and unengaged, was in the habit of opening his heart after another fashion to an old chum and former shipmate, actually serving as second officer on board an Atlantic liner.

First of all he would insist upon the advantages of the Eastern trade, hinting at its superiority to the Western Ocean service. He extolled the sky, the seas, the ships, and the easy life of the Far East. The *Nan-Shan*, he affirmed, was second to none as a sea-boat.

"We have no brass-bound uniforms, but then we are like brothers here," he wrote. "We all mess together and live like fighting-cocks. . . . All the chaps of the black-squad[25] are as decent as they make that kind, and old Sol, the chief, is a dry stick. We are good friends. As to our old man, you could not find a quieter skipper. Sometimes you would think he hadn't sense enough to see anything wrong. And yet it isn't that. Can't be. He has been in command for a good few years now. He doesn't do anything actually foolish, and gets his ship along all right without worrying anybody. I believe he hasn't brains enough to enjoy kicking up a row. I don't take advantage of him. I would scorn it. Outside the routine of duty he doesn't seem to understand more than half of what you tell him. We get a laugh out of this at times; but it is dull, too, to be with a man like this—in the long run. Old Sol says he hasn't much conversation. Conversation! O Lord! He never talks. The other day I had been yarning under the bridge with one of the engineers, and he must have heard us. When I came up to take my watch, he steps out of the chart-room and has a good look all round, peeps over at the sidelights, glances at the compass, squints upward at the stars. That's his regular performance. By-and-by he says: 'Was that you talking just now in the port alleyway?' 'Yes, sir.' 'With the third engineer?' 'Yes, sir.' He walks off to starboard, and sits under the dodger on a little campstool of his, and for half an hour perhaps he makes no sound, except that I heard him sneeze once. Then after a while I hear him getting up over there, and he strolls across to port, where I was. 'I can't understand what you can find to talk about,' says he. 'Two solid hours. I am not blaming you. I see people ashore at it all day long, and then in the evening they sit down and keep at it over the drinks. Must be saying the same things over and over again. I can't understand.'

"Did you ever hear anything like that? And he was so patient about it. It made me quite sorry for him. But he is exasperating too sometimes. Of course one would not do anything to vex him even if it were worth while. But it isn't. He's so jolly innocent that if you were to put your thumb to your nose and wave your fingers at him he would only wonder gravely to himself what got into you. He told me once quite simply that he found it very difficult to make out what made people always act so queerly. He's too dense to trouble about, and that's the truth."

Thus wrote Mr. Jukes to his chum in the Western Ocean trade, out of the fullness of his heart and the liveliness of his fancy.

He had expressed his honest opinion. It was not worth while trying to impress a man of that sort. If the world had been full of such men, life would have probably appeared to Jukes an unentertaining and unprofitable business. He was not alone in his opinion. The sea itself, as if sharing Mr. Jukes's good-natured forbearance, had never put itself out to startle the silent man, who seldom looked up, and wandered innocently over the waters with the only visible purpose of getting food, raiment,²⁶ and house-room for three people ashore. Dirty weather he had known, of course. He had been made wet, uncomfortable, tired in the usual way, felt at the time and presently forgotten. So that upon the whole he had been justified in reporting fine weather at home. But he had never been given a glimpse of immeasurable strength and of immoderate wrath, the wrath that passes exhausted but never appeased—the wrath and fury of the passionate sea. He knew it existed, as we know that crime and abominations exist; he had heard of it as a peaceable citizen in a town hears of battles, famines, and floods,[27] and yet knows nothing of what these things mean—though, indeed, he may have been mixed up in a street row, have gone without his dinner once, or been soaked to the skin in a shower. Captain MacWhirr had sailed over the surface of the oceans as some men go skimming over the years of existence to sink gently into a placid grave, ignorant of life to the last, without ever having been made to see all it may contain of perfidy, of violence, and of terror. There are on sea and land such men thus fortunate—or thus disdained by destiny or by the sea.

II

Observing the steady fall of the barometer, Captain MacWhirr thought, "There's some dirty weather knocking about." This is precisely what he thought. He had had an experience of moderately dirty weather—the term dirty as applied to the weather implying only moderate discomfort to the seaman. Had he been informed by an indisputable authority that the end of the world was to be finally accomplished by a catastrophic disturbance of the atmosphere, he would have assimilated the information under the simple idea of dirty weather, and no other, because he had no experience of cataclysms, and belief does not necessarily imply comprehension. The wisdom of his country had pronounced by means of an Act of Parliament[28] that before he could be considered as fit to take charge of a ship he should be able to answer certain simple questions on the subject of circular storms such as hurricanes, cyclones, typhoons; and apparently he had answered them, since he was now in command of the *Nan-Shan* in the China seas during the season of typhoons.[29] But if he had answered he remembered nothing of it. He was, however, conscious of being made uncomfortable by the clammy heat. He came out on the bridge, and found no relief to this oppression. The air seemed thick. He gasped like a fish, and began to believe himself greatly out of sorts.

The *Nan-Shan* was ploughing a vanishing furrow upon the circle of the sea that had the surface and the shimmer of an undulating piece of grey silk. The sun, pale and without rays, poured down leaden heat in a strangely indecisive light, and the Chinamen were lying prostrate about the decks. Their bloodless, pinched, yellow faces were like the faces of bilious invalids. Captain MacWhirr noticed two of them especially, stretched out on their backs below the bridge. As soon as they had closed their eyes they seemed dead. Three others, however, were quarrelling barbarously away forward; and one big fellow, half naked, with Herculean shoulders, was hanging limply over a winch; another, sitting on the deck, his knees up and his head drooping sideways in a girlish attitude, was plaiting his pigtail with infinite languor depicted in his whole person and in the very movement of his fingers. The smoke struggled with difficulty out of the funnel, and instead of streaming away spread itself out like an infernal sort of cloud, smelling of sulphur and raining soot all over the decks.

"What the devil are you doing there, Mr. Jukes?" asked Captain MacWhirr.

This unusual form of address, though mumbled rather than spoken, caused the body of Mr. Jukes to start as though it had been prodded under the fifth rib. He had had a low bench brought on the bridge, and sitting on it, with a length of rope curled about his feet and a piece of canvas stretched over his knees, was pushing a sail-needle vigorously. He looked up, and his surprise gave to his eyes an expression of innocence and candour.

"I am only roping some of that new set of bags we made last trip for whipping up coals," he remonstrated gently. "We shall want them for the next coaling, sir."

"What became of the others?"

"Why, worn out, of course, sir."

Captain MacWhirr, after glaring down irresolutely at his chief mate, disclosed the gloomy and cynical conviction that more than half of them had been lost overboard, "if only the truth was known," and retired to the other end of the bridge. Jukes, exasperated by this unprovoked attack, broke the needle at the second stitch, and dropping his work got up and cursed the heat in a violent undertone.

The propeller thumped, the three Chinamen forward had given up squabbling very suddenly, and the one who had been plaiting his tail clasped his legs and stared dejectedly over his knees. The lurid sunshine cast faint and sickly shadows. The swell ran higher and swifter every moment, and the ship lurched heavily in the smooth, deep hollows of the sea.

"I wonder where that beastly swell comes from," said Jukes aloud, recovering himself after a stagger.

"North-East," grunted the literal MacWhirr, from his side of the bridge. "There's some dirty weather knocking about. Go and look at the glass."

When Jukes came out of the chart-room, the cast of his countenance had changed to thoughtfulness and concern. He caught hold of the bridge-rail and stared ahead.

The temperature in the engine-room had gone up to 117 degrees. Irritated voices were ascending through the skylight and through the fiddle of the stokehold in a harsh and resonant uproar, mingled with angry clangs and scrapes of metal, as if men with limbs of iron and throats of bronze had been quarrelling down there. The second engineer was falling foul of the stokers for letting the steam go down. He was a man with arms like a blacksmith, and generally feared; but that afternoon the stokers were answering him back recklessly, and slammed the furnace doors with the fury of despair. Then the noise ceased suddenly, and the second engineer appeared, emerging out of the stokehold streaked with grime and soaking wet like a chimney-sweep coming out of a well. As soon as his head was clear of the fiddle he began to scold Jukes for not trimming properly the stokehold ventilators; and in answer Jukes made with his hands deprecatory soothing signs meaning: No wind—can't be helped—you can see for yourself. But the other

wouldn't hear reason. His teeth flashed angrily in his dirty face.
He didn't mind, he said, the trouble of punching their blanked
heads down there, blank his soul, but did the condemned sailors
think you could keep steam up in the God-forsaken boilers
simply by knocking the blanked stokers about? No, by George!
You had to get some draught too—may he be everlastingly
blanked for a swab-headed deck-hand if you didn't! And the
chief, too, rampaging before the steam-gauge and carrying on
like a lunatic up and down the engine-room ever since noon.
What did Jukes think he was stuck up there for, if he couldn't
get one of his decayed, good-for-nothing deck-cripples to turn
the ventilators to the wind?

The relations of the "engine-room" and the "deck" of the
Nan-Shan were, as is known, of a brotherly nature; therefore
Jukes leaned over and begged the other in a restrained tone not
to make a disgusting ass of himself; the skipper was on the
other side of the bridge. But the second declared mutinously
that he didn't care a rap who was on the other side of the
bridge, and Jukes, passing in a flash from lofty disapproval into
a state of exaltation, invited him in unflattering terms to come
up and twist the beastly things to please himself, and catch such
wind as a donkey[30] of his sort could find. The second rushed
up to the fray. He flung himself at the port ventilator as though
he meant to tear it out bodily and toss it overboard. All he
did was to move the cowl round a few inches, with an enormous
expenditure of force, and seemed spent in the effort. He leaned
against the back of the wheel-house, and Jukes walked up
to him.

"Oh, Heavens!" ejaculated the engineer in a feeble voice. He
lifted his eyes to the sky, and then let his glassy stare descend
to meet the horizon that, tilting up to an angle of forty degrees,
seemed to hang on a slant for a while and settled down slowly.
"Heavens! Phew! What's up, anyhow?"

Jukes, straddling his long legs like a pair of compasses, put
on an air of superiority. "We're going to catch it this time," he
said. "The barometer is tumbling down like anything, Harry.
And you trying to kick up that silly row . . ."

The word "barometer" seemed to revive the second engineer's

mad animosity. Collecting afresh all his energies, he directed
Jukes in a low and brutal tone to shove the unmentionable
instrument down his gory throat. Who cared for his crimson
barometer? It was the steam—the steam—that was going
down; and what between the firemen going faint and the chief
going silly, it was worse than a dog's life for him; he didn't care
a tinker's curse how soon the whole show was blown out of
the water. He seemed on the point of having a cry, but after
regaining his breath he muttered darkly, "I'll faint them," and
dashed off. He stopped upon the fiddle long enough to shake
his fist at the unnatural daylight, and dropped into the dark
hole with a whoop.

When Jukes turned, his eyes fell upon the rounded back and
the big red ears of Captain MacWhirr, who had come across.
He did not look at his chief officer, but said at once, "That's a
very violent man, that second engineer."

"Jolly good second, anyhow," grunted Jukes. "They can't
keep up steam," he added rapidly, and made a grab at the rail
against the coming lurch.

Captain MacWhirr, unprepared, took a run and brought
himself up with a jerk by an awning stanchion.

"A profane man," he said obstinately. "If this goes on, I'll
have to get rid of him the first chance."

"It's the heat," said Jukes. "The weather's awful. It would
make a saint swear. Even up here I feel exactly as if I had my
head tied up in a woollen blanket."

Captain MacWhirr looked up. "D'ye mean to say, Mr. Jukes,
you ever had your head tied up in a blanket? What was that
for?"

"It's a manner of speaking, sir," said Jukes stolidly.

"Some of you fellows do go on! What's that about saints
swearing? I wish you wouldn't talk so wild. What sort of saint
would that be that would swear? No more saint than yourself,
I expect. And what's a blanket got to do with it—or the weather
either . . . The heat does not make me swear—does it? It's filthy
bad temper. That's what it is. And what's the good of your
talking like this?"

Thus Captain MacWhirr expostulated against the use of

images in speech, and at the end electrified Jukes by a contemptuous snort, followed by words of passion and resentment: "Damme! I'll fire him out of the ship if he don't look out."

And Jukes, incorrigible, thought: "Goodness me! Somebody's put a new inside to my old man. Here's temper, if you like. Of course it's the weather; what else? It would make an angel quarrelsome—let alone a saint."

All the Chinamen on deck appeared at their last gasp.

At its setting the sun had a diminished diameter and an expiring brown, rayless glow, as if millions of centuries elapsing since the morning had brought it near its end. A dense bank of cloud became visible to the northward; it had a sinister dark olive tint, and lay low and motionless upon the sea, resembling a solid obstacle in the path of the ship. She went floundering towards it like an exhausted creature driven to its death. The coppery twilight retired slowly, and the darkness brought out overhead a swarm of unsteady, big stars, that, as if blown upon, flickered exceedingly and seemed to hang very near the earth. At eight o'clock Jukes went into the chart-room to write up the ship's log.

He copied neatly out of the rough-book the number of miles, the course of the ship, and in the column for "wind" scrawled the word "calm" from top to bottom of the eight hours since noon. He was exasperated by the continuous, monotonous rolling of the ship. The heavy inkstand would slide away in a manner that suggested perverse intelligence in dodging the pen. Having written in the large space under the head of "Remarks" "Heat very oppressive," he stuck the end of the penholder in his teeth, pipe-fashion, and mopped his face carefully.

"Ship rolling heavily in a high cross swell," he began again, and commented to himself, "Heavily is no word for it." Then he wrote: "Sunset threatening, with a low bank of clouds to N. and E. Sky clear overhead."

Sprawling over the table with arrested pen, he glanced out of the door, and in that frame of his vision he saw all the stars flying upwards between the teakwood jambs on a black sky. The whole lot took flight together and disappeared, leaving only a blackness flecked with white flashes, for the sea was as black as the sky and speckled with foam afar. The stars that had flown to the roll came back on the return swing of the ship, rushing downwards in their glittering multitude, not of fiery points, but enlarged to tiny discs brilliant with a clear wet sheen.

Jukes watched the flying big stars for a moment, and then wrote: "8 P.M. Swell increasing. Ship labouring and taking water on her decks. Battened down the coolies for the night. Barometer still falling." He paused, and thought to himself, "Perhaps nothing whatever'll come of it." And then he closed resolutely his entries: "Every appearance of a typhoon coming on."

On going out he had to stand aside, and Captain MacWhirr strode over the doorstep without saying a word or making a sign.

"Shut the door, Mr. Jukes, will you?" he cried from within.

Jukes turned back to do so, muttering ironically: "Afraid to catch cold, I suppose." It was his watch below, but he yearned for communion with his kind; and he remarked cheerily to the second mate: "Doesn't look so bad, after all. Does it?"

The second mate was marching to and fro on the bridge, tripping down with small steps one moment, and the next climbing with difficulty the shifting slope of the deck. At the sound of Jukes's voice he stood still, facing forward, but made no reply.

"Hallo! That's a heavy one," said Jukes, swaying to meet the long roll till his lowered hand touched the planks. This time the second mate made in his throat a noise of an unfriendly nature.

He was an oldish, shabby little fellow, with bad teeth and no hair on his face. He had been shipped in a hurry in Shanghai, that trip when the second officer brought from home had delayed the ship three hours in port by contriving (in some manner Captain MacWhirr could never understand) to fall overboard into an empty coal-lighter lying alongside, and had to be sent ashore to the hospital with concussion of the brain and a broken limb or two.

Jukes was not discouraged by the unsympathetic sound. "The

Chinamen must be having a lovely time of it down there,"
he said. "It's lucky for them the old girl has the easiest roll
of any ship I've ever been in. There now! This one wasn't
so bad."

"You wait," snarled the second mate.

With his sharp nose, red at the tip, and his thin pinched lips,
he always looked as though he were raging inwardly; and he
was concise in his speech to the point of rudeness. All his time
off duty he spent in his cabin with the door shut, keeping so
still in there that he was supposed to fall asleep as soon as he
had disappeared; but the man who came in to wake him for his
watch on deck would invariably find him with his eyes wide
open, flat on his back in the bunk, and glaring irritably from a
soiled pillow. He never wrote any letters, did not seem to hope
for news from anywhere; and though he had been heard once
to mention West Hartlepool,[31] it was with extreme bitterness,
and only in connection with the extortionate charges of a
boarding-house. He was one of those men who are picked up
at need in the ports of the world. They are competent enough,
appear hopelessly hard up, show no evidence of any sort of
vice, and carry about them all the signs of manifest failure.
They come aboard on an emergency, care for no ship afloat,
live in their own atmosphere of casual connection amongst
their shipmates who know nothing of them, and make up their
minds to leave at inconvenient times. They clear out with no
words of leave-taking in some God-forsaken port other men
would fear to be stranded in, and go ashore in company of a
shabby sea-chest, corded like a treasure-box, and with an air
of shaking the ship's dust off their feet.

"You wait," he repeated, balanced in great swings with his
back to Jukes, motionless and implacable.

"Do you mean to say we are going to catch it hot?" asked
Jukes with boyish interest.

"Say? . . . I say nothing. You don't catch me," snapped the
little second mate, with a mixture of pride, scorn, and cunning,
as if Jukes's question had been a trap cleverly detected. "Oh,
no! None of you here shall make a fool of me if I know it," he
mumbled to himself.

Jukes reflected rapidly that this second mate was a mean little beast, and in his heart he wished poor Jack Allen had never smashed himself up in the coal-lighter. The far-off blackness ahead of the ship was like another night seen through the starry night of the earth—the starless night of the immensities beyond the created universe, revealed in its appalling stillness through a low fissure in the glittering sphere of which the earth is the kernel.

"Whatever there might be about," said Jukes, "we are steaming straight into it."

"*You've* said it," caught up the second mate, always with his back to Jukes. "You've said it, mind. Not I."

"Oh, go to Jericho!"[32] said Jukes frankly; and the other emitted a triumphant little chuckle.

"You've said it," he repeated.

"And what of that?"

"I've known some real good men get into trouble with their skippers for saying a dam' sight less," answered the second mate feverishly. "Oh, no! You don't catch me."

"You seem deucedly anxious not to give yourself away," said Jukes, completely soured by such absurdity. "I wouldn't be afraid to say what I think."

"Aye, to me! That's no great trick. I am nobody, and well I know it."

The ship, after a pause of comparative steadiness, started upon a series of rolls, one worse than the other, and for a time Jukes, preserving his equilibrium, was too busy to open his mouth. As soon as the violent swinging had quieted down somewhat, he said: "This is a bit too much of a good thing. Whether anything is coming or not I think she ought to be put head on to that swell. The old man is just gone in to lie down. Hang me if I don't speak to him."

But when he opened the door of the chart-room he saw his captain reading a book. Captain MacWhirr was not lying down: he was standing up with one hand grasping the edge of the bookshelf and the other holding open before his face a thick volume. The lamp wriggled in the gimbals, the loosened books toppled from side to side on the shelf, the long barometer swung in jerky circles, the table altered its slant every moment. In the midst of all this stir and movement Captain MacWhirr, holding on, showed his eyes above the upper edge, and asked, "What's the matter?"

"Swell getting worse, sir."

"Noticed that in here," muttered Captain MacWhirr. "Anything wrong?"

Jukes, inwardly disconcerted by the seriousness of the eyes looking at him over the top of the book, produced an embarrassed grin.

"Rolling like old boots," he said sheepishly.

"Aye! Very heavy—very heavy. What do you want?"

At this Jukes lost his footing and began to flounder.

"I was thinking of our passengers," he said, in the manner of a man clutching at a straw.

"Passengers?" wondered the captain gravely. "What passengers?"

"Why, the Chinamen, sir," explained Jukes, very sick of this conversation.

"The Chinamen! Why don't you speak plainly? Couldn't tell what you meant. Never heard a lot of coolies spoken of as passengers before. Passengers, indeed! What's come to you?"

Captain MacWhirr, closing the book on his forefinger, lowered his arm and looked completely mystified. "Why are you thinking of the Chinamen, Mr. Jukes?" he inquired.

Jukes took a plunge, like a man driven to it. "She's rolling her decks full of water, sir. Thought you might put her head on perhaps—for a while. Till this goes down a bit—very soon, I dare say. Head to the eastward. I never knew a ship roll like this."

He held on in the doorway, and Captain MacWhirr, feeling his grip on the shelf inadequate, made up his mind to let go in a hurry, and fell heavily on the couch.

"Head to the eastward?" he said, struggling to sit up. "That's more than four points off her course."

"Yes, sir. Fifty degrees . . . Would just bring her head far enough round to meet this . . ."

Captain MacWhirr was now sitting up. He had not dropped the book, and he had not lost his place.

"To the eastward?" he repeated, with dawning astonishment. "To the . . . Where do you think we are bound to? You want me to haul a full-powered steamship four points off her course to make the Chinamen comfortable! Now, I've heard more than enough of mad things done in the world—but this . . . If I didn't know you, Jukes, I would think you were in liquor. Steer four points off . . . And what afterwards? Steer four points over the other way, I suppose, to make the course good. What put it into your head that I would start to tack a steamer as if she were a sailing-ship?"

"Jolly good thing she isn't," threw in Jukes, with bitter readiness. "She would have rolled every blessed stick out of her this afternoon."

"Aye! And you just would have had to stand and see them go," said Captain MacWhirr, showing a certain animation. "It's a dead calm, isn't it?"

"It is, sir. But there's something out of the common coming, for sure."

"Maybe. I suppose you have a notion I should be getting out of the way of that dirt," said Captain MacWhirr, speaking with the utmost simplicity of manner and tone, and fixing the oilcloth on the floor with a heavy stare. Thus he noticed neither Jukes's discomfiture nor the mixture of vexation and astonished respect on his face.

"Now, here's this book," he continued with deliberation, slapping his thigh with the closed volume. "I've been reading the chapter on the storms there."

This was true. He had been reading the chapter on the storms. When he had entered the chart-room, it was with no intention of taking the book down. Some influence in the air—the same influence, probably, that caused the steward to bring without orders the captain's sea-boots and oilskin coat up to the chart-room—had as it were guided his hand to the shelf; and without taking the time to sit down he had waded with a conscious effort into the terminology of the subject. He lost himself amongst advancing semi-circles, left- and right-hand quadrants, the curves of the tracks, the probable bearing of the centre, the shifts of wind, and the readings of barometer. He tried to bring all these things into a definite relation to himself, and ended by becoming contemptuously angry with such a lot of words and with so much advice, all head-work and supposition, without a glimmer of certitude.

"It's the damnedest thing, Jukes," he said. "If a fellow was to believe all that's in there, he would be running most of his time all over the sea trying to get behind the weather."

Again he slapped his leg with the book; and Jukes opened his mouth, but said nothing.

"Running to get behind the weather! Do you understand that, Mr. Jukes? It's the maddest thing!" ejaculated Captain MacWhirr, with pauses, gazing at the floor profoundly. "You would think an old woman had been writing this. It passes me. If that thing means anything useful, then it means that I should at once alter the course away, away to the devil somewhere, and come booming down on Fu-chau from the northward at the tail of this dirty weather that's supposed to be knocking about in our way. From the north! Do you understand, Mr. Jukes? Three hundred extra miles to the distance, and a pretty coal bill to show. I couldn't bring myself to do that if every word in there was gospel truth, Mr. Jukes. Don't you expect me . . ."

And Jukes, silent, marvelled at this display of feeling and loquacity.

"But the truth is that you don't know if the fellow is right anyhow. How can you tell what a gale is made of till you get it? He isn't aboard here, is he? Very well. Here he says that the centre of them things bears eight points off the wind; but we haven't got any wind, for all the barometer falling. Where's his centre now?"

"We will get the wind presently," mumbled Jukes.

"Let it come, then," said Captain MacWhirr, with dignified indignation. "It's only to let you see, Mr. Jukes, that you don't find everything in books. All these rules for dodging breezes and circumventing the winds of heaven, Mr. Jukes, seem to me the maddest thing, when you come to look at it sensibly."

He raised his eyes, saw Jukes gazing at him dubiously, and tried to illustrate his meaning.

"About as queer as your extraordinary notion of dodging the ship head to sea, for I don't know how long, to make the Chinamen comfortable; whereas all we've got to do is to take them to Fu-chau, being timed to get there before noon on Friday. If the weather delays me—very well. There's your log-book to talk straight about the weather. But suppose I went swinging off my course and came in two days late, and they asked me: 'Where have you been all that time, Captain?' What could I say to that? 'Went around to dodge the bad weather,' I would say. 'It must've been dam' bad,' they would say. 'Don't know,' I would have to say; 'I've dodged clear of it.' See that, Jukes? I have been thinking it all out this afternoon."

He looked up again in his unseeing, unimaginative way. No one had ever heard him say so much at one time. Jukes, with his arms open in the doorway, was like a man invited to behold a miracle. Unbounded wonder was the intellectual meaning of his eye, while incredulity was seated in his whole countenance.

"A gale is a gale, Mr. Jukes," resumed the captain, "and a full-powered steamship has got to face it. There's just so much dirty weather knocking about the world, and the proper thing is to go through it with none of what old Captain Wilson of the *Melita*[33] calls 'storm strategy.' The other day ashore I heard him hold forth about it to a lot of shipmasters who came in and sat at a table next to mine. It seemed to me the greatest nonsense. He was telling them how he—out-manoeuvred, I think he said—a terrific gale, so that it never came nearer than fifty miles to him. A neat piece of head-work he called it. How he knew there was a terrific gale fifty miles off beats me altogether. It was like listening to a crazy man. I would have thought Captain Wilson was old enough to know better."

Captain MacWhirr ceased for a moment, then said, "It's your watch below, Mr. Jukes?"

Jukes came to himself with a start. "Yes, sir."

"Leave orders to call me at the slightest change," said the captain. He reached up to put the book away, and tucked his legs upon the couch. "Shut the door so that it don't fly open, will you? I can't stand a door banging. They've put a lot of rubbishy locks into this ship, I must say."

Captain MacWhirr closed his eyes.

He did so to rest himself. He was tired, and he experienced that state of mental vacuity which comes at the end of an exhaustive discussion that had liberated some belief matured in the course of meditative years. He had indeed been making his confession of faith, had he only known it; and its effect was to make Jukes, on the other side of the door, stand scratching his head for a good while.

Captain MacWhirr opened his eyes.

He thought he must have been asleep. What was that loud noise? Wind? Why had he not been called? The lamp wriggled in its gimbals, the barometer swung in circles, the table altered its slant every moment; a pair of limp sea-boots with collapsed tops went sliding past the couch. He put out his hand instantly, and captured one.

Jukes's face appeared in a crack of the door; only his face, very red, with staring eyes. The flame of the lamp leaped, a piece of paper flew up, a rush of air enveloped Captain MacWhirr. Beginning to draw on the boot, he directed an expectant gaze at Jukes's swollen, excited features.

"Came on like this," shouted Jukes, "five minutes ago . . . all of a sudden."

The head disappeared with a bang, and a heavy splash and patter of drops swept past the closed door as if a pailful of melted lead had been flung against the house. A whistling could be heard now upon the deep vibrating noise outside. The stuffy chart-room seemed as full of draughts as a shed. Captain MacWhirr collared the other sea-boot on its violent passage along the floor. He was not flustered, but he could not find at once the opening for inserting his foot. The shoes he had flung off were scurrying from end to end of the cabin, gambolling playfully over each other like puppies. As soon as he stood up he kicked at them viciously, but without effect.

He threw himself into the attitude of a lunging fencer to reach after his oilskin coat; and afterwards he staggered all over the confined space while he jerked himself into it. Very grave, straddling his legs far apart, and stretching his neck, he started to tie deliberately the strings of his sou'-wester under his chin, with thick fingers that trembled slightly. He went through all the movements of a woman putting on her bonnet before a glass, with a strained, listening attention, as though he had expected every moment to hear the shout of his name in the confused clamour that had suddenly beset his ship. Its increase filled his ears while he was getting ready to go out and confront whatever it might mean. It was tumultuous and very loud—made up of the rush of the wind, the crashes of the sea, with that prolonged deep vibration of the air, like the roll of an immense and remote drum beating the charge of the gale.

He stood for a moment in the light of the lamp, thick, clumsy, shapeless in his panoply of combat, vigilant and red-faced.

"There's a lot of weight in this," he muttered.

As soon as he attempted to open the door the wind caught it. Clinging to the handle, he was dragged out over the doorstep, and at once found himself engaged with the wind in a sort of personal scuffle whose object was the shutting of that door. At the last moment a tongue of air scurried in and licked out the flame of the lamp.

Ahead of the ship he perceived a great darkness lying upon a multitude of white flashes; on the starboard beam a few amazing stars drooped, dim and fitful, above an immense waste of broken seas, as if seen through a mad drift of smoke.

On the bridge a knot of men, indistinct and toiling, were making great efforts in the light of the wheel-house windows that shone mistily on their heads and backs. Suddenly darkness closed upon one pane, then on another. The voices of the lost group reached him after the manner of men's voices in a gale, in shreds and fragments of forlorn shouting snatched past the ear. All at once Jukes appeared at his side, yelling, with his head down.

"Watch—put in—wheel-house shutters—glass—afraid—blow in."

Jukes heard his commander upbraiding.

"This—come—anything—warning—call me."

He tried to explain, with the uproar pressing on his lips.

"Light air—remained—bridge—sudden—north-east—could turn—thought—you—sure—hear."

They had gained the shelter of the weather-cloth, and could converse with raised voices, as people quarrel.

"I got the hands along to cover up all the ventilators. Good job I had remained on deck. I didn't think you would be asleep, and so . . . What did you say, sir? What?"

"Nothing," cried Captain MacWhirr. "I said—all right."

"By all the powers! We've got it this time," observed Jukes in a howl.

"You haven't altered her course?" inquired Captain Mac-Whirr, straining his voice.

"No, sir. Certainly not. Wind came out right ahead. And here comes the head sea."

A plunge of the ship ended in a shock as if she had landed her forefoot upon something solid. After a moment of stillness a lofty flight of sprays drove hard with the wind upon their faces.

"Keep her at it as long as we can," shouted Captain MacWhirr.

Before Jukes had squeezed the salt water out of his eyes all the stars had disappeared.

III

Jukes was as ready a man as any half-dozen young mates that may be caught by casting a net upon the waters; and though he had been somewhat taken aback by the startling viciousness of the first squall, he had pulled himself together on the instant, had called out the hands, and had rushed them along to secure such openings about the deck as had not been already battened down earlier in the evening. Shouting in his fresh, stentorian voice "Jump, boys, and bear a hand!" he led in the work, telling himself the while that he had "just expected this."

But at the same time he was growing aware that this was rather more than he had expected. From the first stir of the air felt on his cheek the gale seemed to take upon itself the accumulated impetus of an avalanche. Heavy sprays enveloped the *Nan-Shan* from stem to stern, and instantly in the midst of her regular rolling she began to jerk and plunge as though she had gone mad with fright.

Jukes thought, "This is no joke." While he was exchanging explanatory yells with his captain, a sudden lowering of the darkness came upon the night, falling before their vision like something palpable. It was as if the masked lights of the world had been turned down. Jukes was uncritically glad to have his captain at hand. It relieved him as though that man had, by simply coming on deck, taken most of the gale's weight upon his shoulders. Such is the prestige, the privilege, and the burden of command.

Captain MacWhirr could expect no relief of that sort from any one on earth. Such is the loneliness of command. He was trying to see, with that watchful manner of a seaman who stares into the wind's eye as if into the eye of an adversary, to penetrate the hidden intention and guess the aim and force of the thrust. The strong wind swept at him out of a vast obscurity; he felt under his feet the uneasiness of his ship, and he could not even discern the shadow of her shape. He wished it were not so; and very still he waited, feeling stricken by a blind man's helplessness.

To be silent was natural to him, dark or shine. Jukes, at his elbow, made himself heard yelling cheerily in the gusts, "We must have got the worst of it at once, sir." A faint burst of lightning quivered all round, as if flashed into a cavern—into a black and secret chamber of the sea, with a floor of foaming crests.

It unveiled for a sinister, fluttering moment a ragged mass of clouds hanging low, the lurch of the long outlines of the ship, the black figures of men caught on the bridge, heads forward, as if petrified in the act of butting. The darkness palpitated down upon all this, and then the real thing came at last.

It was something formidable and swift, like the sudden smashing of a vial of wrath.[34] It seemed to explode all round the ship with an overpowering concussion and a rush of great waters, as if an immense dam had been blown up to windward. In an instant the men lost touch of each other. This is the disintegrating power of a great wind: it isolates one from one's kind. An earthquake, a landslip, an avalanche, overtake a man incidentally, as it were—without passion. A furious gale attacks him like a personal enemy, tries to grasp his limbs, fastens upon his mind, seeks to rout his very spirit out of him.

Jukes was driven away from his commander. He fancied himself whirled a great distance through the air. Everything disappeared—even, for a moment, his power of thinking; but his hand had found one of the rail-stanchions. His distress was by no means alleviated by an inclination to disbelieve the reality of this experience. Though young, he had seen some bad weather, and had never doubted his ability to imagine the worst; but this was so much beyond his powers of fancy that it appeared incompatible with the existence of any ship whatever. He would have been incredulous about himself in the same way, perhaps, had he not been so harassed by the necessity of exerting a wrestling effort against a force trying to tear him away from his hold. Moreover, the conviction of not being utterly destroyed returned to him through the sensations of being half-drowned, bestially shaken, and partly choked.

It seemed to him he remained there precariously alone with the stanchion for a long, long time. The rain poured on him, flowed, drove in sheets. He breathed in gasps; and sometimes the water he swallowed was fresh and sometimes it was salt. For the most part he kept his eyes shut tight, as if suspecting his sight might be destroyed in the immense flurry of the elements. When he ventured to blink hastily, he derived some moral support from the green gleam of the starboard light shining feebly upon the flight of rain and sprays. He was actually looking at it when its ray fell upon the uprearing sea which put it out. He saw the head of the wave topple over, adding the mite of its crash to the tremendous uproar raging around him, and almost at the same instant the stanchion was wrenched away from his embracing arms. After a crushing thump on his back he found himself suddenly afloat and borne upwards. His first irresistible notion was that the whole China Sea had climbed on the bridge. Then, more sanely, he concluded himself gone overboard. All the time he was being tossed, flung, and rolled in great volumes of water, he kept on repeating mentally, with the utmost precipitation, the words: "My God! My God! My God! My God!"

All at once, in a revolt of misery and despair, he formed the crazy resolution to get out of that. And he began to thresh about with his arms and legs. But as soon as he commenced his wretched struggles he discovered that he had become somehow mixed up with a face, an oilskin coat, somebody's boots. He clawed ferociously all these things in turn, lost them, found them again, lost them once more, and finally was himself caught in the firm clasp of a pair of stout arms. He returned the embrace closely round a thick solid body. He had found his captain.

They tumbled over and over, tightening their hug. Suddenly the water let them down with a brutal bang; and, stranded against the side of the wheel-house, out of breath and bruised, they were left to stagger up in the wind and hold on where they could.

Jukes came out of it rather horrified, as though he had escaped some unparalleled outrage directed at his feelings. It weakened his faith in himself. He started shouting aimlessly to the man he could feel near him in that fiendish blackness, "Is it you, sir? Is it you, sir?" till his temples seemed ready to burst. And he heard in answer a voice, as if crying far away, as if screaming to him fretfully from a very great distance, the one word "Yes!" Other seas swept again over the bridge. He received them defencelessly right over his bare head, with both his hands engaged in holding.

The motion of the ship was extravagant. Her lurches had an appalling helplessness; she pitched as if taking a header into a void, and seemed to find a wall to hit every time. When she rolled she fell on her side headlong, and she would be righted back by such a demolishing blow that Jukes felt her reeling as a clubbed man reels before he collapses. The gale howled and scuffled about gigantically in the darkness, as though the entire world were one black gully. At certain moments the air streamed against the ship as if sucked through a tunnel with a concentrated solid force of impact that seemed to lift her clean out of the water and keep her up for an instant with only a quiver running through her from end to end. And then she would begin her tumbling again as if dropped back into a boiling cauldron. Jukes tried hard to compose his mind and judge things coolly.

The sea, flattened down in the heavier gusts, would uprise and overwhelm both ends of the *Nan-Shan* in snowy rushes of foam, expanding wide, beyond both rails, into the night. And on this dazzling sheet, spread under the blackness of the clouds and emitting a bluish glow, Captain MacWhirr could catch a desolate glimpse of a few tiny specks black as ebony, the tops of the hatches, the battened companions, the heads of the covered winches, the foot of a mast. This was all he could see of his ship. Her middle structure, covered by the bridge which bore him, his mate, the closed wheel-house where a man was steering shut up with the fear of being swept overboard together with the whole thing in one great crash—her middle structure was like a half-tide rock awash upon a coast. It was like an outlying rock with the water boiling up, streaming over, pouring off, beating round—like a rock in the surf to which ship-wrecked people cling before they let go—only it rose, it sank, it rolled continuously, without respite and rest, like a rock that should have miraculously struck adrift from a coast and gone wallowing upon the sea.

The *Nan-Shan* was being looted by the storm with a senseless, destructive fury: trysails torn out of the extra gaskets, double-lashed awnings blown away, bridge swept clean, weather-cloths burst, rails twisted, light-screens smashed—and two of the boats had gone already. They had gone unheard and unseen, melting, as it were, in the shock and smother of the wave. It was only later, when upon the white flash of another high sea hurling itself amidships, Jukes had a vision of two pairs of davits leaping black and empty out of the solid blackness, with one overhauled fall flying and an iron-bound block capering in the air, that he became aware of what had happened within about three yards of his back.

He poked his head forward, groping for the ear of his commander. His lips touched it—big, fleshy, very wet. He cried in an agitated tone, "Our boats are going now, sir."

And again he heard that voice, forced and ringing feebly, but with a penetrating effect of quietness in the enormous discord of noises, as if sent out from some remote spot of peace beyond the black wastes of the gale; again he heard a man's voice—the frail and indomitable sound that can be made to carry an infinity of thought, resolution, and purpose, that shall be pronouncing confident words on the last day, when heavens fall, and justice is done[35]—again he heard it, and it was crying to him, as if from very, very far—"All right."

He thought he had not managed to make himself understood. "Our boats—I say boats—the boats, sir! Two gone!"

The same voice, within a foot of him and yet so remote, yelled sensibly, "Can't be helped."

Captain MacWhirr had never turned his face, but Jukes caught some more words on the wind.

"What can—expect—when hammering through—such—— Bound to leave—something behind—stands to reason."

Watchfully Jukes listened for more. No more came. This was all Captain MacWhirr had to say; and Jukes could picture to himself rather than see the broad squat back before him. An impenetrable obscurity pressed down upon the ghostly glimmers of the sea. A dull conviction seized upon Jukes that there was nothing to be done.

If the steering-gear did not give way, if the immense volumes of water did not burst the deck in or smash one of the hatches, if the engines did not give up, if way could be kept on the ship against this terrific wind, and she did not bury herself in one of these awful seas, of whose white crests alone, topping high above her bows, he could now and then get a sickening glimpse—then there was a chance of her coming out of it. Something within him seemed to turn over, bringing uppermost the feeling that the *Nan-Shan* was lost.

"She's done for," he said to himself, with a surprising mental agitation, as though he had discovered an unexpected meaning in this thought. One of these things was bound to happen.

Nothing could be prevented now, and nothing could be remedied. The men on board did not count, and the ship could not last. This weather was too impossible.

Jukes felt an arm thrown heavily over his shoulders; and to this overture he responded with great intelligence by catching hold of his captain round the waist.

They stood clasped thus in the blind night, bracing each other against the wind, cheek to cheek and lip to ear, in the manner of two hulks lashed stem to stern together.

And Jukes heard the voice of his commander hardly any louder than before, but nearer, as though, starting to march athwart the prodigious rush of the hurricane, it had approached him, bearing that strange effect of quietness like the serene glow of a halo.

"D'ye know where the hands got to?" it asked, vigorous and evanescent at the same time, overcoming the strength of the wind, and swept away from Jukes instantly.

Jukes didn't know. They were all on the bridge when the real force of the hurricane struck the ship. He had no idea where they had crawled to. Under the circumstances they were nowhere, for all the use that could be made of them. Somehow the captain's wish to know distressed Jukes.

"Want the hands, sir?" he cried apprehensively.

"Ought to know," asserted Captain MacWhirr. "Hold hard."

They held hard. An outburst of unchained fury, a vicious rush of the wind absolutely steadied the ship; she rocked only, quick and light like a child's cradle, for a terrific moment of suspense, while the whole atmosphere, as it seemed, streamed furiously past her, roaring away from the tenebrous earth.

It suffocated them, and with eyes shut they tightened their grasp. What from the magnitude of the shock might have been a column of water running upright in the dark, butted against the ship, broke short, and fell on her bridge, crushingly, from on high, with a dead burying weight.

A flying fragment of that collapse, a mere splash, enveloped them in one swirl from their feet over their heads, filling violently their ears, mouths, and nostrils with salt water. It knocked out their legs, wrenched in haste at their arms, seethed away swiftly under their chins; and opening their eyes, they saw the piled-up masses of foam dashing to and fro amongst what looked like the fragments of a ship. She had given way as if driven straight in. Their panting hearts yielded too before the tremendous blow; and all at once she sprang up again to her desperate plunging, as if trying to scramble out from under the ruins.

The seas in the dark seemed to rush from all sides to keep her back where she might perish. There was hate in the way she was handled, and a ferocity in the blows that fell. She was like a living creature thrown to the rage of a mob: hustled terribly, struck at, borne up, flung down, leaped upon. Captain Mac-Whirr and Jukes kept hold of each other, deafened by the noise, gagged by the wind; and the great physical tumult beating about their bodies, brought, like an unbridled display of passion, a profound trouble to their souls. One of those wild and appalling shrieks that are heard at times passing mysteriously overhead in the steady roar of a hurricane, swooped, as if borne on wings, upon the ship, and Jukes tried to outscream it.

"Will she live through this?"

The cry was wrenched out of his breast. It was as unintentional as the birth of a thought in the head, and he heard nothing of it himself. It all became extinct at once—thought, intention, effort—and of his cry the inaudible vibration added to the tempest waves of the air.

He expected nothing from it. Nothing at all. For indeed what answer could be made? But after a while he heard with amazement the frail and resisting voice in his ear, the dwarf sound, unconquered in the giant tumult:

"She may!"

It was a dull yell, more difficult to seize than a whisper. And presently the voice returned again, half submerged in the vast crashes, like a ship battling against the waves of an ocean.

"Let's hope so!" it cried—small, lonely, and unmoved, a stranger to the visions of hope or fear; and it flickered into disconnected words: "Ship . . . This . . . Never . . . Anyhow . . . for the best." Jukes gave it up.

Then, as if it had come suddenly upon the one thing fit to withstand the power of a storm, it seemed to gain force and firmness for the last broken shouts:

"Keep on hammering . . . builders . . . good men. . . . And chance it . . . engines . . . Rout . . . good man."

Captain MacWhirr removed his arm from Jukes's shoulders, and thereby ceased to exist for his mate, so dark it was; Jukes, after a tense stiffening of every muscle, would let himself go limp all over. The gnawing of profound discomfort existed side by side with an incredible disposition to somnolence, as though he had been buffeted and worried into drowsiness. The wind would get hold of his head and try to shake it off his shoulders; his clothes, full of water, were as heavy as lead, cold and dripping like an armour of melting ice; he shivered. It lasted a long time; and with his hands closed hard on his hold, he was letting himself sink slowly into the depths of bodily misery. His mind became concentrated upon himself in an aimless, idle way, and when something pushed lightly at the back of his knees he nearly, as the saying is, jumped out of his skin.

In the start forward he bumped the back of Captain MacWhirr, who didn't move; and then a hand gripped his thigh. A lull had come, a menacing lull of the wind, the holding of a stormy breath—and he felt himself pawed all over. It was the boatswain. Jukes recognised these hands, so thick and enormous that they seemed to belong to some new species of man.

The boatswain had arrived on the bridge, crawling on all fours against the wind, and had found the chief mate's legs with the top of his head. Immediately he crouched and began to explore Jukes's person upwards with prudent, apologetic touches, as became an inferior.

He was an ill-favoured, undersized, gruff sailor of fifty, coarsely hairy, short-legged, long-armed, resembling an elderly ape. His strength was immense; and in his great lumpy paws, bulging like brown boxing-gloves on the end of furry forearms, the heaviest objects were handled like playthings. Apart from the grizzled pelt on his chest, the menacing demeanour, and the hoarse voice, he had none of the classical attributes of his rating. His good nature almost amounted to imbecility; the men did what they liked with him, and he had not an ounce of initiative in his character, which was easy-going and talkative. For these reasons Jukes disliked him; but Captain MacWhirr, to Jukes's scornful disgust, seemed to regard him as a first-rate petty officer.

He pulled himself up by Jukes's coat, taking that liberty with the greatest moderation, and only so far as it was forced upon him by the hurricane.

"What is it, Bo'sun, what is it?" yelled Jukes, impatiently. What could that fraud of a bo'sun want on the bridge? The typhoon had got on Jukes's nerves. The husky bellowings of the other, though unintelligible, seemed to suggest a state of lively satisfaction. There could be no mistake. The old fool was pleased with something.

The boatswain's other hand had found some other body, for in a changed tone he began to inquire: "Is it you, sir? Is it you, sir?" The wind strangled his howls.

"Yes!" cried Captain MacWhirr.

IV

All that the boatswain, out of a superabundance of yells, could make clear to Captain MacWhirr was the bizarre intelligence that "All them Chinamen in the fore 'tween-deck have fetched away, sir."

Jukes to leeward could hear these two shouting within six inches of his face, as you may hear on a still night half a mile away two men conversing across a field. He heard Captain MacWhirr's exasperated "What? What?" and the strained pitch of the other's hoarseness. "In a lump . . . seen them myself . . . Awful sight, sir . . . thought . . . tell you."

Jukes remained indifferent, as if rendered irresponsible by the force of the hurricane, which made the very thought of action utterly vain. Besides, being very young, he had found the occupation of keeping his heart completely steeled against the worst so engrossing that he had come to feel an overpowering dislike towards any other form of activity whatever. He was not scared; he knew this because, firmly believing he would never see another sunrise, he remained calm in that belief.

These are the moments of do-nothing heroics to which even good men surrender at times. Many officers of ships can no doubt recall a case in their experience when just such a trance of confounded stoicism would come all at once over a whole ship's company. Jukes, however, had no wide experience of men or storms. He conceived himself to be calm—inexorably calm; but as a matter of fact he was daunted; not abjectly, but only so far as a decent man may, without becoming loathsome to himself.

It was rather like a forced-on numbness of spirit. The long, long stress of a gale does it; the suspense of the interminably culminating catastrophe; and there is a bodily fatigue in the mere holding on to existence within the excessive tumult; a searching and insidious fatigue that penetrates deep into a man's breast to cast down and sadden his heart, which is incorrigible, and of all the gifts of the earth—even before life itself—aspires to peace.

Jukes was benumbed much more than he supposed. He held on—very wet, very cold, stiff in every limb; and in a momentary hallucination of swift visions (it is said that a drowning man thus reviews all his life) he beheld all sorts of memories altogether unconnected with his present situation. He remembered his father, for instance: a worthy business man, who at an unfortunate crisis in his affairs went quietly to bed and died forthwith in a state of resignation. Jukes did not recall these circumstances, of course, but remaining otherwise unconcerned he seemed to see distinctly the poor man's face; a certain game of nap[36] played when quite a boy in Table Bay[37] on board a ship, since lost with all hands; the thick eyebrows of his first skipper; and without any emotion, as he might years ago have walked listlessly into her room and found her sitting there with a book, he remembered his mother—dead, too, now—the resolute woman, left badly off, who had been very firm in his bringing up.

It could not have lasted more than a second, perhaps not

so much. A heavy arm had fallen about his shoulders; Captain MacWhirr's voice was speaking his name into his ear.

"Jukes! Jukes!"

He detected the tone of deep concern. The wind had thrown its weight on the ship, trying to pin her down amongst the seas. They made a clean breach over her, as over a deep-swimming log; and the gathered weight of crashes menaced monstrously from afar. The breakers flung out of the night with a ghostly light on their crests—the light of sea-foam that in a ferocious, boiling-up pale flash showed upon the slender body of the ship the toppling rush, the downfall, and the seething mad scurry of each wave. Never for a moment could she shake herself clear of the water; Jukes, rigid, perceived in her motion the ominous sign of haphazard floundering. She was no longer struggling intelligently. It was the beginning of the end; and the note of busy concern in Captain MacWhirr's voice sickened him like an exhibition of blind and pernicious folly.

The spell of the storm had fallen upon Jukes. He was pene-trated by it, absorbed by it; he was rooted in it with a rigour of dumb attention. Captain MacWhirr persisted in his cries, but the wind got between them like a solid wedge. He hung round Jukes's neck as heavy as a millstone,[38] and suddenly the sides of their heads knocked together.

"Jukes! Mr. Jukes, I say!"

He had to answer that voice that would not be silenced. He answered in the customary manner: ". . . Yes, sir."

And directly, his heart, corrupted by the storm that breeds a craving for peace, rebelled against the tyranny of training and command.

Captain MacWhirr had his mate's head fixed firm in the crook of his elbow, and pressed it to his yelling lips mysteri-ously. Sometimes Jukes would break in, admonishing hastily: "Look out, sir!" or Captain MacWhirr would bawl an earnest exhortation to "Hold hard, there!" and the whole black uni-verse seemed to reel together with the ship. They paused. She floated yet. And Captain MacWhirr would resume his shouts. ". . . Says . . . whole lot . . . fetched away. . . . Ought to see . . . what's the matter."

Directly the full force of the hurricane had struck the ship, every part of her deck became untenable; and the sailors, dazed and dismayed, took shelter in the port alleyway under the bridge. It had a door aft, which they shut; it was very black, cold, and dismal. At each heavy fling of the ship they would groan all together in the dark, and tons of water could be heard scuttling about as if trying to get at them from above. The boatswain had been keeping up a gruff talk, but a more unreasonable lot of men, he said afterwards, he had never been with. They were snug enough there, out of harm's way, and not wanted to do anything either; and yet they did nothing but grumble and complain peevishly like so many sick kids. Finally, one of them said that if there had been at least some light to see each other's noses by, it wouldn't be so bad. It was making him crazy, he declared, to lie there in the dark waiting for the blamed hooker to sink.

"Why don't you step outside, then, and be done with it at once?" the boatswain turned on him.

This called up a shout of execration. The boatswain found himself overwhelmed with reproaches of all sorts. They seemed to take it ill that a lamp was not instantly created for them out of nothing.[39] They would whine after a light to get drowned by—anyhow! And though the unreason of their revilings was patent—since no one could hope to reach the lamp-room, which was forward—he became greatly distressed. He did not think it was decent of them to be nagging at him like this. He told them so, and was met by general contumely. He sought refuge, therefore, in an embittered silence. At the same time their grumbling and sighing and muttering worried him greatly, but by and-by it occurred to him that there were six globe-lamps hung in the 'tween-deck, and that there could be no harm in depriving the coolies of one of them.

The *Nan-Shan* had an athwartship coal-bunker, which, being at times used as cargo space, communicated by an iron door with the fore 'tween-deck. It was empty then, and its manhole was the foremost one in the alleyway. The boatswain could get in, therefore, without coming out on deck at all; but to his great surprise he found he could induce no one to help him in taking

off the manhole cover. He groped for it all the same, but one
of the crew lying in his way refused to budge.

"Why, I only want to get you that blamed light you are crying
for," he expostulated, almost pitifully.

Somebody told him to go and put his head in a bag. He
regretted he could not recognise the voice, and that it was too
dark to see, otherwise, as he said, he would have put a head on
that son of a sea-cook, anyway, sink or swim. Nevertheless, he
had made up his mind to show them he could get a light, if he
were to die for it.

Through the violence of the ship's rolling, every movement
was dangerous. To be lying down seemed labour enough. He
nearly broke his neck dropping into the bunker. He fell on his
back, and was sent shooting helplessly from side to side in the
dangerous company of a heavy iron bar—a coal-trimmer's slice
probably—left down there by somebody. This thing made him
as nervous as though it had been a wild beast. He could not see
it, the inside of the bunker coated with coal-dust being perfectly
and impenetrably black; but he heard it sliding and clattering,
and striking here and there, always in the neighbourhood of his
head. It seemed to make an extraordinary noise, too—to give
heavy thumps as though it had been as big as a bridge girder.
This was remarkable enough for him to notice while he was
flung from port to starboard and back again, and clawing
desperately the smooth sides of the bunker in the endeavour to
stop himself. The door into the 'tween-deck not fitting quite
true, he saw a thread of dim light at the bottom.

Being a sailor, and a still active man, he did not want much
of a chance to regain his feet; and as luck would have it, in
scrambling up he put his hand on the iron slice, picking it up
as he rose. Otherwise he would have been afraid of the thing
breaking his legs, or at least knocking him down again. At first
he stood still. He felt unsafe in this darkness that seemed to
make the ship's motion unfamiliar, unforeseen, and difficult to
counteract. He felt so much shaken for a moment that he dared
not move for fear of "taking charge again." He had no mind
to get battered to pieces in that bunker.

He had struck his head twice; he was dazed a little. He seemed

to hear yet so plainly the clatter and bangs of the iron slice
flying about his ears that he tightened his grip to prove to
himself he had it there safely in his hand. He was vaguely
amazed at the plainness with which down there he could hear
the gale raging. Its howls and shrieks seemed to take on, in the
emptiness of the bunker, something of the human character, of
human rage and pain—being not vast but infinitely poignant.
And there were, with every roll, thumps too—profound, pon-
derous thumps, as if a bulky object of five-ton weight or so had
got play in the hold. But there was no such thing in the cargo.
Something on deck? Impossible. Or alongside? Couldn't be.

He thought all this quickly, clearly, competently, like a seaman, and in the end remained puzzled. This noise, though,
came deadened from outside, together with the washing and
pouring of water on deck above his head. Was it the wind?
Must be. It made down there a row like the shouting of a big
lot of crazed men. And he discovered in himself a desire for a
light too—if only to get drowned by—and a nervous anxiety
to get out of that bunker as quickly as possible.

He pulled back the bolt; the heavy iron plate turned on its
hinges; and it was as though he had opened the door to the
sounds of the tempest. A gust of hoarse yelling met him; the air
was still; and the rushing of water overhead was covered by a
tumult of strangled, throaty shrieks that produced an effect of
desperate confusion. He straddled his legs the whole width of
the doorway and stretched his neck. And at first he perceived
only what he had come to seek: six small yellow flames swinging
violently on the great body of the dusk.

It was stayed like the gallery of a mine, with a row of stanchions in the middle, and cross-beams overhead, penetrating
into the gloom ahead—indefinitely. And to port there loomed,
like the caving in of one of the sides, a bulky mass with a
slanting outline. The whole place, with the shadows and the
shapes, moved all the time. The boatswain glared; the ship
lurched to starboard, and a great howl came from that mass
that had the slant of fallen earth.

Pieces of wood whizzed past. Planks, he thought, inexpressi-
bly startled, and flinging back his head. At his feet a man went

sliding over, open-eyed, on his back, straining with uplifted arms for nothing; and another came bounding like a detached stone with his head between his legs and his hands clenched. His pigtail whipped in the air; he made a grab at the boatswain's legs, and from his opened hand a bright white disc rolled against the boatswain's foot. He recognised a silver dollar, and yelled at it with astonishment. With a precipitated sound of trampling and shuffling of bare feet, and with guttural cries, the mound of writhing bodies piled up to port detached itself from the ship's side and sliding, inert and struggling, shifted to starboard, with a dull, brutal thump. The cries ceased. The boatswain heard a long moan through the roar and whistling of the wind; he saw an inextricable confusion of heads and shoulders, naked soles kicking upwards, fists raised, tumbling backs, legs, pigtails, faces.

"Good Lord!" he cried, horrified, and banged-to the iron door upon this vision.

This was what he had come on the bridge to tell. He could not keep it to himself; and on board ship there is only one man to whom it is worth while to unburden yourself. On his passage back the hands in the alleyway swore at him for a fool. Why didn't he bring that lamp? What the devil did the coolies matter to anybody? And when he came out, the extremity of the ship made what went on inside of her appear of little moment.

At first he thought he had left the alleyway in the very moment of her sinking. The bridge ladders had been washed away, but an enormous sea filling the after-deck floated him up. After that he had to lie on his stomach for some time, holding to a ring-bolt, getting his breath now and then, and swallowing salt water. He struggled farther on his hands and knees, too frightened and distracted to turn back. In this way he reached the after-part of the wheel-house. In that comparatively sheltered spot he found the second mate. The boatswain was pleasantly surprised—his impression being that everybody on deck must have been washed away a long time ago. He asked eagerly where the captain was.

The second mate was lying low, like a malignant little animal under a hedge.

"Captain? Gone overboard, after getting us into this mess."
The mate, too, for all he knew or cared. Another fool. Didn't
matter. Everybody was going by-and-by.

The boatswain crawled out again into the strength of the
wind; not because he much expected to find anybody, he said,
but just to get away from "that man." He crawled out as
outcasts go to face an inclement world. Hence his great joy at
finding Jukes and the captain. But what was going on in the
'tween-deck was to him a minor matter by that time. Besides,
it was difficult to make yourself heard. But he managed to
convey the idea that the Chinamen had broken adrift together
with their boxes, and that he had come up on purpose to report
this. As to the hands, they were all right. Then, appeased, he
subsided on the deck in a sitting posture, hugging with his
arms and legs the stand of the engine-room telegraph—an iron
casting as thick as a post. When that went, why, he expected
he would go too. He gave no more thought to the coolies.

Captain MacWhirr had made Jukes understand that he wanted
him to go down below—to see.

"What am I to do then, sir?" And the trembling of his whole
wet body caused Jukes's voice to sound like bleating.

"See first . . . bo'sun . . . says . . . adrift."

"That bo'sun is a confounded fool," howled Jukes shakily.

The absurdity of the demand made upon him revolted Jukes.
He was as unwilling to go as if the moment he had left the deck
the ship were sure to sink.

"I must know . . . can't leave . . ."

"They'll settle, sir."

"Fight . . . bo'sun says they fight. . . . Why? Can't have . . .
fighting . . . board ship. . . . Much rather keep you here . . . case
. . . I should . . . washed overboard myself. . . . Stop it . . . some
way. You see and tell me . . . through engine-room tube. Don't
want you . . . come up here . . . too often. Dangerous . . . moving
about . . . deck."

Jukes, held with his head in chancery,[40] had to listen to what
seemed horrible suggestions.

"Don't want . . . you get lost . . . so long . . . ship isn't. . . ."

Rout . . . Good man . . . Ship . . . may . . . through this . . . all right yet."

All at once Jukes understood he would have to go.

"Do you think she may?" he screamed.

But the wind devoured the reply, out of which Jukes heard only the one word, pronounced with great energy: ". . . Always . . ."

Captain MacWhirr released Jukes, and bending over the boatswain, yelled, "Get back with the mate." Jukes only knew that the arm was gone off his shoulders. He was dismissed with his orders—to do what? He was exasperated into letting go his hold carelessly, and on the instant was blown away. It seemed to him that nothing could stop him from being blown right over the stern. He flung himself down hastily, and the boatswain, who was following, fell on him.

"Don't you get up yet, sir," cried the boatswain. "No hurry!"

A sea swept over. Jukes understood the boatswain to splutter that the bridge ladders were gone. "I'll lower you down, sir, by your hands," he screamed. He shouted also something about the smoke-stack being as likely to go overboard as not. Jukes thought it very possible, and imagined the fires out, the ship helpless. . . . The boatswain by his side kept on yelling. "What? What is it?" Jukes cried distressfully; and the other repeated, "What would my old woman say if she saw me now?"

In the alleyway, where a lot of water had got in and splashed in the dark, the men were still as death, till Jukes stumbled against one of them and cursed him savagely for being in the way. Two or three voices then asked, eager and weak, "Any chance for us, sir?"

"What's the matter with you fools?" he said brutally. He felt as though he could throw himself down amongst them and never move any more. But they seemed cheered; and in the midst of obsequious warnings, "Look out! Mind that manhole lid, sir," they lowered him into the bunker. The boatswain tumbled down after him, and as soon as he had picked himself up he remarked, "She would say, 'Serve you right, you old fool, for going to sea.'"

The boatswain had some means, and made a point of alluding

to them frequently. His wife—a fat woman—and two grown-up daughters kept a greengrocer's shop in the East End of London.

In the dark, Jukes, unsteady on his legs, listened to a faint thunderous patter. A deadened screaming went on steadily at his elbow, as it were; and from above the louder tumult of the storm descended upon these near sounds. His head swam. To him, too, in that bunker, the motion of the ship seemed novel and menacing, sapping his resolution as though he had never been afloat before.

He had half a mind to scramble out again; but the remembrance of Captain MacWhirr's voice made this impossible. His orders were to go and see. What was the good of it, he wanted to know. Enraged, he told himself he would see—of course. But the boatswain, staggering clumsily, warned him to be careful how he opened that door; there was a blamed fight going on. And Jukes, as if in great bodily pain, desired irritably to know what the devil they were fighting for.

"Dollars! Dollars, sir. All their rotten chests got burst open. Blamed money skipping all over the place, and they are tumbling after it head over heels—tearing and biting like anything. A regular little hell in there."

Jukes convulsively opened the door. The short boatswain peered under his arm.

One of the lamps had gone out, broken perhaps. Rancorous, guttural cries burst out loudly on their ears, and a strange panting sound, the working of all these straining breasts. A hard blow hit the side of the ship; water fell above with a stunning shock, and in the forefront of the gloom, where the air was reddish and thick, Jukes saw a head bang the deck violently, two thick calves waving on high, muscular arms twined round a naked body, a yellow face, open-mouthed and with a set wild stare, look up and slide away. An empty chest clattered turning over; a man fell head first with a jump, as if lifted by a kick; and farther off, indistinct, others streamed like a mass of rolling stones down a bank, thumping the deck with their feet and flourishing their arms wildly. The hatchway ladder was loaded with coolies swarming on it like bees on a branch. They hung on the steps in a crawling, stirring cluster, beating madly with their fists the underside of the battened hatch, and the headlong rush of the water above was heard in the intervals of their yelling. The ship heeled over more, and they began to drop off: first one, then two, then all the rest went away together, falling straight off with a great cry.

Jukes was confounded. The boatswain, with gruff anxiety, begged him, "Don't you go in there, sir."

The whole place seemed to twist upon itself, jumping incessantly the while; and when the ship rose to a sea Jukes fancied that all these men would be shot upon him in a body. He backed out, swung the door to, and with trembling hands pushed at the bolt. . . .

As soon as his mate had gone Captain MacWhirr, left alone on the bridge, sidled and staggered as far as the wheel-house. Its door being hinged forward, he had to fight the gale for admittance, and when at last he managed to enter, it was with an instantaneous clatter and a bang, as though he had been fired through the wood. He stood within, holding on to the handle.

The steering-gear leaked steam, and in the confined space the glass of the binnacle made a shiny oval of light in a thin white fog. The wind howled, hummed, whistled, with sudden booming gusts that rattled the doors and shutters in the vicious patter of sprays. Two coils of lead-line and a small canvas bag hung on a long lanyard, swung wide off, and came back clinging to the bulkheads. The gratings underfoot were nearly afloat; with every sweeping blow of a sea, water squirted violently through the cracks all round the door, and the man at the helm had flung down his cap, his coat, and stood propped against the gear-casing in a striped cotton shirt open on his breast. The little brass wheel in his hands had the appearance of a bright and fragile toy. The cords of his neck stood hard and lean, a dark patch lay in the hollow of his throat, and his face was still and sunken as in death.

Captain MacWhirr wiped his eyes. The sea that had nearly taken him overboard had, to his great annoyance, washed his sou'-wester hat off his bald head. The fluffy, fair hair, soaked and darkened, resembled a mean skein of cotton threads festooned round his bare skull. His face, glistening with sea water, had been made crimson with the wind, with the sting of sprays. He looked as though he had come off sweating from before a furnace.

"You here?" he muttered heavily.

The second mate had found his way into the wheel-house some time before. He had fixed himself in a corner with his knees up, a fist pressed against each temple; and this attitude suggested rage, sorrow, resignation, surrender, with a sort of concentrated unforgiveness. He said mournfully and defiantly, "Well, it's my watch below now. Ain't it?"

The steam gear clattered, stopped, clattered again; and the helmsman's eyeballs seemed to project out of a hungry face as if the compass-card behind the binnacle glass had been meat. God knows how long he had been left there to steer, as if forgotten by all his shipmates. The bells had not been struck; there had been no reliefs; the ship's routine had gone down wind; but he was trying to keep her head north-north-east. The rudder might have been gone for all he knew, the fires out, the engines broken down, the ship ready to roll over like a corpse. He was anxious not to get muddled and lose control of her head, because the compass-card swung far both ways, wriggling on the pivot, and sometimes seemed to whirl right round. He suffered from mental stress. He was horribly afraid, also, of the wheel-house going. Mountains of water kept on tumbling against it. When the ship took one of her desperate dives the corners of his lips twitched.

Captain MacWhirr looked up at the wheel-house clock. Screwed to the bulkhead, it had a white face on which the black hands appeared to stand quite still. It was half-past one in the morning.

"Another day," he muttered to himself.

The second mate heard him, and lifting his head as one grieving amongst ruins, "You won't see it break," he exclaimed. His wrists and his knees could be seen to shake violently. "No, by God! You won't . . ."

He took his face again between his fists.

The body of the helmsman had moved slightly, but his head didn't budge on his neck—like a stone head fixed to look one way from a column. During a roll that all but took his booted legs from under him, and in the very stagger to save himself, Captain MacWhirr said austerely, "Don't you pay any attention to what that man says." And then, with an indefinable change of tone, very grave, he added, "He isn't on duty."

The sailor said nothing.

The hurricane boomed, shaking the little place, which seemed air-tight; and the light of the binnacle flickered all the time.

"You haven't been relieved," Captain MacWhirr went on, looking down. "I want you to stick to the helm, though, as long as you can. You've got the hang of her. Another man coming here might make a mess of it. Wouldn't do. No child's play. And the hands are probably busy with a job down below. . . . Think you can?"

The steering-gear leaped into an abrupt short clatter, stopped smouldering like an ember; and the still man, with a motionless gaze, burst out, as if all the passion in him had gone into his lips: "By Heavens, sir! I can steer for ever if nobody talks to me."

"Oh! aye! All right. . . ." The captain lifted his eyes for the first time to the man . . . "Hackett."

And he seemed to dismiss this matter from his mind. He stooped to the engine-room speaking-tube, blew in, and bent his head. Mr. Rout below answered, and at once Captain MacWhirr put his lips to the mouthpiece.

With the uproar of the gale around him he applied alternately his lips and his ear, and the engineer's voice mounted to him, harsh and as if out of the heat of an engagement. One of the stokers was disabled, the others had given in, the second engineer and the donkeyman were firing-up. The third engineer was standing by the steam-valve. The engines were being tended by hand. How was it above?

"Bad enough. It mostly rests with you," said Captain Mac-Whirr. Was the mate down there yet? No? Well, he would be presently. Would Mr. Rout let him talk through the speaking-tube?—through the deck speaking-tube, because he—the captain—was going out again on the bridge directly. There was some trouble amongst the Chinamen. They were fighting, it seemed. Couldn't allow fighting anyhow. . . .

Mr. Rout had gone away, and Captain MacWhirr could feel against his ear the pulsation of the engines, like the beat of the ship's heart. Mr. Rout's voice down there shouted something distantly. The ship pitched headlong, the pulsation leaped with a hissing tumult, and stopped dead. Captain MacWhirr's face was impassive, and his eyes were fixed aimlessly on the crouching shape of the second mate. Again Mr. Rout's voice cried out in the depths, and the pulsating beats recommenced, with slow strokes—growing swifter.

Mr. Rout had returned to the tube. "It don't matter much what they do," he said hastily; and then, with irritation, "She takes these dives as if she never meant to come up again."

"Awful sea," said the captain's voice from above.

"Don't let me drive her under," barked Solomon Rout up the pipe.

"Dark and rain. Can't see what's coming," uttered the voice. "Must—keep—her—moving—enough to steer—and chance it," it went on to state distinctly.

"I am doing as much as I dare."

"We are—getting—smashed up—a good deal up here," proceeded the voice mildly. "Doing—fairly well—though. Of course, if the wheel-house should go . . ."

Mr. Rout, bending an attentive ear, muttered peevishly something under his breath.

But the deliberate voice up there became animated to ask: "Jukes turned up yet?" Then, after a short wait, "I wish he would bear a hand. I want him to be done and come up here in case of anything. To look after the ship. I am all alone. The second mate's lost. . . ."

"What?" shouted Mr. Rout into the engine-room, taking his head away. Then up the tube he cried, "Gone overboard?" and clapped his ear to.

"Lost his nerve," the voice from above continued in a matter-of-fact tone. "Damned awkward circumstance."

Mr. Rout, listening with bowed neck, opened his eyes wide

at this. However, he heard something like the sounds of a scuffle and broken exclamations coming down to him. He strained his hearing; and all the time Beale, the third engineer, with his arms uplifted, held between the palms of his hands the rim of a little black wheel projecting at the side of a big copper pipe. He seemed to be poising it above his head, as though it were a correct attitude in some sort of game.

To steady himself, he pressed his shoulder against the white bulkhead, one knee bent, and a sweat-rag tucked in his belt hanging on his hip. His smooth cheek was begrimed and flushed, and the coal dust on his eyelids, like the black pencilling of a make-up, enhanced the liquid brilliance of the whites, giving to his youthful face something of a feminine, exotic, and fascinating aspect. When the ship pitched he would with hasty movements of his hands screw hard at the little wheel.

"Gone crazy," began the captain's voice suddenly in the tube. "Rushed at me. . . . Just now. Had to knock him down. . . . This minute. You heard, Mr. Rout?"

"The devil!" muttered Mr. Rout. "Look out, Beale!"

His shout rang out like the blast of a warning trumpet, between the iron walls of the engine-room. Painted white, they rose high into the dusk of the skylight, sloping like a roof; and the whole lofty space resembled the interior of a monument, divided by floors of iron grating, with lights flickering at different levels, and a mass of gloom lingering in the middle, within the columnar stir of machinery under the motionless swelling of the cylinders. A loud and wild resonance, made up of all the noises of the hurricane, dwelt in the still warmth of the air. There was in it the smell of hot metal, of oil, and a slight mist of steam. The blows of the sea seemed to traverse it in an unringing, stunning shock, from side to side.

Gleams, like pale long flames, trembled upon the polish of metal; from the flooring below, the enormous crank-heads emerged in their turns with a flash of brass and steel—going over; while the connecting-rods, big-jointed like skeleton limbs, seemed to thrust them down and pull them up again with an irresistible precision. And deep in the half-light other rods dodged deliberately to and fro, crossheads nodded, discs of metal rubbed smoothly against each other, slow and gentle, in a commingling of shadows and gleams.

Sometimes all those powerful and unerring movements would slow down simultaneously, as if they had been the functions of a living organism, stricken suddenly by the blight of languor; and Mr. Rout's eyes would blaze darker in his long sallow face. He was fighting this fight in a pair of carpet-slippers. A short shiny jacket barely covered his loins, and his white wrists protruded far out of the tight sleeves, as though the emergency had added to his stature, had lengthened his limbs, augmented his pallor, hollowed his eyes.

He moved, climbing high up, disappearing low down, with a restless, purposeful industry, and when he stood still, holding the guard-rail in front of the starting-gear, he would keep glancing to the right at the steam-gauge, at the water-gauge, fixed upon the white wall in the light of a swaying lamp. The mouths of two speaking-tubes gaped stupidly at his elbow, and the dial of the engine-room telegraph resembled a clock of large diameter, bearing on its face curt words instead of figures. The grouped letters stood out heavily black, around the pivot-head of the indicator, emphatically symbolic of loud exclamations: AHEAD, ASTERN, SLOW, HALF, STAND BY; and the fat black hand pointed downwards to the word FULL, which, thus singled out, captured the eye as a sharp cry secures attention.

The wood-encased bulk of the low-pressure cylinder, frowning portly from above, emitted a faint wheeze at every thrust, and except for that low hiss the engines worked their steel limbs headlong or slow with a silent, determined smoothness. And all this, the white walls, the moving steel, the floor plates under Solomon Rout's feet, the floors of iron grating above his head, the dusk and the gleams, uprose and sank continuously, with one accord, upon the harsh wash of the waves against the ship's side. The whole loftiness of the place, booming hollow to the great voice of the wind, swayed at the top like a tree, would go over bodily, as if borne down this way and that by the tremendous blasts.

"You've got to hurry up," shouted Mr. Rout, as soon as he saw Jukes appear in the stokehold doorway.

Jukes's glance was wandering and tipsy; his red face was puffy, as though he had overslept himself. He had had an arduous road, and had travelled over it with immense vivacity, the agitation of his mind corresponding to the exertions of his body. He had rushed up out of the bunker, stumbling in the dark alleyway amongst a lot of bewildered men who, trod upon, asked "What's up, sir?" in awed mutters all round him—down the stokehold ladder, missing many iron rungs in his hurry, down into a place deep as a well, black as Tophet,[41] tipping over back and forth like a see-saw. The water in the bilges thundered at each roll, and lumps of coal skipped to and fro, from end to end, rattling like an avalanche of pebbles on a slope of iron.

Somebody in there moaned with pain, and somebody else could be seen crouching over what seemed the prone body of a dead man; a lusty voice blasphemed; and the glow under each fire-door was like a pool of flaming blood radiating quietly in a velvety blackness.

A gust of wind struck upon the nape of Jukes's neck, and next moment he felt it streaming about his wet ankles. The stokehold ventilators hummed; in front of the six fire-doors two wild figures, stripped to the waist, staggered and stooped, wrestling with two shovels.

"Hallo! Plenty of draught now," yelled the second engineer at once, as though he had been all the time looking out for Jukes. The donkeyman, a dapper little chap with a dazzling fair skin and a tiny, gingery moustache, worked in a sort of mute transport. They were keeping a full head of steam, and a profound rumbling, as of an empty furniture van trotting over a bridge, made a sustained bass to all the other noises of the place.

"Blowing off all the time," went on yelling the second. With a sound as of a hundred scoured saucepans, the orifice of a ventilator spat upon his shoulder a sudden gush of salt water, and he volleyed a stream of curses upon all things on earth including his own soul, ripping and raving, and all the time attending to his business. With a sharp clash of metal the ardent pale glare of the fire opened upon his bullet head, showing his spluttering lips, his insolent face, and with another clang closed like the white-hot wink of an iron eye.

"Where's the blooming ship? Can you tell me—blast my eyes! Under water—or what? It's coming down here in tons. Are the condemned cowls gone to Hades? Hey? Don't you know anything—you jolly sailor-man you . . . ?"

Jukes, after a bewildered moment, had been helped by a roll to dart through; and as soon as his eyes took in the comparative vastness, peace, and brilliance of the engine-room, the ship, setting her stern heavily in the water, sent him charging head down upon Mr. Rout.

The chief's arm, long like a tentacle, and straightening as if worked by a spring, went out to meet him, and deflected his rush into a spin towards the speaking-tubes. At the same time Mr. Rout repeated earnestly:

"You've got to hurry up, whatever it is."

Jukes yelled "Are you there, sir?" and listened. Nothing. Suddenly the roar of the wind fell straight into his ear, but presently a small voice shoved aside the shouting hurricane quietly.

"You, Jukes?—Well?"

Jukes was ready to talk; it was only time that seemed to be wanting. It was easy enough to account for everything. He could perfectly imagine the coolies battened down in the reeking 'tween-deck, lying sick and scared between the rows of chests. Then one of these chests—or perhaps several at once—breaking loose in a roll, knocking out others, sides splitting, lids flying open, and all these clumsy Chinamen rising up in a body to save their property. Afterwards every fling of the ship would hurl that tramping, yelling mob here and there, from side to side, in a whirl of smashed wood, torn clothing, rolling dollars. A struggle once started, they would be unable to stop themselves. Nothing could stop them now except main force. It was a disaster. He had seen it, and that was all he could say. Some of them must be dead, he believed. The rest would go on fighting. . . . He sent up his words, tripping over each other, crowding the narrow tube. They mounted as if into a silence of an enlightened comprehension dwelling alone up there with a storm. And Jukes wanted to be dismissed from the face of that odious trouble intruding on the great need of the ship.

V

He waited. Before his eyes the engines turned with slow labour, that in the moment of going off into a mad fling would stop dead at Mr. Rout's shout, "Look out, Beale!" They paused in an intelligent immobility, stilled in mid-stroke, a heavy crank arrested on the cant, as if conscious of danger and the passage of time. Then, with a "Now, then!" from the chief, and the sound of a breath expelled through clenched teeth, they would accomplish the interrupted revolution and begin another.

There was the prudent sagacity of wisdom and the deliberation of enormous strength in their movements. This was their work—this patient coaxing of a distracted ship over the fury of the waves and into the very eye of the wind. At times Mr. Rout's chin would sink on his breast, and he watched them with knitted eyebrows as if lost in thought.

The voice that kept the hurricane out of Jukes's ear began: "Take the hands with you . . ." and left off unexpectedly.

"What could I do with them, sir?"

A harsh, abrupt, imperious clang exploded suddenly. The three pairs of eyes flew up to the telegraph dial to see the hand jump from FULL to STOP, as if snatched by a devil. And then these three men in the engine-room had the intimate sensation of a check upon the ship, of a strange shrinking, as if she had gathered herself for a desperate leap.

"Stop her!" bellowed Mr. Rout.

Nobody—not even Captain MacWhirr, who alone on deck had caught sight of a white line of foam coming on at such a height that he couldn't believe his eyes—nobody was to know the steepness of that sea and the awful depth of the hollow the hurricane had scooped out behind the running wall of water.

It raced to meet the ship, and, with a pause, as of girding the loins,[42] the *Nan-Shan* lifted her bows and leaped. The flames in all the lamps sank, darkening the engine-room. One went out. With a tearing crash and a swirling, raving tumult, tons of water fell upon the deck, as though the ship had darted under the foot of a cataract.

Down there they looked at each other, stunned.

"Swept from end to end, by God!" bawled Jukes.

She dipped into the hollow straight down, as if going over the edge of the world. The engine-room toppled forward menacingly, like the inside of a tower nodding in an earthquake. An awful racket, of iron things falling, came from the stokehold. She hung on this appalling slant long enough for Beale to drop on his hands and knees and begin to crawl as if he meant to fly on all fours out of the engine-room, and for Mr. Rout to turn his head slowly, rigid, cavernous, with the lower jaw dropping. Jukes had shut his eyes, and his face in a moment became hopelessly blank and gentle, like the face of a blind man.

At last she rose slowly, staggering, as if she had to lift a mountain with her bows.

Mr. Rout shut his mouth; Jukes blinked; and little Beale stood up hastily.

"Another one like this, and that's the last of her," cried the chief.

He and Jukes looked at each other, and the same thought came into their heads. The captain! Everything must have been swept away. Steering-gear gone—ship like a log. All over directly.

"Rush!" ejaculated Mr. Rout thickly, glaring with enlarged, doubtful eyes at Jukes, who answered him by an irresolute glance.

The clang of the telegraph gong soothed them instantly. The black hand dropped in a flash from STOP to FULL.

"Now then, Beale!" cried Mr. Rout.

The steam hissed low. The piston-rods slid in and out. Jukes put his ear to the tube. The voice was ready for him. It said: "Pick up all the money. Bear a hand now. I'll want you up here." And that was all.

"Sir?" called up Jukes. There was no answer.

He staggered away like a defeated man from the field of battle. He had got, in some way or other, a cut above his left eyebrow—a cut to the bone. He was not aware of it in the least: quantities of the China Sea, large enough to break his neck for him, had gone over his head, had cleaned, washed, and salted that wound. It did not bleed, but only gaped red; and this gash over the eye, his dishevelled hair, the disorder of his clothes, gave him the aspect of a man worsted in a fight with fists.

"Got to pick up the dollars." He appealed to Mr. Rout, smiling pitifully at random.

"What's that?" asked Mr. Rout, wildly. "Pick up . . . ? I don't care. . . ." Then, quivering in every muscle, but with an exaggeration of paternal tone, "Go away now, for God's sake. You deck people'll drive me silly. There's that second mate been going for the old man. Don't you know? You fellows are going wrong for want of something to do. . . ."

At these words Jukes discovered in himself the beginnings of danger. Want of something to do—indeed. . . . Full of hot scorn against the chief, he turned to go the way he had come. In the stokehold the plump donkeyman toiled with his shovel mutely, as if his tongue had been cut out; but the second was carrying on like a noisy, undaunted maniac, who had preserved his skill in the art of stoking under a marine boiler.

"Hallo, you wandering officer! Hey! Can't you get some of your slush-slingers to wind up a few of them ashes? I am getting choked with them here. Curse it! Hallo! Hey! Remember the articles: *Sailors and firemen to assist each other*. Hey! D'ye hear?"

Jukes was climbing out frantically, and the other, lifting up his face after him, howled, "Can't you speak? What are you poking about here for? What's your game, anyhow?"

A frenzy possessed Jukes. By the time he was back amongst the men in the darkness of the alleyway, he felt ready to wring all their necks at the slightest sign of hanging back. The very thought of it exasperated him. *He* couldn't hang back. They shouldn't.

The impetuosity with which he came amongst them carried them along. They had already been excited and startled at all his comings and goings—by the fierceness and rapidity of his movements; and more felt than seen in his rushes, he appeared formidable—busied with matters of life and death that brooked no delay. At his first word he heard them drop into the bunker one after another obediently, with heavy thumps.

They were not clear as to what would have to be done. "What is it? What is it?" they were asking each other. The boatswain tried to explain; the sounds of a great scuffle surprised them; and the mighty shocks, reverberating awfully in the black bunker, kept them in mind of their danger. When the boatswain threw open the door it seemed that an eddy of the hurricane, stealing through the iron sides of the ship, had set all these bodies whirling like dust; there came to them a confused uproar, a tempestuous tumult, a fierce mutter, gusts of screams dying away, and the tramping of feet mingling with the blows of the sea.

For a moment they glared amazed, blocking the doorway. Jukes pushed through them brutally. He said nothing, and simply darted in. Another lot of coolies on the ladder, struggling suicidally to break through the battened hatch to a swamped deck, fell off as before, and he disappeared under them like a man overtaken by a landslide.

The boatswain yelled excitedly: "Come along. Get the mate out. He'll be trampled to death. Come on."

They charged in, stamping on breasts, on fingers, on faces, catching their feet in heaps of clothing, kicking broken wood; but before they could get hold of him Jukes emerged waist deep in a multitude of clawing hands. In the instant he had been lost to view, all the buttons of his jacket had gone, its back had got split up to the collar, his waistcoat had been torn open. The central struggling mass of Chinamen went over to the roll, dark, indistinct, helpless, with a wild gleam of many eyes in the dim light of the lamps.

"Leave me alone—damn you. I am all right," screeched Jukes. "Drive them forward. Watch your chance when she pitches. Forward with 'em. Drive them against the bulkhead. Jam 'em up."

The rush of the sailors into the seething 'tween-deck was like a splash of cold water into a boiling cauldron. The commotion sank for a moment.

The bulk of Chinamen were locked in such a compact scrimmage that, linking their arms and aided by an appalling dive of the ship, the seamen sent it forward in one great shove, like a solid block. Behind their backs small clusters and loose bodies tumbled from side to side.

The boatswain performed prodigious feats of strength. With his long arms open, and each great paw clutching at a stanchion, he stopped the rush of seven entwined Chinamen rolling like a boulder. His joints cracked; he said "Ha!" and they flew apart. But the carpenter showed the greater intelligence. Without saying a word to anybody he went back into the alleyway, to fetch several coils of cargo gear he had seen there—chain and rope. With these life-lines were rigged.

There was really no resistance. The struggle, however it began, had turned into a scramble of blind panic. If the coolies had started up after their scattered dollars they were by that time fighting only for their footing. They took each other by the throat merely to save themselves from being hurled about. Whoever got a hold anywhere would kick at the others who caught at his legs and hung on, till a roll sent them flying together across the deck.

The coming of the white devils[43] was a terror. Had they come to kill? The individuals torn out of the ruck became very limp in the seamen's hands: some, dragged aside by the heels, were passive, like dead bodies, with open, fixed eyes. Here and there a coolie would fall on his knees as if begging for mercy; several, whom the excess of fear made unruly, were hit with hard fists between the eyes, and cowered; while those who were hurt submitted to rough handling, blinking rapidly without a plaint. Faces streamed with blood; there were raw places on the shaven heads, scratches, bruises, torn wounds, gashes. The broken porcelain out of the chests was mostly responsible for the latter. Here and there a Chinaman, wild-eyed, with his tail unplaited, nursed a bleeding sole.

They had been ranged closely, after having been shaken into submission, cuffed a little to allay excitement, addressed in gruff words of encouragement that sounded like promises of evil. They sat on the deck in ghastly, drooping rows, and at the end the carpenter, with two hands to help him, moved busily from place to place, setting taut and hitching the life-lines. The boatswain, with one leg and one arm embracing a stanchion, struggled with a lamp pressed to his breast, trying to get a light, and growling all the time like an industrious gorilla. The figures of seamen stooped repeatedly, with the movements of gleaners, and everything was being flung into the bunker: clothing, smashed wood, broken china, and the dollars too, gathered up in men's jackets. Now and then a sailor would stagger towards the doorway with his arms full of rubbish; and dolorous, slanting eyes followed his movements.

With every roll of the ship the long rows of sitting Celestials would sway forward brokenly, and her headlong dives knocked together the line of shaven polls from end to end. When the wash of water rolling on the deck died away for a moment, it seemed to Jukes, yet quivering from his exertions, that in his mad struggle down there he had overcome the wind somehow: that a silence had fallen upon the ship, a silence in which the sea struck thunderously at her sides.

Everything had been cleared out of the 'tween-deck—all the wreckage, as the men said. They stood erect and tottering above the level of heads and drooping shoulders. Here and there a coolie sobbed for his breath. Where the high light fell, Jukes could see the salient ribs of one, the yellow, wistful face of another; bowed necks; or would meet a dull stare directed at his face. He was amazed that there had been no corpses; but the lot of them seemed at their last gasp, and they appeared to him more pitiful than if they had been all dead.

Suddenly one of the coolies began to speak. The light came and went on his lean, straining face; he threw his head up like a baying hound. From the bunker came the sounds of knocking and the tinkle of some dollars rolling loose; he stretched out his arm, his mouth yawned black, and the incomprehensible guttural hooting sounds, that did not seem to belong to a human language, penetrated Jukes with a strange emotion as if a brute had tried to be eloquent.

Two more started mouthing what seemed to Jukes fierce denunciations; the others stirred with grunts and growls. Jukes ordered the hands out of the 'tween-decks hurriedly. He left last himself, backing through the door, while the grunts rose to a loud murmur and hands were extended after him as after a malefactor. The boatswain shot the bolt, and remarked uneasily, "Seems as if the wind had dropped, sir."

The seamen were glad to get back into the alleyway. Secretly each of them thought that at the last moment he could rush out on deck—and that was a comfort. There is something horribly repugnant in the idea of being drowned under a deck. Now they had done with the Chinamen, they again became conscious of the ship's position.

Jukes on coming out of the alleyway found himself up to the neck in the noisy water. He gained the bridge, and discovered he could detect obscure shapes as if his sight had become preternaturally acute. He saw faint outlines. They recalled not the familiar aspect of the *Nan-Shan*, but something remembered—an old dismantled steamer he had seen years ago rotting on a mudbank. She recalled that wreck.

There was no wind, not a breath, except the faint currents created by the lurches of the ship. The smoke tossed out of the funnel was settling down upon her deck. He breathed it as he passed forward. He felt the deliberate throb of the engines, and heard small sounds that seemed to have survived the great uproar: the knocking of broken fittings, the rapid tumbling of some piece of wreckage on the bridge. He perceived dimly the squat shape of his captain holding on to a twisted bridge-rail, motionless and swaying as if rooted to the planks. The unexpected stillness of the air oppressed Jukes.

"We have done it, sir," he gasped.

"Thought you would," said Captain MacWhirr.

"Did you?" murmured Jukes to himself.

"Wind fell all at once," went on the captain.

Jukes burst out: "If you think it was an easy job——"

But his captain, clinging to the rail, paid no attention. "According to the books the worst is not over yet."

"If most of them hadn't been half dead with seasickness and

fright, not one of us would have come out of that 'tween-deck alive," said Jukes.

"Had to do what's fair by them," mumbled MacWhirr stolidly. "You don't find everything in books."

"Why, I believe they would have risen on us if I hadn't ordered the hands out of that pretty quick," continued Jukes with warmth.

After the whisper of their shouts, their ordinary tones, so distinct, rang out very loud to their ears in the amazing stillness of the air. It seemed to them they were talking in a dark and echoing vault.

Through a jagged aperture in the dome of clouds the light of a few stars fell upon the black sea, rising and falling confusedly. Sometimes the head of a watery cone would topple on board and mingle with the rolling flurry of foam on the swamped deck; and the *Nan-Shan* wallowed heavily at the bottom of a circular cistern of clouds. This ring of dense vapours, gyrating madly round the calm of the centre, encompassed the ship like a motionless and unbroken wall of an aspect inconceivably sinister. Within, the sea, as if agitated by an internal commotion, leaped in peaked mounds that jostled each other, slapping heavily against her sides; and a low moaning sound, the infinite plaint of the storm's fury, came from beyond the limits of the menacing calm. Captain MacWhirr remained silent, and Jukes's ready ear caught suddenly the faint, long-drawn roar of some immense wave rushing unseen under that thick blackness, which made the appalling boundary of his vision.

"Of course," he started resentfully, "they thought we had caught at the chance to plunder them. Of course! You said— pick up the money. Easier said than done. They couldn't tell what was in our heads. We came in, smash!—right into the middle of them. Had to do it by a rush."

"As long as it's done . . ." mumbled the captain, without attempting to look at Jukes. "Had to do what's fair."

"We shall find yet there's the devil to pay when this is over," said Jukes, feeling very sore. "Let them only recover a bit, and you'll see. They will fly at our throats, sir. Don't forget, sir, she isn't a British ship now. These brutes know it well, too. The damn'd Siamese flag."

"We are on board, all the same," remarked Captain MacWhirr.

"The trouble's not over yet," insisted Jukes prophetically, reeling and catching on. "She's a wreck," he added faintly.

"The trouble's not over yet," assented Captain MacWhirr, half aloud. . . . "Look out for her a minute."

"Are you going off the deck, sir?" asked Jukes hurriedly, as if the storm were sure to pounce upon him as soon as he had been left alone with the ship.

He watched her, battered and solitary, labouring heavily in a wild scene of mountainous black waters lit by the gleams of distant worlds. She moved slowly, breathing into the still core of the hurricane the excess of her strength in a white cloud of steam—and the deep-toned vibration of the escape was like the defiant trumpeting of a living creature of the sea impatient for the renewal of the contest. It ceased suddenly. The still air moaned. Above Jukes's head a few stars shone into a pit of black vapours. The inky edge of the cloud-disc frowned upon the ship under the patch of glittering sky. The stars too seemed to look at her intently, as if for the last time, and the cluster of their splendour sat like a diadem on a lowering brow.

Captain MacWhirr had gone into the chart-room. There was no light there; but he could feel the disorder of that place where he used to live tidily. His armchair was upset. The books had tumbled out on the floor; he scrunched a piece of glass under his boot. He groped for the matches, and found a box on a shelf with a deep ledge. He struck one, and puckering the corners of his eyes, held out the little flame towards the barometer whose glittering top of glass and metals nodded at him continuously.

It stood very low—incredibly low, so low that Captain MacWhirr grunted. The match went out, and hurriedly he extracted another, with thick, stiff fingers.

Again a little flame flared up before the nodding glass and metal of the top. His eyes looked at it, narrowed with attention, as if expecting an imperceptible sign. With his grave face he resembled a booted and misshapen pagan burning incense before the oracle of a Joss.[44] There was no mistake. It was the lowest reading he had ever seen in his life.

Captain MacWhirr emitted a low whistle. He forgot himself till the flame diminished to a blue spark, burnt his fingers, and vanished. Perhaps something had gone wrong with the thing!

There was an aneroid glass[45] screwed above the couch. He turned that way, struck another match, and discovered the white face of the other instrument looking at him from the bulkhead, meaningly, not to be gainsaid, as though the wisdom of men were made unerring by the indifference of matter. There was no room for doubt now. Captain MacWhirr pshawed at it, and threw the match down.

The worst was to come, then—and if the books were right this worst would be very bad. The experience of the last six hours had enlarged his conception of what heavy weather could be like. "It'll be terrific," he pronounced mentally. He had not consciously looked at anything by the light of the matches except at the barometer; and yet somehow he had seen that his water-bottle and the two tumblers had been flung out of their stand. It seemed to give him a more intimate knowledge of the tossing the ship had gone through. "I wouldn't have believed it," he thought. And his table had been cleared too; his rulers, his pencils, the inkstand—all the things that had their safe appointed places—they were gone, as if a mischievous hand had plucked them out one by one and flung them on the wet floor. The hurricane had broken in upon the orderly arrangements of his privacy. This had never happened before, and the feeling of dismay reached the very seat of his composure. And the worst was to come yet! He was glad the trouble in the 'tween-deck had been discovered in time. If the ship had to go after all, then, at least, she wouldn't be going to the bottom with a lot of people in her fighting teeth and claw. That would have been odious. And in that feeling there was a humane intention and a vague sense of the fitness of things.

These instantaneous thoughts were yet in their essence heavy and slow, partaking of the nature of the man. He extended his hand to put back the matchbox in its corner of the shelf. There were always matches there—by his order. The steward had his instructions impressed upon him long before. "A box . . . just there, see? Not so very full . . . where I can put my hand on it, steward. Might want a light in a hurry. Can't tell on board ship *what* you might want in a hurry. Mind, now."

And of course on his side he would be careful to put it back in its place scrupulously. He did so now, but before he removed his hand it occurred to him that perhaps he would never have occasion to use that box any more. The vividness of the thought checked him and for an infinitesimal fraction of a second his fingers closed again on the small object as though it had been the symbol of all these little habits that chain us to the weary round of life. He released it at last, and letting himself fall on the settee, listened for the first sounds of returning wind.

Not yet. He heard only the wash of water, the heavy splashes, the dull shocks of the confused seas boarding his ship from all sides. She would never have a chance to clear her decks.

But the quietude of the air was startlingly tense and unsafe, like a slender hair holding a sword suspended over his head.[46] By this awful pause the storm penetrated the defences of the man and unsealed his lips. He spoke out in the solitude and the pitch darkness of the cabin, as if addressing another being awakened within his breast.

"I shouldn't like to lose her," he said half aloud.

He sat unseen, apart from the sea, from his ship, isolated, as if withdrawn from the very current of his own existence, where such freaks as talking to himself surely had no place. His palms reposed on his knees, he bowed his short neck and puffed heavily, surrendering to a strange sensation of weariness he was not enlightened enough to recognise for the fatigue of mental stress.

From where he sat he could reach the door of a washstand locker. There should have been a towel there. There was. Good. . . . He took it out, wiped his face, and afterwards went on rubbing his wet head. He towelled himself with energy in the dark, and then remained motionless with the towel on his knees. A moment passed, of a stillness so profound that no one could have guessed there was a man sitting in that cabin. Then a murmur arose.

"She may come out of it yet."

When Captain MacWhirr came out on deck, which he did brusquely, as though he had suddenly become conscious of having stayed away too long, the calm had lasted already more than fifteen minutes—long enough to make itself intolerable even to his imagination. Jukes, motionless on the forepart of the bridge, began to speak at once. His voice, blank and forced as though he were talking through hard-set teeth, seemed to flow away on all sides into the darkness, deepening again upon the sea.

"I had the wheel relieved. Hackett began to sing out that he was done. He's lying in there alongside the steering-gear with a face like death. At first I couldn't get anybody to crawl out and relieve the poor devil. That bo'sun's worse than no good, I always said. Thought I would have had to go myself and haul out one of them by the neck."

"Ah, well," muttered the captain. He stood watchful by Jukes's side.

"The second mate's in there too, holding his head. Is he hurt, sir?"

"No—crazy," said Captain MacWhirr curtly.

"Looks as if he had a tumble, though."

"I had to give him a push," explained the captain.

Jukes gave an impatient sigh.

"It will come very sudden," said Captain MacWhirr, "and from over there, I fancy. God only knows though. These books are only good to muddle your head and make you jumpy. It will be bad, and there's an end. If we only can steam her round in time to meet it . . ."

A minute passed. Some of the stars winked rapidly and vanished.

"You left them pretty safe?" began the captain abruptly, as though the silence were unbearable.

"Are you thinking of the coolies, sir? I rigged life-lines all ways across that 'tween-deck."

"Did you? Good idea, Mr. Jukes."

"I didn't . . . think you cared to . . . know," said Jukes—the lurching of the ship cut his speech as though somebody had been jerking him around while he talked—"how I got on with . . . that infernal job. We did it. And it may not matter in the end."

"Had to do what's fair, for all—they are only Chinamen. Give them the same chance with ourselves—hang it all. She isn't lost yet. Bad enough to be shut up below in a gale——"

"That's what I thought when you gave me the job, sir," interjected Jukes moodily.

"——without being battered to pieces," pursued Captain MacWhirr with rising vehemence. "Couldn't let that go on in my ship, if I knew she hadn't five minutes to live. Couldn't bear it, Mr. Jukes."

A hollow echoing noise, like that of a shout rolling in a rocky chasm, approached the ship and went away again. The last star, blurred, enlarged, as if returning to the fiery mist of its beginning, struggled with the colossal depth of blackness hanging over the ship—and went out.

"Now for it!" muttered Captain MacWhirr. "Mr. Jukes?"

"Here, sir."

The two men were growing indistinct to each other.

"We must trust her to go through it and come out on the other side. That's plain and straight. There's no room for Captain Wilson's storm-strategy here."

"No, sir."

"She will be smothered and swept again for hours," mumbled the captain. "There's not much left by this time above deck for the sea to take away—unless you or me."

"Both, sir," whispered Jukes breathlessly.

"You are always meeting trouble half way, Jukes," Captain MacWhirr remonstrated quaintly. "Though it's a fact that the second mate is no good. D'ye hear, Mr. Jukes? You would be left alone if . . ."

Captain MacWhirr interrupted himself, and Jukes, glancing on all sides, remained silent.

"Don't you be put out by anything," the captain continued,

mumbling rather fast. "Keep her facing it. They may say what they like, but the heaviest seas run with the wind. Facing it—always facing it—that's the way to get through. You are a young sailor. Face it. That's enough for any man. Keep a cool head."

"Yes, sir," said Jukes, with a flutter of the heart.

In the next few seconds the captain spoke to the engine-room and got an answer.

For some reason Jukes experienced an access of confidence, a sensation that came from outside like a warm breath, and made him feel equal to every demand. The distant muttering of the darkness stole into his ears. He noted it unmoved, out of that sudden belief in himself, as a man safe in a shirt of mail would watch a point.

The ship laboured without intermission amongst the black hills of water, paying with this hard tumbling the price of her life. She rumbled in her depths, shaking a white plumet of steam into the night, and Jukes's thought skimmed like a bird through the engine-room, where Mr. Rout—good man—was ready. When the rumbling ceased it seemed to him that there was a pause of every sound, a dead pause in which Captain MacWhirr's voice rang out startlingly.

"What's that? A puff of wind?"—it spoke much louder than Jukes had ever heard it before—"On the bow. That's right. She may come out of it yet."

The mutter of the winds drew near apace. In the forefront could be distinguished a drowsy waking plaint passing on, and far off the growth of a multiple clamour, marching and expanding. There was the throb as of many drums in it, a vicious rushing note, and like the chant of a tramping multitude.

Jukes could no longer see his captain distinctly. The darkness was absolutely piling itself upon the ship. At most he made out movements, a hint of elbows spread out, of a head thrown up.

Captain MacWhirr was trying to do up the top button of his oilskin coat with unwonted haste. The hurricane, with its power to madden the seas, to sink ships, to uproot trees, to overturn strong walls and dash the very birds of the air to the ground, had found this taciturn man in its path, and, doing its utmost,

had managed to wring out a few words. Before the renewed
wrath of winds swooped on his ship, Captain MacWhirr was
moved to declare, in a tone of vexation, as it were: "I wouldn't
like to lose her."

He was spared that annoyance.

VI

On a bright sunshiny day, with the breeze chasing her smoke
far ahead, the *Nan-Shan* came into Fu-chau. Her arrival was at
once noticed on shore, and the seamen in harbour said: "Look!
Look at that steamer. What's that? Siamese—isn't she? Just
look at her!"

She seemed, indeed, to have been used as a running target
for the secondary batteries of a cruiser. A hail of minor shells
could not have given her upper works a more broken, torn, and
devastated aspect; and she had about her the worn, weary air
of ships coming from the far ends of the world—and indeed
with truth, for in her short passage she had been very far;
sighting, verily, even the coast of the Great Beyond, whence no
ship ever returns to give up her crew to the dust of the earth.[47]
She was incrusted and grey with salt to the trucks of her masts
and to the top of her funnel; as though (as some facetious
seaman said) "the crowd on board had fished her out somewhere from the bottom of the sea and brought her in here for
salvage." And further, excited by the felicity of his own wit, he
offered to give five pounds for her—"as she stands."

Before she had been quite an hour at rest, a meagre little
man, with a red-tipped nose and a face cast in an angry mould,
landed from a sampan on the quay of the Foreign Concession,[48]
and incontinently turned to shake his fist at her.

A tall individual, with legs much too thin for a rotund
stomach, and with watery eyes, strolled up and remarked, "Just
left her—eh? Quick work."

He wore a soiled suit of blue flannel with a pair of dirty
cricketing shoes; a dingy grey moustache drooped from his lip,

and daylight could be seen in two places between the rim and the crown of his hat.

"Hallo! what are you doing here?" asked the ex-second-mate of the *Nan-Shan*, shaking hands hurriedly.

"Standing by for a job—chance worth taking—got a quiet hint," explained the man with the broken hat, in jerky, apathetic wheezes.

The second shook his fist again at the *Nan-Shan*. "There's a fellow there that ain't fit to have the command of a scow," he declared, quivering with passion, while the other looked about listlessly.

"Is there?"

But he caught sight on the quay of a heavy seaman's chest, painted brown under a fringed sailcloth cover, and lashed with new manila line. He eyed it with awakened interest.

"I would talk and raise trouble if it wasn't for that damned Siamese flag. Nobody to go to—or I would make it hot for him. The fraud! Told his chief engineer—that's another fraud for you—I had lost my nerve. The greatest lot of ignorant fools that ever sailed the seas. No! You can't think . . ."

"Got your money all right?" inquired his seedy acquaintance suddenly.

"Yes. Paid me off on board," raged the second mate. "'Get your breakfast on shore,' says he."

"Mean skunk!" commented the tall man vaguely, and passed his tongue on his lips. "What about having a drink of some sort?"

"He struck me," hissed the second mate.

"No! Struck! You don't say?" The man in blue began to bustle about sympathetically. "Can't possibly talk here. I want to know all about it. Struck—eh? Let's get a fellow to carry your chest. I know a quiet place where they have some bottled beer. . . ."

Mr. Jukes, who had been scanning the shore through a pair of glasses, informed the chief engineer afterwards that "our late second mate hasn't been long in finding a friend. A chap looking uncommonly like a bummer.[49] I saw them walk away together from the quay."

The hammering and banging of the needful repairs did not disturb Captain MacWhirr. The steward found in the letter he wrote, in a tidy chart-room, passages of such absorbing interest that twice he was nearly caught in the act. But Mrs. MacWhirr, in the drawing-room of the forty-pound house, stifled a yawn—perhaps out of self-respect—for she was alone.

She reclined in a plush-bottomed and gilt hammock-chair near a tiled fireplace, with Japanese fans on the mantel and a glow of coals in the grate. Lifting her hands, she glanced wearily here and there into the many pages. It was not her fault they were so prosy, so completely uninteresting—from "My darling wife" at the beginning, to "Your loving husband" at the end. She couldn't be really expected to understand all these ship affairs. She was glad, of course, to hear from him, but she had never asked herself why, precisely.

". . . They are called typhoons . . . The mate did not seem to like it . . . Not in books . . . Couldn't think of letting it go on. . . ."

The paper rustled sharply. ". . . A calm that lasted more than twenty minutes," she read perfunctorily; and the next words her thoughtless eyes caught, on the top of another page, were: "see you and the children again. . . ." She had a movement of impatience. He was always thinking of coming home. He had never had such a good salary before. What was the matter now!

It did not occur to her to turn back overleaf to look. She would have found it recorded there that between 4 and 6 A.M. on December 25th, Captain MacWhirr did actually think that his ship could not possibly live another hour in such a sea, and that he would never see his wife and children again. Nobody was to know this (his letters got mislaid so quickly)—nobody whatever but the steward, who had been greatly impressed by that disclosure. So much so, that he tried to give the cook some idea of the "narrow squeak we all had" by saying solemnly, "The old man himself had a dam' poor opinion of our chance."

"How do you know?" asked contemptuously the cook, an old soldier. "He hasn't told you, maybe?"

"Well, he did give me a hint to that effect," the steward brazened it out.

"Get along with you! He will be coming to tell *me* next," jeered the old cook, over his shoulder.

Mrs. MacWhirr glanced farther, on the alert. ". . . Do what's fair. . . . Miserable objects. . . . Only three, with a broken leg each, and one. . . . Thought had better keep the matter quiet . . . hope to have done the fair thing. . . ."

She let fall her hands. No. There was nothing more about coming home. Must have been merely expressing a pious wish. Mrs. MacWhirr's mind was set at ease, and a black marble clock, priced by the local jeweller at £3 18s. 6d., had a discreet stealthy tick.

The door flew open, and a girl in the long-legged, short-frocked period of existence, flung into the room.

A lot of colourless, rather lanky hair was scattered over her shoulders. Seeing her mother, she stood still, and directed her pale prying eyes upon the letter.

"From father," murmured Mrs. MacWhirr. "What have you done with your ribbon?"

The girl put her hands up to her head and pouted.

"He's well," continued Mrs. MacWhirr languidly. "At least I think so. He never says." She had a little laugh. The girl's face expressed a wandering indifference, and Mrs. MacWhirr surveyed her with fond pride.

"Go and get your hat," she said after a while. "I am going out to do some shopping. There is a sale at Linom's."[50]

"Oh, how jolly!" uttered the child impressively in unexpectedly grave vibrating tones, and bounded out of the room.

It was a fine afternoon, with a grey sky and dry sidewalks. Outside the draper's Mrs. MacWhirr smiled upon a woman in a black mantle of generous proportions, armoured in jet and crowned with flowers blooming falsely above a bilious matronly countenance. They broke into a swift little babble of greetings and exclamations both together, very hurried, as if the street were ready to yawn open and swallow all that pleasure before it could be expressed.

Behind them the high glass doors were kept on the swing.

People couldn't pass, men stood aside waiting patiently, and Lydia was absorbed in poking the end of her parasol between the stone flags. Mrs. MacWhirr talked rapidly.

"Thank you very much. He's not coming home yet. Of course it's very sad to have him away, but it's such a comfort to know he keeps so well." Mrs. MacWhirr drew breath. "The climate there agrees with him," she added beamingly as if poor MacWhirr had been away touring in China for the sake of his health.

Neither was the chief engineer coming home yet. Mr. Rout knew too well the value of a good billet.

"Solomon says wonders will never cease," cried Mrs. Rout joyously at the old lady in her armchair by the fire. Mr. Rout's mother moved slightly, her withered hands lying in black half-mittens on her lap.

The eyes of the engineer's wife fairly danced on the paper. "That captain of the ship he is in—a rather simple man, you remember, mother?—has done something rather clever, Solomon says."

"Yes, my dear," said the old woman meekly, sitting with bowed silvery head, and that air of inward stillness character-istic of very old people who seem lost in watching the last flickers of life. "I think I remember."

Solomon Rout, Old Sol, Father Sol, The Chief, "Rout, good man"—Mr. Rout, the condescending and paternal friend of youth, had been the baby of her many children—all dead by this time. And she remembered him best as a boy of ten—long before he went away to serve his apprenticeship in some great engineering works in the North. She had seen so little of him since, she had gone through so many years, that she had now to retrace her steps very far back to recognise him plainly in the mist of time. Sometimes it seemed that her daughter-in-law was talking of some strange man.

Mrs. Rout junior was disappointed. "H'm. H'm." She turned the page. "How provoking! He doesn't say what it is. Says I couldn't understand how much there was in it. Fancy! What could it be so very clever? What a wretched man not to tell us!"

She read on without further remark soberly, and at last sat

looking into the fire. The chief wrote just a word or two of the typhoon; but something had moved him to express an increased longing for the companionship of the jolly woman. "If it hadn't been that mother must be looked after, I would send you your passage-money to-day. You could set up a small house out here. I would have a chance to see you sometimes then. We are not growing younger. . . ."

"He's well, mother," sighed Mrs. Rout, rousing herself.

"He always was a strong healthy boy," said the old woman placidly.

But Mr. Jukes's account was really animated and very full. His friend in the Western Ocean trade imparted it freely to the other officers of his liner. "A chap I know writes to me about an extraordinary affair that happened on board his ship in that typhoon—you know—that we read of in the papers two months ago. It's the funniest thing! Just see for yourself what he says. I'll show you his letter."

There were phrases in it calculated to give the impression of light-hearted, indomitable resolution. Jukes had written them in good faith, for he felt thus when he wrote. He described with lurid effect the scenes in the 'tween-deck. ". . . It struck me in a flash that those confounded Chinamen couldn't tell we weren't a desperate kind of robbers. 'Tisn't good to part the Chinaman from his money if he is the stronger party. We need have been desperate indeed to go thieving in such weather, but what could these beggars know of us? So, without thinking of it twice, I got the hands away in a jiffy. Our work was done—that the old man had set his heart on. We cleared out without staying to inquire how they felt. I am convinced that if they had not been so unmercifully shaken, and afraid—each individual one of them—to stand up, we would have been torn to pieces. Oh! It was pretty complete, I can tell you; and you may run to and fro across the Pond to the end of time before you find yourself with such a job on your hands."

After this he alluded professionally to the damage done to the ship, and went on thus:

"It was when the weather quieted down that the situation became confoundedly delicate. It wasn't made any better by us having been lately transferred to the Siamese flag; though the skipper can't see that it makes any difference—'as long as *we* are on board'—he says. There are feelings that this man simply hasn't got—and there's an end of it. You might just as well try to make a bedpost understand. But apart from this it is an infernally lonely state for a ship to be going about the China seas with no proper consuls, not even a gunboat of her own anywhere, nor a body to go to in case of some trouble.

"My notion was to keep these Johnnies[51] under hatches for another fifteen hours or so; as we weren't much farther than that from Fu-chau. We would find there, most likely, some sort of a man-of-war, and once under her guns we were safe enough; for surely any skipper of a man-of-war—English, French, or Dutch—would see white men through as far as a row on board goes. We could get rid of them and their money afterwards by delivering them to their Mandarin or Taotai,[52] or whatever they call these chaps in goggles you see being carried about in sedan-chairs through their stinking streets.

"The old man wouldn't see it somehow. He wanted to keep the matter quiet. He got that notion into his head, and a steam windlass couldn't drag it out of him. He wanted as little fuss made as possible, for the sake of the ship's name and for the sake of the owners—'for the sake of all concerned,' says he, looking at me very hard. It made me hot.[53] Of course you couldn't keep a thing like that quiet; but the chests had been secured in the usual manner and were safe enough for any earthly gale, while this had been an altogether fiendish business I couldn't give you even an idea of.

"Meantime, I could hardly keep on my feet. None of us had a spell of any sort for nearly thirty hours, and there the old man sat rubbing his chin, rubbing the top of his head, and so bothered he didn't even think of pulling his long boots off.

"'I hope, sir,' says I, 'you won't be letting them out on deck before we make ready for them in some shape or other.' Not, mind you, that I felt very sanguine about controlling these beggars if they meant to take charge. A trouble with a cargo of Chinamen is no child's play. I was dam' tired too. 'I wish,' said I, 'you would let us throw the whole lot of these dollars down to them and leave them to fight it out amongst themselves, while we get a rest.'

"'Now you talk wild, Jukes,' says he, looking up in his slow way that makes you ache all over, somehow. 'We must plan out something that would be fair to all parties.'

"I had no end of work on hand, as you may imagine, so I set the hands going, and then I thought I would turn in a bit. I hadn't been asleep in my bunk ten minutes when in rushes the steward and begins to pull at my leg.

"'For God's sake, Mr. Jukes, come out! Come on deck quick, sir. Oh, do come out!'

"The fellow scared all the sense out of me. I didn't know what had happened. Another hurricane—or what. Could hear no wind.

"'The captain's letting them out. Oh, he is letting them out! Jump on deck, sir, and save us. The chief engineer has just run below for his revolver.'

"That's what I understood the fool to say. However, Father Rout swears he went in there only to get a clean pocket-handkerchief. Anyhow, I made one jump into my trousers and flew on deck aft. There was certainly a good deal of noise going on forward of the bridge. Four of the hands with the bo'sun were at work abaft. I passed up to them some of the rifles all the ships on the China coast carry in the cabin, and led them on the bridge. On the way I ran against Old Sol, looking startled and sucking at an unlighted cigar.

"'Come along,' I shouted to him.

"We charged, the seven of us, up to the chart-room. All was over. There stood the old man with his sea-boots still drawn up to the hips and in shirt-sleeves—got warm thinking it out, I suppose. Bun Hin's dandy clerk at his elbow, as dirty as a sweep, was still green in the face. I could see directly I was in for something.

"'What the devil are these monkey tricks, Mr. Jukes?' asks the old man, as angry as ever he could be. I tell you frankly it made me lose my tongue. 'For God's sake, Mr. Jukes,' says he, 'do take away these rifles from the men. Somebody's sure to get hurt before long if you don't. Damme, if this ship isn't worse than Bedlam!⁵⁴ Look sharp now. I want you up here to help me and Bun Hin's Chinaman to count that money. You wouldn't mind lending a hand, too, Mr. Rout, now you are here. The more of us the better.'

"He had settled it all in his mind while I was having a snooze. Had we been an English ship, or only going to land our cargo of coolies in an English port, like Hong-Kong, for instance, there would have been no end of inquiries and bother, claims for damages and so on. But these Chinamen know their officials better than we do.

"The hatches had been taken off already, and they were all on deck after a night and a day down below. It made you feel queer to see so many gaunt, wild faces together. The beggars stared about at the sky, at the sea, at the ship, as though they had expected the whole thing to have been blown to pieces. And no wonder! They had had a doing that would have shaken the soul out of a white man. But then they say a Chinaman has no soul. He has, though, something about him that is deuced tough. There was a fellow (amongst others of the badly hurt) who had had his eye all but knocked out. It stood out of his head the size of half a hen's egg. This would have laid out a white man on his back for a month; and yet there was that chap elbowing here and there in the crowd and talking to the others as if nothing had been the matter. They made a great hubbub amongst themselves, and whenever the old man showed his bald head on the foreside of the bridge, they would all leave off jawing and look at him from below.

"It seems that after he had done his thinking he made that Bun Hin's fellow go down and explain to them the only way they could get their money back. He told me afterwards that, all the coolies having worked in the same place and for the same length of time, he reckoned he would be doing the fair thing by them as near as possible if he shared all the cash we had picked up equally among the lot. You couldn't tell one man's dollars from another's, he said, and if you asked each man how much money he brought on board he was afraid they would lie, and he would find himself a long way short. I think he was right there. As to giving up the money to any Chinese official he could scare up in Fu-chau, he said he might just as well put the lot in his own pocket at once for all the good it would be to them. I suppose they thought so too.

"We finished the distribution before dark. It was rather a sight; the sea running high, the ship a wreck to look at, these Chinamen staggering up on the bridge one by one for their share, and the old man still booted, and in his shirt-sleeves, busy paying out at the chart-room door, perspiring like anything, and now and then coming down sharp on myself or Father Rout about one thing or another not quite to his mind. He took the share of those who were disabled himself to them on the No. 2 hatch. There were three dollars left over, and these went to the three most damaged coolies, one to each. We turned-to afterwards, and shovelled out on deck heaps of wet rags, all sorts of fragments of things without shape, and that you couldn't give a name to, and let them settle the ownership themselves.

"This certainly is coming as near as can be to keeping the thing quiet for the benefit of all concerned. What's your opinion, you pampered mail-boat swell? The old chief says that this was plainly the only thing that could be done. The skipper remarked to me the other day, 'There are things you find nothing about in books.' I think that he got out of it very well for such a stupid man."

Amy Foster

Kennedy is a country doctor, and lives in Colebrook,[1] on the shores of Eastbay. The high ground rising abruptly behind the red roofs of the little town crowds the quaint High Street against the wall which defends it from the sea. Beyond the sea-wall there curves for miles in a vast and regular sweep the barren beach of shingle, with the village of Brenzett standing out darkly across the water, a spire in a clump of trees; and still further out the perpendicular column of a lighthouse, looking in the distance no bigger than a lead pencil, marks the vanishing-point of the land. The country at the back of Brenzett is low and flat, but the bay is fairly well sheltered from the seas, and occasionally a big ship, windbound or through stress of weather, makes use of the anchoring-ground a mile and a half due north from you as you stand at the back door of the Ship Inn[2] in Brenzett. A dilapidated windmill nearby lifting its shattered arms from a mound no loftier than a rubbish-heap, and a Martello tower[3] squatting at the water's edge half a mile to the south of the Coast-guard cottages, are familiar to the skippers of small craft. These are the official sea-marks for the patch of trustworthy bottom represented on the Admiralty charts by an irregular oval of dots enclosing several figures six, with a tiny anchor engraved among them, and the legend "mud and shells" over all.

The brow of the upland overtops the square tower of the Colebrook Church. The slope is green and looped by a white road. Ascending along this road, you open a valley broad and shallow, a wide green trough of pastures and hedges merging inland into a vista of purple tints and flowing lines closing the view.

In this valley down to Brenzett and Colebrook and up to Darnford, the market town fourteen miles away, lies the practice of my friend Kennedy. He had begun life as surgeon in the Navy, and afterwards had been the companion of a famous traveller, in the days when there were continents with unexplored interiors. His papers on the fauna and flora made him known to scientific societies. And now he had come to a country practice—from choice. The penetrating power of his mind, acting like a corrosive fluid, had destroyed his ambition, I fancy. His intelligence is of a scientific order, of an investigating habit, and of that unappeasable curiosity which believes that there is a particle of a general truth in every mystery.

A good many years ago now, on my return from abroad, he invited me to stay with him. I came readily enough, and as he could not neglect his patients to keep me company, he took me on his rounds—thirty miles or so of an afternoon, sometimes. I waited for him on the roads; the horse reached after the leafy twigs, and, sitting high in the dog-cart,[4] I could hear Kennedy's laugh through the half-open door left open of some cottage. He had a big, hearty laugh that would have fitted a man twice his size, a brisk manner, a bronzed[5] face, and a pair of grey, profoundly attentive eyes. He had the talent of making people talk to him freely, and an inexhaustible patience in listening to their tales.

One day, as we trotted out of a large village into a shady bit of road, I saw on our left hand a low brick cottage, with diamond panes in the windows, a creeper on the end wall, a roof of shingle, and some roses climbing on the rickety trellis-work of the tiny porch. Kennedy pulled up to a walk. A woman, in full sunlight, was throwing a dripping blanket over a line stretched between two old apple-trees. And as the bobtailed, long-necked chestnut, trying to get his head, jerked the left hand, covered by a thick dogskin glove, the doctor raised his voice over the hedge: "How's your child, Amy?"[6]

I had the time to see her dull face, red, not with a mantling blush, but as if her flat cheeks had been vigorously slapped, and to take in the squat figure, the scanty, dusty brown hair drawn into a tight knot at the back of the head. She looked quite young. With a distinct catch in her breath, her voice sounded low and timid.

"He's well, thank you."

We trotted again. "A young patient of yours," I said; and the doctor, flicking the chestnut absently, muttered, "Her husband used to be."

"She seems a dull creature," I remarked listlessly.

"Precisely," said Kennedy. "She is very passive. It's enough to look at the red hands hanging at the end of those short arms, at those slow, prominent brown eyes, to know the inertness of her mind—an inertness that one would think made it everlastingly safe from all the surprises of imagination. And yet which of us is safe? At any rate, such as you see her, she had enough imagination to fall in love. She's the daughter of one Isaac Foster, who from a small farmer has sunk into a shepherd; the beginning of his misfortunes dating from his runaway marriage with the cook of his widowed father—a well-to-do, apoplectic grazier, who passionately struck his name off his will, and had been heard to utter threats against his life. But this old affair, scandalous enough to serve as a motive for a Greek tragedy, arose from the similarity of their characters. There are other tragedies, less scandalous and of a subtler poignancy, arising from irreconcilable differences and from that fear of the Incomprehensible that hangs over all our heads—over all our heads. . . ."

The tired chestnut dropped into a walk; and the rim of the sun, all red in a speckless sky, touched familiarly the smooth top of a ploughed rise near the road as I had seen it times innumerable touch the distant horizon of the sea. The uniform brownness of the harrowed field glowed with a rosy tinge, as though the powdered clods had sweated out in minute pearls of blood the toil of uncounted ploughmen. From the edge of a copse a waggon with two horses was rolling gently along the ridge. Raised above our heads upon the sky-line, it loomed up against the red sun, triumphantly big, enormous, like a chariot of giants drawn by two slow-stepping steeds of legendary proportions. And the clumsy figure of the man plodding at the head of the leading horse projected itself on the background of the Infinite with a heroic uncouthness. The end of his carter's whip quivered high up in the blue. Kennedy discoursed.

"She's the eldest of a large family. At the age of fifteen they put her out to service at the New Barns Farm. I attended Mrs. Smith, the tenant's wife, and saw that girl there for the first time. Mrs. Smith, a genteel person with a sharp nose, made her put on a black dress every afternoon. I don't know what induced me to notice her at all. There are faces that call your attention by a curious want of definiteness in their whole aspect, as, walking in a mist, you peer attentively at a vague shape which, after all, may be nothing more curious or strange than a signpost. The only peculiarity I perceived in her was a slight hesitation in her utterance, a sort of preliminary stammer which passes away with the first word. When sharply spoken to, she was apt to lose her head at once; but her heart was of the kindest. She had never been heard to express a dislike for a single human being, and she was tender to every living creature. She was devoted to Mrs. Smith, to Mr. Smith, to their dogs, cats, canaries; and as to Mrs. Smith's grey parrot, its peculiarities exercised upon her a positive fascination. Nevertheless, when that outlandish bird, attacked by the cat, shrieked for help in human accents, she ran out into the yard stopping her ears, and did not prevent the crime. For Mrs. Smith this was another evidence of her stupidity; on the other hand, her want of charm, in view of Smith's well-known frivolousness, was a great recommendation. Her short-sighted eyes would swim with pity for a poor mouse in a trap, and she had been seen once by some boys on her knees in the wet grass helping a toad in difficulties. If it's true, as some German fellow has said, that without phosphorus there is no thought,[7] it is still more true that there is no kindness of heart without a certain amount of imagination. She had some. She had even more than is necessary to understand suffering and to be moved by pity. She fell in love under circumstances that leave no room for doubt in the matter; for you need imagination to form a notion of beauty at all, and still more to discover your ideal in an unfamiliar shape.

How this aptitude came to her, what it did feed upon, is an inscrutable mystery. She was born in the village, and had never been further away from it than Colebrook or perhaps Darnford. She lived for four years with the Smiths. New Barns is an isolated farmhouse a mile away from the road, and she was content to look day after day at the same fields, hollows, rises; at the trees and the hedgerows; at the faces of the four men about the farm, always the same—day after day, month after month, year after year. She never showed a desire for conversation, and, as it seemed to me, she did not know how to smile. Sometimes of a fine Sunday afternoon she would put on her best dress, a pair of stout boots, a large grey hat trimmed with a black feather (I've seen her in that finery), seize an absurdly slender parasol, climb over two stiles, tramp over three fields and along two hundred yards of road—never further. There stood Foster's cottage. She would help her mother to give their tea to the younger children, wash up the crockery, kiss the little ones, and go back to the farm. That was all. All the rest, all the change, all the relaxation. She never seemed to wish for anything more. And then she fell in love. She fell in love silently, obstinately—perhaps helplessly. It came slowly, but when it came it worked like a powerful spell; it was love as the Ancients understood it: an irresistible and fateful impulse—a possession! Yes, it was in her to become haunted and possessed by a face, by a presence, fatally, as though she had been a pagan worshipper of form under a joyous sky—and to be awakened at last from that mysterious forgetfulness of self, from that enchantment, from that transport, by a fear resembling the unaccountable terror of a brute. . . ."

With the sun hanging low on its western limit, the expanse of the grass-lands framed in the counterscarps of the rising ground took on a gorgeous and sombre aspect. A sense of penetrating sadness, like that inspired by a grave strain of music, disengaged itself from the silence of the fields. The men we met walked past slow, unsmiling, with downcast eyes, as if the melancholy of an overburdened earth had weighted their feet, bowed their shoulders, borne down their glances.

"Yes," said the doctor to my remark, "one would think the earth is under a curse, since of all her children these that cling to her the closest are uncouth in body and as leaden of gait as if their very hearts were loaded with chains. But here on this same road you might have seen amongst these heavy men a being lithe, supple, and long-limbed, straight like a pine with something striving upwards in his appearance as though the heart within him had been buoyant. Perhaps it was only the force of the contrast, but when he was passing one of these villagers here, the soles of his feet did not seem to me to touch the dust of the road. He vaulted over the stiles, paced these slopes with a long elastic stride that made him noticeable at a great distance, and had lustrous black eyes. He was so different from the mankind around that, with his freedom of movement, his soft—a little startled—glance, his olive complexion and graceful bearing, his humanity suggested to me the nature of a woodland creature. He came from there."

The doctor pointed with his whip, and from the summit of the descent seen over the rolling tops of the trees in a park by the side of the road, appeared the level sea far below us, like the floor of an immense edifice inlaid with bands of dark ripple, with still trails of glitter, ending in a belt of glassy water at the foot of the sky. The light blurr of smoke, from an invisible steamer, faded on the great clearness of the horizon like the mist of a breath on a mirror; and, inshore, the white sails of a coaster, with the appearance of disentangling themselves slowly from under the branches, floated clear of the foliage of the trees.

"Shipwrecked in the bay?" I said.

"Yes; he was a castaway.[8] A poor emigrant from Central Europe bound to America and washed ashore here in a storm. And for him, who knew nothing of the earth, England was an undiscovered country.[9] It was some time before he learned its name; and for all I know he might have expected to find wild beasts or wild men here, when, crawling in the dark over the sea-wall, he rolled down the other side into a dyke, where it was another miracle he didn't get drowned. But he struggled instinctively like an animal under a net, and this blind struggle threw him out into a field. He must have been, indeed, of a tougher fibre than he looked to withstand without expiring such buffetings, the violence of his exertions, and so much fear. Later on, in his broken English that resembled curiously the speech of a young child, he told me himself that he put his trust in God, believing he was no longer in this world. And truly— he would add—how was he to know? He fought his way against the rain and the gale on all fours, and crawled at last among some sheep huddled close under the lee[10] of a hedge. They ran off in all directions, bleating in the darkness, and he welcomed the first familiar sound he heard on these shores. It must have been two in the morning then. And this is all we know of the manner of his landing, though he did not arrive unattended by any means. Only his grisly company did not begin to come ashore till much later in the day. . . ."

The doctor gathered the reins, clicked his tongue; we trotted down the hill. Then turning, almost directly, a sharp corner into the High Street, we rattled over the stones and were home.

Late in the evening Kennedy, breaking a spell of moodiness that had come over him, returned to the story. Smoking his pipe, he paced the long room from end to end. A reading-lamp concentrated all its light upon the papers on his desk; and, sitting by the open window, I saw, after the windless, scorching day, the frigid splendour of a hazy sea lying motionless under the moon. Not a whisper, not a splash, not a stir of the shingle, not a footstep, not a sigh came up from the earth below—never a sign of life but the scent of climbing jasmine; and Kennedy's voice, speaking behind me, passed through the wide casement, to vanish outside in a chill and sumptuous stillness.

". . . The relations of shipwrecks in the olden time tell us of much suffering. Often the castaways were only saved from drowning to die miserably from starvation on a barren coast; others suffered violent death or else slavery, passing through years of precarious existence with people to whom their strangeness was an object of suspicion, dislike, or fear. We read about these things, and they are very pitiful. It is indeed hard upon a man to find himself a lost stranger, helpless, incomprehensible, and of a mysterious origin, in some obscure corner of the earth. Yet amongst all the adventurers shipwrecked in all the wild parts of the world, there is not one, it seems to me, that ever had to suffer a fate so simply tragic as the man I am speaking of, the most innocent of adventurers cast out by the sea in the bight of this bay, almost within sight from this very window.

He did not know the name of his ship. Indeed, in the course of time we discovered he did not even know that ships had names—'like Christian people'; and when, one day, from the top of the Talfourd Hill, he beheld the sea lying open to his view, his eyes roamed afar, lost in an air of wild surprise, as though he had never seen such a sight before. And probably he had not. As far as I could make out, he had been hustled together with many others on board an emigrant-ship lying at the mouth of the Elbe,[11] too bewildered to take note of his surroundings, too weary to see anything, too anxious to care. They were driven below into the 'tween-deck and battened down from the very start. It was a low timber dwelling—he would say—with wooden beams overhead, like the houses in his country, but you went into it down a ladder. It was very large, very cold, damp and sombre, with places in the manner of wooden boxes where people had to sleep, one above another, and it kept on rocking all ways at once all the time. He crept into one of these boxes and lay down there in the clothes in which he had left his home many days before, keeping his bundle and his stick by his side. People groaned, children cried, water dripped, the lights went out, the walls of the place creaked, and everything was being shaken so that in one's little box one dared not lift one's head. He had lost touch with his only companion (a young man from the same valley, he said), and all the time a great noise of wind went on outside and heavy blows fell—boom! boom! An awful sickness overcame him, even to the point of making him neglect his prayers. Besides, one could not tell whether it was morning or evening. It seemed always to be night in that place.

Before that he had been travelling a long, long time on the iron track. He looked out of the window, which had a wonderfully clear glass in it, and the trees, the houses, the fields, and the long roads seemed to fly round and round about him till his head swam. He gave me to understand that he had on his passage beheld uncounted multitudes of people—whole nations—all dressed in such clothes as the rich wear. Once he

was made to get out of the carriage, and slept through a night
on a bench in a house of bricks with his bundle under his head;
and once for many hours he had to sit on a floor of flat stones
dozing, with his knees up and with his bundle between his feet.
There was a roof over him, which seemed made of glass, and
was so high that the tallest mountain-pine he had ever seen
would have had room to grow under it. Steam-machines rolled
in at one end and out at the other. People swarmed more than
you can see on a feast-day round the miraculous Holy Image
in the yard of the Carmelite Convent down in the plains where,
before he left his home, he drove his mother in a wooden cart—
a pious old woman who wanted to offer prayers and make a
vow for his safety. He could not give me an idea of how large
and lofty and full of noise and smoke and gloom, and clang of
iron, the place was, but some one had told him it was called
Berlin. Then they rang a bell, and another steam-machine came
in, and again he was taken on and on through a land that
wearied his eyes by its flatness without a single bit of a hill to
be seen anywhere. One more night he spent shut up in a building
like a good stable with a litter of straw on the floor, guarding
his bundle amongst a lot of men, of whom not one could
understand a single word he said. In the morning they were all
led down to the stony shores of an extremely broad muddy
river, flowing not between hills but between houses that seemed
immense. There was a steam-machine that went on the water,
and they all stood upon it packed tight, only now there were
with them many women and children who made much noise.
A cold rain fell, the wind blew in his face; he was wet through,
and his teeth chattered. He and the young man from the same
valley took each other by the hand.

They thought they were being taken to America straightaway,
but suddenly the steam-machine bumped against the side of a
thing like a house on the water. The walls were smooth and
black, and there uprose, growing from the roof as it were, bare
trees in the shape of crosses, extremely high. That's how it
appeared to him then, for he had never seen a ship before. This
was the ship that was going to swim all the way to America.
Voices shouted, everything swayed; there was a ladder dipping

up and down. He went up on his hands and knees in mortal fear of falling into the water below, which made a great splashing. He got separated from his companion, and when he descended into the bottom of that ship his heart seemed to melt suddenly within him.

It was then also, as he told me, that he lost contact for good and all with one of those three men who the summer before had been going about through all the little towns in the foothills of his country. They would arrive on market-days driving in a peasant's cart, and would set up an office in an inn or some other Jew's house. There were three of them, of whom one with a long beard looked venerable; and they had red cloth collars round their necks and gold lace on their sleeves like Government officials. They sat proudly behind a long table; and in the next room, so that the common people shouldn't hear, they kept a cunning telegraph machine, through which they could talk to the Emperor of America. The fathers hung about the door, but the young men of the mountains would crowd up to the table asking many questions, for there was work to be got all the year round at three dollars a day in America, and no military service to do.[12]

But the American Kaiser would not take everybody. Oh no! He himself had a great difficulty in getting accepted, and the venerable man in uniform had to go out of the room several times to work the telegraph on his behalf. The American Kaiser engaged him at last at three dollars, he being young and strong. However, many able young men backed out, afraid of the great distance; besides, only those who had some money could be taken. There were some who sold their huts and their land because it cost a lot of money to get to America; but then, once there, you had three dollars a day, and if you were clever you could find places where true gold could be picked up on the ground. His father's house was getting over-full. Two of his brothers were married and had children. He promised to send money home from America by post twice a year. His father sold an old cow, a pair of piebald mountain ponies of his own raising, and a cleared plot of fair pasture land on the sunny slope of a pine-clad pass to a Jew inn-keeper, in order to pay the people of the ship that took men to America to get rich in a short time.

He must have been a real adventurer at heart, for how many of the greatest enterprises in the conquest of the earth had for their beginning just such a bargaining away of the paternal cow for the mirage of true gold far away! I have been telling you more or less in my own words what I learned fragmentarily in the course of two or three years, during which I seldom missed an opportunity of a friendly chat with him. He told me this story of his adventure with many flashes of white teeth and lively glances of black eyes, at first in a sort of anxious baby-talk, then, as he acquired the language, with great fluency, but always with that singing, soft, and at the same time vibrating intonation that instilled a strangely penetrating power into the sound of the most familiar English words, as if they had been the words of an unearthly language. And he always would come to an end, with many emphatic shakes of his head, upon that awful sensation of his heart melting within him directly he set foot on board that ship. Afterwards there seemed to come for him a period of blank ignorance, at any rate as to facts. No doubt he must have been abominably sea-sick and abominably unhappy—this soft and passionate adventurer, taken thus out of his knowledge, and feeling bitterly as he lay in his emigrant bunk his utter loneliness; for his was a highly sensitive nature. The next thing we know of him for certain is that he had been hiding in Hammond's pig-pound by the side of the road to Norton, six miles, as the crow flies, from the sea. Of these experiences he was unwilling to speak; they seemed to have seared into his soul a sombre sort of wonder and indignation. Through the rumours of the countryside, which lasted for a good many days after his arrival, we know that the fishermen of West Colebrook had been disturbed and startled by heavy knocks against the walls of weatherboard cottages, and by a voice crying piercingly strange words in the night. Several of them turned out even, but, no doubt, he had fled in sudden alarm at their rough angry tones hailing each other in the darkness. A sort of frenzy must have helped him up the steep Norton hill. It was he, no doubt, who early the following

morning had been seen lying (in a swoon, I should say) on the
roadside grass by the Brenzett carrier, who actually got down
to have a nearer look, but drew back, intimidated by the perfect
immobility, and by something queer in the aspect of that tramp,
sleeping so still under the showers. As the day advanced, some
children came dashing into school at Norton in such a fright
that the schoolmistress went out and spoke indignantly to a
'horrid-looking man' on the road. He edged away, hanging his
head, for a few steps, and then suddenly ran off with extraordinary fleetness. The driver of Mr. Bradley's milk-cart made no
secret of it that he had lashed with his whip at a hairy sort of
gipsy fellow who, jumping up at a turn of the road by the
Vents,[13] made a snatch at the pony's bridle. And he caught him
a good one too, right over the face, he said, that made him drop
down in the mud a jolly sight quicker than he had jumped up;
but it was a good half a mile before he could stop the pony.
Maybe that in his desperate endeavours to get help, and in his
need to get in touch with some one, the poor devil had tried to
stop the cart. Also three boys confessed afterwards to throwing
stones at a funny tramp, knocking about all wet and muddy,
and, it seemed, very drunk, in the narrow deep lane by the
limekilns. All this was the talk of three villages for days; but we
have Mrs. Finn's (the wife of Smith's waggoner) unimpeachable
testimony that she saw him get over the low wall of Hammond's[14] pig-pound and lurch straight at her, babbling aloud
in a voice that was enough to make one die of fright. Having
the baby with her in a perambulator, Mrs. Finn called out to
him to go away, and as he persisted in coming nearer, she hit
him courageously with her umbrella over the head, and, without once looking back, ran like the wind with the perambulator
as far as the first house in the village. She stopped then, out of
breath, and spoke to old Lewis, hammering there at a heap of
stones; and the old chap, taking off his immense black wire
goggles, got up on his shaky legs to look where she pointed.
Together they followed with their eyes the figure of the man
running over a field; they saw him fall down, pick himself up,
and run on again, staggering and waving his long arms above
his head, in the direction of the New Barns Farm. From that

moment he is plainly in the toils of his obscure and touching destiny. There is no doubt after this of what happened to him. All is certain now: Mrs. Smith's intense terror; Amy Foster's stolid conviction, held against the other's nervous attack, that the man 'meant no harm'; Smith's exasperation (on his return from Darnford Market) at finding the dog barking himself into a fit, the back door locked, his wife in hysterics; and all for an unfortunate dirty tramp, supposed to be even then lurking in his stackyard. Was he? He would teach him to frighten women.

Smith is notoriously hot-tempered, but the sight of some nondescript and miry creature sitting cross-legged amongst a lot of loose straw, and swinging itself to and fro like a bear in a cage, made him pause. Then this tramp stood up silently before him, one mass of mud and filth from head to foot. Smith, alone amongst his stacks with this apparition, in the stormy twilight ringing with the infuriated barking of the dog, felt the dread of an inexplicable strangeness. But when that being, parting with his black hands the long matted locks that hung before his face, as you part the two halves of a curtain, looked out at him with glistening, wild, black-and-white eyes, the weirdness of this silent encounter fairly staggered him. He had admitted since (for the story has been a legitimate subject of conversation about here for years) that he made more than one step[15] backwards. Then a sudden burst of rapid, senseless speech persuaded him at once that he had to do with an escaped lunatic. In fact, that impression never wore off completely. Smith has not in his heart given up his secret conviction of the man's essential insanity to this very day.

As the creature approached him, jabbering in a most discomposing manner, Smith (unaware that he was being addressed as 'gracious lord,' and adjured in God's name to afford food and shelter) kept on speaking firmly but gently to it, and retreating all the time into the other yard. At last, watching his chance, by a sudden charge he bundled him headlong into the wood-lodge, and instantly shot the bolt. Thereupon he wiped his brow, though the day was cold. He had done his duty to the community by shutting up a wandering and probably dangerous maniac. Smith isn't a hard man at all, but he had room in his brain only for that one idea of lunacy. He was not imaginative enough to ask himself whether the man might not be perishing with cold and hunger. Meantime, at first, the maniac made a great deal of noise in the lodge. Mrs. Smith was screaming upstairs, where she had locked herself in her bedroom; but Amy Foster sobbed piteously at the kitchen-door, wringing her hands and muttering, 'Don't! don't!' I daresay Smith had a rough time of it that evening with one noise and another, and this insane, disturbing voice crying obstinately through the door only added to his irritation. He couldn't possibly have connected this troublesome lunatic with the sinking of a ship in Eastbay, of which there had been a rumour in the Darnford market-place. And I daresay the man inside had been very near to insanity on that night. Before his excitement collapsed and he became unconscious he was throwing himself violently about in the dark, rolling on some dirty sacks, and biting his fists with rage, cold, hunger, amazement, and despair.

He was a mountaineer of the eastern range of the Carpathians,[16] and the vessel sunk the night before in Eastbay was the Hamburg emigrant-ship *Herzogin Sophia-Dorothea*,[17] of appalling memory.

A few months later we could read in the papers the accounts of the bogus 'Emigration Agencies' among the Sclavonian peasantry in the more remote provinces of Austria.[18] The object of these scoundrels was to get hold of the poor ignorant people's homesteads, and they were in league with the local usurers. They exported their victims through Hamburg mostly. As to the ship, I had watched her out of this very window, reaching close-hauled under short canvas into the bay on a dark, threatening afternoon. She came to an anchor, correctly by the chart, off the Brenzett Coastguard station. I remember before the night fell looking out again at the outlines of her spars and rigging that stood out dark and pointed on a background of ragged, slaty clouds like another and a slighter spire to the left of the Brenzett church-tower. In the evening the wind rose. At midnight I could hear in my bed the terrific gusts and the sounds of a driving deluge.

About that time the Coastguardmen thought they saw the

lights of a steamer over the anchoring-ground. In a moment
they vanished; but it is clear that another vessel of some sort
had tried for shelter in the bay on that awful, blind night, had
rammed the German ship amidships (a breach—as one of the
divers told me afterwards—'that you could sail a Thames barge
through'), and then had gone out either scatheless or damaged,
who shall say; but had gone out, unknown, unseen, and fatal,
to perish mysteriously at sea. Of her nothing ever came to light,
and yet the hue and cry that was raised all over the world would
have found her out if she had been in existence anywhere on
the face of the waters.[19]

A completeness without a clue, and a stealthy silence as of a
neatly executed crime, characterise this murderous disaster,
which, as you may remember, had its gruesome celebrity. The
wind would have prevented the loudest outcries from reaching
the shore; there had been evidently no time for signals of distress. It was death without any sort of fuss.[20] The Hamburg
ship, filling all at once, capsized as she sank, and at daylight
there was not even the end of a spar to be seen above water.
She was missed, of course, and at first the Coastguardmen
surmised that she had either dragged her anchor or parted her
cable some time during the night, and had been blown out to
sea. Then, after the tide turned, the wreck must have shifted a
little and released some of the bodies, because a child—a little
fair-haired child in a red frock—came ashore abreast of the
Martello tower. By the afternoon you could see along three
miles of beach dark figures with bare legs dashing in and out
of the tumbling foam, and rough-looking men, women with
hard faces, children, mostly fair-haired, were being carried, stiff
and dripping, on stretchers, on wattles, on ladders, in a long
procession past the door of the Ship Inn, to be laid out in a row
under the north wall of the Brenzett Church.

Officially, the body of the little girl in the red frock is the first
thing that came ashore from that ship. But I have patients
amongst the seafaring population of West Colebrook, and,
unofficially, I am informed that very early that morning two
brothers, who went down to look after their cobble hauled up
on the beach, found, a good way from Brenzett, an ordinary

ship's hencoop lying high and dry on the shore, with eleven drowned ducks inside. Their families ate the birds, and the hencoop was split into firewood with a hatchet. It is possible that a man (supposing he happened to be on deck at the time of the accident) might have floated ashore on that hencoop. He might. I admit it is improbable, but there was the man—and for days, nay, for weeks—it didn't enter our heads that we had amongst us the only living soul that had escaped from that disaster. The man himself, even when he learned to speak intelligibly, could tell us very little. He remembered he had felt better (after the ship had anchored, I suppose), and that the darkness, the wind, and the rain took his breath away. This looks as if he had been on deck some time during that night. But we mustn't forget he had been taken out of his knowledge, that he had been sea-sick and battened down below for four days, that he had no general notion of a ship or of the sea, and therefore could have no definite idea of what was happening to him. The rain, the wind, the darkness he knew; he understood the bleating of the sheep, and he remembered the pain of his wretchedness and misery, his heartbroken astonishment that it was neither seen nor understood, his dismay at finding all the men angry and all the women fierce. He had approached them as a beggar, it is true, he said; but in his country, even if they gave nothing, they spoke gently to beggars. The children in his country were not taught to throw stones at those who asked for compassion. Smith's strategy overcame him completely. The wood-lodge presented the horrible aspect of a dungeon. What would be done to him next? . . . No wonder that Amy Foster appeared to his eyes with the aureole of an angel of light. The girl had not been able to sleep for thinking of the poor man, and in the morning, before the Smiths were up, she slipped out across the back yard. Holding the door of the wood-lodge ajar, she looked in and extended to him half a loaf of white bread— 'such bread as the rich eat in my country,' he used to say.

At this he got up slowly from amongst all sorts of rubbish, stiff, hungry, trembling, miserable, and doubtful. 'Can you eat this?' she asked in her soft and timid voice. He must have taken her for a 'gracious lady.' He devoured ferociously, and tears were falling on the crust. Suddenly he dropped the bread, seized her wrist, and imprinted a kiss on her hand. She was not frightened. Through his forlorn condition she had observed that he was good-looking. She shut the door and walked back slowly to the kitchen. Much later on, she told Mrs. Smith, who shuddered at the bare idea of being touched by that creature.

Through this act of impulsive pity he was brought back again within the pale of human relations with his new surroundings. He never forgot it—never.

That very same morning old Mr. Swaffer (Smith's nearest neighbour) came over to give his advice, and ended by carrying him off. He stood, unsteady on his legs, meek, and caked over in half-dried mud, while the two men talked around him in an incomprehensible tongue. Mrs. Smith had refused to come downstairs till the madman was off the premises; Amy Foster, far from within the dark kitchen, watched through the open back door; and he obeyed the signs that were made to him to the best of his ability. But Smith was full of mistrust. 'Mind, sir! It may be all his cunning,' he cried repeatedly in a tone of warning. When Mr. Swaffer started the mare, the deplorable being sitting humbly by his side, through weakness, nearly fell out over the back of the high two-wheeled cart. Swaffer took him straight home. And it is then that I come upon the scene.

I was called in by the simple process of the old man beckoning to me with his forefinger over the gate of his house as I happened to be driving past. I got down, of course.

'I've got something here,' he mumbled, leading the way to an outhouse at a little distance from his other farm-buildings.

It was there that I saw him first, in a long low room taken upon the space of that sort of coach-house. It was bare and whitewashed, with a small square aperture glazed with one cracked, dusty pane at its further end. He was lying on his back upon a straw pallet; they had given him a couple of horse-blankets, and he seemed to have spent the remainder of his strength in the exertion of cleaning himself. He was almost speechless; his quick breathing under the blankets pulled up to his chin, his glittering, restless black eyes reminded me of a wild bird caught in a snare. While I was examining him, old Swaffer stood silently by the door, passing the tips of his fingers along his shaven upper lip. I gave some directions, promised to send a bottle of medicine, and naturally made some inquiries.

'Smith caught him in the stackyard at New Barns,' said the old chap in his deliberate, unmoved manner, and as if the other had been indeed a sort of wild animal. 'That's how I came by him. Quite a curiosity, isn't he? Now tell me, doctor—you've been all over the world—don't you think that's a bit of a Hindoo we've got hold of here?'

I was greatly surprised. His long black hair scattered over the straw bolster contrasted with the olive pallor of his face. It occurred to me he might be a Basque. It didn't necessarily follow that he should understand Spanish; but I tried him with the few words I know, and also with some French. The whispered sounds I caught by bending my ear to his lips puzzled me utterly. That afternoon the young ladies from the Rectory (one of them read Goethe with a dictionary, and the other had struggled with Dante[21] for years), coming to see Miss Swaffer, tried their German and Italian on him from the doorway. They retreated, just the least bit scared by the flood of passionate speech which, turning on his pallet, he let out at them. They admitted that the sound was pleasant, soft, musical—but, in conjunction with his looks perhaps, it was startling—so excitable, so utterly unlike anything one had ever heard. The village boys climbed up the bank to have a peep through the little square aperture. Everybody was wondering what Mr. Swaffer would do with him.

He simply kept him.

Swaffer would be called eccentric were he not so much respected. They will tell you that Mr. Swaffer sits up as late as ten o'clock at night to read books, and they will tell you also that he can write a cheque for two hundred pounds without thinking twice about it. He himself would tell you that the Swaffers had owned land between this and Darnford for these three hundred years. He must be eighty-five to-day, but he does not look a bit older than when I first came here. He is a great breeder of sheep, and deals extensively in cattle. He attends market-days for miles around in every sort of weather, and drives sitting bowed low over the reins, his lank grey hair curling over the collar of his warm coat, and with a green plaid rug round his legs. The calmness of advanced age gives a solemnity to his manner. He is clean-shaved; his lips are thin and sensitive; something rigid and monachal in the set of his features lends a certain elevation to the character of his face. He has been known to drive miles in the rain to see a new kind of rose in somebody's garden, or a monstrous cabbage grown by a cottager. He loves to hear tell of or to be shown something what he calls 'outlandish.' Perhaps it was just that outland-ishness of the man which influenced old Swaffer. Perhaps it was only an inexplicable caprice. All I know is that at the end of three weeks I caught sight of Smith's lunatic digging in Swaffer's kitchen garden. They had found out he could use a spade. He dug barefooted.

His black hair flowed over his shoulders. I suppose it was Swaffer who had given him the striped old cotton shirt; but he wore still the national brown cloth trousers (in which he had been washed ashore) fitting to the leg almost like tights; was belted with a broad leathern belt studded with little brass discs; and had never yet ventured into the village. The land he looked upon seemed to him kept neatly, like the grounds round a landowner's house; the size of the cart-horses struck him with astonishment; the roads resembled garden walks, and the aspect of the people, especially on Sundays, spoke of opulence. He wondered what made them so hardhearted and their children so bold. He got his food at the back door, carried it in both hands, carefully, to his outhouse, and, sitting alone on his pallet, would make the sign of the cross[22] before he began. Beside the same pallet, kneeling in the early darkness of the short days, he recited aloud the Lord's Prayer before he slept. Whenever he saw old Swaffer he would bow with veneration from the waist, and stand erect while the old man, with his fingers over his upper lip, surveyed him silently. He bowed also to Miss Swaffer, who kept house frugally for her father—a broad-shouldered, big-boned woman of forty-five, with the pocket of her dress full of keys, and a grey, steady eye. She was Church—as people said (while her father was one of the trustees of the Baptist

Chapel)[23]—and wore a little steel cross at her waist. She dressed severely in black, in memory of one of the innumerable Bradleys of the neighbourhood, to whom she had been engaged some twenty-five years ago—a young farmer who broke his neck out hunting on the eve of the wedding-day. She had the unmoved countenance of the deaf, spoke very seldom, and her lips, thin like her father's, astonished one sometimes by a mysteriously ironic curl.

These were the people to whom he owed allegiance, and an overwhelming loneliness seemed to fall from the leaden sky of that winter without sunshine. All the faces were sad. He could talk to no one, and had no hope of ever understanding anybody. It was as if these had been the faces of people from the other world—dead people—he used to tell me years afterwards. Upon my word, I wonder he did not go mad. He didn't know where he was. Somewhere very far from his mountains—somewhere over the water. Was this America, he wondered?

If it hadn't been for the steel cross at Miss Swaffer's belt he would not, he confessed, have known whether he was in a Christian country at all. He used to cast stealthy glances at it, and feel comforted. There was nothing here the same as in his country! The earth and the water were different; there were no images of the Redeemer by the roadside. The very grass was different, and the trees. All the trees but the three old Norway-pines on the bit of lawn before Swaffer's house, and these reminded him of his country. He had been detected once, after dusk, with his forehead against the trunk of one of them, sobbing, and talking to himself. They had been like brothers to him at that time, he affirmed. Everything else was strange. Conceive you the kind of an existence overshadowed, oppressed, by the everyday material appearances, as if by the visions of a nightmare. At night, when he could not sleep, he kept on thinking of the girl who gave him the first piece of bread he had eaten in this foreign land. She had been neither fierce nor angry, nor frightened. Her face he remembered as the only comprehensible face amongst all these faces that were as closed, as mysterious, and as mute as the faces of the dead who are possessed of a knowledge beyond the comprehension of the living. I wonder whether the memory of her compassion prevented him from cutting his throat. But there! I suppose I am an old sentimentalist, and forget the instinctive love of life which it takes all the strength of an uncommon despair to overcome.

He did the work which was given him with an intelligence which surprised old Swaffer. By-and-by it was discovered that he could help at the ploughing, could milk the cows, feed the bullocks in the cattle-yard, and was of some use with the sheep. He began to pick up words, too, very fast; and suddenly, one fine morning in spring, he rescued from an untimely death a grandchild of old Swaffer.

Swaffer's younger daughter is married to Willcox, a solicitor and the Town Clerk[24] of Colebrook. Regularly twice a year they come to stay with the old man for a few days. Their only child, a little girl not three years old at the time, ran out of the house alone in her little white pinafore, and, toddling across the grass of a terraced garden, pitched herself over a low wall head first into the horse-pond in the yard below.

Our man was out with the waggoner and the plough in the field nearest to the house, and as he was leading the team round to begin a fresh furrow, he saw, through the gap of a gate, what for anybody else would have been a mere flutter of something white. But he had straight-glancing, quick, far-reaching eyes, that only seemed to flinch and lose their amazing power before the immensity of the sea. He was barefooted, and looking as outlandish as the heart of Swaffer could desire. Leaving the horses on the turn, to the inexpressible disgust of the waggoner he bounded off, going over the ploughed ground in long leaps, and suddenly appeared before the mother, thrust the child into her arms, and strode away.

The pond was not very deep; but still, if he had not had such good eyes, the child would have perished—miserably suffocated in the foot or so of sticky mud at the bottom. Old Swaffer walked out slowly into the field, waited till the plough came over to his side, had a good look at him, and without saying a word went back to the house. But from that time they laid out his meals on the kitchen table; and at first, Miss Swaffer, all in black and with an inscrutable face, would come and stand in the doorway of the living-room to see him make a big sign of the cross before he fell to. I believe that from that day, too, Swaffer began to pay him regular wages.

I can't follow step by step his development. He cut his hair short, was seen in the village and along the road going to and fro to his work like any other man. Children ceased to shout after him. He became aware of social differences, but remained for a long time surprised at the bare poverty of the churches among so much wealth. He couldn't understand either why they were kept shut up on week-days. There was nothing to steal in them. Was it to keep people from praying too often? The rectory took much notice of him about that time, and I believe the young ladies attempted to prepare the ground for his conversion. They could not, however, break him of his habit of crossing himself, but he went so far as to take off the string with a couple of brass medals the size of a sixpence, a tiny metal cross, and a square sort of scapulary which he wore round his neck. He hung them on the wall by the side of his bed, and he was still to be heard every evening reciting the Lord's Prayer, in incomprehensible words and in a slow, fervent tone, as he had heard his old father do at the head of all the kneeling family, big and little, on every evening of his life. And though he wore corduroys at work, and a slop-made[25] pepper-and-salt suit on Sundays, strangers would turn round to look after him on the road. His foreignness had a peculiar and indelible stamp. At last people became used to see him. But they never became used to him. His rapid, skimming walk; his swarthy complexion; his hat cocked on the left ear; his habit, on warm evenings, of wearing his coat over one shoulder, like a hussar's dolman; his manner of leaping over the stiles, not as a feat of agility, but in the ordinary course of progression—all these peculiarities were, as one may say, so many causes of scorn and offence to the inhabitants of the village. *They* wouldn't in their dinner hour[26] lie flat on their backs on the grass to stare at the sky. Neither did they go about the fields screaming dismal tunes. Many times have I heard his high-pitched voice from behind the ridge of some sloping sheep-walk, a voice light and soaring, like a lark's, but with a melancholy human note, over our fields that hear only the song of birds. And I should be startled myself. Ah! He was different: innocent of heart, and full of good-will, which nobody wanted, this castaway, that, like a man transplanted into another planet, was separated by an immense space from his past and by an immense ignorance from his future. His quick, fervent utterance positively shocked everybody. 'An excitable devil,' they called him. One evening, in the tap-room[27] of the Coach and Horses, (having drunk some whisky), he upset them all by singing a love-song of his country. They hooted him down, and he was pained; but Preble, the lame wheelwright, and Vincent, the fat blacksmith, and the other notables, too, wanted to drink their evening beer in peace. On another occasion he tried to show them how to dance. The dust rose in clouds from the sanded floor; he leaped straight up amongst the deal tables, struck his heels together, squatted on one heel in front of old Preble, shooting out the other leg, uttered wild and exulting cries, jumped up to whirl on one foot, snapping his fingers above his head—and a strange carter who was having a drink in there began to swear, and cleared out with his half-pint in his hand into the bar. But when suddenly he sprang upon a table and continued to dance among the glasses, the landlord interfered. He didn't want any 'acrobat tricks in the tap-room.' They laid their hands on him. Having had a glass or two, Mr. Swaffer's foreigner tried to expostulate; was ejected forcibly; got a black eye.

I believe he felt the hostility of his human surroundings. But he was tough—tough in spirit, too, as well as in body. Only the memory of the sea frightened him, with that vague terror that is left by a bad dream. His home was far away; and he did not want now to go to America. I had often explained to him that there is no place on earth where true gold can be found lying ready and to be got for the trouble of the picking up. How then, he asked, could he ever return home with empty hands when there had been sold a cow, two ponies, and a bit of land to pay for his going? His eyes would fill with tears, and, averting them from the immense shimmer of the sea, he would throw himself face down on the grass. But sometimes, cocking his hat with a little conquering air, he would defy my wisdom. He had found his bit of true gold. That was Amy Foster's heart, which was 'a golden heart, and soft to people's misery,' he would say in the accents of overwhelming conviction.

He was called Yanko.[28] He had explained that this meant Little John; but as he would also repeat very often that he was a mountaineer (some word sounding in the dialect of his country like Goorall)[29] he got it for his surname. And this is the only trace of him that the succeeding ages may find in the marriage register of the parish. There it stands—Yanko Goorall—in the rector's handwriting. The crooked cross made by the castaway, a cross whose tracing no doubt seemed to him the most solemn part of the whole ceremony, is all that remains now to perpetuate the memory of his name.

His courtship had lasted some time—ever since he got his precarious footing in the community. It began by his buying for Amy Foster a green satin ribbon in Darnford. This was what you did in his country. You bought a ribbon at a Jew's stall on a fair-day. I don't suppose the girl knew what to do with it, but he seemed to think that his honourable intentions could not be mistaken.

It was only when he declared his purpose to get married that I fully understood how, for a hundred futile and inappreciable reasons, how—shall I say odious?—he was to all the country-side. Every old woman in the village was up in arms. Smith, coming upon him near the farm, promised to break his head for him if he found him about again. But he twisted his little black moustache with such a bellicose air and rolled such big, black fierce eyes at Smith that this promise came to nothing. Smith, however, told the girl that she must be mad to take up with a man who was surely wrong in his head. All the same, when she heard him in the gloaming whistle from beyond the orchard a couple of bars of a weird and mournful tune, she would drop whatever she had in her hand—she would leave Mrs. Smith in the middle of a sentence—and she would run out to his call. Mrs. Smith called her a shameless hussy. She answered nothing. She said nothing at all to anybody, and went on her way as if she had been deaf. She and I alone in all the land, I fancy, could see his very real beauty. He was very good-looking, and most graceful in his bearing, with that something wild as of a woodland creature in his aspect. Her mother moaned over her dismally whenever the girl came to see her on her day out. The father was surly, but pretended not to know; and Mrs. Finn once told her plainly that 'this man, my dear, will do you some harm some day yet.' And so it went on. They could be seen on the roads, she tramping stolidly in her finery—grey dress, black feather, stout boots, prominent white cotton gloves that caught your eye a hundred yards away; and he, his coat slung picturesquely over one shoulder, pacing by her side, gallant of bearing and casting tender glances upon the girl with the golden heart. I wonder whether he saw how plain she was. Perhaps among types so different from what he had ever seen, he had not the power to judge; or perhaps he was seduced by the divine quality of her pity.

Yanko was in great trouble meantime. In his country you get an old man for an ambassador in marriage affairs. He did not know how to proceed. However, one day in the midst of sheep in a field (he was now Swaffer's under-shepherd with Foster) he took off his hat to the father and declared himself humbly. 'I daresay she's fool enough to marry you,' was all Foster said. 'And then,' he used to relate, 'he puts his hat on his head, looks black at me as if he wanted to cut my throat, whistles the dog, and off he goes, leaving me to do the work.' The Fosters, of course, didn't like to lose the wages the girl earned; Amy used to give all her money to her mother. But there was in Foster a very genuine aversion to that match. He contended that the fellow was very good with sheep, but was not fit for any girl to marry. For one thing, he used to go along the hedges muttering to himself like a dam' fool; and then, these foreigners behave very queerly to women sometimes. And perhaps he would want to carry her off somewhere—or run off himself. It was not safe. He preached it to his daughter that the fellow might ill-use her in some way. She made no answer. It was, they said in the village, as if the man had done something to her. People discussed the matter. It was quite an excitement, and the two went on 'walking out' together in the face of opposition. Then something unexpected happened.

I don't know whether old Swaffer ever understood how much he was regarded in the light of a father by his foreign retainer. Anyway the relation was curiously feudal. So when Yanko asked formally for an interview—'and the Miss too' (he called the severe, deaf Miss Swaffer simply *Miss*)—it was to obtain their permission to marry. Swaffer heard him unmoved, dismissed him by a nod, and then shouted the intelligence into Miss Swaffer's best ear. She showed no surprise, and only remarked grimly, in a veiled blank voice, 'He certainly won't get any other girl to marry him.'

It is Miss Swaffer who has all the credit of the munificence; but in a very few days it came out that Mr. Swaffer had presented Yanko with a cottage (the cottage you've seen this morning) and something like an acre of ground—had made it over to him in absolute property. Willcox expedited the deed, and I remember him telling me he had a great pleasure in making it ready. It recited: 'In consideration of saving the life of my beloved grandchild, Bertha Willcox.'

Of course, after that no power on earth could prevent them from getting married.

Her infatuation endured. People saw her going out to meet him in the evening. She stared with unblinking, fascinated eyes up the road where he was expected to appear, walking freely, with a swing from the hip, and humming one of the love-tunes of his country. When the boy was born, he got elevated at the Coach and Horses, essayed again a song and a dance, and was again ejected. People expressed their commiseration for a woman married to that Jack-in-the-box.[30] He didn't care. There was a man now (he told me boastfully) to whom he could sing and talk in the language of his country, and show how to dance by-and-by.

But I don't know. To me he appeared to have grown less springy of step, heavier in body, less keen of eye. Imagination, no doubt; but it seems to me now as if the net of fate had been drawn closer round him already.

One day I met him on the footpath over the Talfourd Hill.

He told me that 'women were funny.' I had heard already of domestic differences. People were saying that Amy Foster was beginning to find out what sort of man she had married. He looked upon the sea with indifferent, unseeing eyes. His wife had snatched the child out of his arms one day as he sat on the doorstep crooning to it a song such as the mothers sing to babies in his mountains. She seemed to think he was doing it some harm. Women are funny. And she had objected to him praying aloud in the evening. Why? He expected the boy to repeat the prayer aloud after him by-and-by, as he used to do after his old father when he was a child—in his own country. And I discovered he longed for their boy to grow up so that he could have a man to talk with in that language that to our ears sounded so disturbing, so passionate, and so bizarre. Why his wife should dislike the idea he couldn't tell. But that would pass, he said. And tilting his head knowingly, he tapped his breastbone to indicate that she had a good heart: not hard, not fierce, open to compassion, charitable to the poor!

I walked away thoughtfully; I wondered whether his difference, his strangeness, were not penetrating with repulsion that dull nature they had begun by irresistibly attracting. I wondered. . . ."

The doctor came to the window and looked out at the frigid splendour of the sea, immense in the haze, as if enclosing all the earth with all the hearts lost among the passions of love and fear.

"Physiologically, now," he said, turning away abruptly, "it was possible. It was possible."

He remained silent. Then went on——

"At all events, the next time I saw him he was ill—lung trouble. He was tough, but I daresay he was not acclimatised as well as I had supposed. It was a bad winter; and, of course, these mountaineers do get fits of home-sickness; and a state of depression would make him vulnerable. He was lying half-dressed on a couch downstairs.

A table covered with a dark oilcloth took up all the middle of the little room. There was a wicker cradle on the floor, a kettle spouting steam on the hob, and some child's linen lay drying on the fender. The room was warm, but the door opens right into the garden, as you noticed perhaps.

He was very feverish, and kept on muttering to himself. She sat on a chair and looked at him fixedly across the table with her brown, blurred eyes. 'Why don't you have him upstairs?' I asked. With a start and a confused stammer she said, 'Oh! ah! I couldn't sit with him upstairs, sir.'

I gave her certain directions; and going outside, I said again that he ought to be in bed upstairs. She wrung her hands. 'I couldn't. I couldn't. He keeps on saying something—I don't know what.' With the memory of all the talk against the man that had been dinned into her ears, I looked at her narrowly. I looked into her short-sighted eyes, at her dumb eyes that once in her life had seen an enticing shape, but seemed, staring at me, to see nothing at all now. But I saw she was uneasy.

'What's the matter with him?' she asked in a sort of vacant trepidation. 'He doesn't look very ill. I never did see anybody look like this before. . . .'

'Do you think,' I asked indignantly, 'he is shamming?'

'I can't help it, sir,' she said stolidly. And suddenly she clapped her hands and looked right and left. 'And there's the baby. I am so frightened. He wanted me just now to give him the baby. I can't understand what he says to it.'

'Can't you ask a neighbour to come in to-night?' I asked.

'Please, sir, nobody seems to care to come,' she muttered, dully resigned all at once.

I impressed upon her the necessity of the greatest care, and then had to go. There was a good deal of sickness that winter. 'Oh, I hope he won't talk!' she exclaimed softly just as I was going away.

I don't know how it is I did not see—but I didn't. And yet, turning in my trap, I saw her lingering before the door, very still, and as if meditating a flight up the miry road.

Towards the night his fever increased.

He tossed, moaned, and now and then muttered a complaint. And she sat with the table between her and the couch, watching every movement and every sound, with the terror, the unreasonable terror, of that man she could not understand creeping over her. She had drawn the wicker cradle close to her feet. There was nothing in her now but the maternal instinct and that unaccountable fear.

Suddenly coming to himself, parched, he demanded a drink of water. She did not move. She had not understood, though he may have thought he was speaking in English. He waited, looking at her, burning with fever, amazed at her silence and immobility, and then he shouted impatiently, 'Water! Give me water!'

She jumped to her feet, snatched up the child, and stood still. He spoke to her, and his passionate remonstrances only increased her fear of that strange man. I believe he spoke to her for a long time, entreating, wondering, pleading, ordering, I suppose. She says she bore it as long as she could. And then a gust of rage came over him.

He sat up and called out terribly one word—some word. Then he got up as though he hadn't been ill at all, she says. And as in fevered dismay, indignation, and wonder he tried to get to her round the table, she simply opened the door and ran out with the child in her arms. She heard him call twice after her down the road in a terrible voice—and fled. . . . Ah! but you should have seen stirring behind the dull, blurred glance of these eyes the spectre of the fear which had haunted her on that night three miles and a half to the door of Foster's cottage! I did the next day.

And it was I who found him lying face down and his body in a puddle, just outside the little wicket-gate.

I had been called out that night to an urgent case in the village, and on my way home at daybreak passed by the cottage. The door stood open. My man helped me to carry him in. We laid him on the couch. The lamp smoked, the fire was out, the chill of the stormy night oozed from the cheerless yellow paper on the wall. 'Amy!' I called aloud, and my voice seemed to lose itself in the emptiness of this tiny house as if I had cried in a desert.[31] He opened his eyes. 'Gone!' he said distinctly. 'I had only asked for water—only for a little water. . . .'

He was muddy. I covered him up and stood waiting in silence, catching a painfully gasped word now and then. They were no longer in his own language. The fever had left him, taking with it the heat of life. And with his panting breast and lustrous eyes he reminded me again of a wild creature under the net; of a bird caught in a snare. She had left him. She had left him— sick—helpless—thirsty. The spear of the hunter had entered his very soul. 'Why?' he cried in the penetrating and indignant voice of a man calling to a responsible Maker. A gust of wind and a swish of rain answered.

And as I turned away to shut the door he pronounced the word 'Merciful!' and expired.

Eventually I certified heart-failure as the immediate cause of death. His heart must have indeed failed him, or else he might have stood this night of storm and exposure, too. I closed his eyes and drove away. Not very far from the cottage I met Foster walking sturdily between the dripping hedges with his collie at his heels.

'Do you know where your daughter is?' I asked.

'Don't I!' he cried. 'I am going to talk to him a bit. Frightening a poor woman like this.'

'He won't frighten her any more,' I said. 'He is dead.'

He struck with his stick at the mud.

'And there's the child.'

Then, after thinking deeply for a while——

'I don't know that it isn't for the best.'

That's what he said. And she says nothing at all now. Not a word of him. Never. Is his image as utterly gone from her mind as his lithe and striding figure, his carolling voice are gone from our fields? He is no longer before her eyes to excite her imagination into a passion of love or fear; and his memory seems to have vanished from her dull brain as a shadow passes away upon a white screen. She lives in the cottage and works for Miss Swaffer. She is Amy Foster for everybody, and the child is 'Amy Foster's boy.' She calls him Johnny—which means Little John.

It is impossible to say whether this name recalls anything to her. Does she ever think of the past? I have seen her hanging over the boy's cot in a very passion of maternal tenderness. The little fellow was lying on his back, a little frightened at me, but very still, with his big black eyes, with his fluttered air of a bird in a snare. And looking at him I seemed to see again the other one—the father, cast out mysteriously by the sea to perish in the supreme disaster of loneliness and despair."

Falk

A Reminiscence

Several of us, all more or less connected with the sea, were dining in a small river-hostelry[1] not more than thirty miles from London, and less than twenty from that shallow and dangerous puddle to which our coasting men give the grandiose name of "German Ocean."[2] And through the wide windows we had a view of the Thames; an enfilading view down the Lower Hope Reach.[3] But the dinner was execrable, and all the feast was for the eyes.

That flavour of salt-water which for so many of us had been the very water of life permeated our talk. He who hath known the bitterness of the Ocean shall have its taste for ever in his mouth.[4] But one or two of us, pampered by the life of the land, complained of hunger. It was impossible to swallow any of that stuff. And indeed there was a strange mustiness in everything. The wooden dining-room stuck out over the mud of the shore like a lacustrine dwelling; the planks of the floor seemed rotten; a decrepid old waiter tottered pathetically to and fro before an antediluvian and worm-eaten sideboard; the chipped plates might have been disinterred from some kitchen midden near an inhabited lake; and the chops recalled times more ancient still. They brought forcibly to one's mind the night of ages[5] when the primeval man, evolving the first rudiments of cookery from his dim consciousness, scorched lumps of flesh at a fire of sticks in the company of other good fellows; then, gorged and happy, sat him back among the gnawed bones to tell his artless tales of experience—the tales of hunger and hunt—and of women, perhaps!

But luckily the wine happened to be as old as the waiter. So, comparatively empty, but upon the whole fairly happy, we sat back and told our artless tales. We talked of the sea and all its works. The sea never changes, and its works for all the talk of men are wrapped in mystery. But we agreed that the times were changed. And we talked of old ships, of sea-accidents, of break-downs, dismastings; and of a man who brought his ship safe to Liverpool all the way from the River Plate[6] under a jury-rudder. We talked of wrecks, of short rations, and of heroism—or at least of what the newspapers would have called heroism at sea—a manifestation of virtues quite different from the heroism of primitive times. And now and then falling silent all together we gazed at the sights of the river.

A P. & O.[7] boat passed bound down. "One gets jolly good dinners on board these ships," remarked one of our band. A man with sharp eyes read out the name on her bows: *Arcadia*.[8] "What a beautiful model of a ship!" murmured some of us. She was followed by a small cargo-steamer, and the flag they hauled down aboard while we were looking showed her to be a Norwegian. She made an awful lot of smoke; and before it had quite blown away, a high-sided, short wooden barque, in ballast and towed by a paddle-tug, appeared in front of the windows. All her hands were forward busy setting up the headgear; and aft a woman in a red hood, quite alone with the man at the wheel, paced the length of the poop back and forth, with the grey wool of some knitting work in her hands.

"German I should think," muttered one. "The skipper has his wife on board," remarked another; and the light of the crimson sunset all ablaze behind the London smoke, throwing a glow of Bengal light upon the barque's spars, faded away from the Hope Reach.

Then one of us, who had not spoken before, a man of over fifty, that had commanded ships for a quarter of a century, looking after the barque now gliding far away, all black on the lustre of the river, said:

"This reminds me of an absurd episode in my life, now many years ago, when I got first the command of an iron barque, loading then in a certain Eastern seaport.[9] It was also the capital of an Eastern kingdom, lying up a river as might be London lies up this old Thames of ours. No more need be said of the place; for this sort of thing might have happened anywhere where there are ships, skippers, tug-boats, and orphan nieces of indescribable splendour. And the absurdity of the episode concerns only me, my enemy Falk, and my friend Hermann."

There seemed to be something like peculiar emphasis on the words "My friend Hermann," which caused one of us (for we had just been speaking of heroism at sea) to say idly and nonchalantly:

"And was this Hermann a hero?"

"Not at all," said our grizzled friend. "No hero at all. He was a *Schiff-führer*: Ship-conductor. That's how they call a Master Mariner in Germany. I prefer our way. The alliteration is good, and there is something in the nomenclature that gives to us as a body the sense of corporate existence: Apprentice, Mate, Master, in the ancient and honourable craft of the sea. As to my friend Hermann, he might have been a consummate master of the honourable craft, but he was called officially *Schiff-führer*, and had the simple, heavy appearance of a well-to-do farmer, combined with the good-natured shrewdness of a small shopkeeper. With his shaven chin, round limbs, and heavy eyelids he did not look like a toiler, and even less like an adventurer, of the sea.[10] Still, he toiled upon the seas, in his own way, much as a shopkeeper works behind his counter. And his ship was the means by which he maintained his growing family.

She was a heavy, strong, blunt-bowed affair, awakening the ideas of primitive solidity, like the wooden plough of our forefathers. And there were, about her, other suggestions of a rustic and homely[11] nature. The extraordinary timber projections which I have seen in no other vessel made her square stern resemble the tail end of a miller's waggon. But the four stern ports of her cabin, glazed with six little greenish panes each, and framed in wooden sashes painted brown, might have been the windows of a cottage in the country. The tiny white curtains and the greenery of flower-pots behind the glass completed the resemblance. On one or two occasions when passing under her stern I had detected from my boat a round arm in the act of tilting a watering-pot, and the bowed sleek head of a maiden whom I shall always call Hermann's niece, because as a matter of fact I've never heard her name, for all my intimacy with the family.

This, however, sprang up later on. Meantime in common with the rest of the shipping in that Eastern port, I was left in no doubt as to Hermann's notions of hygienic clothing. Evidently he believed in wearing good stout flannel next his skin. On most days little frocks and pinafores could be seen drying in the mizzen rigging of his ship, or a tiny row of socks fluttering on the signal halyards; but once a fortnight the family washing was exhibited in force. It covered the poop entirely. The afternoon breeze would incite to a weird and flabby activity all that crowded mass of clothing, with its vague suggestions of drowned, mutilated, and flattened humanity. Trunks without heads waved at you arms without hands; legs without feet kicked fantastically with collapsible flourishes; and there were long white garments that, taking the wind fairly through their neck-openings edged with lace, became for a moment violently distended as by the passage of obese and invisible bodies. On these days you could make out that ship at a great distance by the multi-coloured grotesque riot going on abaft her mizzen mast.

She had her berth just ahead of me, and her name was *Diana*—Diana not of Ephesus[12] but of Bremen.[13] This was proclaimed in white letters a foot long spaced widely across the stern (somewhat like the lettering of a shop-sign) under the cottage windows. This ridiculously unsuitable name struck one as an impertinence towards the memory of the most charming of goddesses; for, apart from the fact that the old craft was physically incapable of engaging in any sort of chase, there was a gang of four children belonging to her. They peeped over the rail at passing boats and occasionally dropped various objects into them. Thus, sometime before I knew Hermann to speak to, I received on my hat a horrid rag-doll belonging to Hermann's eldest daughter. However, these youngsters were upon the whole well-behaved. They had fair heads, round eyes,

round little knobby noses, and they resembled their father a
good deal.

This *Diana* of Bremen was a most innocent old ship, and
seemed to know nothing of the wicked sea, as there are on
shore households that know nothing of the corrupt world. And
the sentiments she suggested were unexceptionable and mainly
of a domestic order. She was a home. All these dear children
had learned to walk on her roomy quarter-deck. In such
thoughts there is something pretty, even touching. Their teeth,
I should judge, they had cut on the ends of her running-gear.
I have many times observed the baby Hermann (Nicholas)
engaged in gnawing the whipping of the fore-royal brace.
Nicholas' favourite place of residence was under the main fife-
rail. Directly he was let loose he would crawl off there, and the
first seaman who came along would bring him, carefully held
aloft in tarry hands, back to the cabin door. I fancy there must
have been a standing order to that effect. In the course of these
transportations the baby, who was the only peppery person in
the ship, tried to smite these stalwart young German sailors on
the face.

Mrs. Hermann, an engaging, stout housewife, wore on board
baggy blue dresses with white dots. When, as happened once
or twice, I caught her at an elegant little wash-tub rubbing
hard on white collars, baby's socks, and Hermann's summer
neck-ties, she would blush in girlish confusion, and raising her
wet hands greet me from afar with many friendly nods. Her
sleeves would be rolled up to the elbows, and the gold hoop
of her wedding ring glittered among the soapsuds. Her voice
was pleasant; she had a serene brow, smooth bands of very fair
hair, and a good-humoured expression of the eyes. She was
motherly and moderately talkative. When this simple matron
smiled, youthful dimples broke out on her fresh broad cheeks.
Hermann's niece, on the other hand, an orphan and very silent,
I never saw attempt a smile. This, however, was not gloom on
her part but the restraint of youthful gravity.

They had carried her about with them for the last three years,
to help with the children and be company for Mrs. Hermann,
as Hermann mentioned once to me. It had been very necessary

while they were all little, he had added in a vexed manner. It was her arm and her sleek head that I had glimpsed one morning, through the stern-windows of the cabin, hovering over the pots of fuchsias and mignonette; but the first time I beheld her full length I surrendered to her proportions. They fix her in my mind, as great beauty, great intelligence, quickness of wit, or kindness of heart might have made some other woman equally memorable.

With her it was form and size. It was her physical personality that had this imposing charm. She might have been witty, intelligent, and kind to an exceptional degree. I don't know, and this is not to the point. All I know is that she was built on a magnificent scale. Built is the only word. She was constructed, she was erected, as it were, with a regal lavishness. It staggered you to see this reckless expenditure of material upon a chit of a girl. She was youthful and also perfectly mature, as though she had been some fortunate immortal. She was heavy too, perhaps, but that's nothing. It only added to that notion of permanence. She was barely nineteen. But such shoulders! Such round arms! Such a shadowing forth of mighty limbs when with three long strides she pounced across the deck upon the overturned Nicholas—it's perfectly indescribable! She seemed a good, quiet girl, vigilant as to Lena's needs, Gustav's tumbles, the state of Carl's dear little nose—conscientious, hardworking, and all that. But what magnificent hair she had! Abundant, long, thick, of a tawny colour. It had the sheen of precious metals. She wore it plaited tightly into one single tress hanging girlishly down her back and its end reached down to her waist. The massiveness of it surprised you. On my word, it reminded one of a club. Her face was big, comely, of an unruffled expression. She had a good complexion, and her blue eyes were so pale that she appeared to look at the world with the empty white candour of a statue. You could not call her good-looking. It was something much more impressive. The simplicity of her apparel, the opulence of her form, her imposing stature, and the extraordinary sense of vigorous life that seemed to emanate from her like a perfume exhaled by a flower, made her beautiful with a beauty of a rustic and olympian order. To watch her reaching up to the clothes-line with both arms raised high above her head caused you to fall a musing in a strain of pagan piety. Excellent Mrs. Hermann's baggy cotton gowns had some sort of rudimentary frills at neck and bottom, but this girl's print frocks hadn't even a wrinkle; nothing but a few straight folds in the skirt falling to her feet, and these, when she stood still, had a severe and statuesque quality. She was inclined naturally to be still whether sitting or standing. However, I don't mean to say she was statuesque. She was too generously alive; but she could have stood for an allegoric statue of the Earth. I don't mean the worn-out Earth of our possession, but a young Earth, a virginal planet undisturbed by the vision of a future teeming with the monstrous forms of life and death, clamorous with the cruel battles of hunger and thought.

The worthy Hermann himself was not very entertaining, though his English was fairly comprehensible. Mrs. Hermann, who always let off one speech at least at me in an hospitable, cordial tone (and in Platt-Deutsch,[14] I suppose) I could not understand. As to their niece, however satisfactory to look upon (and she inspired you somehow with a hopeful view as to the prospects of mankind), she was a modest and silent presence, mostly engaged in sewing, only now and then, as I observed, falling over that work into a state of maidenly meditation. Her aunt sat opposite her, sewing also, with her feet propped on a wooden footstool. On the other side of the deck Hermann and I would get a couple of chairs out of the cabin and settle down to a smoking-match, accompanied at long intervals by the pacific exchange of a few words. I came nearly every evening. Hermann I would find in his shirt-sleeves. As soon as he returned from the shore on board his ship he commenced operations by taking off his coat; then he put on his head an embroidered round cap with a tassel, and changed his boots for a pair of cloth slippers. Afterwards he smoked at the cabin-door, looking at his children with an air of civic virtue, till they got caught one after another and put to bed in various state-rooms. Lastly, we would drink some beer in the cabin, which was furnished with a wooden table on cross-legs, and with black straight-backed chairs—more like a farm kitchen

than a ship's cuddy. The sea and all nautical affairs seemed
very far removed from the hospitality of this exemplary family.

And I liked this because I had a rather worrying time on
board my own ship. I had been appointed *ex-officio* by the
British Consul to take charge of her after a man who had
died suddenly,[15] leaving for the guidance of his successor some
suspiciously unreceipted bills, a few dry-dock estimates hinting
at bribery, and a quantity of vouchers for three years' extravagant expenditure; all these mixed up together in a dusty old
violin-case lined with ruby velvet. I found besides a large
account-book, which, when opened hopefully, turned out to
my infinite consternation to be filled with verses—page after
page of rhymed doggerel of a jovial and improper character,[16]
written in the neatest minute hand I ever did see. In the same
fiddle-case a photograph of my predecessor, taken lately in
Saigon, represented in front of a garden view, and in company
of a female in strange draperies, an elderly, squat, rugged man
of stern aspect in a clumsy suit of black broadcloth, and with
the hair brushed forward above the temples in a manner
reminding one of a boar's tusks. Of a fiddle, however, the only
trace on board was the case, its empty husk as it were; but of
the two last freights the ship had indubitably earned of late,
there were not even the husks left. It was impossible to say
where all that money had gone to. It wasn't on board. It had
not been remitted home; for a letter from the owners, preserved
in a desk evidently by the merest accident, complained mildly
enough that they had not been favoured by a scratch of the
pen[17] for the last eighteen months. There were next to no stores
on board, not an inch of spare rope or a yard of canvas. The
ship had been run bare, and I foresaw no end of difficulties
before I could get her ready for sea.

As I was young then—not thirty yet—I took myself and my
troubles very seriously. The old mate, who had acted as chief
mourner at the captain's funeral, was not particularly pleased[18]
at my coming. But the fact is the fellow was not legally qualified
for command, and the Consul was bound, if at all possible, to
put a properly certificated man on board. As to the second
mate, all I can say is his name was Tottersen, or something like

that. His practice was to wear on his head, in that tropical climate, a mangy fur cap. He was, without exception, the stupidest man I had ever seen on board ship. And he looked it too. He looked so confoundedly stupid that it was a matter of surprise for me when he answered to his name.

I drew no great comfort from their company, to say the least of it; while the prospect of making a long sea passage with those two fellows was depressing. And my other thoughts in solitude could not be of a gay complexion. The crew was sickly; the cargo was coming very slow; I foresaw I would have lots of trouble with the charterers, and doubted whether they would advance me enough money for the ship's expenses. Their attitude towards me was unfriendly. Altogether I was not getting on. I would discover at odd times (generally about midnight) that I was totally inexperienced, greatly ignorant of business, and hopelessly unfit for any sort of command; and when the steward had to be taken to the hospital ill with choleraic symptoms I felt bereaved of the only decent person at the after end of the ship. He was fully expected to recover, but in the meantime had to be replaced by some sort of servant. And on the recommendation of a certain Schomberg,[19] the proprietor of the smaller of the two hotels in the place, I engaged a Chinaman. Schomberg, a brawny, hairy Alsatian, and an awful gossip, assured me that it was all right. "First-class boy that. Came in the *suite* of his Excellency Tseng the Commissioner, you know. His Excellency Tseng[20] lodged with me here for three weeks."

He mouthed the Chinese Excellency at me with great unction, though the specimen of the "*suite*" did not seem very promising. At the time, however, I did not know what an untrustworthy humbug Schomberg was. The "boy" might have been forty or a hundred and forty for all you could tell—one of those Chinamen of the death's-head type of face and completely inscrutable. Before the end of the third day he had revealed himself as a confirmed opium-smoker, a gambler, a most audacious thief, and a first-class sprinter.[21] When he departed at the top of his speed with thirty-two golden sovereigns of my own hard-earned savings it was the last straw. I had reserved that money in case my difficulties came to the worst. Now it was gone I felt as poor and naked as a fakir. I clung to my ship, for all the bother she caused me, but what I could not bear were the long lonely evenings in her cuddy, where the atmosphere, made smelly by a leaky lamp, was agitated by the snoring of the mate. That fellow shut himself up in his stuffy cabin punctually at eight, and made gross and revolting noises like a water-logged trump.[22] It was odious not to be able to worry oneself in comfort on board one's own ship. Everything in this world, I reflected, even the command of a nice little barque, may be made a delusion and a snare[23] for the unwary spirit of pride in man.

From such reflections I was glad to make my escape on board that Bremen *Diana*. There apparently no whisper of the world's iniquities had ever penetrated. And yet she lived upon the wide sea; and the sea tragic and comic, the sea with its horrors and its peculiar scandals, the sea peopled by men and ruled by iron necessity is indubitably a part of the world. But that patriarchal old tub, like some saintly retreat, echoed nothing of it. She was world-proof. Her venerable innocence apparently had put a restraint on the roaring lusts of the sea. And yet I have known the sea too long to believe in its respect for decency. An elemental force is ruthlessly frank. It may, of course, have been Hermann's skilful seamanship, but to me it looked as if the allied oceans had refrained from smashing these high bulwarks, unshipping the lumpy rudder, frightening the children, and generally opening this family's eyes out of sheer reticence. It looked like reticence. The ruthless disclosure was, in the end, left for a man to make; a man strong and elemental enough and driven to unveil some secrets of the sea by the power of a simple and elemental desire.

This, however, occurred much later, and meantime I took sanctuary in that serene old ship early every evening. The only person on board that seemed to be in trouble was little Lena, and in due course I perceived that the health of the rag-doll was more than delicate. This object led a sort of *in extremis* existence in a wooden box placed against the starboard mooring-bitts, tended and nursed with the greatest sympathy and care by all the children, who greatly enjoyed pulling long faces and moving with hushed footsteps. Only the baby—Nicholas—looked on with a cold, ruffianly leer, as if he had belonged to another tribe altogether. Lena perpetually sorrowed over the box, and all of them were in deadly earnest. It was wonderful the way these children would work up their compassion for that bedraggled thing I wouldn't have touched with a pair of tongs. I suppose they were exercising and developing their racial sentimentalism by the means of that dummy. I was only surprised that Mrs. Hermann let Lena cherish and hug that bundle of rags to that extent; it was so disreputably and completely unclean. But Mrs. Hermann would raise her fine womanly eyes from her needlework to look on with amused sympathy, and did not seem to see it, somehow, that this object of affection was a disgrace to the ship's purity. Purity, not cleanliness, is the word. It was pushed so far that I seemed to detect in this too a sentimental excess, as if dirt had been removed in very love. It is impossible to give you an idea of such a meticulous neatness. It was as if every morning that ship had been arduously explored with—with toothbrushes. Her very bowsprit three times a week had its toilette made with a cake of soap and a piece of soft flannel. Arrayed—I *must* say arrayed—arrayed artlessly in dazzling white paint as to wood and dark green as to ironwork, the simple-minded distribution of these colours evoked the images of simple-minded peace, of Arcadian felicity; and the childish comedy of disease and sorrow struck me sometimes as an abominably real blot upon that ideal state.

I enjoyed it greatly, and on my part I brought a little mild excitement into it. Our intimacy arose from the pursuit of that thief. It was in the evening, and Hermann, who, contrary to his habits, had stayed on shore late that day, was extricating himself backwards out of a little gharry on the river bank, opposite his ship, when the hunt passed. Realising the situation as though he had eyes in his shoulder-blades, he joined us with a leap and took the lead. The Chinaman fled silent like a rapid shadow on the dust of an extremely oriental road. I followed. A long way in the rear my mate whooped like a savage. A young moon threw a bashful light on a plain like a monstrous waste ground: the architectural mass of a Buddhist temple far away projected itself in dead black on the sky. We lost the thief of course; but in my disappointment I had to admire Hermann's presence of mind. The velocity that stodgy man developed in the interests of a complete stranger earned my warm gratitude—there was something truly cordial in his exertions.

He seemed as vexed as myself at our failure, and would hardly listen to my thanks. He said it was "nothings," and invited me on the spot to come on board his ship and drink a glass of beer with him. We poked sceptically for a while amongst the bushes, peered without conviction into a ditch or two. There was not a sound: patches of slime glimmered feebly amongst the reeds. Slowly we trudged back, drooping under the thin sickle of the moon, and I heard him mutter to himself, "*Himmel! Zwei und dreissig Pfund!*" He was impressed by the figure of my loss. For a long time we had ceased to hear the mate's whoops and yells.

Then he said to me, "Everybody has his troubles," and as we went on remarked that he would never have known anything of mine hadn't he by an extraordinary chance been detained on shore by Captain Falk. He didn't like to stay late ashore—he added with a sigh. The something doleful in his tone I put to his sympathy with my misfortune, of course.

On board the *Diana* Mrs. Hermann's fine eyes expressed much interest and commiseration. We had found the two women sewing face to face under the open skylight in the strong glare of the lamp. Hermann walked in first, starting in the very doorway to pull off his coat, and encouraging me with loud, hospitable ejaculations: "Come in! This way! Come in, Captain!" At once, coat in hand, he began to tell his wife all about it. Mrs. Hermann put the palms of her plump hands together; I smiled and bowed with a heavy heart; the niece got up from her sewing to bring Hermann's slippers and his embroidered calotte, which he assumed pontifically, talking (about me) all the time. Billows of white stuff lay between the chairs on the cabin floor; I caught the words "*Zwei und dreissig Pfund*" repeated several times, and presently came the beer, which seemed delicious to my throat, parched with running and the emotions of the chase.

I didn't get away till well past midnight, long after the women had retired. Hermann had been trading in the East for three years or more, carrying freights of rice and timber mostly. His ship was well known in all the ports from Vladivostok to Singapore. She was his own property. The profits had been moderate, but the trade answered well enough while the children were small yet. In another year or so he hoped he would be able to sell the old *Diana* to a firm in Japan for a fair price. He intended to return home, to Bremen, by mail-boat, second class, with Mrs. Hermann and the children. He told me all this stolidly, with slow puffs at his pipe. I was sorry when knocking the ashes out he began to rub his eyes. I would have sat with him till morning. What had I to hurry on board my own ship for? To face the broken rifled drawer in my state-room. Ugh! The very thought made me feel unwell.

I became their daily guest, as you know. I think that Mrs. Hermann from the first looked upon me as a romantic person. I did not, of course, tear my hair *coram populo* over my loss, and she took it for lordly indifference. Afterwards, I daresay, I did tell them some of my adventures—such as they were— and they marvelled greatly at the extent of my experience. Hermann would translate what he thought the most striking passages. Getting up on his legs, and as if delivering a lecture on a phenomenon, he addressed himself, with gestures, to the two women, who would let their sewing sink slowly on their laps. Meantime I sat before a glass of Hermann's beer, trying to look modest. Mrs. Hermann would glance at me quickly, emit slight *"Ach's!"* The girl never made a sound. Never. But she too would sometimes raise her pale eyes to look at me in her unseeing gentle way. Her glance was by no means stupid; it beamed out soft and diffuse as the moonbeams upon a landscape—quite differently from the scrutinising inspection of the stars. You were drowned in it, and imagined yourself to appear blurred. And yet this same glance when turned upon Christian Falk must have been as efficient as the searchlight of a battle-ship.

Falk was the other assiduous visitor on board, but from his behaviour he might have been coming to see the quarter-deck capstan. He certainly used to stare at it a good deal when keeping us company outside the cabin door, with one muscular arm thrown over the back of the chair, and his big shapely legs, in very tight white trousers, extended far out and ending in a pair of black shoes as roomy as punts. On arrival he would shake Hermann's hand with a mutter, bow to the women, and take up his careless and misanthropic attitude by our side. He departed abruptly, with a jump, going through the performance of grunts, handshakes, bows, as if in a panic. Sometimes, with a sort of discreet and convulsive effort, he approached the women and exchanged a few low words with them, half a dozen at most. On these occasions Hermann's usual stare became positively glassy and Mrs. Hermann's kind countenance would colour up. The girl herself never turned a hair.

Falk was a Dane or perhaps a Norwegian, I can't tell now. At all events he was a Scandinavian of some sort, and a bloated monopolist to boot. It is possible he was unacquainted with the word, but he had a clear perception of the thing itself. His tariff of charges for towing ships in and out was the most brutally inconsiderate document of the sort I had ever seen. He was the commander and owner of the only tug-boat on the river, a very trim white craft of 150 tons or more, as elegantly neat as a yacht, with a round wheel-house rising like a glazed turret high above her sharp bows, and with one slender varnished pole-mast forward. I daresay there are yet a few shipmasters afloat who remember Falk and his tug very well. He extracted his pound and a half of flesh[24] from each of us merchant-skippers with an inflexible sort of indifference which made him detested and even feared. Schomberg used to remark: "I won't talk about the fellow. I don't think he has six drinks from year's end to year's end in my place. But my advice is, gentlemen, don't you have anything to do with him, if you can help it."

This advice, apart from unavoidable business relations, was easy to follow because Falk intruded upon no one. It seems absurd to compare a tug-boat skipper to a centaur; but he reminded me somehow of an engraving in a little book I had as a boy, which represented centaurs at a stream, and there was one especially, in the foreground, prancing, bow and arrows in hand, with regular severe features and an immense curled wavy beard, flowing down his breast. Falk's face reminded me of that centaur. Besides, he was a composite creature. Not a man-horse, it is true, but a man-boat. He lived on board his tug, which was always dashing up and down the river from early morn till dewy eve.[25] In the last rays of the setting sun, you could pick out far away down the reach his beard borne high up on the white structure, foaming upstream to anchor for the night. There was the white-clad man's body, and the rich brown patch of the hair, and nothing below the waist but the 'thwart-ship white lines of the bridge-screens, that lead the eye to the sharp white lines of the bows cleaving the muddy water of the river.

Separated from his boat, to me at least he seemed incomplete. The tug herself without his head and torso on the bridge looked mutilated as it were. But he left her very seldom. All the time I remained in harbour I saw him only twice on shore. On the first occasion it was at my charterers, where he came in misanthropically to get paid for towing out a French barque the day before. The second time I could hardly believe my eyes, for I beheld him reclining under his beard in a cane-bottomed chair in the billiard-room of Schomberg's hotel.

It was very funny to see Schomberg ignoring him pointedly. The artificiality of it contrasted strongly with Falk's natural unconcern. The big Alsatian talked loudly with his other customers, going from one little table to the other, and passing Falk's place of repose with his eyes fixed straight ahead. Falk sat there with an untouched glass at his elbow. He must have known by sight and name every white man in the room, but he never addressed a word to anybody. He acknowledged my presence by a drop of his eyelids, and that was all. Sprawling there in the chair, he would, now and again, draw the palms of both his hands down his face, giving at the same time a slight, almost imperceptible, shudder.

It was a habit he had, and of course I was perfectly familiar with it, since you could not remain an hour in his company without being made to wonder at such a movement breaking some long period of stillness. It was a passionate and inexplicable gesture. He used to make it at all sorts of times; as likely

as not after he had been listening to little Lena's chatter about
the suffering doll, for instance. The Hermann children always
besieged him about his legs closely; though, in a gentle way, he
shrank from them a little. He seemed, however, to feel a great
affection for the whole family. For Hermann himself especially.
He sought his company. In this case, for instance, he must
have been waiting for him, because as soon as he appeared
Falk rose hastily, and they went out together. Then Schomberg
expounded in my hearing to three or four people his theory
that Falk was after Captain Hermann's niece, and asserted
confidently that nothing would come of it. It was the same last
year when Captain Hermann was loading here, he said.

Naturally, I did not believe Schomberg, but I own that for a
time I observed closely what went on. All I discovered was some
impatience on Hermann's part. At the sight of Falk stepping
over the gangway, the excellent man would begin to mumble
and chew between his teeth something that sounded like
German swear-words. However, as I've said, I'm not familiar
with the language, and Hermann's soft, round-eyed countenance remained unchanged. Staring stolidly ahead he greeted
him with, "*Wie gehts?*", or in English, "How are you?" with a
throaty enunciation. The girl would look up for an instant and
move her lips slightly; Mrs. Hermann let her hands rest on her
lap to talk volubly to him for a minute or so in her pleasant
voice before she went on with her sewing again. Falk would
throw himself into a chair, stretch his big legs, as like as not
draw his hands down his face passionately. As to myself, he
was not pointedly impertinent: it was rather as though he
could not be bothered with such trifles as my existence; and the
truth is that being a monopolist he was under no necessity to
be amiable. He was sure to get his own extortionate terms out
of me for towage whether he frowned or smiled. As a matter
of fact, he did neither; but before many days elapsed he managed to astonish me not a little and to set Schomberg's tongue
clacking more than ever.

It came about in this way. There was a shallow bar at the
mouth of the river which ought to have been kept down, but
the authorities of the State were piously busy gilding afresh the

great Buddhist Pagoda[26] just then, and I suppose had no money
to spare for dredging operations. I don't know how it may be
now, but at the time I speak of that sandbank was a great
nuisance[27] to the shipping. One of its consequences was that
vessels of a certain draught of water, like Hermann's or mine,
could not complete their loading in the river. After taking in as
much as possible of their cargo, they had to go outside to fill
up. The whole procedure was an unmitigated bore. When you
thought you had as much on board as your ship could carry
safely over the bar, you went and gave notice to your agents.
They, in their turn, notified Falk that so-and-so was ready to
go out. Then Falk (ostensibly when it fitted in with his other
work, but, if the truth were known, simply when his arbitrary
spirit moved him), after ascertaining carefully in the office that
there was enough money to meet his bill, would come along
unsympathetically, glaring at you with his yellow eyes from
the bridge, and would drag you out dishevelled as to rigging,
lumbered as to the decks, with unfeeling haste, as if to
execution. And he would force you too to take the end of his
own wire hawser, for the use of which there was of course
an extra charge. To your shouted remonstrances against that
extortion this towering trunk with one hand on the engine-
room telegraph only shook its bearded head above the splash,
the racket, and the clouds of smoke in which the tug, backing
and filling in the smother of churning paddle-wheels, behaved
like a ferocious and impatient creature. He had her manned by
the cheekiest gang of lascars I ever did see, whom he allowed
to bawl at you insolently, and, once fast, he plucked you out of
your berth as if he did not care what he smashed. Eighteen
miles down the river you had to go behind him, and then three
more along the coast to where a group of uninhabited rocky
islets enclosed a sheltered anchorage. There you would have to
lie at single anchor with your naked spars showing to seaward
over these barren fragments of land scattered upon a very
intensely blue sea. There was nothing to look at besides but a
bare coast, the muddy edge of the brown plain with the sinu-
osities of the river you had left, traced in dull green, and the
Great Pagoda uprising lonely and massive with shining curves

and pinnacles like the gorgeous and stony efflorescence of tropical rocks. You had nothing to do but to wait fretfully for the balance of your cargo, which was sent out of the river with the greatest irregularity. And it was open to you to console yourself with the thought that, after all, this stage of bother meant that your departure from these shores was indeed approaching at last.

We both had to go through that stage, Hermann and I, and there was a sort of tacit emulation between the ships as to which should be ready first. We kept on neck and neck almost to the finish, when I won the race by going personally to give notice in the forenoon; whereas Hermann, who was very slow in making up his mind to go ashore, did not get to the agents' office till late in the day. They told him there that my ship was first on turn for next morning, and I believe he told them he was in no hurry. It suited him better to go the day after.

That evening, on board the *Diana*, he sat with his plump knees well apart, staring and puffing at the curved mouthpiece of his pipe. Presently he spoke with some impatience to his niece about putting the children to bed. Mrs. Hermann, who was talking to Falk, stopped short and looked at her husband uneasily, but the girl got up at once and drove the children before her into the cabin. In a little while Mrs. Hermann had to leave us to quell what, from the sounds inside, must have been a dangerous mutiny. At this Hermann grumbled to himself. For half an hour longer Falk, left alone with us, fidgeted on his chair, sighed lightly, then at last, after drawing his hands down his face, got up, and as if renouncing the hope of making himself understood (he hadn't opened his mouth once) he said in English: "Well. . . . Good night, Captain Hermann." He stopped for a moment before my chair and looked down fixedly; I may even say he glared; and he went so far as to make a deep noise in his throat. There was in all this something so marked that for the first time in our limited intercourse of nods and grunts he excited in me something like interest. But next moment he disappointed me—for he strode away hastily without a nod even.

His manner was usually odd, it is true, and I certainly did

not pay much attention to it; but that sort of obscure intention, which seemed to lurk in his nonchalance like a wary old carp in a pond, had never before come so near the surface. He had distinctly aroused my expectations. I would have been unable to say what it was I expected, but at all events I did not expect the absurd developments he sprung upon me no later than the break of the very next day.

I remember only that there was, on that evening, enough point in his behaviour to make me, after he had fled, wonder audibly what he might mean. To this, Hermann, crossing his legs with a swing and settling himself viciously away from me in his chair, said: "That fellow don't know himself what he means."

There might have been some insight in such a remark. I said nothing, and, still averted, he added: "When I was here last year he was just the same." An eruption of tobacco smoke enveloped his head as if his temper had exploded like gunpowder.

I had half a mind to ask him point blank whether he, at least, didn't know why Falk, a notoriously unsociable man, had taken to visiting his ship with such assiduity. After all, I reflected suddenly, it was a most remarkable thing. I wonder now what Hermann would have said. As it turned out he didn't let me ask. Forgetting all about Falk apparently, he started a monologue on his plans for the future: the selling of the ship, the going home; and falling into a reflective and calculating mood he mumbled between regular jets of smoke about the expense. The necessity of disbursing passage-money for all his tribe seemed to disturb him in a manner that was the more striking because otherwise he gave no signs of a miserly disposition. And yet he fussed over the prospect of that voyage home in a mail boat like a sedentary grocer who has made up his mind to see the world. He was racially thrifty, I suppose, and for him there must have been a great novelty in finding himself obliged to pay for travelling—for sea travelling, which was the normal state of life for the family—from the very cradle for most of them. I could see he grudged prospectively every single shilling which must be spent so absurdly. It was rather funny. He would become doleful over it, and then again, with a fretful sigh, he would suppose there was nothing for it now but to take three second-class tickets—and there were the four children to pay for besides. A lot of money that to spend at once. A big lot of money.

I sat with him listening (not for the first time) to these heart-searchings till I grew thoroughly sleepy, and then I left him and turned in on board my ship. At daylight I was awakened by a yelping of shrill voices, accompanied by a great commotion in the water, and the short, bullying blasts of a steam-whistle. Falk with his tug had come for me.

I began to dress. It was remarkable that the answering noise on board my ship together with the patter of feet above my head ceased suddenly. But I heard more remote guttural cries which seemed to express surprise and annoyance. Then the voice of my mate reached me howling expostulations to somebody at a distance. Other voices joined, apparently indignant; a chorus of something that sounded like abuse replied. Now and then the steam-whistle screeched.

Altogether that unnecessary uproar was distracting, but down there in my cabin I took it calmly. In another moment, I thought, I should be going down that wretched river, and in another week at the most I should be totally quit of the odious place and all the odious people in it.

Greatly cheered by the idea, I seized the hair-brushes and looking at myself in the glass began to use them. Suddenly a hush fell upon the noise outside, and I heard (the ports of my cabin were thrown open)—I heard a deep calm voice, not on board my ship, however, hailing resolutely in English, but with a strong foreign twang, "Go ahead!"

There may be tides in the affairs of men which taken at the flood ... and so on.[28] Personally I am still on the look-out for that important turn. I am, however, afraid that most of us are fated to flounder for ever in the dead water of a pool whose shores are arid indeed. But I know that there are often in men's affairs unexpectedly—even irrationally—illuminating moments when an otherwise insignificant sound, perhaps only some perfectly commonplace gesture, suffices to reveal to us all the unreason, all the fatuous unreason, of our complacency. "Go ahead" are not particularly striking words even when pronounced with a foreign accent; yet they petrified me in the very act of smiling at myself in the glass. And then, refusing to believe my ears, but already boiling with indignation, I ran out of the cabin and up on deck.

It was incredibly true. It was perfectly true. I had no eyes for anything but the *Diana*. It was she that was being taken away. She was already out of her berth and shooting athwart the river. "The way this loonatic plucked that ship out is a caution," said the awed voice of my mate close to my ear. "Hey! Hallo! Falk! Hermann! What's this infernal[29] trick?" I yelled in a fury.

Nobody heard me. Falk certainly could not hear me. His tug was turning at full speed away under the other bank. The wire hawser between her and the *Diana*, stretched as taut as a harpstring, vibrated alarmingly.

The high black craft careened over to the awful strain. A loud crack came out of her, followed by the tearing and splintering of wood. "There!" said the awed voice in my ear. "He's carried away their towing chock." And then, with enthusiasm, "Oh! Look! Look, sir! Look at them Dutchmen[30] skipping out of the way on the forecastle. I hope to goodness he'll break a few of their shins before he's done with 'em."

I yelled my vain protests. The rays of the rising sun coursing level along the plain warmed my back, but I was hot enough with rage. I could not have believed that a simple towing operation could suggest so plainly the idea of abduction, of rape. Falk was simply running off with the *Diana*.

The white tug careered out into the middle of the river. The red floats of her paddle-wheels revolving with mad rapidity tore up the whole reach into foam. The *Diana* in mid-stream waltzed round with as much grace as an old barn, and flew after her ravisher. Through the ragged fog of smoke driving headlong upon the water I had a glimpse of Falk's square motionless shoulders under a white hat as big as a cart-wheel, of his red face, his yellow staring eyes, his great beard. Instead of keeping a look-out ahead, he was deliberately turning his back on the river to glare at his tow. The tall heavy craft, never so used

before in her life, seemed to have lost her senses; she took a
wild sheer against her helm, and for a moment came straight
at us, menacing and clumsy, like a runaway mountain. She
piled up a streaming, hissing, boiling wave halfway up her blunt
stem; my crew let out one great howl—and then we held our
breaths. It was a near thing. But Falk had her! He had her in
his clutch. I fancied I could hear the steel hawser ping as it
surged across the *Diana*'s forecastle, with the hands on board
of her bolting away from it in all directions. It was a near thing.
Hermann, with his hair rumpled, in a snuffy[31] flannel shirt and
a pair of mustard-coloured trousers, had rushed to help with
the wheel. I saw his terrified round face; I saw his very teeth
uncovered by a sort of ghastly fixed grin; and in a great leaping
tumult of water between the two ships the *Diana* whisked past
so close that I could have flung a hair-brush at his head, for, it
seems, I had kept them in my hands all the time. Meanwhile
Mrs. Hermann sat placidly on the skylight, with a woollen
shawl on her shoulders. The excellent woman in response to
my indignant gesticulations fluttered a handkerchief, nodding
and smiling in the kindest way imaginable. The boys, only
half-dressed, were jumping about the poop in great glee, dis-
playing their gaudy braces; and Lena in a short scarlet petticoat,
with peaked elbows and thin bare arms, nursed the rag-doll
with devotion. The whole family passed before my sight as if
dragged across a scene of unparalleled violence. The last I saw
was Hermann's niece with the baby Hermann in her arms
standing apart from the others. Magnificent in her close-fitting
print frock, she displayed something so commanding in the
manifest perfection of her figure that the sun seemed to be rising
for her alone. The flood of light brought out the opulence of
her form and the vigour of her youth in a glorifying way. She
went by perfectly motionless and as if lost in meditation; only
the hem of her skirt stirred in the draught; the sun-rays broke
on her sleek tawny hair; that bald-headed ruffian, Nicholas,
was whacking her on the shoulder. I saw his tiny fat arm rise
and fall in a workmanlike manner. And then the four cottage
windows of the *Diana* came into view retreating swiftly down
the river. The sashes were up, and one of the white calico

curtains fluttered straight out like a streamer above the agitated water of the wake.

To be thus tricked out of one's turn was an unheard-of occurrence. In my agent's office, where I went to complain at once, they protested with apologies they couldn't understand how the mistake arose; but Schomberg, when I dropped in later to get some tiffin, though surprised to see me, was perfectly ready with an explanation. I found him seated at the end of a long narrow table, facing his wife—a scraggy little woman, with long ringlets and a blue tooth, who smiled abroad stupidly and looked frightened when you spoke to her. Between them a waggling punkah fanned twenty cane-bottomed chairs and two rows of shiny plates. Three Chinamen in white jackets loafed with napkins in their hands around that desolation. Schomberg's pet *table d'hôte* was not much of a success that day. He was feeding himself furiously and seemed to overflow with bitterness.

He began by ordering in a brutal voice the chops to be brought back for me, and turning in his chair: "Mistake, they told you? Not a bit of it! Don't you believe it for a moment, Captain! Falk isn't a man to make mistakes unless on purpose." His firm conviction was that Falk had been trying all along to curry favour on the cheap with Hermann. "On the cheap—mind you! It doesn't cost him a cent to put that insult upon you, and Captain Hermann gets in a day ahead of your ship. Time's money! Eh? You are very friendly with Captain Hermann, I believe, but a man is bound to be pleased at any little advantage he may get. Captain Hermann is a good business man, and there's no such thing as a friend in business. Is there?" He leaned forward and began to cast stealthy glances as usual. "But Falk is, and always was, a miserable fellow. I would despise him."

I muttered, grumpily, that I had no particular respect for Falk.

"I would despise him," he insisted, with an appearance of anxiety which would have amused me if I had not been fathoms deep in discontent. To a young man fairly conscientious and as well-meaning as only the young can be, the current ill-usage of

life comes with a peculiar cruelty. Youth that is fresh enough
to believe in guilt, in innocence, and in itself will always doubt
whether it has not perchance deserved its fate. Sombre of mind
and without appetite, I struggled with the chop while Mrs.
Schomberg sat with her everlasting stupid grin and Schomberg's
talk gathered way like a slide of rubbish.

"Let me tell you. It's all about that girl. I don't know what
Captain Hermann expects, but if he asked me I could tell him
something about Falk. He's a miserable fellow. That man is a
perfect slave. That's what I call him. A slave. Last year I started
this *table d'hôte*, and sent cards out, you know. You think he
had one meal in the house? Give the thing a trial? Not once.
He has got hold now of a Madras cook—a blamed fraud that
I hunted out of my cookhouse with a rattan. He was not fit to
cook for white men. No, not for the white men's dogs either;
but, see, any damned native that can boil a pot of rice is good
enough for Mr. Falk. Rice and a little fish he buys for a few
cents from the fishing-boats outside is what he lives on. You
would hardly credit it, eh? A white man, too. . . ."

He wiped his lips, using the napkin with indignation, and
looking at me. It flashed through my mind in the midst of my
depression that if all the meat in the town was like these *table
d'hôte* chops, Falk wasn't so far wrong. I was on the point of
saying this, but Schomberg's stare was intimidating. "He's a
vegetarian, perhaps," I murmured instead.

"He's a miser. A miserable miser," affirmed the hotel-keeper
with great force. "The meat here is not so good as at home, of
course. And dear, too. But look at me. I only charge a dollar[32]
for the tiffin, and one dollar and fifty cents for the dinner. Show
me anything cheaper. Why am I doing it? There's little profit
in this game. Falk wouldn't look at it. I do it for the sake of a
lot of young white fellows here that hadn't a place where they
could get a decent meal and eat it decently in good company.
There's first-rate company always at my table."

The convinced way he surveyed the empty chairs made me
feel as if I had intruded upon a tiffin of ghostly presences.

"A white man should eat like a white man, dash it all," he
burst out impetuously. "Ought to eat meat, must eat meat. I

manage to get meat for my patrons all the year round. Don't I?
I am not catering for a dam' lot of coolies. Have another chop,
Captain. . . . No? You, boy—take away!"

He threw himself back and waited grimly for the curry. The
half-closed jalousies darkened the room pervaded by the smell
of fresh whitewash; a swarm of flies buzzed and settled in
turns, and poor Mrs. Schomberg's smile seemed to express the
quintessence of all the imbecility that had ever spoken, had ever
breathed, had ever been fed on infamous buffalo meat within
these bare walls. Schomberg did not open his lips till he was
ready to thrust therein a spoonful of greasy rice. He rolled his
eyes ridiculously before he swallowed the hot stuff, and only
then broke out afresh.

"It is the most degrading thing. They take the dish up to the
wheel-house for him with a cover on it, and he shuts both the
doors before he begins to eat. Fact! Must be ashamed of himself.
Ask the engineer. He can't do without an engineer—don't you
see—and as no respectable man can be expected to put up with
such a table, he allows them fifteen dollars a month extra mess
money. I assure you it is so! You just ask Mr. Ferdinand da
Costa. That's the engineer he has now. You may have seen
him about my place, a delicate dark young man, with very fine
eyes and a little moustache. He arrived here a year ago from
Calcutta. Between you and me, I guess the money-lenders there
must have been after him. He rushes here for a meal every
chance he can get, for just please tell me what satisfaction is
that for a well-educated young fellow to feed all alone in his
cabin—like a wild beast? That's what Falk expects his engineers
to put up with for fifteen dollars extra. And the rows on board
every time a little smell of cooking gets about the deck! You
wouldn't believe! The other day da Costa got the cook to fry a
steak for him—a turtle-steak it was too, not beef at all—and
the fat caught or something. Young da Costa himself was telling
me of it here in this room. 'Mr. Schomberg'—says he—'if I
had let a cylinder cover blow off through the skylight by my
negligence Captain Falk couldn't have been more savage. He
frightened the cook so that he won't put anything on the fire
for me now.' Poor da Costa had tears in his eyes. Only try to put

yourself in his place, Captain: a sensitive, gentlemanly young fellow. Is he expected to eat his food raw? But that's your Falk all over. Ask any one you like. I suppose the fifteen dollars extra he has to give keep on rankling—in there."

And Schomberg tapped his manly breast. I sat half-stunned by his irrelevant babble. Suddenly he gripped my forearm in an impressive and cautious manner, as if to lead me into a very cavern of confidence.

"It's nothing but enviousness," he said in a lowered tone, which had a stimulating effect upon my wearied hearing. "I don't suppose there is one person in this town that he isn't envious of. I tell you he's dangerous. Even I myself am not safe from him. I know for certain he tried to poison. . . ."

"Oh, come now," I cried, revolted.

"But I know for certain. The people themselves came and told me of it. He went about saying everywhere I was a worse pest to this town than the cholera. He had been talking against me ever since I opened this hotel. And he poisoned Captain Hermann's mind too. Last time the *Diana* was loading here Captain Hermann used to come in every day for a drink or a cigar. This time he hasn't been here twice in a week. How do you account for that?"

He squeezed my arm till he extorted from me some sort of mumble.

"He makes ten times the money I do. I've another hotel to fight against, and there is no other tug on the river. I am not in his way, am I? He wouldn't be fit to run an hotel if he tried. But that's just his nature. He can't bear to think I am making a living. I only hope it makes him properly wretched. He's like that in everything. He would like to keep a decent table well enough. But no—for the sake of a few cents. Can't do it. It's too much for him. That's what I call being a slave to it. But he's mean enough to kick up a row when his nose gets tickled a bit. See that? That just paints him. Miserly and envious. You can't account for it any other way. Can you? I have been studying him these three years."

He was anxious I should assent to his theory. And indeed on thinking it over it would have been plausible enough if there hadn't been always the essential falseness of irresponsibility in Schomberg's chatter. However, I was not disposed to investigate the psychology of Falk. I was engaged just then in eating despondently a piece of stale Dutch cheese, being too much crushed to care what I swallowed myself, let alone bothering my head about Falk's ideas of gastronomy. I could expect from their study no clue to his conduct in matters of business, which seemed to me totally unrestrained by morality or even by the commonest sort of decency. How insignificant and contemptible I must appear for the fellow to dare treat me like this—I reflected suddenly, writhing in silent agony. And I consigned Falk and all his peculiarities to the devil with so much mental fervour as to forget Schomberg's existence, till he grabbed my arm urgently. "Well, you may think and think till every hair of your head falls off, Captain; but you can't explain it in any other way."

For the sake of peace and quietness I admitted hurriedly that I couldn't; persuaded that now he would leave off. But the only result was to make his moist face shine with the pride of cunning. He removed his hand for a moment to scare a black mass of flies off the sugar-basin and caught hold of my arm again.

"To be sure. And in the same way everybody is aware he would like to get married. Only he can't. Let me quote you an instance. Well, two years ago a Miss Vanlo, a very ladylike girl, came from home to keep house for her brother Fred, who had an engineering shop for small repairs by the water-side. Suddenly Falk takes to going up to their bungalow after dinner, and sitting for hours in the verandah saying nothing. The poor girl couldn't tell for the life of her what to do with such a man, so she would keep on playing the piano and singing to him evening after evening till she was ready to drop. And it wasn't as if she had been a strong young woman either. She was thirty, and the climate had been playing the deuce with her. Then—don't you know—Fred had to sit up with them for propriety, and during whole weeks on end never got a single chance to get to bed before midnight. That was not pleasant for a tired man, was it? And besides Fred had worries then because his shop didn't pay and he was dropping money fast. He just longed to get away from here and try his luck somewhere else, but for the sake of his sister he hung on and on till he ran himself into debt over his ears, I can tell you. I, myself, could show a handful of his chits for meals and drinks in my drawer. I could never find out tho' where he found all the money at last. Can't be but he must have got something out of that brother of his, a coal merchant in Port Said.[33] Anyhow he paid everybody before he left, but the girl nearly broke her heart. Disappointment, of course, and at her age, don't you know. . . . Mrs. Schomberg here was very friendly with her, and she could tell you. Awful despair. Fainting fits. It was a scandal. A notorious scandal. To the extent that old Mr. Siegers[34]—not your present charterer, but Mr. Siegers the father, the old gentleman who retired from business on a fortune and got buried at sea going home—*he* had to interview Falk in his private office. He was a man who could speak like a Dutch Uncle,[35] and, besides, Messrs. Siegers had been helping Falk with a good bit of money from the start. In fact you may say they made him as far as that goes. It so happened that just at the time he turned up here, their firm was chartering a lot of sailing-ships every year, and it suited their business that there should be good towing facilities on the river. See? . . . Well, there's always an ear at the keyhole, isn't there? In fact," he lowered his tone confidentially, "in this case a good friend of mine; a man you can see here any evening; only they conversed rather low. Anyhow my friend's certain that Falk was trying to make all sorts of excuses, and old Mr. Siegers was coughing a lot. And yet Falk wanted all the time to be married too. Why! It's notorious the man has been longing for years to make a home for himself. Only he can't face the expense. When it comes to putting his hand in his pocket—it chokes him off. That's the truth and no other. I've always said so, and everybody agrees with me by this time. What do you think of that, eh?"

He appealed confidently to my indignation, but having a mind to annoy him I remarked that "It seemed to me very pitiful—if true."

He bounced in his chair as if I had run a pin into him. I don't know what he might have said, only at that moment we heard through the half-open door of the billiard-room the footsteps of two men entering from the verandah, a murmur of two voices; at the sharp tapping of a coin on a table Mrs. Schomberg half rose irresolutely. "Sit still," he hissed at her, and then, in an hospitable, jovial tone, contrasting amazingly with the angry glance that had made his wife sink in her chair, he cried very loud: "Tiffin still going on in here, gentlemen."

There was no answer, but the voices dropped suddenly. The head Chinaman went out. We heard the clink of ice in the glasses, pouring sounds, the shuffling of feet, the scraping of chairs. Schomberg, after wondering in a low mutter who the devil could be there at this time of the day, got up napkin in hand to peep through the doorway cautiously. He retreated rapidly on tip-toe, and whispering behind his hand informed me that it was Falk, Falk himself who was in there, and, what's more, he had Captain Hermann with him.

The return of the tug from the outer Roads was unexpected but possible, for Falk had taken away the *Diana* at half-past five, and it was now two o'clock. Schomberg wished me to observe that neither of these men would spend a dollar on a tiffin, which they must have wanted. But by the time I was ready to leave the dining-room Falk had gone. I heard the last of his big boots on the planks of the verandah. Hermann was sitting quite alone in the large, wooden room with the two lifeless billiard-tables shrouded in striped covers, mopping his face diligently. He wore his best go-ashore clothes, a stiff collar, black coat, large white waistcoat, grey trousers. A white cotton sunshade with a cane handle reposed between his legs, his side-whiskers were neatly brushed, his chin had been freshly shaved; and he only distantly resembled the dishevelled and terrified man in a snuffy night-shirt and ignoble old trousers I had seen in the morning hanging on to the wheel of the *Diana*.

He gave a start at my entrance, and addressed me at once in some confusion, but with genuine eagerness. He was anxious to make it clear he had nothing to do with what he called the "tam' pizness" of the morning. It was most inconvenient. He had reckoned upon another day up in town to settle his bills and sign certain papers. There were also some few stores to

come, and sundry pieces of "my ironwork," as he called it
quaintly, landed for repairs, had been left behind. Now he
would have to hire a native boat to take all this out to the ship.
It would cost five or six dollars perhaps. He had had no warning
from Falk. Nothing. . . . He hit the table with his dumpy fist. . . .
Der verfluchte Kerl came in the morning like a "tam' ropper,"
making a great noise, and took him away. His mate was not
prepared, his ship was moored fast—he protested it was shameful to come upon a man in that way. Shameful! Yet such was
the power Falk had on the river that when I suggested in a
chilling tone that he might have simply refused to have his ship
moved, Hermann was quite startled at the idea. I never realised
so well before that this is an age of steam. The exclusive possession of a marine boiler had given Falk the whip-hand of us
all. Hermann, recovering, put it to me appealingly that I knew
very well how unsafe it was to contradict that fellow. At this
I only smiled distantly.

"*Der Kerl!*" he cried. He was sorry he had not refused. He
was indeed. The damage! The damage! What for all that damage! There was no occasion for damage. Did I know how much
damage he had done? It gave me a certain satisfaction to tell
him that I had heard his old waggon of a ship crack fore and
aft as she went by. "You passed close enough to me," I added
significantly.

He threw both his hands up to heaven at the recollection.
One of them grasped by the middle the white parasol, and he
resembled curiously a caricature of a shopkeeping citizen in one
of his own German comic papers. "*Ach!* That was dangerous,"
he cried. I was amused. But directly he added with an appearance of simplicity, "The side of your iron ship would have been
crushed in like—like this matchbox."

"Would it?" I growled, much less amused now; but by the
time I had decided that this remark was not meant for a dig at
me he had worked himself into a high state of resentfulness
against Falk. The inconvenience, the damage, the expense!
Gottverdammt! Devil take the fellow. Behind the bar Schomberg, with a cigar in his teeth, pretended to be writing with a
pencil on a large sheet of paper; and as Hermann's excitement

increased it made me comfortingly aware of my own calmness
and superiority. But it occurred to me, while I listened to his
revilings, that after all the good man had come up in the tug.
There perhaps—since he must come to town—he had no
option. But evidently he had had a drink with Falk, either
accepted or offered. How was that? So I checked him by saying
loftily that I hoped he would make Falk pay for every penny of
the damage.

"That's it! That's it! Go for him," called out Schomberg from
the bar, flinging his pencil down and rubbing his hands.

We ignored his noise. But Hermann's excitement suddenly
went off the boil as when you remove a saucepan from the fire.
I urged on his consideration that he had done now with Falk
and Falk's confounded tug. He, Hermann, would not, perhaps,
turn up again in this part of the world for years to come, since
he was going to sell the *Diana* at the end of this very trip ("Go
home passenger in a mail-boat," he murmured mechanically).
He was therefore safe from Falk's malice. All he had to do was
to race off to his consignees and stop payment of the towage
bill before Falk had the time to get in and lift the money.

Nothing could have been less in the spirit of my advice than
the thoughtful way in which he set about to make his parasol
stay propped against the edge of the table.

While I watched his concentrated efforts with astonishment
he threw at me one or two perplexed, half-shy glances. Then
he sat down. "That's all very well," he said reflectively.

It cannot be doubted that the man had been thrown off his
balance by being hauled out of the harbour against his wish.
His stolidity had been profoundly stirred, else he would never
have made up his mind to ask me unexpectedly whether I had
not remarked that Falk had been casting eyes upon his niece.
"No more than myself," I answered with literal truth. The girl
was of the sort one necessarily casts eyes at in a sense. She made
no noise, but she filled most satisfactorily a good bit of space.

"But you, Captain, are not the same kind of man," observed
Hermann.

I was not, I am happy to say, in a position to deny this.
"What about the lady?" I could not help asking. At this he

gazed for a time into my face, earnestly, and made as if to change the subject. I heard him beginning to mutter something unexpected, about his children growing old enough to require schooling. He would have to leave them ashore with their grandmother when he took up that new command he expected to get in Germany.

This constant harping on his domestic arrangements was funny. I suppose it must have been like the prospect of a complete alteration in his life. An epoch. He was going, too, to part with the *Diana*! He had served in her for years. He had inherited her. From an uncle, if I remember rightly. And the future loomed big before him, occupying his thought exclusively with all its aspects as on the eve of a venturesome enterprise. He sat there frowning and biting his lip, and suddenly he began to fume and fret.

I discovered to my momentary amusement that he seemed to imagine I could, should, or ought, have caused Falk in some way to pronounce himself. Such a hope was incomprehensible, but funny. Then the contact with all this foolishness irritated me. I said crossly that I had seen no symptoms, but if there were any—since he, Hermann, was so sure—then it was still worse. What pleasure Falk found in humbugging people in just that way I couldn't say. It was, however, my solemn duty to warn him. It had lately, I said, come to my knowledge that there was a man (not a very long time ago either) who had been taken in just like this.

All this passed in undertones, and at this point Schomberg, exasperated at our secrecy, went out of the room slamming the door with a crash that positively lifted us in our chairs. This, or else what I had said, huffed my Hermann. He supposed, with a contemptuous toss of his head towards the door which trembled yet, that I had got hold of some of that man's silly tales. It looked, indeed, as though his mind had been thoroughly poisoned against Schomberg. "His tales were—they were," he repeated, seeking for the word—"trash." They were trash, he reiterated, and moreover I was young yet . . .

This horrid aspersion (I regret I am no longer exposed to that sort of insult) made me huffy too. I felt ready in my own mind to back up every assertion of Schomberg's and on any subject. In a moment, devil only knows why, Hermann and I were looking at each other most inimically. He caught up his hat without more ado and I gave myself the pleasure of calling after him:

"Take my advice and make Falk pay for breaking up your ship. You aren't likely to get anything else out of him."

When I got on board my ship later on, the old mate, who was very full of the events of the morning, remarked:

"I saw the tug coming back from the outer Roads just before two P.M." (He never by any chance used the words morning or afternoon. Always P.M. or A.M., log-book style.) "Smart work that. Man's always in a state of hurry. He's a regular chucker-out, ain't he, sir? There's a few pubs I know of in the East End of London[36] that would be all the better for one of his sort around the bar." He chuckled at his joke. "A regular chucker-out. Now he has fired out that Dutchman head over heels, I suppose our turn's coming to-morrow morning."

We were all on deck at break of day (even the sick—poor devils—had crawled out) ready to cast off in the twinkling of an eye.[37] Nothing came. Falk did not come. At last, when I began to think that probably something had gone wrong in his engine-room, we perceived the tug going by, full pelt, down the river, as if we hadn't existed. For a moment I entertained the wild notion that he was going to turn round in the next reach. Afterwards I watched his smoke appear above the plain, now here, now there, according to the windings of the river. It disappeared. Then without a word I went down to breakfast. I just simply went down to breakfast.

Not one of us uttered a sound till the mate, after imbibing— by means of suction out of a saucer—his second cup of tea, exclaimed: "Where the devil is the man gone to?"

"Courting!" I shouted, with such a fiendish laugh that the old chap didn't venture to open his lips any more.

I started to the office perfectly calm. Calm with excessive rage. Evidently they knew all about it already, and they treated me to a show of consternation. The manager, a soft-footed, immensely obese man, breathing short, got up to meet me, while all round the room the young clerks, bending over the papers on their desks, cast upward glances in my direction. The fat man, without waiting for my complaint, wheezing heavily and in a tone as if he himself were incredulous, conveyed to me the news that Falk—Captain Falk—had declined—had absolutely declined—to tow my ship—to have anything to do with my ship—this day or any other day. Never!

I did my best to preserve a cool appearance, but, all the same, I must have shown how much taken aback I was. We were talking in the middle of the room. Suddenly behind my back some ass blew his nose with great force, and at the same time another quill-driver[38] jumped up and went out on the landing hastily. It occurred to me I was cutting a foolish figure there. I demanded angrily to see the principal in his private room.

The skin of Mr. Siegers' head showed dead white between the iron-grey streaks of hair lying plastered cross-wise from ear to ear over the top of his skull in the manner of a bandage. His narrow sunken face was of a uniform and permanent terra-cotta colour, like a piece of pottery. He was sickly, thin, and short, with wrists like a boy of ten. But from that debile body there issued a bullying voice, tremendously loud, harsh, and resonant, as if produced by some powerful mechanical contrivance in the nature of a fog-horn. I do not know what he did with it in the private life of his home, but in the larger sphere of business it presented the advantage of overcoming arguments without the slightest mental effort, by the mere volume of sound. We had had several passages of arms. It took me all I knew to guard the interests of my owners—whom, *nota bene*, I had never seen—while Siegers (who had made their acquaintance some years before, during a business tour in Australia) pretended to the knowledge of their innermost minds, and, in the character of "our very good friends," threw them perpetually at my head.

He looked at me with a jaundiced eye (there was no love lost between us), and declared at once that it was strange, very strange. His pronunciation of English was so extravagant that I can't even attempt to reproduce it. For instance, he said "Fferie strantch." Combined with the bellowing intonation it made the language of one's childhood sound weirdly startling, and even

if considered purely as a kind of unmeaning noise it filled you
with astonishment at first. "They had," he continued, "been
acquainted with Captain Falk for very many years, and never
had any reason. . . ."

"That's why I come to you, of course," I interrupted. "I've
the right to know the meaning of this infernal nonsense." In
the half-light of the room, which was greenish, because of the
tree-tops screening the window, I saw him writhe his meagre
shoulders. It came into my head, as disconnected ideas will
come at all sorts of times into one's head, that this, most likely,
was the very room where, if the tale were true, Falk had been
lectured by Mr. Siegers, the father. Mr. Siegers' (the son's)
overwhelming voice, in brassy blasts, as though he had been
trying to articulate his words through a trombone, was expressing his great regret at conduct characterised by a very marked
want of discretion . . . As I lived, I was being lectured too!
His deafening gibberish was difficult to follow, but it was *my*
conduct—mine!—that . . . Damn! I wasn't going to stand this.

"What on earth are you driving at?" I asked in a passion. I
put my hat on my head (he never offered a seat to anybody), and
as he seemed for the moment struck dumb by my irreverence,
I turned my back on him and marched out. His vocal arrangements blared after me a few threats of coming down on the
ship for the demurrage of the lighters, and all the other expenses
consequent upon the delays arising from my frivolity.

Once outside in the sunshine my head swam. It was no longer
a question of mere delay. I perceived myself involved in hopeless
and humiliating absurdities that were leading me to something
very like a disaster. "Let us be calm," I muttered to myself, and
ran into the shade of a leprous wall. From that short side-street
I could see the broad main thoroughfare, ruinous and gay,
running away between stretches of decaying masonry, bamboo
fences, ranges of arcades of brick and plaster, hovels of lath
and mud, lofty temple gates of carved timber, huts of rotten
mats—an immensely wide thoroughfare, loosely packed as far
as the eye could reach with a barefooted and brown multitude
paddling ankle-deep in the dust. For a moment I felt myself
about to go out of my mind with worry and desperation.

Some allowance must be made for the feelings of a young man new to responsibility. I thought of my crew. Half of them were ill, and I really began to think that some of them would end by dying on board if I couldn't get them out to sea soon. Obviously I should have to take my ship down the river, either working under canvas or dredging with the anchor down; operations which, in common with many modern sailors, I only knew theoretically. And I almost shrank from undertaking them shorthanded and without local knowledge of the river-bed, which is so necessary for the confident handling of the ship. There were no pilots, no beacons, no buoys of any sort; but there was a very devil of a current for anybody to see, no end of shoal places, and at least two obviously awkward turns of the channel between me and the sea. But how dangerous these turns were I could not tell. I didn't even know what my ship was capable of! I had never handled her in my life. A misunderstanding between a man and his ship, in a difficult river with no room to make it up, is bound to end in trouble for the man. On the other hand, it must be owned I had not much reason to count upon a general run of good luck. And suppose I had the misfortune to pile her up high and dry on some beastly shoal? That would have been the final undoing of that voyage. It was plain that if Falk refused to tow me out he would also refuse to pull me off. This meant—what? A day lost at the very best; but more likely a whole fortnight of frizzling on some pestilential mudflat, of desperate work, of discharging cargo; more than likely it meant borrowing money at an exorbitant rate of interest—from the Siegers' gang too at that. They were a power in the port. And that elderly seaman of mine, Gambril, had looked pretty ghastly when I went forward to dose him with quinine[39] that morning. *He* would certainly die—not to speak of two or three others that seemed nearly as bad, and of the rest of them just ready to catch any tropical disease going. Horror, ruin, and everlasting remorse. And no help. None. I had fallen amongst a lot of unfriendly lunatics!

At any rate, if I must take my ship down myself it was my duty to procure if possible some local knowledge. But that was not easy. The only person I could think of for that service was a certain Johnson, formerly captain of a country ship, but now spliced to a country wife and gone utterly to the bad. I had only heard of him in the vaguest way, as living concealed in the thick of two hundred thousand natives, and only emerging into the light of day for the purpose of hunting up some brandy. I had a notion that if I could lay my hands on him I would sober him on board my ship and use him for a pilot. Better than nothing. Once a sailor always a sailor—and he had known the river for years. But in our Consulate (where I arrived dripping after a sharp walk) they could tell me nothing. The excellent young men on the staff, though willing to help me, belonged to a sphere of the white colony for which that sort of Johnson does not exist. Their suggestion was that I should hunt the man up myself with the help of the Consulate's constable— an ex-sergeant-major of a regiment of hussars.

This man, whose usual duty apparently consisted in sitting behind a little table in an outer room of Consular offices, when ordered to assist me in my search for Johnson displayed lots of energy and a marvellous amount of local knowledge of a sort. But he did not conceal an immense and sceptical contempt for the whole business. We explored together on that afternoon an infinity of infamous grog shops, gambling dens, opium dens. We walked up narrow lanes where our gharry—a tiny box of a thing on wheels, attached to a jibbing Burmah pony— could by no means have passed. The constable seemed to be on terms of scornful intimacy with Maltese, with Eurasians, with Chinamen, with Klings, and with the sweepers attached to a temple, with whom he talked at the gate. We interviewed also through a grating in a mud wall closing a blind alley an immensely corpulent Italian, who, the ex-sergeant-major remarked to me perfunctorily, had "killed another man last year." Thereupon he addressed him as "Antonio" and "Old Buck," though that bloated carcase, apparently more than half filling the sort of cell wherein it sat, recalled rather a fat pig in a stye. Familiar and never unbending, the sergeant chucked— absolutely chucked—under the chin a horribly wrinkled and shrivelled old hag propped on a stick, who had volunteered some sort of information; and with the same stolid face he kept up an animated conversation with the groups of swathed brown women, who sat smoking cheroots on the doorsteps of a long range of clay hovels. We got out of the gharry and clambered into dwellings airy like packing crates, or descended into places sinister like cellars. We got in, we drove on, we got out again for the sole purpose, as it seemed, of looking behind a heap of rubble. The sun declined; my companion was curt and sardonic in his answers, but it appears we were just missing Johnson all along. At last our conveyance stopped once more with a jerk, and the driver jumping down opened the door.

A black mudhole blocked the lane. A mound of garbage crowned with the dead body of a dog arrested us not. An empty Australian beef tin bounded cheerily before the toe of my boot. Suddenly we clambered through a gap in a prickly fence. . . .

It was a very clean native compound; and the big native woman, with bare brown legs as thick as bed-posts, pursuing on all fours a silver dollar that came rolling out from somewhere, was Mrs. Johnson herself. "Your man's at home," said the ex-sergeant, and stepped aside in complete and marked indifference to anything that might follow. Johnson—at home —stood with his back to a native house built on posts and with its walls made of mats. In his left hand he held a banana. Out of the right he dealt another dollar into space. The woman captured this one on the wing, and there and then plumped down on the ground to look at us with greater comfort.

"My man" was sallow of face, grizzled, unshaven, muddy on elbows and back; where the seams of his serge coat yawned you could see his white nakedness. The vestiges of a paper collar encircled his neck. He looked at us with a grave, swaying surprise. "Where do you come from?" he asked. My heart sank. How could I have been stupid enough to waste energy and time for this?

But having already gone so far I approached a little nearer and declared the purpose of my visit. He would have to come at once with me, sleep on board my ship, and to-morrow, with the first of the ebb, he would give me his assistance in getting my ship down to the sea, without steam. A six-hundred-ton barque, drawing nine feet aft. I proposed to give him eighteen dollars for his local knowledge; and all the time I was speaking he kept on considering attentively the various aspects of the banana, holding first one side up to his eye, then the other.

"You've forgotten to apologise," he said at last with extreme precision. "Not being a gentleman yourself, you don't know apparently when you intrude upon a gentleman. I am one. I wish you to understand that when I am in funds I don't work, and now . . ."

I would have pronounced him perfectly sober had he not paused in great concern to try and brush a hole off the knee of his trousers.

"I have money—and friends. Every gentleman has. Perhaps you would like to know my friend? His name is Falk. You could borrow some money. Try to remember. F-A-L-K. Falk." Abruptly his tone changed. "A noble heart," he said muzzily.

"Has Falk been giving you some money?" I asked, appalled by the detailed finish of the dark plot.

"Lent me, my good man, not given me," he corrected suavely. "Met me taking the air last evening, and being as usual anxious to oblige—Hadn't you better go to the devil out of my compound?"

And upon this, without other warning, he let fly with the banana which missed my head, and took the constable just under the left eye. He rushed at the miserable Johnson, stammering with fury. They fell. . . . But why dwell on the wretchedness, the breathlessness, the degradation, the senselessness, the weariness, the ridicule and humiliation, and—and—the perspiration, of these moments? I dragged the ex-hussar off. He was like a wild beast. It seems he had been greatly annoyed at losing his free afternoon on my account. The garden of his bungalow required his personal attention, and at the slight blow of the banana the brute in him had broken loose. We left Johnson on his back, still black in the face, but beginning to kick feebly. Meantime, the big woman had remained sitting on the ground, apparently paralysed with extreme terror.

For half an hour we jolted inside our rolling box, side by side, in profound silence. The ex-sergeant was busy staunching the blood of a long scratch on his cheek. "I hope you're satisfied," he said suddenly. "That's what comes of all that tomfool business. If you hadn't quarrelled with that tug-boat skipper over some girl or other, all this wouldn't have happened."

"You heard *that* story?" I said.

"Of course I heard. And I shouldn't wonder if the Consul-General himself doesn't come to hear of it. How am I to go before him to-morrow with that thing on my cheek—I want to know. It's *you* who ought to have got this!"

After that, till the gharry stopped and he jumped out without leave-taking, he swore to himself steadily, horribly, muttering great, purposeful, trooper oaths, to which the worst a sailor can do is like the prattle of a child. For my part I had just the strength to crawl into Schomberg's coffee-room, where I wrote at a little table a note to the mate instructing him to get every-thing ready for dropping down the river next day. I couldn't face my ship. Well! she had a clever sort of skipper and no mistake—poor thing! What a horrid mess! I took my head between my hands. At times the obviousness of my innocence would reduce me to despair. What had I done? If I had done something to bring about the situation I should at least have learned not to do it again. But I felt guiltless to the point of imbecility. The room was empty yet; only Schomberg prowled round me goggle-eyed and with a sort of awed respectful curi-osity. No doubt he had set the story going himself; but he was a good-hearted chap, and I am really persuaded he participated in all my troubles. He did what he could for me. He ranged aside the heavy matchstand,[40] set a chair straight, pushed a spittoon slightly with his foot—as you show small attentions to a friend under a great sorrow—sighed, and at last, unable to hold his tongue:

"Well! I warned you, Captain. That's what comes of running your head against Mr. Falk. Man'll stick at nothing."

I sat without stirring, and after surveying me with a sort of commiseration in his eyes, he burst out in a hoarse whisper: "But for a fine lump of a girl, she's a fine lump of a girl." He made a loud smacking noise with his thick lips. "The finest lump of a girl that I ever . . ." he was going on with great unction, but for some reason or other broke off. I fancied myself throwing something at his head. "I don't blame you, Captain. Hang me if I do," he said with a patronising air.

"Thank you," I said resignedly. It was no use fighting against this false fate. I don't know even if I was sure myself where the truth of the matter began. The conviction that it would end disastrously had been driven into me by all the successive shocks my sense of security had received. I began to ascribe an extra-ordinary potency to agents in themselves powerless. It was as if Schomberg's baseless gossip had the power to bring about the thing itself or the abstract enmity of Falk could put my ship ashore.

I have already explained how fatal this last would have been. For my further action, my youth, my inexperience, my very real concern for the health of my crew must be my excuse. The action itself, when it came, was purely impulsive. It was set in movement quite undiplomatically and simply by Falk's appearance in the doorway of the coffee-room.

The room was full by then and buzzing with voices. I had been looked at with curiosity by every one, but how am I to describe the sensation produced by the appearance of Falk himself blocking the doorway? The tension of expectation could be measured by the profundity of the silence that fell upon the very click of the billiard-balls. As to Schomberg, he looked extremely frightened; he hated mortally any sort of row (*fracas* he called it) in his establishment. *Fracas* was bad for business, he affirmed; but, in truth, this specimen of portly, middle aged manhood was of a timid disposition. I don't know what, con-sidering my presence in the place, they all hoped would come of it. A sort of stag fight, perhaps. Or they may have supposed Falk had come in only to annihilate me completely. As a matter of fact, Falk had come in because Hermann had asked him to inquire after the precious white cotton parasol which, in the worry and excitement of the previous day, he had forgotten at the table where we had held our little discussion.

It was this that gave me my opportunity. I don't think I would have gone to seek Falk out. No. I don't think so. There are limits. But there was an opportunity and I seized it—I have already tried to explain why. Now I will merely state that, in my opinion, to get his sickly crew into the sea air and secure a quick despatch for his ship a skipper would be justified in going to any length, short of absolute crime. He should put his pride in his pocket; he may accept confidences; he must explain his innocence as if it were a sin; he may take advantage of misconceptions, of desires, and of weaknesses; he ought to conceal his horror and other emotions, and, if the fate of a human being, and that human being a magnificent young girl, is strangely involved—why, he should contemplate that fate (whatever it might seem to be) without turning a hair. And all these things I have done; the explaining, the listening, the pretending—even to the discretion—and nobody, not even Hermann's niece, I believe, need throw stones at me now. Schomberg at all events needn't, since from first to last, I am happy to say, there was not the slightest *"fracas."*

Overcoming a nervous contraction of the windpipe, I had managed to exclaim "Captain Falk!" His start of surprise was perfectly genuine, but afterwards he neither smiled nor scowled. He simply waited. Then, when I had said, "I must have a talk with you," and had pointed to a chair at my table, he moved up to me, though he didn't sit down. Schomberg, however, with a long tumbler in his hand, was making towards us prudently, and I discovered then the only sign of weakness in Falk. He had for Schomberg a repulsion resembling that sort of physical fear some people experience at the sight of a toad. Perhaps to a man so essentially and silently concentrated upon himself (though he could talk well enough, as I was to find out presently) the other's irrepressible loquacity, embracing every human being within range of the tongue, might have appeared unnatural, disgusting, and monstrous. He suddenly gave signs of restiveness—positively like a horse about to rear, and, muttering hurriedly as if in great pain, "No. I can't stand that fellow," seemed ready to bolt. This weakness of his gave me the advantage at the very start. "Verandah," I suggested, as if rendering him a service, and walked him out by the arm. We stumbled over a few chairs; we had the feeling of open space before us, and felt the fresh breath of the river—fresh, but tainted. The

Chinese theatres across the water made, in the sparsely twinkling masses of gloom an Eastern town presents at night, blazing
centres of light, and of a distant and howling uproar. I felt
him become suddenly tractable again like an animal, like a
good-tempered horse when the object that scares him is
removed. Yes. I felt in the darkness there how tractable he
was, without my conviction of his inflexibility—tenacity,
rather, perhaps—being in the least weakened. His very arm
abandoning itself to my grasp was as hard as marble—like a
limb of iron. But I heard a tumultuous scuffling of boot-soles
within. The unspeakable idiots inside were crowding to the
windows, climbing over each other's backs behind the blinds,
billiard-cues and all. Somebody broke a window-pane, and with
the sound of falling glass, so suggestive of riot and devastation,
Schomberg reeled out after us in a state of funk which had
prevented his parting with his brandy and soda. He must have
trembled like an aspen leaf. The piece of ice in the long tumbler
he held in his hand tinkled with an effect of chattering teeth. "I
beg you, gentlemen," he expostulated thickly. "Come! Really,
now, I must insist . . ."

How proud I am of my presence of mind! "Hallo," I said
instantly in a loud and naïve tone, "somebody's breaking your
windows, Schomberg. Would you please tell one of your boys
to bring out here a pack of cards and a couple of lights? And
two long drinks. Will you?"

To receive an order soothed him at once. It was business.
"Certainly," he said in an immensely relieved tone. The night
was rainy, with wandering gusts of wind, and while we waited
for the candles Falk said, as if to justify his panic, "I don't
interfere in anybody's business. I don't give any occasion for
talk. I am a respectable man. But this fellow is always making
out something wrong, and can never rest till he gets somebody
to believe him."

This was the first of my knowledge of Falk. This desire
of respectability, of being like everybody else, was the only
recognition he vouchsafed to the organisation of mankind. For
the rest he might have been the member of a herd, not of a
society. Self-preservation was his only concern. Not selfishness,

but mere self-preservation. Selfishness presupposes consciousness, choice, the presence of other men; but his instinct acted
as though he were the last of mankind nursing that law like the
only spark of a sacred fire. I don't mean to say that living naked
in a cavern would have satisfied him. Obviously he was the
creature of the conditions to which he was born. No doubt
self-preservation meant also the preservation of these conditions. But essentially it meant something much more simple,
natural, and powerful. How shall I express it? It meant the
preservation of the five senses of his body—let us say—taking
it in its narrowest as well as in its widest meaning. I think you
will admit before long the justice of this judgment. However,
as we stood there together in the dark verandah I had judged
nothing as yet—and I had no desire to judge—which is an idle
practice anyhow. The light was long in coming.

"Of course," I said in a tone of mutual understanding, "it
isn't exactly a game of cards I want with you."

I saw him draw his hands down his face—the vague stir of
the passionate and meaningless gesture; but he waited in silent
patience. It was only when the lights had been brought out that
he opened his lips. I understood his mumble to mean that he
"didn't know any game."

"Like this, Schomberg and all the other fools will have to
keep off," I said, tearing open the pack. "Have you heard that
we are universally supposed to be quarrelling about a girl? You
know who, of course. I am really ashamed to ask, but is it
possible that you do me the honour to think me dangerous?"

As I said these words I felt how absurd it was and also I
felt flattered—for, really, what else could it be? His answer,
spoken in his usual dispassionate undertone, made it clear that
it was so, but not precisely as flattering as I supposed. He
thought me dangerous with Hermann, more than with the girl
herself; but, as to quarrelling, I saw at once how inappropriate
the word was. We had no quarrel. Natural forces are not quarrelsome. You can't quarrel with the wind that inconveniences
and humiliates you by blowing off your hat in a street full of
people. He had no quarrel with me. Neither would a boulder,
falling on my head, have had. He fell upon me in accordance

with the law by which he was moved—not of gravitation, like a detached stone, but of self-preservation. Of course this is giving it a rather wide interpretation. Strictly speaking, he had existed and could have existed without being married. Yet he told me that he had found it more and more difficult to live alone. Yes. He told me this in his low, careless voice, to such a pitch of confidence had we arrived at the end of half an hour.

It took me just about that time to convince him that I had never dreamed of marrying Hermann's niece. Could any necessity have been more extravagant? And the difficulty was the greater because he was so hard hit that he couldn't imagine anybody being able to remain in a state of indifference. Any man with eyes in his head, he seemed to think, could not help coveting so much bodily magnificence. This profound belief was conveyed by the manner he listened sitting sideways to the table and playing absently with a few cards I had dealt to him at random. And the more I saw into him the more I saw of him. The wind swayed the lights so that his sunburnt face, whiskered to the eyes, seemed to successively flicker crimson at me and to go out. I saw the extraordinary breadth of the high cheek-bones, the perpendicular style of the features, the massive forehead, steep like a cliff, denuded at the top, largely uncovered at the temples. The fact is I had never before seen him without his hat; but now, as if my fervour had made him hot, he had taken it off and laid it gently on the floor. Something peculiar in the shape and setting of his yellow eyes gave them the provoking silent intensity which characterised his glance. But the face was thin, furrowed, worn; I discovered that through the bush of his hair, as you may detect the gnarled shape of a tree trunk lost in a dense undergrowth. These overgrown cheeks were sunken. It was an anchorite's bony head fitted with a Capuchin's beard and adjusted to a herculean body. I don't mean athletic. Hercules, I take it, was not an athlete. He was a strong man, susceptible to female charms, and not afraid of dirt. And thus with Falk, who was a strong man. He was extremely strong, just as the girl (since I must think of them together) was magnificently attractive by the masterful power of flesh and blood, expressed in shape, in size, in attitude—that is by a straight appeal to the senses. His mind meantime, preoccupied with respectability, quailed before Schomberg's tongue and seemed absolutely impervious to my protestations; and I went so far as to protest that I would just as soon think of marrying my mother's (dear old lady!) faithful female cook as Hermann's niece. Sooner, I protested, in my desperation, much sooner; but it did not appear that he saw anything outrageous in the proposition, and in his sceptical immobility he seemed to nurse the argument that at all events the cook was very, very far away. It must be said that, just before, I had gone wrong by appealing to the evidence of my manner whenever I called on board the *Diana*. I had never attempted to approach the girl, or to speak to her, or even to look at her in any marked way. Nothing could be clearer. But, as his own idea of—let us say— courting seemed to consist precisely in sitting silently for hours in the vicinity of the beloved object, that line of argument inspired him with distrust. Staring down his extended legs he let out a grunt—as much as to say, "That's all very fine, but you can't throw dust in *my* eyes."

At last I was exasperated into saying, "Why don't you put the matter at rest by talking to Hermann?" and I added sneer-ingly: "You don't expect me perhaps to speak for you?"

To this he said, very loud for him, "Would you?"

And for the first time he lifted his head to look at me with wonder and incredulity. He lifted his head so sharply that there could be no mistake. I had touched a spring. I saw the whole extent of my opportunity, and could hardly believe in it.

"Why . . . Speak to . . . Well, of course," I proceeded very slowly, watching him with great attention, for, on my word, I feared a joke. "Not, perhaps, to the young lady herself. I can't speak German, you know. But . . ."

He interrupted me with the earnest assurance that Hermann had the highest opinion of me; and at once I felt the need for the greatest possible diplomacy at this juncture. So I demurred just enough to draw him on. Falk sat up, but except for a very noticeable enlargement of the pupils, till the irises of his eyes were reduced to two narrow yellow rings, his face, I should judge, was incapable of expressing excitement. "Oh, yes! Hermann did have the greatest . . ."

"Take up your cards. Here's Schomberg peeping at us through the blind!" I said.

We went through the motions of what might have been a game of écarté. Presently the intolerable scandalmonger withdrew, probably to inform the people in the billiard-room that we two were gambling on the verandah like mad.

We were not gambling, but it was a game; a game in which I felt I held the winning cards. The stake, roughly speaking, was the success of the voyage—for me; and he, I apprehended, had nothing to lose. Our intimacy matured rapidly, and before many words had been exchanged I perceived that the excellent Hermann had been making use of me. That simple and astute Teuton had been, it seems, holding me up to Falk in the light of a rival. I was young enough to be shocked at so much duplicity. "Did he tell you that in so many words?" I asked with indignation.

Hermann had not. He had given hints only; and of course it had not taken very much to alarm Falk; but, instead of declaring himself, he had taken steps to remove the family from under my influence. He was perfectly straightforward about it—as straightforward as a tile falling on your head. There was no duplicity in that man; and when I congratulated him on the perfection of his arrangements—even to the bribing of the wretched Johnson against me—he had a genuine movement of protest. Never bribed. He knew the man wouldn't work as long as he had a few cents in his pocket to get drunk on, and, naturally (he said—"*naturally*") he let him have a dollar or two. He was himself a sailor, he said, and anticipated the view another sailor, like myself, was bound to take. On the other hand, he was sure that I should have to come to grief. He hadn't been knocking about for the last seven years up and down that river for nothing. It would have been no disgrace to me; but he asserted confidently I would have had my ship very awkwardly ashore at a spot two miles below the Great Pagoda. . . .

And with all that he had no ill-will. That was evident. This was a crisis in which his only object had been to gain time, I fancy. And presently he mentioned that he had written for some jewellery, real good jewellery—had written to Hong-Kong for it. It would arrive in a day or two.

"Well, then," I said cheerily, "everything is all right. All you've got to do is to present it to the lady together with your heart, and live happy ever after."

Upon the whole he seemed to accept that view as far as the girl was concerned, but his eyelids drooped. There was still something in the way. For one thing Hermann disliked him so much. As to me, on the contrary, it seemed as though he could not praise me enough. Mrs. Hermann too. He didn't know why they disliked him so. It made everything most difficult.

I listened impassive, feeling more and more diplomatic. His speech was not transparently clear. He was one of those men who seem to live, feel, suffer in a sort of mental twilight. But as to being fascinated by the girl and possessed by the desire of home life with her—it was as clear as daylight. So much being at stake, he was afraid of putting it to the hazard of the declaration. Besides, there was something else. And with Hermann being so set against him . . .

"I see," I said thoughtfully, while my heart beat fast with the excitement of my diplomacy. "I don't mind sounding Hermann. In fact, to show you how mistaken you were, I am ready to do all I can for you in that way."

A light sigh escaped him. He drew his hands down his face, and it emerged, bony, unchanged of expression, as if all the tissues had been ossified. All the passion was in those big brown hands. He was satisfied. Then there was that other matter. If there were anybody on earth it was I who could persuade Hermann to take a reasonable view! I had a knowledge of the world and lots of experience. Hermann admitted this himself. And then I was a sailor too. Falk thought that a sailor would be able to understand certain things best. . . .

He talked as if the Hermanns had been living all their life in a rural hamlet, and I alone had been capable, with my practice in life, of a large and indulgent view of certain occurrences. That was what my diplomacy was leading me to. I began suddenly to dislike it.

"I say, Falk," I asked quite brusquely, "you haven't already a wife put away somewhere?"

The pain and disgust of his denial were very striking. Couldn't I understand that he was as respectable as any white man hereabouts; earning his living honestly. He was suffering from my suspicion, and the low undertone of his voice made his protestations sound very pathetic. For a moment he shamed me, but, my diplomacy notwithstanding, I seemed to develop a conscience, as if in very truth it were in my power to decide the success of this matrimonial enterprise. By pretending hard enough we come to believe anything—anything to our advantage. And I had been pretending very hard, because I meant yet to be towed safely down the river. But through conscience or stupidity, I couldn't help alluding to the Vanlo affair. "You acted rather badly there. Didn't you?" was what I ventured actually to say—for the logic of our conduct is always at the mercy of obscure and unforeseen impulses.

His dilated pupils swerved from my face, glancing at the window with a sort of scared fury. We heard behind the blinds the continuous and sudden clicking of ivory, a jovial murmur of many voices, and Schomberg's deep manly laugh.

"That confounded old woman of a hotel-keeper then would never, never let it rest!" Falk exclaimed. "Well, yes! It had happened two years ago." When it came to the point he owned he couldn't make up his mind to trust Fred Vanlo—no sailor, a bit of a fool too. He could not trust him, but, to stop his row, he had lent him enough money to pay all his debts before he left. I was greatly surprised to hear this. Then Falk could not be such a miser after all. So much the better for the girl. For a time he sat silent; then he picked up a card, and while looking at it said:

"You need not think of anything bad. It was an accident. I've been unfortunate once."

"Then in heaven's name say nothing about it."

As soon as these words were out of my mouth I fancied I had said something immoral. He shook his head negatively. It had to be told. He considered it proper that the relations of the lady should know. No doubt—I thought to myself—had

Miss Vanlo not been thirty and damaged by the climate he would have found it possible to entrust Fred Vanlo with this confidence. And then the figure of Hermann's niece appeared before my mind's eye, with the wealth of her opulent form, her rich youth, her lavish strength. With that powerful and immaculate vitality, her girlish form must have shouted aloud of life to that man, whereas poor Miss Vanlo could only sing sentimental songs to the strumming of a piano.

"And that Hermann hates me, I know it!" he cried in his undertone, with a sudden recrudescence of anxiety. "I must tell them. It is proper that they should know. You would say so yourself."

He then murmured an utterly mysterious allusion to the necessity for peculiar domestic arrangements. Though my curiosity was excited I did not want to hear any of his confidences. I feared he might give me a piece of information that would make my assumed *rôle* of match-maker odious—however unreal it was. I was aware that he could have the girl for the asking; and keeping down a desire to laugh in his face, I expressed a confident belief in my ability to argue away Hermann's dislike for him. "I am sure I can make it all right," I said. He looked very pleased.

And when we rose not a word had been said about towage! Not a word! The game was won and the honour was safe. Oh! blessed white cotton umbrella! We shook hands, and I was holding myself with difficulty from breaking into a step-dance of joy when he came back, striding all the length of the verandah, and said doubtfully:

"I say, Captain, I have your word? You—you—won't turn round?"

Heavens! The fright he gave me. Behind his tone of doubt there was something desperate and menacing. The infatuated ass. But I was equal to the situation.

"My dear Falk," I said, beginning to lie with a glibness and effrontery that amazed me even at the time—"confidence for confidence." (He had made no confidences.) "I will tell you that I am already engaged to an extremely charming girl at home, and so you understand . . ."

He caught my hand and wrung it in a crushing grip.

"Pardon me. I feel it every day more difficult to live alone . . ."

"On rice and fish," I interrupted smartly, giggling with the sheer nervousness of a danger escaped.

He dropped my hand as if it had become suddenly red-hot. A moment of profound silence ensued, as though something extraordinary had happened.

"I promise you to obtain Hermann's consent," I faltered out at last, and it seemed to me that he could not help seeing through that humbugging promise. "If there's anything else to get over I shall endeavour to stand by you," I conceded further, feeling somehow defeated and overborne, "but you must do your best yourself."

"I have been unfortunate once," he muttered unemotionally, and turning his back on me he went away, thumping slowly the plank floor as if his feet had been shod with iron.

Next morning, however, he was lively enough as man-boat, a combination of splashing and shouting; of the insolent commotion below with the steady overbearing glare of the silent head-piece above. He turned us out most unnecessarily at an ungodly hour, but it was nearly eleven in the morning before he brought me up a cable's length from Hermann's ship. And he did it very badly too, in a hurry, and nearly contriving to miss altogether the patch of good holding ground, because, forsooth, he had caught sight of Hermann's niece on the poop. And so did I; and probably as soon as he had seen her himself. I saw the modest, sleek glory of the tawny head, and the full, grey shape of the girlish print frock she filled so perfectly, so satisfactorily, with the seduction of unfaltering curves—a very nymph of Diana the Huntress. And *Diana* the ship sat, high-walled and as solid as an institution, on the smooth level of the water, the most uninspiring and respectable craft upon the seas, useful and ugly, devoted to the support of domestic virtues like any grocer's shop on shore. At once Falk steamed away; for there was some work for him to do. He would return in the evening.

He ranged close by us, passing out dead slow, without a hail. The beat of the paddle-wheels reverberating amongst the stony

islets, as if from the ruined walls of a vast arena, filled the
anchorage confusedly with the clapping sounds of a mighty and
leisurely applause. Abreast of Hermann's ship he stopped the
engines; and a profound silence reigned over the rocks, the
shore, and the sea, for the time it took him to raise his hat aloft
before the nymph of the grey print frock. I had snatched up my
binoculars, and I can answer for it she didn't stir a limb, standing by the rail shapely and erect, with one of her hands grasping
a rope at the height of her head, while the way of the tug carried
slowly past her the lingering and profound homage of the man.
There was for me an enormous significance in the scene, the
sense of having witnessed a solemn declaration. The die was
cast.[41] After such a manifestation he couldn't back out. And I
reflected that it was nothing whatever to me now. With a rush
of black smoke belching suddenly out of the funnel, and a
mad swirl of paddle-wheels provoking a burst of weird and
precipitated clapping, the tug shot out of the desolate arena.
The rocky islets lay on the sea like the heaps of a cyclopean
ruin on a plain; the centipedes and scorpions lurked under the
stones; there was not a single blade of grass in sight anywhere,
not a single lizard sunning himself on a boulder by the shore.
When I looked again at Hermann's ship the girl had disappeared. I could not detect the smallest dot of a bird on the
immense sky, and the flatness of the land continued the flatness
of the sea to the naked line of the horizon.

This is the setting now inseparably connected with my knowledge of Falk's misfortune. My diplomacy had brought me
there, and now I had only to wait the time for taking up the
rôle of an ambassador. My diplomacy was a success; my ship
was safe; old Gambril would probably live; a feeble sound of a
tapping hammer came intermittently from the *Diana*. During
the afternoon I looked at times at the old homely ship, the
faithful nurse of Hermann's progeny, or yawned towards the
distant temple of Buddha, like a lonely hillock on the plain,
where shaven priests cherish the thoughts of that Annihilation
which is the worthy reward of us all. Unfortunate! He had been
unfortunate once. Well, that was not so bad as life goes. And
what the devil could be the nature of that misfortune? I

remembered that I had known a man before who had declared himself to have fallen, years ago, a victim to misfortune; but this misfortune, whose effects appeared permanent (he looked desperately hard up) when considered dispassionately, seemed indistinguishable from a breach of trust. Could it be something of that nature? Apart, however, from the utter improbability that he would offer to talk of it even to his future uncle-in-law I had a strange feeling that Falk's physique unfitted him for that sort of delinquency. As the person of Hermann's niece exhaled the profound physical charm of feminine form, so her adorer's big frame embodied to my senses the hard, straight masculinity that would conceivably kill but would not condescend to cheat. The thing was obvious. I might just as well have suspected the girl of a curvature of the spine. And I perceived that the sun was about to set.

The smoke of Falk's tug hove in sight, far away at the mouth of the river. It was time for me to assume the character of an ambassador, and the negotiation would not be difficult except in the matter of keeping my countenance. It was all too extravagantly nonsensical, and I conceived that it would be best to compose for myself a grave demeanour. I practised this in my boat as I went along, but the bashfulness that came secretly upon me the moment I stepped on the deck of the *Diana* is inexplicable. As soon as we had exchanged greetings Hermann asked me eagerly if I knew whether Falk had found his white parasol.

"He's going to bring it to you himself directly," I said with great solemnity. "Meantime I am charged with an important message for which he begs your favourable consideration. He is in love with your niece. . . ."

"*Ach so!*" he hissed with an animosity that made my assumed gravity change into the most genuine concern. What meant this tone? And I hurried on.

"He wishes, with your consent of course, to ask her to marry him at once—before you leave here, that is. He would speak to the Consul."

Hermann sat down and smoked violently. Five minutes passed in that furious meditation, and then, taking the long

pipe out of his mouth, he burst into a hot diatribe against
Falk—against his cupidity, his stupidity (a fellow that can
hardly be got to say "yes" or "no" to the simplest question)—
against his outrageous treatment of the shipping in port
(because he saw they were at his mercy)—and against his
manner of walking, which to his (Hermann's) mind showed a
conceit positively unbearable. The damage to the old *Diana*
was not forgotten, of course, and there was nothing of any
nature said or done by Falk (even to the last offer of refreshment
in the hotel) that did not seem to have been a cause of offence.
"Had the cheek" to drag him (Hermann) into that coffee-
room; as though a drink from him could make up for forty-
seven dollars and fifty cents of damage in the cost of wood
alone—not counting two days' work for the carpenter. Of
course he would not stand in the girl's way. He was going home
to Germany. There were plenty of poor girls walking about in
Germany.

"He's very much in love," was all I found to say.

"Yes," he cried. "And it is time too after making himself and
me talked about ashore the last voyage I was here, and then
now again; coming on board every evening unsettling the girl's
mind, and saying nothing. What sort of conduct is that?"

The seven thousand dollars the fellow was always talking
about did not, in his opinion, justify such behaviour. Moreover,
nobody had seen them. He (Hermann) seriously doubted if
there were seven thousand cents, and the tug, no doubt, was
mortgaged up to the top of the funnel to the firm of Siegers.
But let that pass. He wouldn't stand in the girl's way. Her head
was so turned that she had become no good to them of late.
Quite unable even to put the children to bed without her aunt.
It was bad for the children; they got unruly; and yesterday he
actually had to give Gustav a thrashing.

For that, too, Falk was made responsible apparently. And
looking at my Hermann's heavy, puffy, good-natured face, I
knew he would not exert himself till greatly exasperated, and,
therefore, would thrash very hard, and being fat would resent
the necessity. How Falk had managed to turn the girl's head
was more difficult to understand. I supposed Hermann would

know. And then hadn't there been Miss Vanlo? It could not be his silvery tongue, or the subtle seduction of his manner; he had no more of what is called "manner" than an animal—which, however, on the other hand, is never, and can never be called, vulgar. Therefore it must have been his bodily appearance, exhibiting a virility of nature as exaggerated as his beard, and resembling a sort of constant ruthlessness. It was seen in the very manner he lolled in the chair. He meant no offence, but his intercourse was characterised by that sort of frank disregard of susceptibilities a man of six foot seven, living in a world of dwarfs, would naturally assume, without in the least wishing to be unkind. But amongst men of his own stature, or nearly, this frank use of his advantages, in such matters as the awful towage bills for instance, caused much impotent gnashing of teeth.[42] When attentively considered it seemed appalling at times. He was a strange beast. But maybe women liked it. Seen in that light he was well worth taming, and I suppose every woman at the bottom of her heart considers herself as a tamer of strange beasts. But Hermann arose with precipitation to carry the news to his wife. I had barely the time, as he made for the cabin door, to grab him by the seat of his inexpressibles.[43] I begged him to wait till Falk in person had spoken with him. There remained some small matter to talk over, as I understood.

He sat down again at once, full of suspicion.

"What matter?" he said surlily. "I have had enough of his nonsense. There's no matter at all, as he knows very well; the girl has nothing in the world. She came to us in one thin dress when my brother died, and I have a growing family."

"It can't be anything of that kind," I opined. "He's desperately enamoured of your niece. I don't know why he did not say so before. Upon my word, I believe it is because he was afraid to lose, perhaps, the felicity of sitting near her on your quarter-deck."

I intimated my conviction that his love was so great as to be in a sense cowardly. The effects of a great passion are unaccountable. It has been known to make a man timid. But Hermann looked at me as if I had foolishly raved; and the twilight was dying out rapidly.

"You don't believe in passion, do you, Hermann?" I said cheerily. "The passion of fear will make a cornered rat courageous. Falk's in a corner. He will take her off your hands in one thin frock just as she came to you. And after ten years' service it isn't a bad bargain," I added.

Far from taking offence, he resumed his air of civic virtue. The sudden night came upon him while he stared placidly along the deck, bringing in contact with his thick lips, and taking away again after a jet of smoke, the curved mouthpiece fitted to the stem of his pipe. The night came upon him and buried in haste his whiskers, his globular eyes, his puffy pale face, his fat knees, and the vast flat slippers on his fatherly feet. Only his short arms in respectable white shirt-sleeves remained very visible, propped up like the flippers of a seal reposing on the strand.

"Falk wouldn't settle anything about repairs. Told me to find out first how much wood I should require and he would see," he remarked; and after he had spat peacefully in the dusk we heard over the water the beat of the tug's floats. There is, on a calm night, nothing more suggestive of fierce and headlong haste than the rapid sound made by the paddle-wheels of a boat threshing her way through a quiet sea; and the approach of Falk towards his fate seemed to be urged by an impatient and passionate desire. The engines must have been driven to the very utmost of their revolutions. We heard them slow down at last, and, vaguely, the white hull of the tug appeared moving against the black islets, whilst a slow and rhythmical clapping as of thousands of hands rose on all sides. It ceased all at once, just before Falk brought her up. A single brusque splash was followed by the long-drawn rumbling of iron links running through the hawse-pipe. Then a solemn silence fell upon the Roadstead.

"He will soon be here," I murmured, and after that we waited for him without a word. Meantime, raising my eyes, I beheld the glitter of a lofty sky above the *Diana*'s mastheads. The multitude of stars gathered into clusters, in rows, in lines, in masses, in groups, shone all together, unanimously—and the few isolated ones, blazing by themselves in the midst of dark

patches, seemed to be of a superior kind and of an inextinguishable nature. But long striding footsteps were heard hastening
along the deck; the high bulwarks of the *Diana* made a deeper
darkness. We rose from our chairs quickly, and Falk, appearing
before us, all in white, stood still.

Nobody spoke at first, as though we had been covered with
confusion. His arrival was fiery, but his white bulk, of indefinite
shape and without features, made him loom up like a man of
snow.

"The captain here has been telling me . . ." Hermann began
in a homely and amicable voice; and Falk had a low, nervous
laugh. His cool, negligent undertone had no inflexions, but the
strength of a powerful emotion made him ramble in his speech.
He had always desired a home. It was difficult to live alone,
though he was not answerable. He was domestic; there had
been difficulties; but since he had seen Hermann's niece he
found that it had become at last impossible to live by himself.
"I mean—impossible," he repeated with no sort of emphasis
and only with the slightest of pauses, but the word fell into my
mind with the force of a new idea.

"I have not said anything to her yet," Hermann observed
quietly. And Falk dismissed this by a "That's all right. Certainly.
Very proper." There was a necessity for perfect frankness—in
marrying, especially. Hermann seemed attentive, but he seized
the first opportunity to ask us into the cabin. "And by-the-by,
Falk," he said innocently, as we passed in, "the timber came to
no less than forty-seven dollars and fifty cents."

Falk, uncovering his head, lingered in the passage. "Some
other time," he said; and Hermann nudged me angrily—I don't
know why. The girl alone in the cabin sat sewing at some
distance from the table. Falk stopped short in the doorway.
Without a word, without a sign, without the slightest inclination of his bony head, by the silent intensity of his look alone,
he seemed to lay his herculean frame at her feet. Her hands
sank slowly on her lap, and raising her clear eyes,[44] she let her
soft, beaming glance enfold him from head to foot like a slow
and pale caress. He was very hot when he sat down; she, with
bowed head, went on with her sewing; her neck was very white

under the light of the lamp; but Falk, hiding his face in the palms of his hands, shuddered faintly. He drew them down, even to his beard, and his uncovered eyes astonished me by their tense and irrational expression—as though he had just swallowed a heavy gulp of alcohol. It passed away while he was binding us to secrecy. Not that he cared, but he did not like to be spoken about; and I looked at the girl's marvellous, at her wonderful, at her regal hair, plaited tight into that one astonishing and maidenly tress. Whenever she moved her well-shaped head it would stir stiffly to and fro on her back. The thin cotton sleeve fitted the irreproachable roundness of her arm like a skin; and her very dress, stretched on her bust, seemed to palpitate like a living tissue with the strength of vitality animating her body. How good her complexion was, the outline of her soft cheek, and the small convoluted conch of her rosy ear! To pull her needle she kept the little finger apart from the others; it seemed a waste of power to see her sewing— eternally sewing—with that industrious and precise movement of her arm, going on eternally upon all the oceans, under all the skies, in innumerable harbours. And suddenly I heard Falk's voice declare that he could not marry a woman unless she knew of something in his life that had happened ten years ago. It was an accident. An unfortunate accident. It would affect the domestic arrangements of their home, but, once told, it need not be alluded to again for the rest of their lives. "I should want my wife to feel for me," he said. "It has made me unhappy." And how could he keep the knowledge of it to himself—he asked us—perhaps through years and years of companionship? What sort of companionship would that be? He had thought it over. A wife must know. Then why not at once? He counted on Hermann's kindness for presenting the affair in the best possible light. And Hermann's countenance, mystified before, became very sour. He stole an inquisitive glance at me. I shook my head blankly. Some people thought, Falk went on, that such an experience changed a man for the rest of his life. He couldn't say. It was hard, awful, and not to be forgotten, but he did not think himself a worse man than before. Only he talked in his sleep now, he believed. . . . At last I began to think he had accidentally killed some one, perhaps a friend—his own father maybe, when he went on to say that probably we were aware he never touched meat. Throughout he spoke English, of course on my account.

He swayed forward heavily.

The girl, with her hands raised before her pale eyes, was threading her needle. He glanced at her, and his mighty trunk overshadowed the table, bringing nearer to us the breadth of his shoulders, the thickness of his neck, and that incongruous, anchorite head, burnt in the desert, hollowed and lean as if by excesses of vigils and fasting. His beard flowed imposingly downwards, out of sight, between the two brown hands gripping the edge of the table, and his persistent glance made sombre by the wide dilations of the pupils, fascinated.

"Imagine to yourselves," he said in his ordinary voice, "that I have eaten man."

I could only ejaculate a faint "Ah!" of complete enlightenment. But Hermann, dazed by the excessive shock, actually murmured, "*Himmel!* What for?"

"It was my terrible misfortune to do so," said Falk in a measured undertone. The girl, unconscious, sewed on. Mrs. Hermann was absent in one of the state-rooms, sitting up with Lena, who was feverish; but Hermann suddenly put both his hands up with a jerk. The embroidered calotte fell, and, in the twinkling of an eye, he had rumpled his hair all ends up in a most extravagant manner. In this state he strove to speak; with every effort his eyes seemed to start further out of their sockets; his head looked like a mop. He choked, gasped, swallowed, and managed to shriek out the one word, "Beast!"

From that moment till Falk went out of the cabin the girl, with her hands folded on the work lying in her lap, never took her eyes off him. His own, in the blindness of his heart, darted all over the cabin, only seeking to avoid the sight of Hermann's raving. It was ridiculous, and was made almost terrible by the stillness of every other person present. It was contemptible, and was made appalling by the man's overmastering horror of this awful sincerity, coming to him suddenly, with the confession of such a fact. He walked with great strides; he gasped. He

wanted to know from Falk how dared he to come and tell him
this? Did he think himself a proper person to be sitting in this
cabin where his wife and children lived? Tell his niece! Expected
him to tell his niece! His own brother's daughter! Shameless!
Did I ever hear tell of such impudence?—he appealed to me.
"This man here ought to have gone and hidden himself out of
sight instead of . . ."

"But it's a great misfortune for me. But it's a great misfortune
for me," Falk would ejaculate from time to time.

However, Hermann kept on running frequently against the
corners of the table. At last he lost a slipper, and crossing his
arms on his breast, walked up with one stockinged foot very
close to Falk, in order to ask him whether he did think there
was anywhere on earth a woman abandoned enough to mate
with such a monster. "Did he? Did he? Did he?" I tried to
restrain him. He tore himself out of my hands; he found his
slipper, and, endeavouring to put it on, stormed standing on
one leg—and Falk, with a face unmoved and averted eyes,
grasped all his mighty beard in one vast palm.

"Was it right then for me to die myself?" he asked thoughtfully. I laid my hand on his shoulder.

"Go away," I whispered imperiously, without any clear
reason for this advice, except that I wished to put an end to
Hermann's odious noise. "Go away."

He looked searchingly for a moment at Hermann before he
made a move. I left the cabin too to see him out of the ship.
But he hung about the quarter-deck.

"It is my misfortune," he said in a steady voice.

"You were stupid to blurt it out in such a manner. After all,
we don't hear such confidences every day."

"What does the man mean?" he mused in deep undertones.
"Somebody had to die—but why me?"

He remained still for a time in the dark—silent, almost invisible. All at once he pinned my elbows to my sides. I felt utterly
powerless in his grip, and his voice, whispering in my ear,
vibrated.

"It's worse than hunger. Captain, do you know what that
means? And I could kill then—or be killed. I wish the crowbar

had smashed my skull ten years ago. And I've got to live now. Without her. Do you understand? Perhaps many years. But how? What can be done? If I had allowed myself to look at her once I would have carried her off before that man in my hands—like this."

I felt myself snatched off the deck, then suddenly dropped— and I staggered backwards, feeling bewildered and bruised. What a man! All was still; he was gone. I heard Hermann's voice declaiming in the cabin, and I went in.

I could not at first make out a single word, but Mrs. Hermann, who, attracted by the noise, had come in some time before, with an expression of surprise and mild disapproval, depicted broadly on her face, was giving now all the signs of profound, helpless agitation. Her husband shot a string of guttural words at her, and instantly putting out one hand to the bulkhead as if to save herself from falling, she clutched the loose bosom of her dress with the other. He harangued the two women extraordinarily, with much of his shirt hanging out of his waistbelt, stamping his foot, turning from one to the other, sometimes throwing both his arms together, straight up above his rumpled hair, and keeping them in that position while he uttered a passage of loud denunciation; at others folding them tight across his breast—and then he hissed with indignation, elevating his shoulders and protruding his head. The girl was crying.

She had not changed her attitude. From her steady eyes that, following Falk in his retreat, had remained fixed wistfully on the cabin door, the tears fell rapid, thick, on her hands, on the work in her lap, warm and gentle like a shower in spring. She wept without grimacing, without noise—very touching, very quiet, with something more of pity than of pain in her face, as one weeps in compassion rather than in grief—and Hermann, before her, declaimed. I caught several times the word *"Mensch,"* man; and also *"Fressen,"* which last I looked up afterwards in my dictionary. It means "Devour." Hermann seemed to be requesting an answer of some sort from her; his whole body swayed. She remained mute and perfectly still; at last his agitation gained her; she put the palms of her hands together, her full lips parted, no sound came. His voice scolded shrilly, his arms went like a windmill—suddenly he shook a thick fist at her. She burst out into loud sobs. He seemed stupefied.

Mrs. Hermann rushed forward babbling rapidly. The two women fell on each other's necks, and, with an arm round her niece's waist, she led her away. Her own eyes were simply streaming; her face was flooded. She shook her head back at me negatively, I wonder why to this day. The girl's head dropped heavily on her shoulder. They disappeared.

Then Hermann sat down and stared at the cabin floor.

"We don't know all the circumstances," I ventured to break the silence. He retorted tartly that he didn't want to know of any. According to his ideas no circumstances could excuse a crime—and certainly not such a crime. This was the opinion generally received. The duty of a human being was to starve. Falk therefore was a beast, an animal; base, low, vile, despicable, shameless, and deceitful. He had been deceiving him since last year. He was, however, inclined to think that Falk must have gone mad quite recently; for no sane person, without necessity, uselessly, for no earthly reason, and regardless of another's self-respect and peace of mind, would own to having devoured human flesh. "Why tell?" he cried. "Who was asking him?" It showed Falk's brutality because after all he had selfishly caused him (Hermann) much pain. He would have preferred not to know that such an unclean creature had been in the habit of caressing his children. He hoped I would say nothing of all this ashore, though. He wouldn't like it to get about that he had been intimate with an eater of men[45]—a common cannibal. As to the scene he had made (which I judged quite unnecessary) he was not going to inconvenience and restrain himself for a fellow that went about courting and upsetting girls' heads, while he knew all the time that no decent housewifely girl could think of marrying him. At least he (Hermann) could not conceive how any girl could. Fancy Lena! ... No, it was impossible. The thoughts that would come into their heads every time they sat down to a meal. Horrible! Horrible!

"You are too squeamish, Hermann," I said.

He seemed to think it was eminently proper to be squeamish if the word meant disgust at Falk's conduct; and turning up his eyes sentimentally he drew my attention to the horrible fate of the victims—the victims of that Falk. I said that I knew nothing about them. He seemed surprised. Could not anybody imagine without knowing? He, for instance, felt he would like to avenge them. But what if, said I, there had not been any? They might have died as it were, naturally—of starvation. He shuddered. But to be eaten—after death! To be devoured! He gave another deep shudder, and asked suddenly, "Do you think it is true?"

His indignation and his personality together would have been enough to spoil the reality of the most authentic thing. When I looked at him I doubted the story; but the remembrance of Falk's words, looks, gestures, invested it not only with an air of reality but with the absolute truth of primitive passion.

"It is true just as much as you are able to make it; and exactly in the way you like to make it. For my part, when I hear you clamouring about it, I don't believe it is true at all."

And I left him pondering. The men in my boat, lying at the foot of *Diana*'s side-ladder, told me that the captain of the tug had gone away in his gig some time ago.

I let my fellows pull an easy stroke; because of the heavy dew the clear sparkle of the stars seemed to fall on me cold and wetting. There was a sense of lurking gruesome horror some-where in my mind, and it was mingled with clear and grotesque images. Schomberg's gastronomic tittle-tattle was responsible for these; and I half-hoped I should never see Falk again. But the first thing my anchor-watchman told me was that the captain of the tug was on board. He had sent his boat away and was now waiting for me in the cuddy.

He was lying full length on the stern settee, his face buried in the cushions. I had expected to see it discomposed, contorted, despairing. It was nothing of the kind; it was just as I had seen it twenty times, steady and glaring from the bridge of the tug. It was immovably set and hungry, dominated like the whole man by the singleness of one instinct.

He wanted to live. He had always wanted to live. So we all do—but in us the instinct serves a complex conception, and in

him this instinct existed alone. There is in such simple development a gigantic force, and like the pathos of a child's naïve and
uncontrolled desire. He wanted that girl, and the utmost that
can be said for him was that he wanted that particular girl alone.
I think I saw then the obscure beginning, the seed germinating in
the soil of an unconscious need, the first shoot of that tree
bearing now for a mature mankind the flower and the fruit, the
infinite gradation in shades and in flavour of our discriminating
love. He was a child. He was as frank as a child too. He was
hungry for the girl, terribly hungry, as he had been terribly
hungry for food.

Don't be shocked if I declare that in my belief it was the same
need, the same pain, the same torture. We are in his case allowed
to contemplate the foundation of all the emotions—that one
joy which is to live, and the one sadness at the root of the
innumerable torments. It was made plain by the way he talked.
He had never suffered so. It was gnawing; it was fire; it was
there, like this! And after pointing below his breastbone, he
made a hard wringing motion with his hands. And I assure you
that, seen as I saw it with my bodily eyes, it was anything but
laughable. And again, as he was presently to tell me (alluding
to an early incident of the disastrous voyage when some damaged meat had been flung overboard), he said that a time soon
came when his heart ached (that was the expression he used),
and he was ready to tear his hair out at the thought of all that
rotten beef thrown away.

I had heard all this; I witnessed his physical struggles, seeing
the working of the rack and hearing the true voice of pain. I
witnessed it all patiently, because the moment I came into the
cuddy he had called upon me to stand by him—and this, it
seems, I had diplomatically promised.

His agitation was impressive and alarming in the little cabin,
like the floundering of a great whale driven into a shallow cove
in a coast. He stood up; he flung himself down headlong; he
tried to tear the cushion with his teeth; and again hugging it
fiercely to his face he let himself fall on the couch. The whole
ship seemed to feel the shock of his despair; and I contemplated
with wonder the lofty forehead, the noble touch of time on the

uncovered temples, the unchanged hungry character of the face—so strangely ascetic and so incapable of portraying emotion.

What should he do? He had lived by being near her. He had sat—in the evening—I knew?—all his life! She sewed. Her head was bent—so. Her head—like this—and her arms. Ah! Had I seen? Like this.

He dropped on a stool, bowed his powerful neck whose nape was red, and with his hands stitched the air, ludicrous, sublimely imbecile, and comprehensible.

And now he couldn't have her? No! That was too much. After thinking too that . . . What had he done? What was my advice? Take her by force? No? Mustn't he? Who was there then to kill him? For the first time I saw one of his features move; a fighting teeth-baring curl of the lip. . . . "Not Hermann, perhaps." He lost himself in thought as though he had fallen out of the world.

I may note that the idea of suicide apparently did not enter his head for a single moment. It occurred to me to ask:

"Where was it that this shipwreck of yours took place?"

"Down south," he said vaguely with a start.

"You are not down south now," I said. "Violence won't do. They would take her away from you in no time. And what was the name of the ship?"

"*Borgmester Dahl*,"[46] he said. "It was no shipwreck."

He seemed to be waking up by degrees from that trance, and waking up calmed.

"Not a shipwreck? What was it?"

"Break-down," he answered, looking more like himself every moment. By this only I learned that it was a steamer. I had till then supposed they had been starving in boats or on a raft—or perhaps on a barren rock.

"She did not sink, then?" I asked in surprise. He nodded. "We sighted the southern ice," he pronounced dreamily.

"And you alone survived?"

He sat down. "Yes. It was a terrible misfortune for me. Everything went wrong. All the men went wrong. I survived."

Remembering the things one reads of, it was difficult to

realise the true meaning of his answers. I ought to have seen at once—but I did not; so difficult is it for our minds, remembering so much, instructed so much, informed of so much, to get in touch with the real actuality at our elbow. And with my head full of preconceived notions as to how a case of "cannibalism and suffering at sea" should be managed I said: "You were then so lucky in the drawing of lots?"

"Drawing of lots?" he said. "What lots? Do you think I would have allowed my life to go for the drawing of lots?"

Not if he could help it, I perceived, no matter what other life went.

"It was a great misfortune. Terrible. Awful," he said. "Many heads went wrong, but the best men would live."

"The toughest, you mean," I said. He considered the word. Perhaps it was strange to him, though his English was so good.

"Yes," he asserted at last. "The best. It was everybody for himself at last and the ship open to all."

Thus from question to question I got the whole story. I fancy it was the only way I could that night have stood by him. Outwardly at least he was himself again; the first sign of it was the return of that incongruous trick he had of drawing both his hands down his face—and it had its meaning now, with that slight shudder of the frame and the passionate anguish of these hands uncovering a hungry immovable face, the wide pupils of the intent, silent, fascinating eyes.

It was an iron steamer of a most respectable origin. The burgomaster of Falk's native town had built her. She was the first steamer ever launched there. The burgomaster's daughter had christened her. Country people drove in carts from miles around to see her. He told me all this. He got the berth as, what we should call, a chief mate. He seemed to think it had been a feather in his cap; and, in his own corner of the world, this lover of life was of good parentage.

The burgomaster had advanced ideas in the shipowning line. At that time not everyone would have known enough to think of despatching a cargo steamer to the Pacific. But he loaded her with pitch-pine deals[47] and sent her off to hunt for her luck. Wellington was to be the first port, I fancy. It doesn't matter, because in latitude 44° south and somewhere halfway between Good Hope and New Zealand the tail-shaft broke and the propeller dropped off.

They were steaming then with a fresh gale on the quarter and all their canvas set, to help the engines. But by itself the sail power was not enough to keep way on her. When the propeller went the ship broached-to at once, and the masts got whipped overboard.

The disadvantage of being dismasted consisted in this, that they had nothing to hoist flags on to make themselves visible at a distance. In the course of the first few days several ships failed to sight them; and the gale was drifting them out of the usual track. The voyage had been, from the first, neither very successful nor very harmonious. There had been quarrels on board. The captain was a clever, melancholic man, who had no unusual grip on his crew. The ship had been amply provisioned for the passage, but, somehow or other, several barrels of meat were found spoiled on opening, and had been thrown overboard soon after leaving home, as a sanitary measure. Afterwards the crew of the *Borgmester Dahl* thought of that rotten carrion with tears of regret, covetousness, and despair.

She drove south. To begin with, there had been an appearance of organisation, but soon the bonds of discipline became relaxed. A sombre idleness succeeded. They looked with sullen eyes at the horizon. The gales increased: she lay in the trough, the seas made a clean breach over her. On one frightful night, when they expected their hulk to turn over with them every moment, a heavy sea broke on board, deluged the store-rooms and spoiled the best part of the remaining provisions. It seems the hatch had not been properly secured. This instance of neglect is characteristic of utter discouragement. Falk tried to inspire some energy into his captain, but failed. From that time he retired more into himself, always trying to do his utmost in the situation. It grew worse. Gale succeeded gale, with black mountains of water hurling themselves on the *Borgmester Dahl*. Some of the men never left their bunks; many became quarrelsome. The chief-engineer, an old man, refused to speak at all to anybody. Others shut themselves up in their berths to cry.

On calm days the inert steamer rolled on a leaden sea under a murky sky, or showed, in sunshine, the squalor of sea waifs, the dried white salt, the rust, the jagged broken places. Then the gales came again. They kept body and soul together on short rations. Once, an English ship, scudding in a storm, tried to stand by them, heaving-to pluckily under their lee. The seas swept her decks; the men in oilskins clinging to her rigging looked at them, and they made desperate signs over their shattered bulwarks. Suddenly her main-topsail went, yard and all, in a terrific squall; she had to bear up under bare poles and disappeared.

Other ships had spoken to them before, but at first they had refused to be taken off, expecting the assistance of some steamer. There were very few steamers in those latitudes then; and when they desired to leave this dead and drifting carcase, no ship came in sight. They had drifted south out of men's knowledge. They failed to attract the attention of a lonely whaler; and very soon the edge of the polar ice-cap rose from the sea and closed the southern horizon like a wall. One morning they were alarmed by finding themselves floating amongst detached pieces of ice. But the fear of sinking passed away like their vigour, like their hopes; the shocks of the floes knocking against the ship's side could not rouse them from their apathy; and the *Borgmester Dahl* drifted out again, unharmed, into open water. They hardly noticed the change.

The funnel had gone overboard in one of the heavy rolls; two of their three boats had disappeared, washed away in bad weather, and the davits swung to and fro, unsecured, with chafed ropes' ends waggling to the roll. Nothing was done on board, and Falk told me how he had often listened to the water washing about the dark engine-room where the engines, stilled for ever, were decaying slowly into a mass of rust, as the stilled heart decays within the lifeless body. At first, after the loss of the motive power, the tiller had been thoroughly secured by lashings. But in course of time these had rotted, chafed, rusted, parting one by one; and the rudder, freed, banged heavily to and fro night and day, sending dull shocks through the whole frame of the vessel. This was dangerous. Nobody cared enough to lift a little finger. He told me that even now sometimes waking up at night, he fancied he could hear the dull vibrating thuds. The pintles were carried away, and it dropped off at last.

The final catastrophe came with the sending off of their one remaining boat. It was Falk who had managed to preserve her intact, and now it was agreed that some of the hands should sail away into the track of the shipping to procure assistance. She was provisioned with all the food they could spare for the six who were to go. They waited for a fine day. It was long in coming. At last one morning they lowered her into the water.

Directly, in that demoralised crowd, trouble broke out. Two men who had no business there had jumped into the boat under the pretence of unhooking the tackles, while some sort of squabble arose on the deck amongst these weak, tottering spectres of a ship's company. The captain, who had been for days living secluded and unapproachable in the chart-room, came to the rail. He ordered the two men to come up on board and menaced them with his revolver. They pretended to obey, but suddenly cutting the boat's painter, gave a shove against the ship's side and made ready to hoist the sail.

"Shoot, sir! Shoot them down!" cried Falk, "and I will jump overboard to regain the boat." But the captain, after taking aim with an irresolute arm, turned suddenly away.

A howl of rage arose. Falk dashed into his cabin for his own pistol. When he returned it was too late. Two more men had leaped into the water, but the fellows in the boat beat them off with the oars, hoisted the boat's lug, and sailed away. They were never heard of again.

Consternation and despair possessed the remaining ship's company, till the apathy of utter hopelessness reasserted its sway. That day a fireman committed suicide, running up on deck with his throat cut from ear to ear, to the horror of all hands. He was thrown overboard. The captain had locked himself in the chart-room, and Falk, knocking vainly for admittance, heard him reciting over and over again the names of his wife and children, not as if calling upon them or commending them to God, but in a mechanical voice like an exercise of memory. Next day the doors of the chart-room were swinging open to the roll of the ship, and the captain had disappeared. He must during the night have jumped into the sea. Falk locked both the doors and kept the keys.

The organised life of the ship had come to an end. The solidarity of the men had gone. They became indifferent to each other. It was Falk who took in hand the distribution of such food as remained. They boiled their boots for soup to eke out the rations, which only made their hunger more intolerable. Sometimes whispers of hate were heard passing between the languid skeletons that drifted endlessly to and fro, north and south, east and west, upon that carcase of a ship.

And in this lies the grotesque horror of this sombre story. The last extremity of sailors, overtaking a small boat or a frail craft, seems easier to bear, because of the direct danger of the seas. The confined space, the close contact, the imminent menace of the waves, seem to draw men together, in spite of madness, suffering, and despair. But there was a ship—safe, convenient, roomy: a ship with beds, bedding, knives, forks, comfortable cabins, glass and china, and a complete cook's galley, pervaded, ruled, and possessed by the pitiless spectre of starvation. The lamp oil had been drunk, the wicks cut up for food, the candles eaten. At night she floated dark in all her recesses, and full of fears. One day Falk came upon a man gnawing a splinter of pine wood. Suddenly he threw the piece of wood away, tottered to the rail, and fell over. Falk, too late to prevent the act, saw him claw the ship's side desperately before he went down. Next day another man did the same thing, after uttering horrible imprecations. But this one somehow managed to get hold of the broken rudder chains and hung on there, silently. Falk set about trying to save him, and all the time the man, holding with both hands, looked at him anxiously with his sunken eyes. Then, just as Falk was ready to put his hand on him, the man let go his hold and sank like a stone. Falk reflected on these sights. His heart revolted against the horror of death, and he said to himself that he would struggle for every precious minute of his life.

One afternoon—as the survivors lay about on the after-

deck—the carpenter, a tall man with a black beard, spoke of
the last sacrifice. There was nothing eatable left on board.
Nobody said a word to this; but that company separated
quickly, these listless feeble spectres slunk off one by one to
hide in fear of each other. Falk and the carpenter remained on
deck together. Falk liked the big carpenter. He had been the
best man of the lot, helpful and ready as long as there was
anything to do, the longest hopeful, and had preserved to the
last some vigour and decision of mind.

They did not speak to each other. Henceforth no voices were
to be heard conversing sadly on board that ship. After a time
the carpenter tottered away forward; but, later on, Falk going
to drink at the fresh-water pump, had the inspiration to turn
his head. The carpenter had stolen upon him from behind, and,
summoning all his strength, was aiming with a crowbar a blow
at the back of his skull.

Dodging just in time, Falk made his escape and ran into his
cabin. While he was loading his revolver there, he heard the
sound of heavy blows struck upon the bridge. The locks of
the chart-room doors were slight, they flew open, and the carpenter, possessing himself of the captain's revolver, fired a shot
of defiance.

Falk was about to go on deck and have it out at once, when
he remarked that one of the ports of his cabin commanded the
approaches to the fresh-water pump. Instead of going out he
remained in and secured the door. "The best man shall survive,"
he said to himself—and the other, he reasoned, must at some
time or other come there to drink. These starving men would
drink often to cheat the pangs of their hunger. But the carpenter
too must have noticed the position of the port. They were the
two best men in the ship, and the game was with them. All the
rest of the day Falk saw no one and heard no sound. At night
he strained his eyes. It was dark—he heard a rustling noise
once, but he was certain that no one could have come near the
pump. It was to the left of his deck port, and he could not have
failed to see a man, for the night was clear and starry. He
saw nothing; towards morning another faint noise made him
suspicious. Deliberately and quietly he unlocked his door. He

had not slept, and had not given way to the horror of the situation. He wanted to live.

But during the night the carpenter, without at all trying to approach the pump, had managed to creep quietly along the starboard bulwark, and, unseen, had crouched down right under Falk's deck port. When daylight came he rose up suddenly, looked in, and putting his arm through the round brass-framed opening, fired at Falk within a foot. He missed—and Falk, instead of attempting to seize the arm holding the weapon, opened his door unexpectedly, and with the muzzle of his long revolver nearly touching the other's side, shot him dead.

The best man had survived. Both of them had at the beginning just strength enough to stand on their feet, and both had displayed pitiless resolution, endurance, cunning, and courage—all the qualities of classic heroism. At once Falk threw overboard the captain's revolver. He was a born monopolist. Then after the report of the two shots, followed by a profound silence, there crept out into the cold, cruel dawn of Antarctic regions, from various hiding-places, over the deck of that dismantled corpse of a ship floating on a grey sea ruled by iron necessity and with a heart of ice—there crept into view one by one, cautious, slow, eager, glaring, and unclean, a band of hungry and livid skeletons. Falk faced them, the possessor of the only fire-arm on board, and the second-best man—the carpenter—was lying dead between him and them.

"He was eaten, of course," I said.

He bent his head slowly, shuddered a little, drawing his hands over his face, and said, "I had never any quarrel with that man. But there were our lives between him and me."

Why continue the story of that ship, that story before which, with its fresh-water pump like a spring of death, its man with the weapon, the sea ruled by iron necessity, its spectral band swayed by terror and hope, its mute and unhearing heaven? The fable of the *Flying Dutchman*[48] with its convention of crime and its sentimental retribution fades like a graceful wraith, like a wisp of white mist. What is there to say that every one of us cannot guess for himself? I believe Falk began by going through the ship, revolver in hand, to annex all the matches. Those

starving wretches had plenty of matches! He had no mind to
have the ship set on fire under his feet, either from hate or
from despair. He lived in the open, camping on the bridge,
commanding all the after-deck and the only approach to the
pump. He lived! Some of the others lived too—concealed, anxious, coming out one by one from their hiding-places at the
seductive sound of a shot. And he was not selfish. They shared,
but only three of them all were alive when a whaler, returning
from her cruising-ground, nearly ran over the water-logged hull
of the *Borgmester Dahl*, which, it seems, in the end had in some
way sprung a leak in both her holds, but being loaded with
deals could not sink.

"They all died," Falk said. "These three, too, afterwards. But
I would not die. All died, all! under this terrible misfortune.
But was I too to throw away my life? Could I? Tell me, Captain?
I was alone there, quite alone, just like the others. Each man
was alone. Was I to give up my revolver? Who to? Or was I to
throw it into the sea? What would have been the good? Only
the best man would survive. It was a great, terrible, and cruel
misfortune."

He had survived! I saw him before me as though preserved
for a witness to the mighty truth of an unerring and eternal
principle. Great beads of perspiration stood on his forehead.
And suddenly it struck the table with a heavy blow, as he fell
forward throwing his hands out.

"And this is worse," he cried. "This is a worse pain! This is
more terrible."

He made my heart thump with the profound conviction of
his cry. And after he had left me alone I called up before my
mental eye the image of the girl weeping silently, abundantly,
patiently, and as if irresistibly. I thought of her tawny hair. I
thought how, if unplaited, it would have covered her all round
as low as the hips, like the hair of a siren. And she had bewitched
him. Fancy a man who would guard his own life with the
inflexibility of a pitiless and immovable fate, being brought to
lament that once a crowbar had missed his skull! The sirens
sing and lure to death, but this one had been weeping silently
as if for the pity of his life. She was the tender and voiceless

siren of this appalling navigator. He evidently wanted to live his whole conception of life. Nothing else would do. And she too was a servant of that life that, in the midst of death, cries aloud to our senses. She was eminently fitted to interpret for him its feminine side. And in her own way, and with her own profusion of sensuous charms, she also seemed to illustrate the eternal truth of an unerring principle. I don't know though what sort of principle Hermann illustrated when he turned up early on board my ship with a most perplexed air. It struck me, however, that he too would do his best to survive. He seemed greatly calmed on the subject of Falk, but still very full of it.

"What is it you said I was last night? You know," he asked after some preliminary talk. "Too—too—I don't know. A very funny word."

"Squeamish?" I suggested.

"Yes. What does it mean?"

"That you exaggerate things—to yourself. Without inquiry, and so on."

He seemed to turn it over in his mind. We went on talking. This Falk was the plague of his life. Upsetting everybody like this! Mrs. Hermann was unwell rather this morning. His niece was crying still. There was nobody to look after the children. He struck his umbrella on the deck. She would be like that for months. Fancy carrying all the way home, second class, a perfectly useless girl who is crying all the time. It was bad for Lena, too, he observed; but on what grounds I could not guess. Perhaps of the bad example. That child was already sorrowing and crying enough over the rag-doll. Nicholas was really the least sentimental person of the family.

"Why does she weep?" I asked.

"From pity," cried Hermann.

It was impossible to make out women. Mrs. Hermann was the only one he pretended to understand. She was very, very upset and doubtful.

"Doubtful about what?" I asked.

He averted his eyes and did not answer this. It was impossible to make them out. For instance, his niece was weeping for Falk. Now he (Hermann) would like to wring his neck—but then . . .

He supposed he had too tender a heart. "Frankly," he asked at last, "what do you think of what we heard last night, Captain?"

"In all these tales," I observed, "there is always a good deal of exaggeration."

And not letting him recover from his surprise I assured him that I knew all the details. He begged me not to repeat them. His heart was too tender. They made him feel unwell. Then, looking at his feet and speaking very slowly, he supposed that he need not see much of them after they were married. For, indeed, he could not bear the sight of Falk. On the other hand, it was ridiculous to take home a girl with her head turned. A girl that weeps all the time and is of no help to her aunt.

"Now you will be able to do with one cabin only on your passage home," I said.

"Yes, I had thought of that," he said brightly, almost. Yes! Himself, his wife, four children—one cabin might do. Whereas if his niece went . . .

"And what does Mrs. Hermann say to it?" I inquired.

Mrs. Hermann did not know whether a man of that sort could make a girl happy—she had been greatly deceived in Captain Falk. She had been very upset last night.

Those good people did not seem to be able to retain an impression for a whole twelve hours. I assured him on my own personal knowledge that Falk possessed in himself all the qualities to make his niece's future prosperous. He said he was glad to hear this, and that he would tell his wife. Then the object of the visit came out. He wished me to help him to resume relations with Falk. His niece, he said, had expressed the hope I would do so in my kindness. He was evidently anxious that I should, for though he seemed to have forgotten nine-tenths of his last night's opinions and the whole of his indignation, yet he evidently feared to be sent to the right-about.[49] "You told me he was very much in love," he concluded slyly, and leered in a sort of bucolic way.

As soon as he had left my ship I called Falk on board by signal—the tug still lying at the anchorage. He took the news with calm gravity, as though he had all along expected the stars to fight for him in their courses.[50]

I saw them once more together, and only once—on the quarter-deck of the *Diana*. Hermann sat smoking with a shirt-sleeved elbow hooked over the back of his chair. Mrs. Hermann was sewing alone. As Falk stepped over the gangway, Hermann's niece, with a slight swish of the skirt and a swift friendly nod to me, glided past my chair.

They met in sunshine abreast of the mainmast. He held her hands and looked down at them, and she looked up at him with her candid and unseeing glance. It seemed to me they had come together as if attracted, drawn, and guided to each other by a mysterious influence. They were a complete couple. In her grey frock, palpitating with life, generous of form, olympian and simple, she was indeed the siren to fascinate that dark navigator, this ruthless lover of the five senses. From afar I seemed to feel the masculine strength with which he grasped those hands she had extended to him with a womanly swiftness. Lena, a little pale, nursing her beloved lump of dirty rags, ran towards her big friend; and then in the drowsy silence of the good old ship Mrs. Hermann's voice rang out so changed that it made me spin round in my chair to see what was the matter.

"Lena, come here!" she screamed. And this good-natured matron gave me a wavering glance, dark and full of fearsome distrust. The child ran back, surprised, to her knee. But the two, standing before each other in sunlight with clasped hands, had heard nothing, had seen nothing and no one. Three feet away from them in the shade a seaman sat on a spar, very busy splicing a strop, and dipping his fingers into a tar-pot, as if utterly unaware of their existence.

When I returned in command of another ship, some five years afterwards, Mr. and Mrs. Falk had left the place. I should not wonder if Schomberg's tongue had succeeded at last in scaring Falk away for good; and, indubitably, there was a tale still going about the town of a certain Falk, owner of a tug, who had won his wife at cards from the captain of an English ship."

To-morrow

What was known of Captain Hagberd in the little seaport of Colebrook[1] was not exactly in his favour. He did not belong to the place. He had come to settle there under circumstances not at all mysterious—he used to be very communicative about them at the time—but extremely morbid and unreasonable. He was possessed of some little money evidently, because he bought a plot of ground, and had a pair of ugly yellow brick cottages run up very cheaply. He occupied one of them himself and let the other to Josiah Carvil—blind Carvil, the retired boat-builder—a man of evil repute as a domestic tyrant.

These cottages had one wall in common, shared in a line of iron railing dividing their front gardens; a wooden fence separated their back gardens. Miss Bessie Carvil was allowed, as it were of right, to throw over it the tea-cloths, blue rags, or an apron that wanted drying.

"It rots the wood, Bessie my girl," the captain would remark mildly, from his side of the fence, each time he saw her exercising that privilege.

She was a tall girl; the fence was low, and she could spread her elbows on the top. Her hands would be red with the bit of washing she had done, but her forearms were white and shapely, and she would look at her father's landlord in silence—in an informed silence which had an air of knowledge, expectation, and desire.

"It rots the wood," repeated Captain Hagberd. "It is the only unthrifty, careless habit I know in you. Why don't you have a clothes-line out in your back yard?"

Miss Carvil would say nothing to this—she only shook her

head negatively. The tiny back yard on her side had a few stone-bordered little beds of black earth, in which the simple flowers she found time to cultivate appeared somehow extravagantly overgrown, as if belonging to an exotic clime; and Captain Hagberd's upright, hale person, clad in No. 1 sail-cloth[2] from head to foot, would be emerging knee-deep out of rank grass and the tall weeds on his side of the fence. He appeared, with the colour and uncouth stiffness of the extraordinary material in which he chose to clothe himself—"for the time being," would be his mumbled remark to any observation on the subject—like a man roughened out of granite, standing in a wilderness not big enough for a decent billiard-room. A heavy figure of a man of stone, with a red handsome face, a blue wandering eye, and a great white beard flowing to his waist and never trimmed as far as Colebrook knew.

Seven years before, he had seriously answered, "Next month, I think," to the chaffing attempt to secure his custom made by that distinguished local wit, the Colebrook barber, who happened to be sitting insolently in the tap-room[3] of the New Inn near the harbour, where the captain had entered to buy an ounce of tobacco. After paying for his purchase with three half-pence extracted from the corner of a handkerchief which he carried in the cuff of his sleeve, Captain Hagberd went out. As soon as the door was shut the barber laughed. "The old one and the young one will be strolling arm in arm to get shaved in my place presently. The tailor shall be set to work, and the barber, and the candlestick maker; high old times are coming for Colebrook; they are coming, to be sure. It used to be 'next week,' now it has come to 'next month,' and so on—soon it will be next spring, for all I know."

Noticing a stranger listening to him with a vacant grin, he explained, stretching out his legs cynically, that this queer old Hagberd, a retired coasting-skipper, was waiting for the return of a son of his. The boy had been driven away from home, he shouldn't wonder; had run away to sea and had never been heard of since. Put to rest in Davy Jones's locker[4] this many a day, as likely as not. That old man came flying to Colebrook three years ago all in black broadcloth (had lost his wife lately

then), getting out of a third-class smoker[5] as if the devil had
been at his heels; and the only thing that brought him down
was a letter—a hoax probably. Some joker had written to him
about a seafaring man with some such name who was supposed
to be hanging about some girl or other, either in Colebrook or
in the neighbourhood. "Funny, ain't it?" The old chap had
been advertising in the London papers for Harry Hagberd, and
offering rewards for any sort of likely information. And the
barber would go on to describe, with sardonic gusto, how that
stranger in mourning had been seen exploring the country, in
carts, on foot, taking everybody into his confidence, visiting all
the inns and alehouses for miles around, stopping people on
the road with his questions, looking into the very ditches
almost; first in the greatest excitement, then with a plodding
sort of perseverance, growing slower and slower; and he could
not even tell you plainly how his son looked. The sailor was
supposed to be one of two that had left a timber ship, and to
have been seen dangling after some girl; but the old man
described a boy of fourteen or so—"a clever-looking, high-
spirited boy." And when people only smiled at this he would
rub his forehead in a confused sort of way before he slunk off,
looking offended. He found nobody, of course; not a trace of
anybody—never heard of anything worth belief, at any rate;
but he had not been able somehow to tear himself away from
Colebrook.

"It was the shock of this disappointment, perhaps, coming
soon after the loss of his wife, that had driven him crazy on that
point," the barber suggested, with an air of great psychological
insight. After a time the old man abandoned the active search.
His son had evidently gone away; but he settled himself to
wait. His son had been once at least in Colebrook in preference
to his native place. There must have been some reason for it,
he seemed to think, some very powerful inducement, that would
bring him back to Colebrook again.

"Ha, ha, ha! Why, of course, Colebrook. Where else? That's
the only place in the United Kingdom for your long-lost
sons. So he sold up his old home in Colchester,[6] and down he
comes here. Well, it's a craze, like any other. Wouldn't catch

me going crazy over any of my youngsters clearing out. I've got eight of them at home."[7] The barber was showing off his strength of mind in the midst of a laughter that shook the tap-room.

Strange, though, that sort of thing, he would confess, with the frankness of a superior intelligence, seemed to be catching. His establishment, for instance, was near the harbour, and whenever a sailorman came in for a hair-cut or a shave—if it was a strange face he couldn't help thinking directly, "Suppose he's the son of old Hagberd!" He laughed at himself for it. It was a strong craze. He could remember the time when the whole town was full of it. But he had his hopes of the old chap yet. He would cure him by a course of judicious chaffing. He was watching the progress of the treatment. Next week—next month—next year! When the old skipper had put off the date of that return till next year, he would be well on his way to not saying any more about it. In other matters he was quite rational, so this, too, was bound to come. Such was the barber's firm opinion.

Nobody had ever contradicted him; his own hair had gone grey since that time, and Captain Hagberd's beard had turned quite white, and had acquired a majestic flow over the No. 1 canvas[8] suit, which he had made for himself secretly with tarred twine, and had assumed suddenly, coming out in it one fine morning, whereas the evening before he had been seen going home in his mourning of broadcloth. It caused a sensation in the High Street—shopkeepers coming to their doors, people in the houses snatching up their hats to run out—a stir at which he seemed strangely surprised at first, and then scared; but his only answer to the wondering questions was that startled and evasive, "For the present."

That sensation had been forgotten long ago; and Captain Hagberd himself, if not forgotten, had come to be disregarded—the penalty of dailiness—as the sun itself is disregarded unless it makes its power felt heavily. Captain Hagberd's movements showed no infirmity: he walked stiffly in his suit of canvas, a quaint and remarkable figure; only his eyes wandered more furtively perhaps than of yore. His manner abroad had lost its excitable watchfulness; it had become puzzled and diffident, as though he had suspected that there was somewhere about him something slightly compromising, some embarrassing oddity; and yet had remained unable to discover what on earth this something wrong could be.

He was unwilling now to talk with the townsfolk. He had earned for himself the reputation of an awful skinflint, of a miser, in the matter of living. He mumbled regretfully in the shops, bought inferior scraps of meat after long hesitations; and discouraged all allusions to his costume. It was as the barber had foretold. For all one could tell, he had recovered already from the disease of hope; and only Miss Bessie Carvil knew that he said nothing about his son's return because with him it was no longer "next week," "next month," or even "next year." It was "to-morrow."

In their intimacy of back yard and front garden he talked with her paternally, reasonably, and dogmatically, with a touch of arbitrariness. They met on the ground of unreserved confidence, which was authenticated by an affectionate wink now and then. Miss Carvil had come to look forward rather to these winks. At first they had discomposed her: the poor fellow was mad. Afterwards she had learned to laugh at them: there was no harm in him. Now she was aware of an unacknowledged, pleasurable, incredulous emotion, expressed by a faint blush. He winked not in the least vulgarly; his thin red face, with a well-modelled curved nose, had a sort of distinction—the more so that when he talked to her he looked with a steadier and more intelligent glance. A handsome, hale, upright, capable man, with a white beard. You did not think of his age. His son, he affirmed, had resembled him amazingly from his earliest babyhood.

Harry would be one-and-thirty next July, he declared. Proper age to get married with a nice, sensible girl that could appreciate a good home. He was a very high-spirited boy. High-spirited husbands were the easiest to manage. These mean, soft chaps, that you would think butter wouldn't melt in their mouths, were the ones to make a woman thoroughly miserable. And there was nothing like home—a fireside—a good roof: no turning out of your warm bed in all sorts of weather. "Eh, my dear?"

Captain Hagberd had been one of those sailors that pursue their calling within sight of land. One of the many children of a bankrupt farmer, he had been apprenticed hurriedly to a coasting-skipper, and had remained on the coast all his sea life. It must have been a hard one at first: he had never taken to it; his affection turned to the land, with its innumerable houses, with its quiet lives gathered round its firesides. Many sailors feel and profess a rational dislike for the sea, but his was a profound and emotional animosity, as if the love of the stabler element had been bred into him through many generations.

"People did not know what they let their boys in for when they let them go to sea," he expounded to Bessie. "As soon make convicts of them at once." He did not believe you ever got used to it. The weariness of such a life got worse as you got older. What sort of trade was it in which more than half your time you did not put your foot inside your house? Directly you got out to sea you had no means of knowing what went on at home. One might have thought him weary of distant voyages; and the longest he had ever made had lasted a fortnight, of which the most part had been spent at anchor, sheltering from the weather. As soon as his wife had inherited a house and enough to live on (from a bachelor uncle who had made some money in the coal business) he threw up his command of an East-coast collier with a feeling as though he had escaped from the galleys. After all these years he might have counted on the fingers of his two hands all the days he had been out of sight of England.[9] He had never known what it was to be out of soundings. "I have never been further than eighty fathoms from the land" was one of his boasts.

Bessie Carvil heard all these things. In front of their cottage grew an under-sized ash; and on summer afternoons she would bring out a chair on the grass-plot and sit down with her sewing. Captain Hagberd, in his canvas suit, leaned on a spade. He dug every day in his front plot. He turned it over and over several times every year, but was not going to plant anything "just at present."

To Bessie Carvil he would state more explicitly: "Not till our Harry comes home to-morrow." And she had heard this formula of hope so often that it only awakened the vaguest pity in her heart for that hopeful old man.

Everything was put off in that way, and everything was being prepared likewise for to-morrow. There was a boxful of packets of various flower-seeds to choose from, for the front garden. "He will doubtless let you have your say about that, my dear," Captain Hagberd intimated to her across the railing.

Miss Bessie's head remained bowed over her work. She had heard all this so many times. But now and then she would rise, lay down her sewing, and come slowly to the fence. There was a charm in these gentle ravings. He was determined that his son should not go away again for the want of a home all ready for him. He had been filling the other cottage with all sorts of furniture. She imagined it all new, fresh with varnish, piled up as in a warehouse. There would be tables wrapped up in sacking; rolls of carpets thick and vertical like fragments of columns; the gleam of white marble tops in the dimness of the drawn blinds. Captain Hagberd always described his purchases to her carefully, as to a person having a legitimate interest in them The overgrown yard of his cottage could be laid over with concrete . . . after to-morrow.

"We may just as well do away with the fence. You could have your drying-line out, quite clear of your flowers." He winked, and she would blush faintly.

This madness that had entered her life through the kind impulses of her heart had reasonable details. What if some day his son returned? But she could not even be quite sure that he ever had a son; and if he existed anywhere, he had been too long away. When Captain Hagberd got excited in his talk she would steady him by a pretence of belief, laughing a little to salve her conscience.

Only once she had tried pityingly to throw some doubt on that hope doomed to disappointment, but the effect of her attempt had scared her very much. All at once over that man's face there came an expression of horror and incredulity, as though he had seen a crack open out in the firmament.

"You—you—you don't think he's drowned!"

For a moment he seemed to her ready to go out of his mind, for in his ordinary state she thought him more sane than people gave him credit for. On that occasion the violence of the emotion was followed by a most paternal and complacent recovery.

"Don't alarm yourself, my dear," he said a little cunningly. "The sea can't keep him. He does not belong to it. None of us Hagberds ever did belong to it. Look at me; I didn't get drowned. Moreover, he isn't a sailor at all; and if he is not a sailor, he's bound to come back. There's nothing to prevent him coming back. . . ."

His eyes began to wander.

"To-morrow."

She never tried again, for fear the man should go out of his mind on the spot. He depended on her. She seemed the only sensible person in the town; and he would congratulate himself frankly before her face on having secured such a level-headed wife for his son. The rest of the town, he confided to her once, in a fit of temper, was certainly queer. The way they looked at you—the way they talked to you! He had never got on with any one in the place. Didn't like the people. He would not have left his own country if it had not been clear that his son had taken a fancy to Colebrook.

She humoured him in silence, listening patiently by the fence; crocheting with downcast eyes. Blushes came with difficulty on her dead-white complexion, under the negligently twisted opulence of mahogany-coloured hair. Her father was frankly carroty.

She had a full figure; a tired, unrefreshed face. When Captain Hagberd vaunted the necessity and propriety of a home and the delights of one's own fireside, she smiled a little, with her lips only. Her home delights had been confined to the nursing of her father during the ten best years of her life.

A bestial roaring coming out of an upstairs window would interrupt their talk. She would begin at once to roll up her crochet-work or fold her sewing, without the slightest sign of haste. Meanwhile the howls and roars of her name would go on, making the fishermen strolling upon the sea-wall on the other side of the road turn their heads towards the cottages. She would go in slowly at the front door, and a moment after-wards there would fall a profound silence. Presently she would reappear, leading by the hand a man, gross and unwieldy like a hippopotamus, with a bad-tempered, surly face.

He was a widowed boat-builder, whom blindness had over-taken years before in the full flush of business. He behaved to his daughter as if she had been responsible for its incurable character. He had been heard to bellow at the top of his voice, as if to defy Heaven, that he did not care: he had made enough money to have ham and eggs for his breakfast every morning. He thanked God for it, in a fiendish tone as though he were cursing.

Captain Hagberd had been so unfavourably impressed by his tenant that once he told Miss Bessie, "He is a very extravagant fellow, my dear."

She was knitting that day, finishing a pair of socks for her father, who expected her to keep up the supply dutifully. She hated knitting, and, as she was just at the heel part, she had to keep her eyes on her needles.

"Of course it isn't as if he had a son to provide for," Captain Hagberd went on a little vacantly. "Girls, of course, don't require so much—h'm—h'm. They don't run away from home, my dear."

"No," said Miss Bessie, quietly.

Captain Hagberd, amongst the mounds of turned-up earth, chuckled. With his maritime rig, his weather-beaten face, his beard of Father Neptune,[10] he resembled a deposed sea-god who had exchanged the trident for the spade.

"And he must look upon you as already provided for, in a manner. That's the best of it with the girls. The husbands . . ." He winked. Miss Bessie, absorbed in her knitting, coloured faintly.

"Bessie! my hat!" old Carvil bellowed out suddenly. He had been sitting under the tree mute and motionless, like an idol of some remarkably monstrous superstition. He never opened his mouth but to howl for her, at her, sometimes about her; and then he did not moderate the terms of his abuse. Her system

was never to answer him at all; and he kept up his shouting till
he got attended to—till she shook him by the arm, or thrust
the mouthpiece of his pipe between his teeth. He was one of
the few blind people who smoke. When he felt the hat being
put on his head he stopped his noise at once. Then he rose, and
they passed together through the gate.

He weighed heavily on her arm. During their slow, toilful
walks she appeared to be dragging with her for a penance the
burden of that infirm bulk. Usually they crossed the road at
once (the cottages stood in the fields near the harbour, two
hundred yards away from the end of the street), and for a long,
long time they would remain in view, ascending imperceptibly
the flight of wooden steps that led to the top of the sea-wall.
It ran on from east to west, shutting out the Channel like a
neglected railway embankment, on which no train had ever
rolled within memory of man. Groups of sturdy fishermen
would emerge upon the sky, walk along for a bit, and sink
without haste. Their brown nets, like the cobwebs of gigantic
spiders, lay on the shabby grass of the slope; and, looking up
from the end of the street, the people of the town would recognise the two Carvils by the creeping slowness of their gait.
Captain Hagberd, pottering aimlessly about his cottages, would
raise his head to see how they got on in their promenade.

He advertised still in the Sunday papers for Harry Hagberd.
These sheets were read in foreign parts to the end of the world,
he informed Bessie. At the same time he seemed to think that
his son was in England—so near to Colebrook that he would
of course turn up "to-morrow." Bessie, without committing
herself to that opinion in so many words, argued that in that
case the expense of advertising was unnecessary; Captain
Hagberd had better spend that weekly half-crown on himself.
She declared she did not know what he lived on. Her argumen-
tation would puzzle him and cast him down for a time. "They
all do it," he pointed out. There was a whole column devoted
to appeals after missing relatives. He would bring the news-
paper to show her. He and his wife had advertised for years;
only she was an impatient woman. The news from Colebrook
had arrived the very day after her funeral; if she had not been

so impatient she might have been here now, with no more
than one day more to wait. "You are not an impatient woman,
my dear."

"I've no patience with you sometimes," she would say.

If he still advertised for his son he did not offer rewards
for information any more; for, with the muddled lucidity of
a mental derangement, he had reasoned himself into a conviction as clear as day-light that he had already attained all that
could be expected in that way. What more could he want?
Colebrook was the place, and there was no need to ask for
more. Miss Carvil praised him for his good sense, and he was
soothed by the part she took in his hope, which had become
his delusion; in that idea which blinded his mind to truth and
probability, just as the other old man in the other cottage had
been made blind, by another disease, to the light and beauty of
the world.

But anything he could interpret as a doubt—any coldness of
assent, or even a simple inattention to the development of his
projects of a home with his returned son and his son's wife—
would irritate him into flings and jerks and wicked side-glances.
He would dash his spade into the ground and walk to and fro
before it. Miss Bessie called it his tantrums. She shook her finger
at him. Then, when she came out again, after he had parted
with her in anger, he would watch out of the corner of his eyes
for the least sign of encouragement to approach the iron railings
and resume his fatherly and patronising relations.

For all their intimacy, which had lasted some years now, they
had never talked without a fence or a railing between them.
He described to her all the splendours accumulated for the
setting-up of their housekeeping, but had never invited her to
an inspection. No human eye was to behold them till Harry
had his first look. In fact, nobody had ever been inside his
cottage; he did his own housework, and he guarded his son's
privilege so jealously that the small objects of domestic use he
bought sometimes in the town were smuggled rapidly across
the front garden under his canvas coat. Then, coming out,
he would remark apologetically, "It was only a small kettle,
my dear."

And, if not too tired with her drudgery, or worried beyond endurance by her father, she would laugh at him with a blush, and say: "That's all right, Captain Hagberd; I am not impatient."

"Well, my dear, you haven't long to wait now," he would answer with a sudden bashfulness, and looking uneasily, as though he had suspected that there was something wrong somewhere.

Every Monday she paid him his rent over the railings. He clutched the shillings greedily. He grudged every penny he had to spend on his maintenance, and when he left her to make his purchases his bearing changed as soon as he got into the street. Away from the sanction of her pity, he felt himself exposed without defence. He brushed the walls with his shoulder. He mistrusted the queerness of the people; yet, by then, even the town children had left off calling after him, and the tradesmen served him without a word. The slightest allusion to his clothing had the power to puzzle and frighten especially, as if it were something utterly unwarranted and incomprehensible.

In the autumn, the driving rain drummed on his sail-cloth suit saturated almost to the stiffness of sheet-iron, with its surface flowing with water. When the weather was too bad, he retreated under the tiny porch, and, standing close against the door, looked at his spade left planted in the middle of the yard. The ground was so much dug up all over, that as the season advanced it turned to a quagmire. When it froze hard, he was disconsolate. What would Harry say? And as he could not have so much of Bessie's company at that time of the year, the roars of old Carvil, that came muffled through the closed windows, calling her indoors, exasperated him greatly.

"Why don't that extravagant fellow get you a servant?" he asked impatiently one mild afternoon. She had thrown something over her head to run out for a while.

"I don't know," said the pale Bessie, wearily, staring away with her heavy-lidded, grey, and unexpectant glance. There were always smudgy shadows under her eyes, and she did not seem able to see any change or any end to her life.

"You wait till you get married, my dear," said her only friend, drawing closer to the fence. "Harry will get you one."

His hopeful craze seemed to mock her own want of hope
with so bitter an aptness that in her nervous irritation she
could have screamed at him outright. But she only said in
self-mockery, and speaking to him as though he had been sane,
"Why, Captain Hagberd, your son may not even want to
look at me."

He flung his head back and laughed his throaty affected
cackle of anger.

"What! That boy? Not want to look at the only sensible girl
for miles around? What do you think I am here for, my dear—
my dear—my dear? . . . What? You wait. You just wait. You'll
see to-morrow. I'll soon——"

"Bessie! Bessie! Bessie!" howled old Carvil inside. "Bessie!—
my pipe!" That fat blind man had given himself up to a very
lust of laziness. He would not lift his hand to reach for the
things she took care to leave at his very elbow. He would not
move a limb; he would not rise from his chair; he would not put
one foot before another, in that parlour (where he knew his
way as well as if he had his sight), without calling her to his
side and hanging all his atrocious weight on her shoulder. He
would not eat one single mouthful of food without her close
attendance. He had made himself helpless beyond his affliction,
to enslave her better. She stood still for a moment, setting her
teeth in the dusk, then turned and walked slowly indoors.

Captain Hagberd went back to his spade. The shouting in
Carvil's cottage stopped, and after a while the window of the
parlour downstairs was lit up. A man coming from the end of
the street with a firm leisurely step passed on, but seemed to
have caught sight of Captain Hagberd, because he turned back
a pace or two. A cold white light lingered in the western sky.
The man leaned over the gate in an interested manner.

"You must be Captain Hagberd," he said, with easy
assurance.

The old man spun round, pulling out his spade, startled by
the strange voice.

"Yes, I am," he answered nervously.

The other, smiling straight at him, uttered very slowly:
"You've been advertising for your son, I believe?"

"My son Harry," mumbled Captain Hagberd, off his guard for once. "He's coming home to-morrow."

"The devil he is!" The stranger marvelled greatly, and then went on, with only a slight change of tone: "You've grown a beard like Father Christmas himself."

Captain Hagberd drew a little nearer, and leaned forward over his spade. "Go your way," he said, resentfully and timidly at the same time, because he was always afraid of being laughed at. Every mental state, even madness, has its equilibrium based upon self-esteem. Its disturbance causes unhappiness; and Captain Hagberd lived amongst a scheme of settled notions which it pained him to feel disturbed by people's grins. Yes, people's grins were awful. They hinted at something wrong: but what? He could not tell; and that stranger was obviously grinning—had come on purpose to grin. It was bad enough on the streets, but he had never before been outraged like this.

The stranger, unaware how near he was of having his head laid open with a spade, said seriously: "I am not trespassing where I stand, am I? I fancy there's something wrong about your news. Suppose you let me come in."

"*You* come in!" murmured old Hagberd, with inexpressible horror.

"I could give you some real information about your son—the very latest tip, if you care to hear."

"No," shouted Hagberd. He began to pace wildly to and fro, he shouldered his spade, he gesticulated with his other arm. "Here's a fellow—a grinning fellow, who says there's something wrong. I've got more information than you're aware of. I've all the information I want. I've had it for years—for years—for years—enough to last me till to-morrow. Let you come in, indeed! What would Harry say?"

Bessie Carvil's figure appeared in black silhouette on the parlour window; then, with the sound of an opening door, flitted out before the other cottage, all black, but with something white over her head. These two voices beginning to talk suddenly outside (she had heard them indoors) had given her such an emotion that she could not utter a sound.

Captain Hagberd seemed to be trying to find his way out of

a cage. His feet squelched in the puddles left by his industry. He stumbled in the holes of the ruined grass-plot. He ran blindly against the fence.

"Here, steady a bit!" said the man at the gate, gravely stretching his arm over and catching him by the sleeve. "Somebody's been trying to get at you. Hallo! what's this rig you've got on? Storm canvas, by George!" He had a big laugh. "Well, you *are* a character!"

Captain Hagberd jerked himself free, and began to back away shrinkingly. "For the present," he muttered, in a crestfallen tone.

"What's the matter with him?" The stranger addressed Bessie with the utmost familiarity, in a deliberate, explanatory tone. "I didn't want to startle the old man." He lowered his voice as though he had known her for years. "I dropped into a barber's on my way, to get a twopenny shave, and they told me there he was something of a character. The old man has been a character all his life."

Captain Hagberd, daunted by the allusion to his clothing, had retreated inside, taking his spade with him; and the two at the gate, startled by the unexpected slamming of the door, heard the bolts being shot, the snapping of the lock, and the echo of an affected gurgling laugh within.

"I didn't want to upset him," the man said, after a short silence. "What's the meaning of all this? He isn't quite crazy."

"He has been worrying a long time about his lost son," said Bessie, in a low apologetic tone.

"Well, I am his son."

"Harry!" she cried—and was profoundly silent.

"Know my name? Friends with the old man, eh?"

"He's our landlord," Bessie faltered out, catching hold of the iron railing.

"Owns both them rabbit-hutches, does he?" commented young Hagberd, scornfully. "Just the thing he would be proud of. Can you tell me who's that chap coming to-morrow? You must know something of it. I tell you, it's a swindle on the old man—nothing else."

She did not answer, helpless before an insurmountable

difficulty, appalled before the necessity, the impossibility and
the dread of an explanation in which she and madness seemed
involved together.

"Oh—I am so sorry," she murmured.

"What's the matter?" he said, with serenity. "You needn't
be afraid of upsetting me. It's the other fellow that'll be upset
when he least expects it. I don't care a hang; but there will be
some fun when he shows his mug to-morrow. I don't care *that*
for the old man's pieces, but right is right. You shall see me put
a head on that coon[11]—whoever he is!"

He had come nearer, and towered above her on the other
side of the railings. He glanced at her hands. He fancied she
was trembling, and it occurred to him that she had her part
perhaps in that little game that was to be sprung on his old man
to-morrow. He had come just in time to spoil their sport. He
was entertained by the idea—scornful of the baffled plot. But all
his life he had been full of indulgence for all sorts of women's
tricks. She really was trembling very much; her wrap had slipped
off her head. "Poor devil!" he thought. "Never mind about
that chap. I daresay he'll change his mind before to-morrow.
But what about me? I can't loaf about the gate till the morning."

She burst out: "It is *you*—you yourself that he's waiting for.
It is *you* who come to-morrow."

He murmured "Oh! It's me!" blankly, and they seemed to
become breathless together. Apparently he was pondering over
what he had heard; then, without irritation, but evidently perplexed, he said: "I don't understand. I hadn't written or anything. It's my chum who saw the paper and told me—this very
morning. . . . Eh? what?"

He bent his ear; she whispered rapidly, and he listened for a
while, muttering the words "yes" and "I see" at times. Then,
"But why won't to-day do?" he queried at last.

"You didn't understand me!" she exclaimed, impatiently.
The clear streak of light under the clouds died out in the west.
Again he stooped slightly to hear better; and the deep night
buried everything of the whispering woman and the attentive
man, except the familiar contiguity of their faces, with its air
of secrecy and caress.

He squared his shoulders; the broad-brimmed shadow of a hat sat cavalierly on his head. "Awkward this, eh?" he appealed to her. "To-morrow? Well, well! Never heard tell of anything like this. It's all to-morrow, then, without any sort of to-day, as far as I can see."

She remained still and mute.

"And you have been encouraging this funny notion," he said.

"I never contradicted him."

"Why didn't you?"

"What for should I?" she defended herself. "It would only have made him miserable. He would have gone out of his mind."

"His mind!" he muttered, and heard a short nervous laugh from her.

"Where was the harm? Was I to quarrel with the poor old man? It was easier to half believe it myself."

"Aye, aye," he meditated, intelligently. "I suppose the old chap got around you somehow with his soft talk. You are good-hearted."

Her hands moved up in the dark nervously. "And it might have been true. It was true. It has come. Here it is. This is the to-morrow we have been waiting for."

She drew a breath, and he said, good-humouredly: "Aye, with the door shut. I wouldn't care if . . . And you think he could be brought round to recognise me . . . Eh? What? . . . You could do it? In a week you say? H'm, I daresay you could— but do you think I could hold out a week in this dead-alive place? Not me! I want either hard work, or an all-fired racket, or more space than there is in the whole of England. I have been in this place, though, once before, and for more than a week. The old man was advertising for me then, and a chum I had with me had a notion of getting a couple of quid out of him by writing a lot of silly nonsense in a letter. That lark did not come off, though. We had to clear out—and none too soon. But this time I've a chum waiting for me in London, and besides . . ."

Bessie Carvil was breathing quickly.

"What if I tried a knock at the door?" he suggested.

"Try," she said.

Captain Hagberd's gate squeaked, and the shadow of the son moved on, then stopped with another deep laugh in the throat, like the father's, only soft and gentle, thrilling to the woman's heart, awakening to her ears.

"He isn't frisky—is he? I would be afraid to lay hold of him. The chaps are always telling me I don't know my own strength."

"He's the most harmless creature that ever lived," she interrupted.

"You wouldn't say so if you had seen him chasing me upstairs with a hard leather strap," he said. "I haven't forgotten it in sixteen years."

She got warm from head to foot under another soft, subdued laugh. At the rat-tat-tat of the knocker her heart flew into her mouth.

"Hey, dad! Let me in. I am Harry, I am. Straight! Come back home a day too soon."

One of the windows upstairs ran up.

"A grinning information fellow," said the voice of old Hagberd, up in the darkness. "Don't you have anything to do with him. It will spoil everything."

She heard Harry Hagberd say, "Hallo, dad," then a clanging clatter. The window rumbled down, and he stood before her again.

"It's just like old times. Nearly walloped the life out of me to stop me going away, and now I come back he throws a confounded shovel at my head to keep me out. It grazed my shoulder."

She shuddered.

"I wouldn't care," he began, "only I spent my last shillings on the railway fare and my last twopence on a shave—out of respect for the old man."

"Are you really Harry Hagberd?" she asked swiftly. "Can you prove it?"

"Can I prove it? Can any one else prove it?" he said jovially. "Prove with what? What do I want to prove? There isn't a single corner in the world, barring England, perhaps, where you could not find some man, or more likely a woman, that would remember me for Harry Hagberd. I am more like Harry

Hagberd than any man alive; and I can prove it to you in a minute, if you will let me step inside your gate."

"Come in," she said.

He entered then the front garden of the Carvils. His tall shadow strode with a swagger; she turned her back on the window and waited, watching the shape, of which the footfalls seemed the most material part. The light fell on a tilted hat; a powerful shoulder that seemed to cleave the darkness; on a leg stepping out. He swung about and stood still, facing the illuminated parlour window at her back, turning his head from side to side, laughing softly to himself.

"Just fancy, for a minute, the old man's beard stuck on to my chin. Hey? Now say. I was the very spit of him from a boy."

"It's true," she murmured to herself.

"And that's about as far as it goes. He was always one of your domestic characters. Why, I remember how he used to go about looking very sick for three days before he had to leave home on one of his trips to South Shields[12] for coal. He had a standing charter from the gas-works. You would think he was off on a whaling cruise—three years and a tail. Ha, ha! Not a bit of it. Ten days on the outside. The *Skimmer of the Seas*[13] was a smart craft. Fine name, wasn't it? Mother's uncle owned her. . . ."

He interrupted himself, and in a lowered voice, "Did he ever tell you what mother died of?" he asked.

"Yes," said Miss Bessie, bitterly: "from impatience."

He made no sound for a while; then brusquely: "They were so afraid I would turn out badly that they fairly drove me away. Mother nagged at me for being idle, and the old man said he would cut my soul out of my body rather than let me go to sea.[14] Well, it looked as if he would do it too—so I went. It looks to me sometimes as if I had been born to them by a mistake—in that other hutch of a house."

"Where ought you to have been born by rights?" Bessie Carvil interrupted him, defiantly.

"In the open, upon a beach, on a windy night," he said, quick as lightning. Then he mused slowly. "They were characters, both of them, by George; and the old man keeps it up well—

don't he? A damned shovel on the—— Hark! who's that making that row? 'Bessie, Bessie.' It's in your house."

"It's for me," she said with indifference.

He stepped aside, out of the streak of light. "Your husband?" he inquired, with the tone of a man accustomed to unlawful trysts. "Fine voice for a ship's deck in a thundering squall."

"No; my father. I am not married."

"You seem a fine girl, Miss Bessie, dear," he said at once. She turned her face away.

"Oh, I say, what's up? Who's murdering him?"

"He wants his tea."[15] She faced him, still and tall, with averted head, with her hands hanging clasped before her.

"Hadn't you better go in?" he suggested, after watching for a while the nape of her neck, a patch of dazzling white skin and soft shadow above the sombre line of her shoulders. Her wrap had slipped down to her elbows. "You'll have all the town coming out presently. I'll wait here a bit."

Her wrap fell to the ground, and he stooped to pick it up; she had vanished. He threw it over his arm, and approaching the window squarely he saw a monstrous form of a fat man in an arm-chair, an unshaded lamp, the yawning of an enormous mouth in a big flat face encircled by a ragged halo of hair, Miss Bessie's head and bust. The shouting stopped; the blind ran down. He lost himself in thinking how awkward it was. Father mad; no getting into the house. No money to get back; a hungry chum in London who would begin to think he had been given the go-by. "Damn!" he muttered. He could break the door in, certainly; but they would perhaps bundle him into chokey for that without asking questions—no great matter, only he was confoundedly afraid of being locked up,[16] even in mistake. He turned cold at the thought. He stamped his feet on the sodden grass.

"What are you? A sailor?" said an agitated voice.

She had flitted out, a shadow herself, attracted by the reckless shadow waiting under the wall of her home.

"Anything. Enough of a sailor to be worth my salt before the mast. Came home that way this time."

"Where do you come from?" she asked.

"Right away from a jolly good spree," he said, "by the London train—see? Ough! I hate being shut up in a train. I don't mind a house so much."

"Ah," she said, "that's lucky."

"Because in a house you can at any time open the blamed door and walk away straight before you."

"And never come back?"

"Not for sixteen years at least," he laughed. "To a rabbit-hutch, and get a confounded old shovel . . ."

"A ship is not so very big," she taunted.

"No, but the sea is great."

She dropped her head, and as if her ears had been opened to the voices of the world, she heard, beyond the rampart of sea-wall, the swell of yesterday's gale breaking on the beach with monotonous and solemn vibrations, as if all the earth had been a tolling bell.

"And then, why, a ship's a ship. You love her and leave her; and a voyage isn't a marriage." He quoted the sailor's saying lightly.

"It is not a marriage," she whispered.

"I never took a false name, and I've never yet told a lie to a woman. What lie? Why, *the* lie——. Take me or leave me, I say: and if you take me, then it is . . ." He hummed a snatch very low, leaning against the wall.

> Oh, ho, ho Rio!
> And fare thee well,
> My bonnie young girl,
> We're bound to Rio Grande.

"Capstan song,"[17] he explained. Her teeth chattered.

"You are cold," he said. "Here's that affair of yours I picked up." She felt his hands about her, wrapping her closely. "Hold the ends together in front," he commanded.

"What did you come here for?" she asked, repressing a shudder.

"Five quid," he answered, promptly. "We let our spree go on a little too long and got hard up."

"You've been drinking?" she said.

"Blind three days; on purpose. I am not given that way—
don't you think. There's nothing and nobody that can get over
me unless I like. I can be as steady as a rock. My chum sees the
paper this morning, and says he to me: 'Go on, Harry: loving
parent. That's five quid sure.' So we scraped all our pockets for
the fare. Devil of a lark!"

"You have a hard heart, I am afraid," she sighed.

"What for? For running away? Why! he wanted to make
a lawyer's clerk of me—just to please himself. Master in his
own house; and my poor mother egged him on—for my
good, I suppose. Well, then—so long; and I went. No, I tell
you: the day I cleared out, I was all black and blue from his
great fondness for me. Ah! he was always a bit of a character.
Look at that shovel now. Off his chump? Not much. That's just
exactly like my dad. He wants me here just to have somebody to
order about. However, we two were hard up; and what's five
quid to him—once in sixteen hard years?"

"Oh, but I am sorry for you. Did you never want to come
back home?"

"Be a lawyer's clerk and rot here—in some such place as
this?" he cried in contempt. "What! if the old man set me up
in a home to-day, I would kick it down about my ears—or else
die there before the third day was out."

"And where else is it that you hope to die?"

"In the bush somewhere; in the sea; on a blamed mountain-
top for choice. At home? Yes! the world's my home; but I
expect I'll die in a hospital some day. What of that? Any place
is good enough, as long as I've lived; and I've been everything
you can think of almost but a tailor or a soldier. I've been a
boundary rider;[18] I've sheared sheep; and humped my swag;
and harpooned a whale. I've rigged ships, and prospected for
gold, and skinned dead bullocks—and turned my back on more
money than the old man would have scraped in his whole life.
Ha, ha!"

He overwhelmed her. She pulled herself together and managed to utter, "Time to rest now."

He straightened himself up, away from the wall, and in a severe voice said, "Time to go."

But he did not move. He leaned back again, and hummed thoughtfully a bar or two of an outlandish tune.

She felt as if she were about to cry. "That's another of your cruel songs," she said.

"Learned it in Mexico—in Sonora."[19] He talked easily. "It is the song of the Gambusinos.[20] You don't know? The song of restless men. Nothing could hold them in one place—not even a woman. You used to meet one of them now and again, in the old days, on the edge of the gold country, away north there beyond the Rio Gila. I've seen it. A prospecting engineer in Mazatlan[21] took me along with him to help look after the waggons. A sailor's a handy chap to have about you anyhow. It's all a desert: cracks in the earth that you can't see the bottom of; and mountains—sheer rocks standing up high like walls and church spires, only a hundred times bigger. The valleys are full of boulders and black stones. There's not a blade of grass to see; and the sun sets more red over that country than I have seen it anywhere—blood-red and angry. It *is* fine."

"You do not want to go back there again?" she stammered out.

He laughed a little. "No. That's the blamed gold country. It gave me the shivers sometimes to look at it—and we were a big lot of men together, mind; but these Gambusinos wandered alone. They knew that country before anybody had ever heard of it. They had a sort of gift for prospecting, and the fever of it was on them too; and they did not seem to want the gold very much. They would find some rich spot, and then turn their backs on it; pick up perhaps a little—enough for a spree—and then be off again, looking for more. They never stopped long where there were houses; they had no wife, no chick, no home, never a chum. You couldn't be friends with a Gambusino; they were too restless—here to-day, and gone, God knows where, to-morrow. They told no one of their finds, and there has never been a Gambusino well off. It was not for the gold they cared; it was the wandering about looking for it in the stony country that got into them and wouldn't let them rest; so that no woman yet born could hold a Gambusino for more than a week. That's what the song says. It's all about a pretty girl that tried hard to keep hold of a Gambusino lover, so that he should bring her lots of gold. No fear! Off he went, and she never saw him again."

"What became of her?" she breathed out.

"The song don't tell. Cried a bit, I daresay. They were the fellows: kiss and go. But it's the looking for a thing—a something . . . Sometimes I think I am a sort of Gambusino myself."

"No woman can hold you, then," she began in a brazen voice, which quavered suddenly before the end.

"No longer than a week," he joked, playing upon her very heartstrings with the gay, tender note of his laugh, "and yet I am fond of them all. Anything for a woman of the right sort. The scrapes they got me into, and the scrapes they got me out of! I love them at first sight. I've fallen in love with you already, Miss—Bessie's your name—eh?"

She backed away a little, and with a trembling laugh: "You haven't seen my face yet."

He bent forward gallantly. "A little pale: it suits some. But you are a fine figure of a girl, Miss Bessie."

She was all in a flutter. Nobody had ever said so much to her before.

His tone changed. "I am getting middling hungry, though. Had no breakfast to-day. Couldn't you scare up some bread from that tea for me, or——"

She was gone already. He had been on the point of asking her to let him come inside. No matter. Anywhere would do. Devil of a fix! What would his chum think?

"I didn't ask you as a beggar," he said, jestingly, taking a piece of bread-and-butter from the plate she held before him. "I asked as a friend. My dad is rich, you know."

"He starves himself for your sake."

"And I have starved for his whim," he said, taking up another piece.

"All he has in the world is for you," she pleaded.

"Yes, if I come here to sit on it like a dam' toad in a hole. Thank you; and what about the shovel, eh? He always had a queer way of showing his love."

"I could bring him round in a week," she suggested timidly.

He was too hungry to answer her; and, holding the plate submissively to his hand, she began to whisper up to him in a quick, panting voice. He listened, amazed, eating slower and slower, till at last his jaws stopped altogether. "That's his game, is it?" he said, in a rising tone of scathing contempt. An ungovernable movement of his arm sent the plate flying out of her fingers. He shot out a violent curse.

She shrank from him, putting her hand against the wall.

"No!" he raged. "He expects! Expects *me*—for his rotten money! ... Who wants his home? Mad—not he! Don't you think? He wants his own way. He wanted to turn me into a miserable lawyer's clerk, and now he wants to make of me a blamed tame rabbit in a cage. Of me! Of me!" His subdued angry laugh frightened her now.

"The whole world ain't a bit too big for me to spread my elbows in, I can tell you—what's your name—Bessie—let alone a dam' parlour in a hutch. Marry! He wants me to marry and settle! And as likely as not he has looked out the girl too—dash my soul! And do you know the Judy,[22] may I ask?"

She shook all over with noiseless dry sobs; but he was fuming and fretting too much to notice her distress. He bit his thumb with rage at the mere idea. A window rattled up.

"A grinning information fellow," pronounced old Hagberd dogmatically, in measured tones. And the sound of his voice seemed to Bessie to make the night itself mad—to pour insanity and disaster on the earth. "Now I know what's wrong with the people here, my dear. Why, of course! With this mad chap going about. Don't you have anything to do with him, Bessie. Bessie, I say!"

They stood as if dumb. The old man fidgeted and mumbled to himself at the window. Suddenly he cried, piercingly: "Bessie— I see you. I'll tell Harry."

She made a movement as if to run away, but stopped and

raised her hands to her temples. Young Hagberd, shadowy and big, stirred no more than a man of bronze. Over their heads the crazy night whimpered and scolded in an old man's voice.

"Send him away, my dear. He's only a vagabond. What you want is a good home of your own. That chap has no home— he's not like Harry. He can't be Harry. Harry is coming to-morrow. Do you hear? One day more,"[23] he babbled more excitedly. "Never you fear—Harry shall marry you."

His voice rose very shrill and mad against the regular deep soughing of the swell coiling heavily about the outer face of the sea-wall.

"He will have to. I shall make him, or if not"—he swore a great oath—"I'll cut him off with a shilling to-morrow, and leave everything to you. I shall. To you. Let him starve."

The window rattled down.

Harry drew a deep breath, and took one step towards Bessie. "So it's you—the girl," he said, in a lowered voice. She had not moved, and she remained half turned away from him, pressing her head in the palms of her hands. "My word!" he continued, with an invisible half-smile on his lips. "I have a great mind to stop. . . ."

Her elbows were trembling violently.

"For a week," he finished without a pause.

She clapped her hands to her face.

He came up quite close, and took hold of her wrists gently. She felt his breath on her ear.

"It's a scrape I am in—this, and it is you that must see me through." He was trying to uncover her face. She resisted. He let her go then, and stepping back a little, "Have you got any money?" he asked. "I must be off now."

She nodded quickly her shamefaced head, and he waited, looking away from her, while, trembling all over and bowing her neck, she tried to find the pocket of her dress.

"Here it is!" she whispered. "Oh, go away! Go away for God's sake! If I had more—more—I would give it all to forget—to make you forget."

He extended his hand. "No fear! I haven't forgotten a single one of you in the world. Some gave me more than money—but

I am a beggar now—and you women always had to get me out of my scrapes."

He swaggered up to the parlour window, and in the dim light filtering through the blind, looked at the coin lying in his palm. It was a half-sovereign. He slipped it into his pocket. She stood a little on one side, with her head drooping, as if wounded; with her arms hanging passive by her side, as if dead.

"You can't buy me in," he said, "and you can't buy yourself out."

He set his hat firmly with a little tap, and next moment she felt herself lifted up in the powerful embrace of his arms. Her feet lost the ground; her head hung back; he showered kisses on her face with a silent and overmastering ardour, as if in haste to get at her very soul. He kissed her pale cheeks, her hard forehead, her heavy eyelids, her faded lips; and the measured blows and sighs of the rising tide accompanied the enfolding power of his arms, the overwhelming might of his caresses. It was as if the sea, breaking down the wall protecting all the homes of the town, had sent a wave over her head. It passed on; she staggered backwards, with her shoulders against the wall, exhausted, as if she had been stranded there after a storm and a shipwreck.

She opened her eyes after a while; and, listening to the firm, leisurely footsteps going away with their conquest, began to gather her skirts, staring all the time before her. Suddenly she darted through the open gate into the dark and deserted street.

"Stop!" she shouted. "Don't go!"

And listening with an attentive poise of the head, she could not tell whether it was the beat of the swell or his fateful tread that seemed to fall cruelly upon her heart. Presently every sound grew fainter, as though she were slowly turning into stone. A fear of this awful silence came to her—worse than the fear of death. She called upon her ebbing strength for the final appeal:

"Harry!"

Not even the dying echo of a footstep. Nothing. The thundering of the surf, the voice of the restless sea itself, seemed stopped. There was not a sound—no whisper of life, as though she were alone and lost in that stony country of which she had heard, where madmen go looking for gold and spurn the find.

Captain Hagberd, inside his dark house, had kept on the alert. A window ran up; and in the silence of the stony country a voice spoke above her head, high up in the black air—the voice of madness, lies and despair[24]—the voice of inextinguishable hope. "Is he gone yet—that information fellow? Do you hear him about, my dear?"

She burst into tears. "No! no! no! I don't hear him any more," she sobbed.

He began to chuckle up there triumphantly. "You frightened him away. Good girl. Now we shall be all right. Don't you be impatient, my dear. One day more."

In the other house old Carvil, wallowing regally in his armchair, with a globe-lamp burning by his side on the table, yelled for her, in a fiendish voice: "Bessie! Bessie! You, Bessie!"

She heard him at last, and, as if overcome by fate, began to totter silently back towards her stuffy little inferno of a cottage. It had no lofty portal, no terrific inscription of forfeited hopes[25]—she did not understand wherein she had sinned.

Captain Hagberd had gradually worked himself into a state of noisy happiness up there.

"Go in! Keep quiet!" she turned upon him tearfully, from the doorstep below.

He rebelled against her authority in his great joy at having got rid at last of that "something wrong." It was as if all the hopeful madness of the world had broken out to bring terror upon her heart, with the voice of that old man shouting of his trust in an everlasting to-morrow.

Appendix: Author's Note

The main characteristic of this volume consists in this, that all the stories composing it belong not only to the same period but have been written one after another in the order in which they appear in the book.[1]

The period is that which follows on my connection with *Blackwood's Magazine*.[2] I had just finished writing "The End of the Tether"[3] and was casting about for some subject which could be developed in a shorter form than the tales in the volume of *Youth*[4] when the instance of a steamship full of returning coolies from Singapore to some port in northern China occurred to my recollection. Years before I had heard it being talked about in the East as a recent occurrence. It was for us merely one subject of conversation amongst many others of the kind. Men earning their bread in any very specialized occupation will talk shop, not only because it is the most vital interest of their lives but also because they have not much knowledge of other subjects. They have never had the time to get acquainted with them. Life, for most of us, is not so much a hard as an exacting taskmaster.

I never met anybody personally concerned in this affair, the interest of which for us was, of course, not the bad weather but the extraordinary complication brought into the ship's life at a moment of exceptional stress by the human element below her deck. Neither was the story itself ever enlarged upon in my hearing. In that company each of us could imagine easily what the whole thing was like. The financial difficulty of it, presenting also a human problem, was solved by a mind much too simple to be perplexed by anything in the world except men's idle talk for which it was not adapted.

From the first the mere anecdote, the mere statement I might say, that such a thing had happened on the high seas, appeared to me a sufficient subject for meditation. Yet it was but a bit of a sea yarn after all. I felt that to bring out its deeper significance which was quite apparent to me, something other, something more was required: a

leading motive that would harmonize all these violent noises, and a
point of view that would put all that elemental fury into its proper
place.

What was needed of course was Captain MacWhirr.[5] Directly I
perceived him I could see that he was the man for the situation. I don't
mean to say that I ever saw Captain MacWhirr in the flesh, or had ever
come in contact with his literal mind and his dauntless temperament.
MacWhirr is not an acquaintance of a few hours, or a few weeks, or
a few months. He is the product of twenty years of life. My own life.
Conscious invention had little to do with him. If it is true that Captain
MacWhirr never walked and breathed on this earth (which I find for
my part extremely difficult to believe) I can also assure my readers
that he is perfectly authentic. I may venture to assert the same of every
aspect of the story, while I confess that the particular typhoon of the
tale was not a typhoon of my actual experience.

At its first appearance "Typhoon," the story, was classed by some
critics as a deliberately intended storm-piece.[6] Others picked out
MacWhirr, in whom they perceived a definite symbolic intention.
Neither was exclusively my intention. Both the typhoon and Captain
MacWhirr presented themselves to me as the necessities of the deep
conviction with which I approached the subject of the story. It was
their opportunity. It was also my opportunity; and it would be vain
to discourse about what I made of it in a handful of pages, since the
pages themselves are here, between the covers of this volume, to speak
for themselves.

This is a belated reflection. If it had occurred to me before it would
have perhaps done away with the existence of this Author's Note;
for, indeed, the same remark applies to every story in this volume.
None of them are stories of experience in the absolute sense of the
word. Experience in them is but the canvas of the attempted picture.
Each of them has its more than one intention. With each the question
is what the writer has done with his opportunity; and each answers
the question for itself in words which, if I may say so without undue
solemnity, were written with a conscientious regard for the truth of
my own sensations. And each of those stories, to mean something,
must justify itself in its own way to the conscience of each successive
reader.

"Falk" – the second story in the volume – offended the delicacy of
one critic[7] at least by certain peculiarities of its subject. But what is
the subject of "Falk"? I personally do not feel so very certain about
it. He who reads must find out for himself. My intention in writing
"Falk" was not to shock anybody. As in most of my writings I insist

not on the events but on their effect upon the persons in the tale. But in everything I have written there is always one invariable intention, and that is to capture the reader's attention, by securing his interest and enlisting his sympathies for the matter in hand, whatever it may be, within the limits of the visible world and within the boundaries of human emotions.

I may safely say that Falk is absolutely true to my experience of certain straightforward characters combining a perfectly natural ruthlessness with a certain amount of moral delicacy. Falk obeys the law of self-preservation without the slightest misgivings as to his right, but at a crucial turn of that ruthlessly preserved life he will not condescend to dodge the truth. As he is presented as sensitive enough to be affected permanently by a certain unusual experience, that experience had to be set by me before the reader vividly; but it is not the subject of the tale. If we go by mere facts then the subject is Falk's attempt to get married; in which the narrator of the tale finds himself unexpectedly involved both on its ruthless and its delicate side.

"Falk" shares with one other of my stories ("The Return" in the *Tales of Unrest* volume) the distinction of never having been serialized. I think the copy was shown to the editor of some magazine who rejected it indignantly on the sole ground that "the girl never says anything." This is perfectly true. From first to last Hermann's niece utters no word in the tale – and it is not because she is dumb, but for the simple reason that whenever she happens to come under the observation of the narrator she has either no occasion or is too profoundly moved to speak.[8] The editor, who obviously had read the story, might have perceived that for himself. Apparently he did not, and I refrained from pointing out the impossibility to him because, since he did not venture to say that "the girl" did not live, I felt no concern at his indignation.

All the other stories were serialized. "Typhoon" appeared in the early numbers of the *Pall Mall Magazine*, then under the direction of the late Mr. Halkett.[9] It was on that occasion, too, that I saw for the first time my conceptions rendered by an artist in another medium. Mr. Maurice Grieffenhagen[10] knew how to combine in his illustrations the effect of his own most distinguished personal vision with an absolute fidelity to the inspiration of the writer. "Amy Foster" was published in *The Illustrated London News* with a fine drawing of Amy on her day out giving tea to the children at her home, in a hat with a big feather. "To-morrow" appeared first in the *Pall Mall Magazine*. Of that story I will only say that it struck many people by its adaptability to the stage and that I was induced to dramatize it under the title

of *One Day More*; up to the present my only effort in that direction.[11]
I may also add that each of the four stories on their appearance
in book form was picked out on various grounds as the "best of
the lot" by different critics, who reviewed the volume with a warmth
of appreciation and understanding, a sympathetic insight and a
friendliness of expression for which I cannot be sufficiently grateful.

J. C.

1919.

NOTES

1. *written ... book*: Conrad, in fact, wrote 'Falk' (January–May
    1901) before 'Amy Foster' (May–June 1901).
2. *Blackwood's Magazine*: Familiarly called 'Maga', the wide cir-
    culation magazine (established 1817) published fiction as well
    as articles on current events and general topics. Conrad first
    appeared in it with 'Karain: A Memory' (1897). The monthly
    also serialized his 'Youth, A Narrative' (1898), 'The Heart of
    Darkness' (1899), *Lord Jim* (1899–1900) and 'The End of the
    Tether' (1902).
3. *finished ... Tether*: Conrad, in fact, composed 'The End of the
    Tether' between March and mid-October 1902, *after* he had
    written all the stories in this volume. He completed 'Typhoon'
    between September 1900 and January 1901, and then went
    on to write 'Falk' and 'Amy Foster' (see note 1), finishing 'To-
    morrow' in January 1902.
4. *shorter form ... Youth*: The volume *Youth: A Narrative and Two
    Other Stories* (1902). It includes 'Heart of Darkness' and 'The End
    of the Tether', both of novella length; 'Typhoon' and 'Falk' are
    both somewhat shorter but not markedly so.
5. *Captain MacWhirr*: See 'Typhoon', note 1.
6. *storm-piece*: ' "Typhoon" is the most elaborate storm piece that
    one can recall in English literature', 'The Sea between Covers:
    Mr. Joseph Conrad's New Book', *The Daily Mail*, 22 April 1903,
    p. 4 (rpt. Sherry, ed., 1973, p. 146).
7. *one critic*: In his review in *Bookman*, A. T. Quiller-Couch (1863–
    1944), short-story writer, poet and man of letters wrote ' "Falk"
    is spoilt for me by a natural repugnance, which perhaps has
    nothing to do with criticism', 'Four Tales by Joseph Conrad',
    June 1903, 108–9 (rpt. Sherry 1973, pp. 155–7).

8.   *too ... speak*: A commonplace. Conrad cites it in French to Henry James in a letter of 24 July 1915: 'Quand je suis ému je deviens muet' (*Letters*, vol. V, p. 492).

9.   *Pall Mall Magazine ... Halkett*: Launched in 1893, the *Pall Mall Magazine* contained a medley ranging from serious poetry and fiction to more popular items and photographic essays. George Roland Halkett (1834–1909) edited the monthly from 1901 to 1905.

10. *Grieffenhagen*: Born in London of Danish parents, Maurice William Grieffenhagen (1862–1931), studied at the Royal Academy Schools, becoming a successful magazine and book illustrator during the 1890s, and after 1900 mainly shifting his interest to portraiture and decorative painting.

11. *One Day More ... direction*: Produced with mixed success by the London Stage Society in late June 1905, the play was published in the *English Review* in 1913. Conrad thought the original actors 'awful' (letter to Christopher Sandeman, 27 March 1917, private collection), and in 'The Censor of Plays' (1907) remembered 'the freezing atmosphere of that auditorium ... cold enough to preserve a dead sheep to the end of ages'(*Notes on Life and Letters*, ed. J. H. Stape, Cambridge University Press, 2004, p. 65). Conrad later dramatized *The Secret Agent*, which had a brief London run in November 1922.

Notes

Topics adequately covered in a standard desk dictionary are not glossed here. The Glossary deals with nautical terms. In the notes below, where a place-name has changed since writing, the present-day name is given only on the first occurrence. The Riverside Shakespeare (2nd edition, 1997) is used for quotations from Shakespeare's plays, and biblical quotations are from the King James Bible.

Conrad drew on, and borrowed from, a large number of sources; the notes indicate the most important of these and do not attempt to catalogue all the source materials that he might have used.

Abbreviations

Letters   *The Collected Letters of Joseph Conrad*, ed. Frederick R. Karl and Laurence Davies, with Owen Knowles (vol. VI), J. H. Stape (vol. VII) and Gene M. Moore (vol. VIII), 8 vols. (Cambridge: Cambridge University Press, 1983–).

OED   *The Oxford English Dictionary of the English Language*, 2nd edn (Oxford: Oxford University Press, 1989).

Sherry 1966   Norman Sherry, *Conrad's Eastern World* (Cambridge: Cambridge University Press, 1966).

Sherry 1973   Norman Sherry, ed., *Conrad: The Critical Heritage* (London: Routledge, 1973).

EPIGRAPH

Far . . . hall: From the long poem *Endymion: A Poetic Romance*, III, 866–8 (1818) by the Romantic poet John Keats (1795–1821).

DEDICATION

R. B. Cunninghame Graham: Robert Bontine Cunninghame Graham (1852–1936) and Conrad began an enduring friendship in 1897. A socialist, although according to some scholars the rightful King of Scotland, he represented north-west Lanarkshire in Parliament (1885–92), and was gaoled for a month for his part in the Bloody Sunday demonstration of 1887. Graham worked and travelled widely in South America, drawing on his experiences for tales, sketches, essays and histories of the Spanish conquest.

TYPHOON

1. *Captain MacWhirr*: The name is taken from Captain John McWhir (1858–95), of County Down, under whom Conrad served in 1887 in the *Highland Forest*, an iron barque sailing from Amsterdam to Semarang, Java. Conrad also recollects him as the 'Scotch captain' of Chapter 2 of *Lord Jim.*

2. *Nan-Shan*: The name of a ship with a large contingent of Chinese (some 500) that Conrad had seen in Singapore harbour when serving in the *Vidar* as chief mate (August 1887 to January 1888). Nanshan is a district on the Liaotung Peninsula in north-east China. In Mandarin, the words mean 'south mountain'.

3. *blessed gamp*: 'Blessed' is a commonplace polite euphemism or circumlocution for 'damned', perhaps a response to critics who had complained about salty language in *The Nigger of the 'Narcissus'* (see also note 30). A gamp is a very large, bulgy and loosely tied cotton umbrella, named after Mrs Sarah Gamp, a monthly nurse in Charles Dickens's *Martin Chuzzlewit* (1843–4). The word is no longer current.

4. *Talcahuano*: A Pacific port town in south-central Chile, the outport for the city of Concepción. The port attracted British commercial interests.

5. *Fu-chau*: Fuchau (also Foochow or Foochowfoo; now Fuzhou) was among the original five treaty ports, the others being Canton (now Guanzhou), Amoy (now Xiamen), Ningpo (now Ningbo) and Shanghai. These were provided for by the Anglo-Chinese Treaty of Nanking of August 1842, which restored peaceful relations between China and Great Britain after the First Opium War. Closed to foreign trade, China formally conceded international trade rights through this legal instrument.

6. *Fo-kien*: Present-day Fukien Province, on the Strait of Taiwan.
7. *various tropical colonies*: Presumably British ones, which included the Federated Malay States (Penang, Singapore and the Dindings) and British India, which included Burma.
8. *pigtails*: In Imperial China, the wearing of the pigtail was not a matter of fashion but obligatory. Although living abroad, the coolies here have maintained the custom.
9. *Celestial*: A Chinese person, possibly with some mild humour implied in the usage; from the 'Celestial Empire' with its 'Celestial Emperor', translations into English of the name of the Chinese nation and its paramount leader.
10. *sticks of incense*: Joss sticks, used in invoking the gods' favour as well as in Buddhist rituals and on ancestral altars.
11. *Formosa Channel*: The present-day Strait of Taiwan, the Island of Formosa ('Beautiful Island') being the name given to the island by the Portuguese in the mid-sixteenth century.
12. *Dumbarton*: Like Glasgow, situated on the River Clyde, a great nineteenth-century Scottish industrial town and shipping port.
13. *Siam–Messrs. Sigg and Son*: Siam: the name, until 1939, of the nation now Thailand. The company mentioned here is based on the Swiss firm Jucker & Sigg & Co. of Bangkok, ships' chandlers and dealers in teak, rice and general merchandise, established in 1882 by Albert Jucker (1844–85) in partnership with Henry Sigg. Conrad had dealings with the firm as captain of the *Otago* in 1888. In *Lord Jim*, the firm is recalled as Yucker Brothers and in 'Falk' as Siegers.
14. *little straws*: That is, small things matter, a variation on the idea of 'the straw that breaks the camel's back'. Cf. 'There were little hints then that I did not take, little straws in the wind that I did not see, little incidents the gravity of which I did not realise', Jack London, *John Barleycorn* (1913).
15. *British register . . . Siamese flag*: By law, ships were either 'home' or 'country' registered, the latter being registered in colonial ports; here registration is transferred to another nation, local registry involving savings on port fees. Previously simply red, from 1855 to 1916 the Siamese flag featured a centrally placed white elephant upon a red background. The white elephant, held to be sacred, was and is a royal prerogative.
16. *Noah's Ark elephant*: A topical reference: during the mid- and late-Victorian period, a Noah's Ark replete with various animals carved in wood was a highly popular toy, particularly among

well-to-do families. Owing to their biblical theme, sets were often played with only on Sundays.

17. *International Signal Code-book*: In 1855, Great Britain's Board of Trade replaced and amalgamated earlier signalling regimes with the International Code of Signals (published as *The Commercial Code of Signals for the Use of All Nations* in 1857) as a means of improving and standardizing maritime communication in order to ensure navigational safety. It took some decades to come into universal use.

18. *upside-down*: The hanging of an ensign upside down was one way for a ship to signal that she was in distress and requiring assistance.

19. *Bun Hin*: The most important Chinese ship-owner in Singapore in the 1880s. The name Bun Hin also occurs in *An Outcast of the Islands* (1896), again in connection with the counting of money.

20. *seven-years'-men*: Persons working on contract (in effect, indentured) for seven years, with outward and return passage as part of their terms.

21. *John*: That is, 'John Chinaman', a nickname for a Chinese person or for the Chinese collectively. Its usage ran from the relatively benign to the caricatural or depreciatory. The *OED* dates its first use to 1818.

22. *Teddington*: At the time an independent village on the western bank of the Thames, now a south-western suburb of London, about twelve miles from the capital's centre.

23. *the engineers ... wonders*: 'They that go down to the sea in ships, that do business in great waters; These see the works of the Lord, and his wonders in the deep', Psalm 107:23–4.

24. *Solomon's wisdom*: After King Solomon, a Jewish king (tenth century BC), the son of King David in the Old Testament, and proverbial for his wisdom. The Apocrypha contain a book entitled 'The Wisdom of Solomon'.

25. *black-squad*: The crew assigned to the engine-room – stokers and firemen – whose faces would be smeared with coal.

26. *food, raiment*: 'And having food and raiment let us be therewith content', 1 Timothy 6:8.

27. *battles, famines, and floods*: The phrasing derives from the Litany of the Saints, an antiphonal prayer; the officiating priest intones '*A peste, fame et bello*' (From pestilence, famine and war), to which the congregation responds '*Libera nos, Domine*' (Deliver us, O Lord).

28. *Act of Parliament*: The professionalization of the British Merchant Service dates to the Merchant Shipping Act of 1854, which regulated all aspects of shipboard conduct. Alluded to specifically is the examination system for ranks and certification by the Board of Trade.

29. *season of typhoons*: Typhoons occur off China from May to December. They are rare in the latter month, the vast majority occurring between July and September.

30. *donkey*: A common euphemism for the impolite 'ass'. Others in the story include 'gory' and 'crimson' for 'bloody', and 'curse' and 'condemned' for 'damn' and 'damned', respectively.

31. *West Hartlepool*: At the time a boom town on England's northeast coast. Founded in the mid-nineteenth century, the town was strategically placed, having good access to the sea, to County Durham's coal mines and Yorkshire's iron-ore mines.

32. *go to Jericho*: A phrase used optatively or imperatively to imply the desire to see no more of a person or that one is indifferent to what becomes of him or her.

33. *Melita*: The name of the ship, under the command of Captain G. Moretz, in which Conrad travelled from Singapore to Bangkok on 24–28 January 1888 to take captaincy of the *Otago*, his first and only command.

34. *vial of wrath*: Cf. 'And one of the four beasts gave unto the seven angels seven golden vials full of the wrath of God', Revelation 15:7.

35. *heavens . . . done*: A play on the Latin tag '*Fiat justitia ruat caelum*' (Let justice be done though the heavens fall). Conrad also recalls the phrase at the close of *Heart of Darkness*.

36. *game of nap*: A late-nineteenth-century British trick-taking card game (nap for 'Napoleon') in which players each receive five cards.

37. *Table Bay*: An inlet of the Atlantic Ocean off south-western South Africa that forms Cape Town's harbour.

38. *round . . . millstone*: A commonplace from the New Testament: 'It were better for him that a millstone were hanged about his neck, and he cast into the sea, than that he should offend one of these little ones', Luke 17:2 (see also Matthew 18:6). Cf. Conrad to Austin Harrison, 7 January 1913: 'a novel hangs round my neck like a millstone' (*Letters*, vol. V, p. 161).

39. *created . . . nothing*: An allusion to the theological proposition of creation '*ex nihilo*' (Latin: out of nothing), which posits that God created the Universe from no pre-existent matter.

40. *head in chancery*: A boxing hold that often finishes off one's

opponent. It involves a complex manoeuvre that results in the opponent's head being held in such a way that his unprotected face can be pummelled at will.

41. *black as Tophet*: A synonym for hell. In the Old Testament, Tophet is a place near Jerusalem, in the Valley of Hinnom, associated with the worship of strange gods. The phrase was proverbial. Cf. 'whose sin is as black as Tophet's midnight', Sermon 1726, 17 June 1883, by C. H. Spurgeon (1834–92); 'It's as black as Tophet, here ahead!', *In a Hollow of the Hills* (1895), Chapter 1, by Bret Harte (1836–1902) and 'He's as black as Tophet by birth', *Kingsblood Royal* (1947), Chapter 20, by Sinclair Lewis (1885–1951).

42. *girding the loins*: Proverbial for preparing for a difficult or brave action, derived from 'Gird up now thy loins like a man', Job 38:3.

43. *white devils*: The translation of Chinese racist slang (Cantonese: '*gweilo*') referring to Europeans or persons of European background. A less literal translation is 'foreign devil'.

44. *a Joss*: A Chinese divinity, often a household god, worshipped as an idol.

45. *aneroid glass*: That is, an aneroid barometer, which uses a small, flexible metal box called an aneroid cell. The box is tightly sealed after some air is removed, so that small changes in external air pressure cause the cell to expand or contract. This expansion and contraction drives a series of mechanical levers displayed on the barometer's face.

46. *hair . . . head*: An allusion to the famous story recounted by Cicero that Damocles, one of the courtiers of Dionysius of Syracuse (*c.* 430–367 BC), having extolled the tyrant's good fortune was invited to taste of it and at a banquet looked up to find a sword hanging above his head suspended by a horsehair.

47. *Great Beyond . . . earth*: Possibly a distant echo of 'The undiscover'd country from whose bourn / No traveller returns', Shakespeare, *Hamlet*, III.i.78–9, a phrase Conrad uses several times in his writings (see 'Amy Foster', p. 92). The phrase 'the dust of the earth' occurs ten times in the Bible (three in Genesis).

48. *Foreign Concession*: That is, the territory ceded by China for the use of foreign powers under the terms of the Treaty of Nanking (see note 5).

49. *bummer*: An idler or loafer, American slang derived from the German *Bummler*; a name for frequenters of low taverns and in the United States after the Civil War for army hangers-on.

50. *Linom's*: Lewis, Hyland, & Linom, established in Kent as whole-
     sale and family drapers at Ashford, Folkestone, Hastings, Pluck-
     ley, Ramsgate and Tenterden, were in some locations also ladies'
     outfitters, silk mercers and dealers in home furnishings. Conrad
     patronized the firm (*Letters*, vol. III, pp. 252, 264).

51. *these Johnnies*: That is, 'these fellows', 'Johnnie' being mildly
     contemptuous or humorous for a class of men or an individual.
     Now dated and a conscious archaism.

52. *Taotai*: A provincial official in charge of a district's civil and
     military affairs.

53. *hot*: The typescript and the first edition have 'angry hot'; how-
     ever, it appears that Conrad simply forgot to delete his initial
     inscription when he struck upon 'hot' and that this odd, even
     impossible, phrasing went unnoticed by his typist and was
     also missed by Conrad when he read both the serial and book
     proofs.

54. *worse than Bedlam*: That is, 'worse than a mental institution',
     from a hospice established at the Priory of St Mary of Bethlehem
     in 1247. The word 'Bedlam' (Bethlehem shortened to 'Bethlem'
     and then altered in pronunciation and spelling) in the sense of
     an asylum for the mentally deranged dates to about 1450, the
     OED's first citations being from the early sixteenth century. Cf.
     also: 'they . . . kept up a din and a racket that was worse than
     Bedlam itself', *Innocents Abroad* (1869), Pt 1, Chapter 7, by
     Mark Twain (1835–1910).

AMY FOSTER

1. *Colebrook*: Aside from Brenzett, a real-life village lying in the
    centre of Kent's Romney Marshes, the story's place-names are
    fictional, the area evoked being rural south-west Kent as well as
    the Romney Marshes and Hythe. Darnford, a market town,
    stands in for Canterbury. Conrad had learned from his friend
    and then-collaborator Ford Madox Ford (né Hueffer, 1873–
    1939) of the germ of the story about a castaway in this area (see
    note 8).

2. *Ship Inn*: The real-life Ship Inn, a public house in Dymchurch,
    dates to the fifteenth century and had connections to smuggling.

3. *Martello tower*: A small, circular or ovoid and squat fort erected
    for coastal defence to repel a possible invasion during the Napo-
    leonic Wars. The name comes from an edifice of this type in

Martello, Corsica. More than a hundred such towers stretching along the coast of Sussex, Kent and East Anglia were built from about 1805 to 1812.

4. *dog-cart*: An open vehicle with two transverse seats back to back, the seat at the rear was originally made to shut so as to form a box for dogs.

5. *bronzed*: Not, as might first appear, a Gallicism. The expression was common in the period: for example, 'The sweat burst through the skin of his forehead in tiny beads, and he paused and mopped his bronzed face with his handkerchief', Jack London, *Martin Eden* (1909), Chapter 1, and 'He threw his head back and let the warm sun beat down upon his bronzed face', Edgar Rice Burroughs, *The Mucker* (1914), Chapter 4.

6. *Amy*: Conrad's wife claimed that 'The actual character, Amy Foster, was for many years in our service, and it was her animal-like capacity for sheer uncomplaining endurance that inspired Conrad' (Jessie Conrad, *Joseph Conrad as I Knew Him*, London: Heinemann, 1926, p. 118). To whatever degree this needs to be taken with a grain of salt, the individual Mrs Conrad referred to was Nellie Lyons (1883–1919) of Sturry, Kent, who entered the Conrads' service in 1898 and died in it. She never married. Conrad apparently borrowed the surnames of several of his neighbours for this story, one of whom was a John Foster, aged 44, listed in the 1901 Census as 'Shepherd on farm'. He married Alma (née Paine in 1860 in Sussex) in 1884. She had formerly worked as a domestic servant. See also note 14.

7. *German . . . thought*: Jacobus Albertus Willebrordus Moleschott (1822–93), a Dutch medical doctor, philosopher and physiologist, who taught at Heidelberg, Zurich, Turin and Rome. Moleschott's famous aphorism '*Ohne Phosphor kein Gedanke*' from his *Lehre der Nahrungsmittel* (1850), II.i.4, pithily sums up his belief in the material basis of emotion and thought. Conrad uses the phrase in a letter to Marguerite Poradowska of 16 October [1891] (*Letters*, vol. I, p. 97).

8. *a castaway*: One of the story's original titles (another was 'The Husband'), whose germ came from Conrad's then friend and collaborator Ford Madox Hueffer who recounted the fate of a German castaway on the Kentish coast thus: 'He had nothing, no clothes, no food; he came ashore on a winter's night . . . He knocked at doors, tried to make himself understood. The Marsh people thought him either a lunatic or a supernatural visitor. He got the name of Mad Jack. Knowing nothing of the country,

nothing of the language, he could neither ask his way nor read the names on signposts, and even if he read them, they meant nothing to him', *The Cinque Ports: A Historical and Descriptive Record* (London: Blackwood, 1900), p. 163.

9. *undiscovered country*: See 'Typhoon', note 47.

10. *under the lee*: Having both a physical and immaterial sense: 'in the protection of'. (As a nautical term, it indicates protection from the wind.)

11. *mouth of the Elbe*: The town so situated is Cuxhaven, but, as identified later, the ship's port is clearly Hamburg, a major departure point during the late nineteenth century for emigrants from Eastern Europe to the United States.

12. *no military service to do*: Compulsory military service was a commonplace throughout Europe, Britain being an exception among the Great Powers.

13. *the Vents*: The name of a house, either Postling Vents or The Vents, in the village of Postling, Kent, where the Conrads lived at Pent Farm from October 1898 to September 1907.

14. *Mrs Finn's . . . waggoner . . . Hammond's*: Possible recollections of neighbours at Postling: on the same page of the 1901 Census listing the Conrads at Pent Farm are Daniel Finn, aged 42, a 'carter on farm' and his wife Alice, aged 35, employed as a grocer's shop assistant, living at 71 Lyminge Road. Other neighbours included John C. Hammon, aged 75, and Frederic R. Hammon, aged 42, both graziers. Mrs Charlotte Finn, aged 46, the wife of Isaac Finn, aged 53, an agricultural labourer, resided at 82 Postling Street. The former looked after the Conrads' house and dog during their absence in Montpellier in 1907.

15. *made . . . one step*: A Polonism (*zrobić krok*) or Gallicism (*faire un pas*), idiomatic English requiring, of course, that steps be 'taken'. This phrasing, somewhat varied, also occurs in *An Outcast of the Islands* (1896), 'An Outpost of Progress' (1897), *Lord Jim* (1900) and *The Secret Agent* (1907).

16. *the Carpathians*: A meandering mountain range extending nearly 1,000 miles and traversing Central and Eastern Europe, with the population largely concentrated in agricultural valleys.

17. *Herzogin Sophia-Dorothea*: Literally, the Duchess Sophia-Dorothea. The forenames were traditional ones in the German ruling family, the Hanovers.

18. *Sclavonian . . . Austria*: An alternative spelling for Slavonian, meaning, ethnographically, a Slav. At the time of the story's action, Austria-Hungary included much of present-day southern

Poland and Galicia, the province in which the Tatra Mountains (see note 29) are located.

19. *face of the waters*: Cf. 'And the Spirit of God moved upon the face of the waters', and 'And the waters prevailed, and were increased greatly upon the earth; and the ark went upon the face of the waters', Genesis 1:2 and 7:18.

20. *death . . . fuss*: An echo of the phrase '*La mort sans phrases*' (Death – with no need for discussion), a contemptuous phrase varyingly attributed to the Abbé de Sièyes and to Danton on voting for the death sentence at the trial of Louis XVI. Conrad recalls it in a letter to Henry Arthur Jones of 7 November 1922 (*Letters*, vol. VII, p. 571).

21. *Goethe . . . Dante*: The German Romantic writer Johann Wolfgang von Goethe (1749–1832), author of *Faust*, and Dante Alighieri (1265–1321), author of *La divina commedia* (The Divine Comedy, 1307–21) are representative figures of European culture and humanism. (In context, the aspirations of 'the young ladies of the Rectory' towards learning and gentility are suggested.)

22. *sign of the cross*: A pious gesture, Roman Catholic but retained by the High Anglican Church. In essence a brief prayer, it often introduces and closes longer prayers (here 'Grace before Meals'). In danger, the gesture seeks divine protection or assistance.

23. *Church . . . Chapel*: 'Church' is the established Church of England, whereas 'chapel' designates non-conformist Protestant sects. The former had more social cachet.

24. *Town Clerk*: A public official in charge of the records, correspondence and accounts of the town and who assists in superintending its general business.

25. *slop-made*: That is, ready-made (as opposed to tailored) clothing, and with the secondary meaning of cheap or poor-quality garments.

26. *dinner hour*: That is, the mid-day meal; cf. 'it occurs to me that perhaps it was their dinner hour; it was certainly near twelve', H. G. Wells, *Tono-Bungay* (1908), Book 3, Chapter 3.

27. *tap-room*: Named for having beer on tap, the room favoured by locals and offering cheaper drink than the bar, which was generally patronized by an itinerant clientele.

28. *Yanko*: A dialectical variant of the diminutive Janek, the Polish proper name being Jan (John).

29. *Goorall*: A corruption or attempted Anglicization of the Polish *góral* (highlander), a sheep-keeping and agricultural people of a

highly independent and intensely Roman Catholic character, who emerged as a distinct culture in the Tatra Mountains (part of the Carpathian chain) of southern Poland in around 1600.

30. *Jack-in-the-box*: A once popular mechanical toy for children, known from at least the late seventeenth century, in the form of a music box. Winding caused a tune to be played at the end of which a puppet – a garish 'jack' – would pop up and bob crazily.

31. *cried in a desert*: An echo of a phrase appearing in all four Gospels, announcing the mission of John the Baptist: 'I am the voice of one crying in the wilderness, Make straight the way of the Lord', John 1:23. Cf. also the eighteenth-century hymn 'Redeemer of Israel': 'How long we have wandered as strangers in sin, / And cried in the desert for Thee!'

FALK: A REMINISCENCE

1. *river-hostelry*: Either the Bull Inn, immortalized in Charles Dickens's *Pickwick Papers* (1836–7), at Chatham, or The Lobster Smack Inn at Hole Haven, both connected with Conrad's excursions in G. F. W. Hope's yacht the *Nellie* in 1891. Hope describes the latter's cooking as 'excellent but plain' in 'Friend of Conrad' (*Conrad between the Lines: Documents in a Life*, ed. Gene M. Moore, Allan H. Simmons and J. H. Stape Amsterdam: Rodopi, 2000, p. 43).

2. *"German Ocean"*: The North Sea, derived from the Roman name for this body of water, *Mare Germanicum* or *Oceanus Germanicus*. The name, in common use, appeared on maps until the early twentieth century.

3. *Lower Hope Reach*: A stretch of the Thames about 30 miles from London Bridge. In *The Mirror of the Sea* (1906), Conrad recalls the shore view thus: 'on the slight turn of the Lower Hope Reach, clusters of factory chimneys come distinctly into view, tall and slender above the squat ranges of cement works in Grays and Greenhithe' (Chapter 31).

4. *He who . . . his mouth*: The inflated, even pompous, language recalls the flavour and style of the King James Bible (1611).

5. *night of ages*: Cf. 'Then Greece arose, and to its bards and sages, / In dream, the golden-pinioned Genii came, / Even where they slept amid the night of ages', *The Revolt of Islam* (1818), Canto I, xxxii.1–3, by Percy Bysshe Shelley (1792–1822), and 'The double night of ages, and of her, / Night's daughter, Ignorance,

hath wrapt and wrap / All round us', *Childe Harold's Pilgrimage*, Canto IV (1818), lxxxi.1–3, by Lord Byron (1788–1824).

6. *the River Plate*: The English name for the Rio de la Plata, the muddy estuary of the Paraná and Uruguay Rivers, forming part of the border between Argentina and Uruguay and supporting the capital cities Buenos Aires and Montevideo.

7. *P. & O.*: The Peninsular and Oriental Steam Navigation Company (established 1834), providing service first to the Peninsula (Spain and Portugal), quickly expanded to become the major passenger carrier to India and the Far East.

8. *Arcadia*: In Greek mythology, a utopian garden paradise of serenity and happiness and of pastoral character, enjoying endless summer. It was inhabited by dryads, naiads, satyrs and fauns.

9. *Eastern seaport*: Details identify the location as Bangkok, the capital of Siam (now Thailand), lying about 15 miles inland, the city's access to the sea being the sinuous Chao Phraya River.

10. *toiler . . . sea*: Perhaps a recollection of the title of Victor Hugo's novel *Les Travailleurs de la mer* (1866), translated into English as *The Toilers of the Sea*. Conrad read the book in childhood, and his father translated it into Polish (unpublished).

11. *homely*: In British English, that which is comfortable and suggesting the domestic; the North American equivalent is 'homey', 'homely' meaning unattractive.

12. *Diana . . . Ephesus*: A fertility goddess worshipped throughout Asia Minor. The particular recollection here is of her statue, preserved at Ephesus (now in Turkey), featuring her multiple breasts and wearing a garment of animal heads. The Roman goddess Diana, a goddess associated with the hunt and chastity, is recalled in the phrase two sentences later 'in any sort of chase'.

13. *Bremen*: On the Weser River, Bremen, a major German port city, was and is a significant commercial and industrial centre.

14. *Platt-Deutsch*: Literally, 'flat' or 'low' German, a collective name for those German dialects not High German, and mainly associated with the German spoken in northern Germany.

15. *appointed . . . suddenly*: A biographical detail that has a significant role in the plot of Conrad's *The Shadow-Line* (1916). While in Singapore in January 1888, Conrad, through the port's Harbour Master, was given the command of an Australian-owned barque, the *Otago*, then moored in Bangkok. He made his way there, replacing the ship's captain, who had recently died.

16. *extravagant . . . improper character*: In *The Shadow-Line*,

Conrad similarly imputes a louche aspect and unprofessional conduct to his predecessor, the Scottish-born John Snadden (1837–87). Snadden made his career in Eastern waters, but Conrad's other details are invented, an acquaintance of Snadden going so far as to call them 'absurd' (letter from A. T. Saunders to *The Nautical Magazine*, June 1921, in Sherry 1966, p. 322).

17. *scratch of the pen*: Cf. 'The accounts which you enclosed are no doubt all in order but I have had no means of comparing them with other documents as the late Captain never favored me with the scratch of a pen from the time of leaving Newcastle in August last', Henry Simpson & Sons to Conrad, 5 April 1888 (*A Portrait in Letters: Correspondence to and about Conrad*, ed. J. H. Stape and Owen Knowles, Amsterdam: Rodopi, 1996, p. 3).

18. *not particularly pleased*: Conrad also dramatizes antagonism between a captain appointed over a mate in two stories, both with a partly autobiographical basis. In *Lord Jim*, Captain Brierly's first mate Mr Jones is passed over for command (Chapter 6), and *The Shadow-Line,* Part III, records similar tensions after the death of a captain and his replacement by a newcomer to the ship.

19. *Schomberg*: This hotel-keeper of unappealing aspect is treated with similar hostility in the Bangkok chapters of *Lord Jim*, where he plays a minor role, and in *Victory*, where he is important to the plot. In the latter novel his enterprise is located at Surabaya. This character may owe something to the German proprietors Schulmacher and Ulrich of Bangkok's Universal Hotel or to Guldberg, another German hotel-keeper in Bangkok.

20. *His Excellency Tseng*: Cf. Conrad on his experience in Siam in a letter to Bertrand Russell of 22–23 October 1922: 'I also received many kindnesses at the hands of various Chinese. This with the addition of an evening's conversation with the secretary of His Excellency Tseng on a verandah of an hotel' (*Letters*, vol. VII, p. 542).

21. *thief . . . sprinter*: Again, a detail with a biographical basis. *The Bangkok Times* of 1 February 1888 reports as follows:

A Chinese 'boy' employed on the barque Otago managed the other day to steal 15 gold mohurs from a sailor on board, and then to abscond. The captain and mate, however, met the juvenile thief a few hours afterwards in Mr Clarke's compound and arrested him. Whilst being conducted to the Bang Rak Police Station, he unfortunately managed to bolt and has not been seen since. (Quoted in Sherry 1966, p. 234)

In his correspondence Conrad identifies himself as the victim:

> I have always liked the Chinese, even those who tried to kill me (and some other people) in the yard of a private house in Chantabun, even (but not so much) the fellow who stole all my money one night in Bangkok, but brushed and folded my clothes neatly for me to dress in the morning, before vanishing into the depths of Siam. (Conrad to Bertrand Russell, 22–23 October 1922, *Letters*, vol. VII, p. 542)

22. *trump*: An archaic or poetic word for trumpet.
23. *a delusion and a snare*: Usually 'a snare and delusion', a familiar version of Lord Chief Justice Thomas, Baron Denman's warning that trial by jury, if tampered with, would become 'a delusion, a mockery and a snare': *Regina* vs. O'Connell, House of Lords, 4 September 1844.
24. *pound . . . flesh*: Derived from Shakespeare's *Merchant of Venice*, an expression meaning precise repayment of a debt, whatever the suffering involved for the debtor.
25. *from . . . eve*: A commonplace derived from Milton's description of the fall of the devil Mulciber:

> Men call'd him *Mulciber*; and how he fell
> From Heav'n, they fabl'd, thrown by angry *Jove*
> Sheer o're the Chrystal Battlements: from Morn
> To Noon he fell, from Noon to dewy Eve
> (*Paradise Lost* (1674), l.740–3)

26. *great Buddhist Pagoda*: The so-called 'Temple in the River' (in Thai, *Phra Chedi Klang Nam*) at Paknam, erected in the early eighteenth century by royal order. At the time of writing, it was located on an island (now silted up) about 3 miles up the mouth of the Chao Phraya. Featuring a pagoda and gilt spire, it was noteworthy on making one's way up or down the river. The first Buddhist structure encountered by nineteenth-century travellers to Siam, the temple complex was much remarked upon in travellers' accounts. Conrad refers to it as 'the great Paknam pagoda' in the first paragraph of 'The Secret Sharer' (1907).
27. *shallow bar . . . nuisance*: A historically accurate description of

navigation at the Bight of Bangkok: 'We make use of the floodtide to cross the bar, the half-muddy, half-sandy mass of which, during the low tide, shows, as far as the eye can see, a bamboo forest stuck into the soil', Lucien Fournereau, *Le Tour de monde*, 1894 (translated as *Bangkok in 1892*, Bangkok: White Lotus Press, 1998, p. 7).

28. *tides . . . so on*: Apparently an allusion to Byron's throwaway reference to Brutus's famous urging of his men to seize an opportunity in Shakespeare's *Julius Caesar*: 'There is a tide in the affairs of men, / which taken at the flood – you know the rest', *Don Juan* (1819), VI.i.1–2. The omitted words are: 'leads on to fortune'.

29. *infernal*: A common euphemism for 'damned', considered coarse at the time of writing.

30. *Dutchmen*: Now obsolete, the term during Conrad's time could be used to refer to anyone of Teutonic origin (*Deutsch*); hence, Germans would be referred to as 'Dutch'. The usage remains in 'Pennsylvania Dutch'.

31. *snuffy*: That is, soiled by snuff, implying that the item in question is stained and discoloured.

32. *dollar*: The currency of the Straits Settlements, that is, between 1867 and 1900 the British colonies of Penang, the Dindings, Malacca (in present-day Peninsular Malaysia) and Singapore. The word derives from the German *thaler*.

33. *Port Said*: An Egyptian port town situated at the mouth of the Suez Canal (opened 1869) and founded at the time the canal was dug. A coaling-station, it also had commercial facilities and firms engaged in repairing ships.

34. *Mr. Siegers*: See 'Typhoon', note 13.

35. *Dutch Uncle*: Proverbial for a plain- or even sharp-speaking critic or advisor.

36. *East End of London*: At the time the populous, poorer section of the city, the home likewise to its industries and port.

37. *twinkling of an eye*: 'We shall all be changed. / In a moment, in the twinkling of an eye': 1 Corinthians 15:51–2. The phrase occurs in 'The Order for the Burial of the Dead at Sea', *The Book of Common Prayer* (1623), which Conrad knew from burials at sea.

38. *quill-driver*: A common pejorative term for a person employed in writing and record-keeping.

39. *Gambril . . . quinine*: The subject of cholera and a crew member named Gambril figure importantly in *The Shadow-Line*.

40. *matchstand*: A small bowl or tray, usually in porcelain and sometimes attached to an ashtray, for the storage of matches.

41. *The die was cast*: Julius Caesar's words, pronounced on crossing the Rubicon, a small river forming the border between Italy and the Province of Cisalpine Gaul. Doing so without the permission of the Roman Senate, which was required of military commanders, he in effect declared war on Pompey and his supporters in the Senate in January 49 BC.

42. *gnashing of teeth*: A commonplace derived from the New Testament, in which the phrase occurs seven times; cf. 'there shall be weeping and gnashing of teeth', Matthew 8:12.

43. *inexpressibles*: Colloquial for 'trousers', by Conrad's time the periphrasis had become almost wholly jocular. The *OED*'s first citation dates from 1790.

44. *clear eyes*: The phrase is probably influenced by the Polish *jasne* or French *clair*, both translated into English as 'clear' but connoting brightness or luminousness as English does not. There is, however, some precedent in English; cf. 'her eyes were so clear and bright that few would wish them darker', Anne Brontë, *Agnes Grey* (1847), Chapter 7. Conrad elsewhere uses 'clear' where 'bright' would be more idiomatic: 'clear stars' and 'clear sunshine' in *Lord Jim* and 'clear dress' in *Nostromo*.

45. *eater of men*: Either a translation of or influenced by the German 'Menschenfresser' (cannibal).

46. *Borgmester Dahl*: That is, 'Burgomaster Dahl', burgomaster being the Danish equivalent of a mayor.

47. *pitch-pine deals*: A deal is a slice sawn from a log and usually understood to be more than seven inches wide and not more than three thick. In the British timber trade, a deal is understood to be nine inches (17.7 cm) wide, not more than three (7.6 cm) thick, and at least six feet (1.8 m) long. Pitch pine is a species of pine tree with specially resinous wood from which 'pitch' or turpentine is extracted.

48. *Flying Dutchman*: The legend is of a cursed ship so named and manned by the dead. Her captain is doomed to sail the seas in it until he finds a faithful woman. It is perhaps most notably recollected in the opera *Der fliegende Holländer* (1843) by Richard Wagner (1813–83) and in *The Phantom Ship* (1838–9) by Captain Frederick Marryat (1792–1848), captain in the Royal Navy and author of sea novels.

49. *sent to the right-about*: Originally a military term meaning 'to retreat' or 'to flee'; by extension and in general use, 'to be sent packing'.

50. *stars . . . courses*: 'They fought from heaven; the stars in their

courses fought against Sisera', Judges 5:20. Cf. 'I had not known for weeks whether the sun shone upon the earth and whether the stars above still moved on their appointed courses', Conrad, *A Personal Record* (1908–9; book 1912), Chapter 5.

TO-MORROW

Title: The title derives from, and puns on, the old saw 'Tomorrow never comes.' The original title was 'The Son'.

1.   *Colebrook*: As in 'Amy Foster', this is a fictional place-name, with the Kentish coast being evoked. The manuscript suggests that Conrad drew on the Cinque Port of Winchelsea, 2 miles from Rye: 'Brenzett had had a history in its time and had known a prosperity for whose return it sat waiting. . . . It was only quaint in its garb of umber walls and red roofs jostling against each other on the slight rise above the tidal creek' (Berg Collection, New York Public Library).

2.   *No. 1 sail-cloth*: Sail-cloth used for clothing, made of lightweight cotton, linen or flax, and much lighter than the cloth used for making sails, which is often of canvas.

3.   *tap-room*: See 'Amy Foster', note 27.

4.   *Davy Jones's locker*: Nautical slang for a watery grave. Of unknown origins, its first cited use in the *OED* is 1751. In effect, malevolent sea monsters eager to devour human prey, Davy Jones and his wife figure in ceremonies of Crossing the Line.

5.   *third-class smoker*: A railway carriage permitting smoking. At the time, accommodation was first and third class only, the latter used by almost all passengers.

6.   *Colchester*: This Essex town on the River Colne, which boasts of being the oldest recorded one in Britain, was long famous for its oyster fishery.

7.   *eight . . . at home*: In the 1860s, somewhat before the story's time-frame, the average family in Great Britain comprised 6.2 members, with one family in ten having ten or more children.

8.   *No. 1 canvas*: The thickest (and hence heaviest) grade of canvas.

9.   *East-coast collier . . . out of sight of England*: Conrad may be drawing on his earliest experiences in England for Hagberd. During his time in Lowestoft in the summer of 1878, he had been friendly with Norfolk-born Captain William Cook (b. 1837), who commanded the *Skimmer of the Seas*. The story's emphasis

on Hagberd's extreme domesticity may owe something to the fact that his part-model was the father of six children when Conrad knew him. (He had two more before 1881.) Master of a collier that made unvarying rounds from Lowestoft, Cook had reputedly never been out of sight of land, earning from wags the nickname 'The Great Circumnavigator' (see Sir Hugh Clifford, *A Talk on Joseph Conrad and His Work*, The English Association, Ceylon Branch, Colombo: H. W. Cave, 1927).

10. *Father Neptune*: The Roman god of the sea and of earthquakes (his brothers Jupiter ruled the sky and Pluto the underworld). Neptune's attribute was a magical trident that allowed him control over water. Usually depicted as heavily bearded, he was, like the sea, of temperamental character.

11. *coon*: In British mid- and late-nineteenth century usage, a sly or shrewd individual. Conrad uses it of himself in this sense in a letter to R. B. Cunninghame Graham of 18 May 1904 (*Letters*, vol. III, p. 140), a sense used also in *The Nigger of the 'Narcissus'* and *Chance*. For a discussion, see Jeremy Hawthorn, 'The Use of "Coon" in Conrad: British Slang or Racist Slur?', *The Conradian* 30.1 (2005), pp. 111–17.

12. *South Shields*: A port town on the North Sea on the Tyne estuary near Newcastle.

13. *Skimmer of the Seas*: The name is taken from the *Skimmer of the Sea*, a three-masted coasting schooner (built 1855, gross tonnage 215), owned by Joseph Saul (1816–93) of Lowestoft, in which Conrad made three voyages as an ordinary seaman in the summer of 1878 from Lowestoft to Newcastle.

14. *let me go to sea*: An autobiographical reference: after his parents' deaths, Conrad was placed in the care of relatives who were hostile to his desire to go to sea. He recounts overcoming their opposition in *A Personal Record* (1908–09; book version 1912), Chapter 2.

15. *tea*: In the story's social context, the evening meal (not 'afternoon tea' as taken in polite society), and not necessarily involving the taking of tea.

16. *afraid ... locked up*: Cf. *Lord Jim*, Ch. 38:

> this man, who would stake his existence on a whim with a bitter and jeering recklessness, stood in mortal fear of imprisonment. He had an unreasoning cold-sweat, nerve-shaking, blood-to-water-turning sort of horror at the bare possibility of being locked up – the sort of terror a superstitious man would feel at the thought of

being embraced by a spectre. (*Lord Jim*, ed. Allan H. Simmons, Harmondsworth: Penguin, 2007, pp. 270–71).

17. *Oh, ho ... Capstan song*: There are several versions of the 'Rio Grande' shanty, the destination being Rio Grande del Sul, a port and province in Brazil, and the occasion the departure for the gold rush. The song was sung on departing from the English west coast (but also became popular in the United States) at the anchor-capstan, on heaving up the anchor. The version here resembles the following chorus: 'An' a-away Rio! A-way, you Rio! / It's Fa-are ye well, my bonny young girl. For we're bound t' Ri-i-o Grande!' (*Capstan Bars*, ed. David W. Bone, Edinburgh: Porpoise Press, 1931).

18. *boundary rider*: (Australia and New Zealand): A horseman responsible for keeping a station's fencing in good repair.

19. *Sonora*: A state in north-west Mexico on the Pacific Ocean and south of the present-day American states of Arizona and New Mexico.

20. *Gambusinos*: In ore-processing and mining terminology, small-scale prospectors or miners; by extension, greedy persons or fortune hunters (Spanish).

21. *Rio Gila ... Mazatlan*: Respectively, a river flowing through present-day Arizona and New Mexico, and a coastal town (in Spanish, Mazátlan) in central Mexico on the Pacific coast.

22. *the Judy*: Originally from the Punch and Judy show, but colloquial or slang for any girl or woman. The *OED*'s first usage in this sense dates to 1812.

23. *One day more*: Conrad used this title for his dramatic adaptation of this story, performed by the Stage Society, London, in June 1905.

24. *madness ... despair*: Cf. 'An impenetrable mystery seems destined to hang forever over this act of madness and despair', *The Secret Agent* (1907), Chapter 12. Conrad may have borrowed the phrase from Maupassant's short story 'Rosalie Prudent' in the collection *La petite Rocque* (1886).

25. *inferno ... forfeited hopes*: An echo of 'Give up all hope, ye who enter here', the sign placed above the entrance to the Underworld in the *Inferno* by Dante, the first part of *La divina commedia* (see 'Amy Foster', note 21).

Glossary of Nautical Terms

This glossary briefly explains all nautical terms and the vocabulary related to shipping as used in *Typhoon and Other Stories*. Admiral W. H. Smyth's *The Sailor's Word-Book: An Alphabetical Digest of Nautical Terms* (London, 1867) can be recommended as providing useful detailed descriptions relevant to the period in which Conrad was writing.

abaft: in the after part or *stern* half of the ship

aft: 'after', in or near a ship's hinder part or *stern*

after-deck: the part of a ship's deck amidships towards the *stern*

after-part: the rear part of a ship

anchor-watchman: the man assigned to the *watch* while the ship is at anchor

articles: the agreement between the captain and crew as to terms of service and conditions of employment

astern: towards the rear (*aft*) of the ship; behind a ship's *stern*

barque: (also spelled bark) traditionally, a small sailing ship, although by Conrad's time larger steamers were so referred to

batten down: to fasten with battens (narrow strips of wood)

before the mast: to be employed not as an officer but as an ordinary seaman

Bengal light: a kind of firework producing a steady and vivid bluish light, used for signalling

bilge: the broadest part of a ship's bottom

billet: a job or position in a ship

binnacle: the stand on which the ship's compass is mounted

bo'sun (also boatswain; pronounced 'bosun'): the petty officer in charge of a ship's rigging, sails, anchors and cables

bow: the forward part of a ship, from the point at which she begins to curve to the *stem bowsprit*: a large *spar* or boom running out from the *stem* of a vessel, to which the foremast stays are fastened

brace: a rope by which a *yard* is swung and secured on a square-rigged ship

bridge: elevated platform above the upper deck from which the ship is navigated

bridge-rail: a rail attached to the *bridge*

bridge-screens: the screens shielding and separating off the ship's *bridge*

broached-to: turned to face the wind

bulkhead: an upright partition forming a ship's cabins or dividing the hold into watertight compartments

bulwark: raised woodwork running along a ship's sides above the level of the deck

bunker: a bin or tank for storing fuel

canvas set: that is, with the sails unfurled so as to take the wind

capstan: a rotating cylinder used as a pulley or winch to position heavy objects

charterers: a firm that hires out a vessel under a charter-party, a contract made between the ship's owners and hirers for the safe delivery of a ship's cargo

chart-room: the navigating officer's domain, with nautical tables, charts and instruments to plot the ship's courses and measure distances

chronometer: highly accurate time-piece for calculating a ship's position

close-hauled: with the sails flat (that is, away from square) so that the ship is able to make progress while pointing into the wind

coal-trimmer: an individual responsible for evenly stowing coal in a steamer so as to ensure the ship's stability

coamings: the raised borders about the edges of the *hatches* and scuttles, which prevent water on deck from entering below

cobble (English north-east coast): a sea-going fishing boat

coming-to: stopping by turning towards the wind

companion: (a) covering or skylight over the entrance to a vessel's stairways; (b) ladder or staircase connecting two decks

compass card: a freely pivoting circular disk carrying the magnetic needles of a compass and marked with its thirty-two points and the 360 degrees of the circle

country ship: a vessel registered not in London but in a colonial port

cowl: a wire cage at the top of a funnel

crank: a handle or arm attached at right angles to a shaft and transmitting rotary motion

crank-heads: the tops of *cranks*

cross swell: the sea running contrary to the wind, usually caused by cyclonic conditions

crosshead: bar at the end of a steam-engine's piston-rod that communicates motion to the connecting-rods

cuddy: in a larger vessel, the saloon under the *poop*; in a small vessel, a small cabin

davits: small cranes, usually paired, for suspending or lowering a lifeboat

deck: a platform built into a ship, covering in the space below and serving as a floor

deck locker: a storage unit located on deck and used to hold equipment

demurrage: payment by the freighter in compensation for detaining a ship beyond the agreed-upon time

derrick: a mast or *spar* supported at the top by stays or guys, with suitable tackle for hoisting heavy weights

dodger: a canvas screen on the *bridge* affording shelter from inclement weather

donkeyman: person responsible for operating an auxiliary steam-engine (the donkey-engine), and assisting in the engine-room

drawing . . . aft: requiring a given number of feet of water at the *stern*

draws over: having a depth of a specified number of feet in the water

dredging with the anchor down: proceeding downstream with the lowered anchor as a guide

fall: (a) the loose end of a rope to which power is applied for hoisting up; (b) an apparatus for lowering bales

fiddle: a steel grate over the boiler-room's *hatch*

fife-rail: a rail at the base of a mast, fitted with belaying-pins

fireman: a man responsible for attending to the fire used to operate a steam-engine

float: one of the blades of a ship's *paddle-wheel*

fore and aft: from *stem* to *stern*, that is, lengthwise

fore 'tween-deck (*foreward 'tween-deck*): the space between two decks, particularly towards the ship's front

forebitts: the frame comprised of two oak pillars, bolted upright to beams below the deck, to which anchor-cables or mooring-*hawsers* are fastened *forecastle* (pronounced 'fok-sal'): a compartment forward of the mast where the seamen have their berths

fore-deck: the area of a boat's deck in front of the mast

forefoot: point where a ship's *stem* meets the foremost end of her keel

foreman: a person exercising authority and control over workers

fore-royal brace: rope of the foremast's uppermost sail

foreward: towards the ship's front

friction winches: machines for hoisting, fitted with a brake to prevent the drum's cones from being overhauled by the load when they are not in contact with the gear wheel

gangway: a narrow platform or plank used for walking from the ship to the shore or from the *quarter-deck* to the *forecastle*, allowing convenient access from one to the other

gaskets: lines used to secure a furled sail to its *yard*

gear-casing: the case or covering in which the ship's steering gear is stored

gimbals: two concentric metal rings joined so as to counteract a ship's rolling and pitching and thus allowing a compass, *chronometer* or lamp to stay level

gins: mechanical apparatuses used for hoisting heavy weights, a crane

gunny-bags: strong bags made from 'gunny' (jute) and used for storing coarse commodities

halyards: ropes or tackle used to raise or lower a sail, flag or *yard*

hatches: (a) squared openings in the deck to afford passage up or down; (b) the covering of these openings

hatchway: an opening in the deck of a ship for lowering cargo into the hold and forming a passage from one deck to another

hawse-pipe: a metal tube through which the anchor-cable runs, fitted to prevent the cable from damaging the ship's *bows*

hawser: rope or cable, or rope used in towing

headgear: the rigging (sails) on the forepart of a ship

head-sheets: ropes attached to the lower corners of the *fore and aft* sails, serving to move or extend them

heaving-to: that is, immobilized as the result of manipulating the engine or sails, and thus mounting up or rising repeatedly near another object

heel over: to tilt or incline towards one side; to list

helm: the handle or *tiller* (in large ships the wheel) by which the *rudder* is managed; occasionally extended to include the whole steering-gear *hooker*: (sailor slang) a ship overly long in service and in poor condition

in ballast: not carrying or loaded with a cargo but filled with material to balance or stabilize a ship

jury-rudder: a makeshift *rudder*, replacing one damaged or lost

keelson: (pronounced 'kelson'): a piece of timber laid on the middle of the floor timbers over the keel and binding the floor timbers to the keel

lanyard: a line or short rope used for securing or attaching
lascars: seamen of East Indian origin (Urdu)
lashings: cords for fastening down a movable object
lead-line: a line, wire or cord used to measure depth and weighted at one end with a plummet (a sounding lead) to do so
lee: the direction towards which the wind blows
leeward (prounced 'loo'ard'): direction of the ship in relation to the wind, down-wind as opposed to up-wind
life-lines: ropes extended on the deck to provide protection to the crew in inclement weather
lighters: boats used for loading and unloading a ship's cargo
lines: ropes
log, log-book: the official record of a ship's movements and activities
lug (lug-sail): a four-cornered sail, bent upon a *yard* and slung at about a third or a quarter of its length, and thus hanging obliquely

mainmast: a ship's principal mast
main-topsail. the mainmast's second sail, just above the mainsail
man-of-war: a government ship intended to protect national interests and fitted out for combat
masthead: the highest part of a vessel's mast
mizzen mast: a sailing ship's third, aftermost, mast
mizzen rigging: the sails on a sailing ship's *mizzen mast*
moored: secured to the shore by cables or at anchor
mooring-bitts: the strong posts, usually in pairs, on the deck of a ship for securing mooring and other lines

off-shore tack: part of a zigzag course moving away from the shore
old man: (sailor slang) the captain or master mariner
on the cant: in a slanting position

on the quarter: in a direction approximately midway between *astern* and on the beam (in a line with the beams, or at a right angle with the keel)

Ordinary Seaman: the lowest ranking seaman, having at least nine months but fewer than three years of service at sea

paddle-tug: a tugboat propelled by a *paddle-wheel* at its *stern*

paddle-wheels: large, typically steam-driven, wheels with paddles or boards fitted round their circumference, at the *stern* or on each side of a ship, and propelling it by rotating about a horizontal axis that pushes the lower paddle-boards backward through the water

painter: a rope used for securing a boat to a fixed point

pintles: steering mechanisms consisting of hinged vertical plates

pole-mast: a mast formed of a single *spar*

poop: raised deck at the *stern*, which in larger ships contains accommodation for the master and officers

port: (a) the left-hand side of a ship, as one faces forwards (cf. *starboard*); (b) an opening in the ship's side, a window

port alleyway: a passageway on the ship's portside

ports: normally, openings in a ship's side; in 'Falk' simply windows in the captain's cabin

punt: a flat-bottomed shallow boat, broad and square at both ends, propelled by means of a long pole thrust against the bottom of a river or shallow water

quarter: either side of the rear part of a ship, between the beam and the *stern*; hence, 'on the quarter': between 'abeam' and '*astern*'

quarter-deck: that part of the upper deck extending between the *stern* and the after-mast, used as a promenade by officers or passengers

reach: (a) the portion of a river, channel or lake that lies between two bends; (b) as much as can be seen in one view

ring-bolt: a bolt having a ring fitted through its eye

roads, roadstead: sheltered expanse of water near shore where ships may ride safely at anchor

rolling chocks: pieces of timber or steel plates fitted longitudinally on a ship's bottom, so that she may take the ground readily without damage to her bottom

rudder: a broad, flat wooden piece for steering attached to a ship's stern-post

running-gear: a ship's ropes, usually run through pulleys

sampan: (Mandarin = boat) applied by Europeans in the China Seas to any small boat of the Chinese pattern

scow: a large flat-bottomed boat with broad, square ends and carrying cargo in an open hold

sea-way: 'in rough seas' or, by extension, 'in heavy weather'

ship's articles: a binding written agreement between the master and crew laying out duties and terms of employment, including rates of pay, each crewman's capacity, the date of the voyage's beginning and its duration and, occasionally, the foodstuffs provided on a daily basis

short canvas: with the area of the sails exposed to the wind reduced

short rations: less than the daily amount of nourishment specified in the *ship's articles*

signal halyards: rope or tackle used for raising or lowering a signal flag

slice: a metal bar with a blade for clearing furnaces of clinkers and other debris

sounding: ascertaining the depth of water by means of a *lead-line*

spar: stout wooden pole used for a mast, gaff or boom

stanchion: an upright bar or post serving as a support

starboard: when looking forward, the right-hand side of a vessel

state-room: a captain's or superior officer's room on board ship

steam gear: device supplying the power necessary to move the *rudder*

stem: the curved upright timber at a ship's *bow*, into which the bow's planks are joined

stern: the rear of a vessel

stern-windows: those windows facing the ship's *stern*

stokehold: compartment housing the boilers, where the furnaces are stoked

stokers: those responsible for tending a steamer's furnaces

strop: a ring of rope with its ends spliced together, used on a mast, *yard* or rope

tack: steer a zigzag course to enable the ship to sail into the wind by shifting the tacks (the ropes and so forth used to manage the lower square sails) and bracing the *yards* in order to turn the ship's head to the wind

tackles: a rope and pulley-block used to raise or shift a ship's boat

tail-shaft: in a screw steamship, the section of the shaft (a long, cylindrical, rotating rod upon which are fixed the parts for transmitting motive power in a machine) nearest the propeller *'thwart-ship* (from 'athwart'): across the course or direction of the ship

tiller: horizontal bar fitted to the head of the ship's *rudder* for steering

topside: a ship's upper deck, exposed to the open air

towing chock: a cradle in which a ship's towing gear is secured on deck

trimming: to turn towards the wind

truck: a disc-shaped block of wood fixed to the top of a mast, containing small holes for *signal halyards*

trysails: used chiefly as a storm sail, a *fore and aft* sail, bent to a gaff and hoisted on a lower or small mast called the trysail mast

turned-to: settled into work

'tween-deck (between-deck): the deck below the main deck, frequently used for stowing cargo

under bare poles: to sail without sails set on the masts

watch: (a) any of the four-hour periods beginning at midnight and again at noon during which part of the ship's crew are on duty; (b) the officers and crew on duty during a specified watch

way: the progress of a ship or boat through the water; the impetus gained by a vessel in motion

weather-cloths: pieces of canvas fitted on ridge ropes and *stanchions* above the *bulwarks* or the tarpaulins used to cover the hammocks when stowed

wheel-house: a structure on the bridge enclosing the ship's wheel and providing protection for the helmsman

whipping: a binding of twine round the end of a rope

whipping up: hoisting cargo (usually said of coal) into the ship's hold by means of a pulley or rope

winch: a fixed motor-driven or hand-powered machine used for hoisting or hauling, having a drum round which a rope is wound or a deck-mounted drum with a handle offering mechanical advantage used to trim the sheets or *halyards*

windlass: a rotating cylinder for raising or lowering an anchor

yard: a wooden *spar*, tapering at the ends, slung horizontally across a mast to suspend a square sail

Glossary of Foreign Words and Phrases

ach: (German) oh

ach so: (German) I see

coram populo: (Latin) in public, in the public arena

der verfluchte Kerl: (German) the damned fellow

écarté: (French) a card game for two persons, played with a pack of thirty-two cards

ex officio: (Latin) by virtue of his / her office

gharry: (Hindi, later Anglo-Indian) small box-like horse- or pony-drawn carriage for hire

Gottverdammt: (German) God damn it

Himmel! Zwei und dreissig Pfund: (German) Good heavens! Thirty-two pounds

in extremis: (Latin) at the last gasp

Klings: (Malay: *Keling*) persons from continental India settled in Malaya

nota bene: (Latin) note well; please take note of

punkah: (Anglo-Indian, from Hindi) a large overhead swinging fan, made from cloth or palm fronds, hung from the ceiling and pulled by a rope by a servant or slave to ventilate and cool a room

table d'hôte: (French) a public table in a hotel dining room, but often used to imply a fixed bill of fare

tiffin: (colonial English) meal taken at midday

PENGUIN CLASSICS

UNDER WESTERN EYES
JOSEPH CONRAD

'It was myself, after all, whom I have betrayed most basely'

Razumov is a university student of uncertain – possibly noble – parentage, who dreams of making his way in the academic world. But his solitary, industrious existence in St Petersburg is shattered by the appearance of his fellow student, the revolutionary terrorist Victor Haldin. Thrust into a world of state politics and espionage, Razumov is also brought into contact with Haldin's trusting sister Natalia in Geneva. When he falls in love with her he becomes caught in a tragic web and finds his identity torn apart. Exploring the conflict between East and West, this is a powerful and profound story of tyranny, guilt, loyalty and betrayal.

Part of a major series of new editions of Conrad's most famous works in Penguin Classics, this volume contains a chronology, further reading, notes and an introduction discussing the novel in the context of Conrad's troubled life, his mistrust of political institutions and his ambivalent attitude towards Russia's history and people.

Edited with notes and a glossary by Stephen Donovan
With an introduction by Allan H. Simmons
General editor J. H. Stape

PENGUIN CLASSICS

THE BEAST WITHIN
EMILE ZOLA

'He was driven by a single overriding need; he must appease the beast that raged within him'

Roubaud is consumed by a jealous rage when he discovers a sordid secret about his lovely young wife's past. The only way he can rest is by forcing her to help him murder the man involved, but there is a witness – Jacques Lantier, a fellow railway employee. Jacques, meanwhile, must contend with his own terrible impulses, for every time he sees a woman he feels an overwhelming desire to kill. In the company of Roubaud's wife, Séverine, he finds peace briefly, yet his feelings for her soon bring disastrous consequences. The seventeenth novel in the Rougon-Macquart cycle, *The Beast Within* (1890) is one of Zola's most dark and violent works – a tense thriller of political corruption and a graphic exploration of the criminal mind.

Roger Whitehouse's vivid translation is accompanied by an introduction discussing Zola's depiction of the railways, politics and the legal system and the influence of the studies of criminology and the Jack the Ripper murders on his novel. This edition also includes a chronology, suggestions for further reading and notes.

Translated with an introduction and notes by Roger Whitehouse

PENGUIN CLASSICS

HASHISH
HENRY DE MONFREID

'I didn't even know exactly what hashish was ... I knew only two things – that it was grown in Greece, and sold very dear in Egypt'

Henry de Monfreid was a nobleman, writer, smuggler and adventurer who travelled the world during the 1920s with his wife and young daughter in search of excitement and quick money. First seeking his fortune by becoming a collector and merchant of the fabled Gulf pearls, he was then drawn into the shadowy world of arms trading, slavery and drugs. When he decided to set out on his own, transporting hashish from Piraeus to Suez, his daring and initiative compensated for his lack of knowledge and experience. Written with an engaging wit and charm, Hashish describes de Monfreid's fail safe hiding places for contraband, how to catch a water turtle and the aphrodisiac properties of shark's meat – and is alive with the people he encountered on his travels, from paunchy customs officials and Bedouin camel-drivers, to a marooned Dankali fisherman and a jovial Greek undertaker.

This edition also includes a map of the Gulf of Suez.

PENGUIN CLASSICS

COLD COMFORT FARM
STELLA GIBBONS

'I saw something nasty in the woodshed'

When sensible, sophisticated Flora Poste is orphaned at nineteen, she decides her only choice is to descend upon relatives in deepest Sussex. At the aptly named Cold Comfort Farm, she meets the doomed Starkadders: cousin Judith, heaving with remorse for unspoken wickedness; Amos, preaching fire and damnation; their sons, lustful Seth and despairing Reuben; child of nature Elfine; and crazed old Aunt Ada Doom, who has kept to her bedroom for the last twenty years. But Flora loves nothing better than to organize other people. Armed with common sense and a strong will, she resolves to take each of the family in hand. A hilarious and merciless parody of rural melodramas, *Cold Comfort Farm* (1932) is one of the best-loved comic novels of all time.

This new Penguin Classics edition includes an introduction by Lynne Truss discussing Stella Gibbons's unconventional life and career and her exuberant, satirical voice.

'Brilliant ... very probably the funniest book ever written' Julie Burchill, *Sunday Times*

'Literary bliss' *Guardian*

With an introduction by Lynne Truss

PENGUIN CLASSICS

KING SOLOMIN'S MINES
H. RIDER HAGGARD

'There at the end of the long stone table ... sat Death himself'

Onboard a ship bound for Natal, adventurer Allan Quartermain meets Sir Henry Curtis and Captain John Good. His new friends have set out to find Sir Henry's younger brother, who vanished seeking King Solomon's legendary diamond mines in the African interior. By strange chance, Quartermain has a map to the mines, drawn in blood, and agrees to join the others on their perilous journey. The travellers face many dangers on their quest – the baking desert heat, the hostile lost tribe they discover and the evil 'wise woman' who holds the secret of the diamond mines. *King Solomon's Mines* (1885) is a brilliant work of adventure romance that has gripped readers for generations.

In his preface Giles Foden considers Haggard's treatment of the cultural stereotypes of the time, while Robert Hampson's introduction discusses the explorations and empire building that inspired Haggard's writing. This edition also includes further reading, an appendix and notes.

'Enchantment is just what Rider Haggard exercised ... his books live today with undiminished vitality' Graham Greene

Edited with an introduction and notes by Robert Hampson
Preface by Giles Foden

PENGUIN CLASSICS

A DEAD MAN'S MEMOIR (A THEATRICAL NOVEL)
MIKHAIL BULGAKOV

'I confess quite frankly that what I produced was some kind of gibberish'

Sergei Maksudov has failed as a novelist and made a farce of a suicide attempt, but only after a surprise break as a playwright on the Moscow stage does his turmoil truly begin. Thrown uncomprehending into theatre life, he soon sees his beloved play dragged into chaos by inflated egos, jealous critics, literary double-dealers, communist censors and insanely bad acting. Full of affectionately drawn characters, *A Dead Man's Memoir* is a brilliant, absurdist tale of the exhilaration and black desperation wrought on one man by his turbulent love affair with the theatre. Based on his own experiences at the famous Moscow Art Theatre of the 1920s and 30s, it reaches its comic height in a merciless lampooning of Stanislavsky's fashionable stage techniques.

Andrew Bromfield's powerful new translation is accompanied by an introduction by Keith Gessen, which discusses the autobiographical basis of these fictionalized memoirs and Bulgakov's artistic integrity in the face of Soviet repression. This edition also contains notes and a chronology.

Translated with notes by Andrew Bromfield

With a new introduction by Keith Gessen

PENGUIN CLASSICS

THE ROAD TO OXIANA
ROBERT BYRON

'Neither an Afghan saddle nor the pangs of starvation could spoil the beauty of our ride among the glistening silver hills'

In 1933 Robert Byron began a journey to Persia and Afghanistan, via Jerusalem, Damascus and Baghdad, in search of the origins of Islamic architecture. *The Road to Oxiana* is the record of his ten-month voyage and the characters, landscapes and buildings he encountered: from diary entries, historical vignettes, comic conversations and magnificent evocations of architecture. At once poetic, scholarly and acidly humorous, Byron's travel journal is a passionate ode to the pursuit of experience and a portrait of an extraordinary traveller.

In his new introduction, Colin Thubron discusses Byron's life and travels, and the impact *The Road to Oxiana* had on travel writing.

'One of the best, most learned and most entertaining of all books of literary travel'
Independent

'What *Ulysses* is to the novel between the wars and what *The Waste Land* is to poetry, *The Road to Oxiana* is to the travel book' Paul Fussell

With an introduction by Colin Thubron

THE STORY OF PENGUIN CLASSICS

Before 1946 ... 'Classics' are mainly the domain of academics and students; readable editions for everyone else are almost unheard of. This all changes when a little-known classicist, E. V. Rieu, presents Penguin founder Allen Lane with the translation of Homer's *Odyssey* that he has been working on in his spare time.

1946 Penguin Classics debuts with *The Odyssey*, which promptly sells three million copies. Suddenly, classics are no longer for the privileged few.

1950s Rieu, now series editor, turns to professional writers for the best modern, readable translations, including Dorothy L. Sayers's *Inferno* and Robert Graves's unexpurgated *Twelve Caesars*.

1960s The Classics are given the distinctive black covers that have remained a constant throughout the life of the series. Rieu retires in 1964, hailing the Penguin Classics list as 'the greatest educative force of the twentieth century.'

1970s A new generation of translators swells the Penguin Classics ranks, introducing readers of English to classics of world literature from more than twenty languages. The list grows to encompass more history, philosophy, science, religion and politics.

1980s The Penguin American Library launches with titles such as *Uncle Tom's Cabin*, and joins forces with Penguin Classics to provide the most comprehensive library of world literature available from any paperback publisher.

1990s The launch of Penguin Audiobooks brings the classics to a listening audience for the first time, and in 1999 the worldwide launch of the Penguin Classics website extends their reach to the global online community.

The 21st Century Penguin Classics are completely redesigned for the first time in nearly twenty years. This world-famous series now consists of more than 1300 titles, making the widest range of the best books ever written available to millions – and constantly redefining what makes a 'classic'.

The Odyssey continues ...

The best books ever written

PENGUIN CLASSICS

SINCE 1946

Find out more at www.penguinclassics.com